Exploring with Him

Ella Jane Book Two

Edward Green

Cover Designed by Edward Green

Paperback ISBN-13: 978-1-916638-06-8

eBook ISBN-13: 978-1-916638-07-5

The first book in his series is **Meeting Him** - I recommend reading this first

https://mybook.to/EllaJaneMeetingHim

Having been flirting and playing online for for some time with a mysterious dominant, young author Ella Jane finds herself on the way to a writing conference he's also attending. Not only that it turns out that he's a highly successful writer. She flies coach to New York to meet him while his Gulfstream arrows over the Atlantic.

Both of them are in for more than either expects.

Ella Jane's story continues in **Travelling with Him – due out September 2023**

https://mybook.to/TravellingWithHim

The erotic adventure continues as they leave New York to do a number of book signings around the US, and for him to visit various parts of his far flung business empire. On the way they continue to explore Ella Jane's boundaries and the limits of one another's endurance and imagination

If you enjoyed reading about Ella Jane, you may enjoy **Meredith's Journey Begins**

Meredith Webb has built herself a pleasant, though unchallenging life, with a decent job she doesn't strive too hard at. Oh, and she has two cats she loves very much.

William Farrow on the other hand, knows there's something missing from his.

Reader Comments:

"A richly crafted journey into passion"

"Tantalisingly teasing"

"Stylish, smart and captivating! Sprinkled with moments of spine tingling awkwardness and evocativeness."

Get it here: https://mybook.to/MeredithsJourneyBegins

This book contains:

Descriptions of sexual acts including consensual sexual violence

Forthright defences of freedom of speech and human bodily autonomy

Moderate alcohol consumption

Consumption and enjoyment of bacon, cheese and other delicacies

Exercise

People enjoying themselves in New York

New Yorkers behaving with consideration and humour

British people who've never enslaved anyone (other than consensually and with safe words in play)

A person who travels by private jet but doesn't object to others travelling by car

Contents

Introduction

Continuing on from Meeting Him – The Ella Jane Stories (Him and Her) Book 1

New York's morning has dawned grey and miserable through the windows of the St Regis's Presidential Suite.

He and Ella Jane are finishing breakfast the morning after their night at the Metropolitan Opera, and he has a plan to ease them down from the excitement of the night before. He might be learning, but Ella Jane is a lesson not even he can learn in so short a time.

Her Massage

Having got her set up working, he goes and gets his own laptop and a robe for her, pours them each some pink grapefruit then tops the glasses up with orange.

Ella Jane smiles at the taste of the drink, though she frowns at being expected to dress, until the butler arrives to clear away the breakfast things.

"It's only fair."

"It is."

The duty butler clears the obviously finished plates and uses a tilt of his head to ask whether she should leave the unfinished pastries.

He gives a dignified half nod, but Ella Jane's smile is radiant. "Please, they're *so* good!"

So she returns Ella Jane's smile then turns back to Him. "Would there be anything else sir?"

"Not right now, thank you."

As soon as they're alone again she slips the soft cotton robe off again.

"Warm?"

"No, well, yes, but not too warm. I just want to make sure you remember not to write all day."

He chuckles, "Have you seen the weather?"

Ella Jane hadn't paid much attention to it earlier beyond registering the darker than usual grey, but now she walks to the windows. They're flecked with raindrops, and there's a steady drizzle beyond. "Yuck, is it going to be like this all day?"

"Till late afternoon, I'm afraid."

A range of emotions flicker across her face, starting with irritation, but softening rapidly, until at last she asks, "How are we going to keep ourselves amused?"

"I told you, we're going to write." He blinks and offers her a mild smiling look as her expression and state of undress shout, *I'm young and attractive and naked and we don't have to be anywhere!*

He reads the exasperation on her face and issues a warning. "Is that expression saying *I'm going to kill* you or a *what are we going to do after we've written*?"

She answers, "It's a *what are we going to do after we've written.*" Though she has to fight her mood and her facial muscles to hold them back from offering angrier opinions."

He beams and kisses her cheek, "Good girl." then steers, her hands to her keyboard.

He keeps her at the table until she's talked through some ideas with him and written a thousand words of notes. She isn't prepared to look him in the eye and admit the exercise was useful instead hoping he'll turn his attention to other matters, but he asks, "Did you have a productive writing sprint?"

She clenches her lips. The truth is, that she had, but she'd not only worked on Abigail, and she doesn't want any questions about the new story yet, not till she's sure she's captured the intensity, and not till they know each other better. It had been one thing sending him her erotic stories before they met, showing him the beginnings of one inspired by her time with him feels quite another.

"Are you trying not to admit that it was?" His face is so serious, and he's so right, and when she scowls at him and tries to maintain the expression, he's amused. "Would you like to join me back on holiday now?"

She nods.

"Would you like to close your eyes then?"

Her smile sparkles and her eyes light up before she closes them.

Once they're closed, he rises silently and makes his way around to her, places a blindfold over her eyes and checks its positioning then touches her arm. "Stand please." She cooperates, allowing him to guide her to her feet. "Are you ready for me to take my pleasure in you?" She nods again. "Good girl."

With that he leads her and as she follows. She remembers the thousands of messages they've exchanged on the subjects of pleasure, of pain, and of bondage. She remembers the dozens of things he's done with her in the few days since they've met and thinks how they add to those messages.

During their long exchanges before they decided to meet in the flesh he'd said he would do many things to and with her. Reading his messages and sending excited replies to them, then and re-read their conversations in the privacy of her room for months was one thing. A thing very far removed from her present reality. Now she's with him and has experienced the proof of his ability to do those things, just so long as she's brave enough and passionate enough to endure them.

The sight that greets her in the second bedroom when he lifts the blindfold from her eyes isn't something she expects. For one thing, there are no restraints mounted on it.

"A massage bed?"

"Yes, we have time today, so a massage bed."

"I don't know how to give you a massage."

"Then it's a good thing it's not me getting the massage."

"I didn't ask for a massage."

"Have you had a massage?"

"When I was at college."

"Have you ever had a proper one?"

"How do you know it wasn't?"

He looks at her, and his eyes speak of the years of difference in their experiences while his frame remains still, powerful, confident. "Probably not a proper one, not what you'd call that anyway." She sets her jaw. "I didn't enjoy lying there getting poked."

"Then this," he declares, "will be a revelation." She hesitates, and the line of his brow hardens as he leans his head forward, and slowly enunciates, "Trust...me," his voice silk over steel.

"You don't have to; can't you just do things to me."

He nods. "I can." Then he states quite firmly, "The thing I want to do to you right now is give you a massage." He softens his voice, "Aren't you a little achy from all that being tied up and made to exercise?"

She bites her lip as the colour spreads from her cheeks. "Mmm, those and other things."

"Well then," comes out with a firm edge, one that sets Ella Jane into heel-dug-in mode, though she's not certain whether it's just the *make me* kind.

"What if I don't want to?"

There's both iron and sarcasm in his voice as he observes, "Then you can say *red*."

"The most Domly of answers. How about if I resist?" She stretches the word about then blinks twice when she finishes speaking.

"Then I'll force you, so long as you don't safeword."

He has her trapped between seeming unreasonable and being cooperative again. "So, I'm going to have a massage?"

"Yes." He goes on to offer the carrot. "There are oils, towels, and a few little surprises." He's honey toned, but then injects a note of command, "I wish to give you a massage, and I'm going to do it."

"Whether I want you to or not?"

"I refer you to my previous reference to safewording."

"What if I don't enjoy it?"

"If you don't you can amber, but that's not going to happen, now, *on the bed*."

Ella Jane tries narrowing her eyes at him, but this time his look of impending thunder turns her insides to playful mush, making her want his hands on her, and that's exactly what he's demanding. She hops up, though rather than lying face down with her face over the hole, she lies on her back further down and stretches her limbs out to the bed's corners.

"Not this time."

She pouts and waggles her hands and feet as though her wrists and ankles were already secured.

"Don't you ever get tired of being tied up?" He asks with his voice laced with faux exasperation.

"I haven't yet." Her words carry all the self-satisfaction of a child who's being told off having already eaten the whole cake.

That provokes a renewed darkening of his expression as he steps towards her. "How shall I put this?" He raises his right hand with his index finger extended, then slowly and deliberately trails it from the instep of her left foot to the palm of her right hand. The touch he applies as he does so is firm, and it comes achingly close to her opening and then over her mons and her up over the tensing of her convex abdomen and between her breasts. She arches in the hope of drawing his attention to them.

He sees, but doesn't detour, choosing instead to mock her renewed need with his eyes. "If you're a good girl today, I might tie you up next time."

Ella Jane licks her lips and blinks then arches her body and rubs her head against the massage bed. She watches until his face betrays signs of amusement and asks, "Not tonight?" with a winsome smile.

He moves his fingertip from her right palm to her left and draws the other line of the St. Andrews Cross shape in which she has arranged her body as he rumbles, "If you aren't careful, I might tie you to the bed and leave you in here as a punishment for your sass."

The threat doesn't have the apparent desired effect, causing her to smile and blush rather than appear cowed. Nevertheless, he completes his caress before looking her in the eye with a brow raised. "Did I say something funny?"

"No! But when you touch me like that and talk like that the prospect of you punishing me is just hot." She chews a lip as his eyes ask hers whether her voice is telling the truth, and when they say yes, he repeats his lengthways caresses with his full open hand.

As he does so, he rumbles, "Even if the punishment's something dull?"

"Yes. I mean, I'd rather you did something sexily mean but..." She chuckles and sighs until he finished the second stroke.

He frowns then closes his eyes for a moment. "Whatever am I to do with you?"

"Sexily mean things, I said." She says it with her, *I'm handing in a paper that I know is going to get an A grade*, smile plastered over her face.

His fingers and thumbs tease and threaten the tips of her breasts. "It's a good job I've got 2,000 messages from you saying how much you like me doing sexily mean things."

"It is. Technically, encouraging you to do them is an act of service."

Her logic is impeccable and just too damned funny for him to be able to answer her right away. It takes him a good half minute to manage to reply while keeping his face straight. "I'll discuss that with you *if* you earn yourself the tied-up version."

"I'll be good! Do you want me face up or face down?"

He unscrews the jar of coconut oil and scrapes a half handful of the marbled white waxy oil into his hands. "Seeing as how you appear to have got yourself comfortable, we may as well start this way up."

While he rubs the oil between his warm hands to melt it, Ella Jane lies back and wriggles against the soft towels with her back arched and her thighs parted, whether consciously or unconsciously making it clear where she wants him to begin.

"Are you trying to earn a whacking?" His voice is stern, and though she keeps her face straight, she can't stop her cheeks from colouring. "Well, you aren't getting it until I've finished."

"That's so unfair!"

He lays his slick hands on her, left at her shoulder and right at her hip. "And that's a second whacking, but you aren't getting that until I've finished either." With that he begins working the rich oil and its sweet scent into her skin with slow figure of eight motions that tease around her breasts and opening without getting close enough to do more than build a pleasant congestion.

She closes her eyes to allow herself to focus on the sensation instead of studying him or trying to encourage or provoke. She opens them again when his hands lift away, and watches him gather and liquefy more oil. Then she coos as she rubs the back of her head against the padding when they return to her and extend the slickened areas to her thighs and shoulders.

Satisfied for now, he brings his hands to the sides of her neck and caresses downwards to the top of her ribcage. Here he applies light pinching strokes along lengths of her collar bones, then sinks a deep force along the fibres of her shoulder muscles and down those of her upper arms. He repeats this motion until her body and breathing anticipate the repetition, and on until she lets out a long soft groan before returning to the jar and gathering more oil.

He uses this to coat her forearms and hands. As he does so, her eyes study his rapt expression. At first, he's too focused on what his hands are doing to pay any heed, but as he settles into the rhythm of the new strokes, he's able to spare her a look and a smile. He then bends and gives her a brush-lipped kiss before he straightens again to set his attention on her face. His eyes study hers as the magic of touch dissolves her focus with more long, slow strokes.

Having brought her to a state of sleeping cat relaxation, he takes her left arm and applies a flat grip of his straight thumb and forefinger across her forearm just below her elbow; slowly increasing his pressure for a softly spoken count of ten then eases it. He moves to a point an inch lower and repeats. When he reaches her palm, he counts even slower, and she sighs thinking he's finished but instead he applies the same ageless artfulness to each pad of each of her fingers and then to those of her thumb.

He repeats the ritual on her right arm and hand and then goes back, and in place of static pressure, his hands work in infinitesimally show motion before moving back to her left, once again working in a pattern she learns easily.

She's crooning contentedly and viewing him through lidded eyes by the time he finishes with her arms for the time being.

"Legs next." His voice is so quiet and so deep that she misses anything but the sound and presence of him and that he'd spoken words.

"Hmm?"

The contented rumble that follows is even deeper, but she makes out his, "I said legs next."

"Hmm, okay." She eases them further apart. Then, when he ahems, her eyes open to reveal dilated pupils and her lips curve into a guilt-free, but entirely uninnocent caricature of an innocent smile.

He narrows his eyes and raises the flat of a hand, but her response to that is to raise her hips offering her opening as a target. As she does so, she takes her lower lip between her teeth. That wins her a hint of a smile. "We're going to have a long *conversation* about your attitude when I've finished," he says with more than a hint of warning hardness, and the unstated, *But for now you will behave* carries such force and certainty that she meekly goes back to lying flat.

"Sorry, Sir."

"That's okay." He goes to the jar and scraps out more oil. "I know you're feeling..."

"Playful?"

"Yes, something like that." His enunciation hardens again, "But right now I want you to relax, enjoy and *trust me*." He then lays his oil laden hands on her thighs.

Ella Jane bites her lip and mouths a sorry, then lets out an audible, "Oh!" Having spread the rich slickness along her upper legs, his fingers repeat the movement with greater force and infinitely greater slowness, sinking into her muscles with his iron strength.

He makes a second such pass and her eyes close, a third and she lets out a sigh. After a fourth he returns to the jar, and she opens her eyes to watch him dig out and melt more oil then come back to her. This time he uses both hands on her right leg, and she raises her arms and rests her head on them so she can watch him work.

She sees the muscles of his shoulders bunch and thick veins stand out on his forearms. His crazily intense workouts have already given her a clue how his lower arms had got so big. But feeling the power his hands put into her is another.

He becomes rapt in concentration again, and she watches him in fascination, as the almost painfully intense force he applies melts her flesh. A rumble of amusement escapes his lips and breaks her reverie as he prepares to do the same to her left leg.

"Huh?"

He chuckles again, "You were humming."

"Oh, was I? Must have been happy." She waves her left leg in the air, and when he catches it, her eyes seek his in playful hope that he will dare her to say or do something wrong. When his face retains a serious calm, she pouts. When that too fails to alter his mood, she subsides, surrendering herself to his touch once more.

As with her arms, the foreknowledge she has from how he massaged her other limb aides her in her relaxation and appreciation. It's as though the tissue of her right leg has passed messages of what to expect, along with details of each highlight, to her left. As a result, her flesh thrums with anticipation ahead of his touch.

Having reached her foot and lavished his skills on each toe while she smiled at how deliciously not quite ticklish his touch is, he goes for the jar again. She watches him while she stretches and purrs, studying his broad back and heavy shoulders through half-lidded eyes.

First, he smothers her in the thick, sweet, freshly-melted oil, ensuring he spreads it's slickness over every inch of her body from her shoulders and thighs. He works unhurriedly. The strokes and circles of his hands and forearms move ever closer to the tips of her breasts and the folds of her opening. Now that she's deeper in the experience of the long sensual massage, her efforts to provoke and entice are more muted, which is just as well, because at times his eyebrows twitch and his humming acquires an edge of growl.

It's hard to stay still, hard to not try to insist that he quench the fire his touch has been slowly building, but she subsides. But she finds the idea of not continuing to experience all he wishes to give unbearable.

At length his hands circle close to the buds of her breasts and press strongly onto the bones of her pelvis. They find the point at the top of her pubic bone where he's pressed so often in the last few days though no one, not even she herself, had ever pressed before and the same rush of sexual heat surges. He presses yet more slowly and more firmly still and she gasps aloud, breathes out, "Fuck!" as he chuckles and mewls her loss as his hand sweeps away.

Next, he spirals slow figures-of-eight over her chest, and she guesses, hopes, and senses that he will at last reach their eager tips, and so he does. He continues until her breathing accelerates, and then adjusts his stance and his pattern, caressing one breast and now the other. Then one with either hand. When he moves away this time though, there's no mewl of loss, rather, an arching of herself in offering as his left hand slides to her shoulder and his right glides downward. There's only one place on the front of her body left for him to massage and his inexorably slow touch is heading directly there.

His hand passes down, over and around, his thumb, little finger, and the sides of his hand framing her vulva and his heel pressing into her mons with a slowly building force. Her lidded eyes see the muscles of his shoulder and arm bunch and a deep welling of heat floods from within the bone under his hand. He presses there, holds, cupping her tender swollen outer lips and delicate folds while the power and mass of his body flow into her until a long ragged sigh escapes from her lips. Only then do his three longest fingers curl further, slipping between her outer and inner lips and along the line of her opening. His ring and index fingers soon reach and press into hard bone adding their notes to that of the slow heat still flowing from under the heel of his hand. His middle finger has further to go before it finds such resistance, curls around the lower edge of her pubic bone and inside her, hooking her most intimate self, exerting physical power and declaring an intimate ownership.

His grip now has her, though after the long awakening of her entire body in place of an immediate sexual thrill. A wave of heat and erotic tension blossoms from her clit and pubic bone then spread through her whole self. It isn't orgasm as she understands it, rather it fills her, flowing along every fibre of her being and bringing with it a sense of completeness and connection. It's something different, something unique even in her days with him and beyond comparison to anything before.

He maintains the pressure until the ripples flowing through her body ease, then backs it off with a slowness still more glacial than his usual until it eases to nothing.

"Can you turn over now?"

"Hmm?"

He chuckles softly and repeats himself.

Ella Jane moves slowly, and he helps her turn. It takes her a while to settle with her head in position at the table's face hole and he uses that time to load his hands with oil again.

When she'd been lying on her back, he'd begun at her shoulders and hip, and worked inwards and outwards from there, but with her lying face down he begins at the base of her spine leaning his strength into the strong bones of her hips. He applies his hands open palmed to the crest of her pelvis centrally at first, acclimatising her body to the power he exerts, then moves out in slow motions to her right, walks around the bed and repeats himself on the left side of her body. Next he works the points where the muscles of her back and legs attach and into the tendons that connect them.

He rumbles, "Am I pressing too hard?" and she responds with a purr to the sound of his voice and the feeling of his strength on her rather than to the words.

From there, he moves on to sweeping from her pelvis to her spine below her ribs and on up between her shoulder blades. The first passes he applies are slow with the heels of his hands. He builds on the initial motion, pressing the heel of one hand with that of his other and moving still more slowly. Next his knuckles flow into meeting places between her vertebrae and then his finger and thumb tips work their ways into the spaces between her ribs and under her shoulder-blades that she had no idea could be touched, let alone wonderfully.

She rouses slowly as his hands find muscles she didn't realise she had and works them as easily as if her body were printed with a map of them. They find aches she'd forgotten too, and tensions she realises she's carried so long their easing brings her close to tears.

As she relaxes still further, his hands work their way deeper into her joints, their slow power forces and seduces its way so far into her body that she fears they will cause injury. Yet any trace of pain passes, and they move on leaving only a deep glowing warmth and a sense that she can reach beyond the confines of her being.

At length he returns to focusing his attentions on her hips. He begins out wide pressing inwards, building up to using so much of his strength that his body shakes with exertion and liquid honey flows from where his hands clamp onto her. He eases, moves down to the points of her hips and repeats.

Moving lower, he adjusts to working on one leg at a time, the heel of his hand outside and full open palm on the inside. Sweat drips onto her, and he apologises, taking a pause to towel his face and chest and take a swig of water before he continues down to her knee.

He repeats the process without interruption starting just below the crest of her hips and making his way down to where her hamstrings thin. Then he applies light comforting pressure to the back of her knee before moving around the bed to begin work on her other leg and drinking again.

After finishing her other thigh, he gathers her hair and lifts it laying it so as to leave her slender neck uncovered and available. He then oils the heavy muscles of his forearms and runs their lengths across her shoulders and the length of her neck finishing each motion with his fingertips deep in her flesh where the muscles of her neck meet the back of her skull. She lets out a low hum, and he continues first from one side and then the other until her trance like state returns.

That achieved, he moves to the end of the bed and takes her arms from her sides raising them above her head. He sinks his thumbs, slowing into the point at which her collar bones meet the tops of her shoulders with yet more slow power.

As he withdraws that force, he touches his lips to the top of her head and murmurs, "All good." But she doesn't reply.

Next he presses into the curves of her buttocks and the lines of her thighs. He uses the same strength and long strokes of his hands and arms as when he caresses her or brings her to orgasm but as she lies on the massage bed he applies them slower and more powerfully. So much so that even the strong muscles and bones of her hips, bum and upper thighs fill with a suffusing warmth that kisses the borderline of pain. Every part of his hands seems to know where every muscle and bone in her body is, which are stiff or tense and pleasurable to have touched.

She coos and stretches when he lifts her foot and sweeps strong thumbs down its sole then lets out little sighs as he presses the pads of each of her toes and circles with gentle force.

When he rumbles, "Nice?"

Her voice dreamily answers, "Mhm, I've gone all floppy."

His hands become heavier and slower and Ella Jane sinks further into her reverie.

As he works on her, he sometimes explains what he's doing in the voice that turns into a soothing background rumble as the works pass into Ella Jane's ears. At other times, he croons and hums happily to himself.

At last, he places one hand on either side of her hips and lifts to enable him to slip one arm under her while he uses his other to slide a pad beneath her hips.

The half-aware Ella Jane murmurs as he lowers her and, briefly opening her eyes, lets out a contented purr, when he eases her feet to the sides of the bed.

With her in this position, he massages her inner thighs and buttocks until she begins to rock against his touch. Only then he presses over her rosebud and perineum, at first with stationary hands but then with a rocking and circling of his hand that accents and adds to her onanistic enjoyment.

He presses the pad of his thumb over her tight rosebud with the same slow power, pushing her sensitive skin into the muscle beneath until her outer ring accepts him and her inner begins to respond before stopping. He then rocks his strength, his thumb circling against her sensitivity, awakening the need within her entrance, though the pressure is at her other opening.

Ella Jane sighs as he continues, presses up against him and finds that by doing so she forces her breasts more firmly into the bed's padding. She lets out a chuckle at the sensations this adds, at his refusal to be tempted or provoked, and as a release from the growing tension in her body.

As her response becomes more passionate, his touch becomes more intimate. He slides his fingers into her entrance, applying pressure to her fourchette at very back of her opening and gripping through the little pad of erectile tissue that separates it from his thumb against her rosebud.

His lack of rush and the way in which he has prepared the rest of her body causes the sensations he creates to spread further and deeper, suffusing her being.

At first, she doesn't register when he reaches one hand away, but she does recognise the feeling of steel inside her. She's unsure whether it's her nJoy he uses or one of his own toys, but whichever it is, he slides it just far enough that when he presses down onto the inside of her pubic bone, it causes a warming shudder to run through her body.

He takes that shudder as his signal to apply the pads of his middle finger over her hood and clit and circle there.

With his massage having broken down every tension in her, there's no place for the rising tide to break until it fills her. When it does so, it spills over and takes her everything with it.

It's all he can do to hold her still while her convulsions play out, and for Ella Jane the following time is a haze.

Her Actual Punishment

Ella Jane's world is still and silent save for the warmth of his presence and of his hand holding hers. She shifts, and feels the weight of towels on her, opens her eyes and sees him sitting on a chair by the massage bed wearing headphones and turning his attention from his tablet to her.

"Did you enjoy your massage?"

"I'm not sure I should tell you how much I enjoyed it."

"And why might that be?"

She smiles dazedly, "I think your head's already too big as it is."

"Oh, you do, do you?"

"Uh-huh, I didn't even know an orgasm could last that long."

"If we practice, they can last longer."

Her laugh comes out softly and she squeezes his hand, "Is nothing ever enough for you?"

"That was. I enjoyed it, particularly when you stopped trying to goof around."

"Sorry."

She lies there and he sits and after a while he asks, "Would you like some water?"

Hearing the question awakens her realisation, and she rolls onto her side and greedily swigs down half of the bottle he offers. “So thirsty!”

“Mhm, cumming is hard work.”

Her cheeks rosy. “Ha, it’s a tough job but somebody’s got to do it.”

“Ready to move around?”

“Yes, just about.”

“Good. I want you to show me your ring gag.” She turns to go with a ‘yes, sir’, but he stops her before she’s gone a step, “I’ll be in the office. Bring it to me there.”

Ella Jane happily scampers off to the master bedroom and the wardrobe in the bottom of which her bag, and her few secret toys, are concealed. It isn’t just the ring gag in there. Her nasal and anal hooks are there too, and she takes a moment to consider taking those to him as well. However, the firmness in his voice when he sent her serves as a warming, and her suspicion that her effort to seduce him part way through her massage may have already got him more annoyed than amused convinces her that this is *not* the time. That decided, she returns them and the bag. Then she hurries back to him with her gag, nervous but eager to try it with a partner for the first time.

He’s working rather than waiting when she arrives, and he makes her wait before signalling with his eyes for her to move to his side. When she does, he motions for her to wait again before using a hand gesture to command her to kneel. This is a first between them, and that adds to her growing certainty that she has messed up big time, prompt her to lower herself meekly into a formal slave pose with her head lowered, knees spread and the precious leather and metal device raised like an offering on the palms of her hands.

He still doesn’t respond immediately, preferring to finish typing his current thoughts before swinging his chair around to face her.

She’s so close that his knees brush her naked body as he turns, and her breath catches at the contact.

“Let me see this.” He lifts the gag from her unresisting fingers. “How long have you had this?”

"About a year, Sir. Since before we started talking."

"And you haven't worn it with anyone before?"

"No, Sir, I...I haven't had the right time, or the right person."

"But you're ready now?"

Ella Jane nods, "Yes, Sir."

"Good."

At that she raises her eyes and sees the pleasure in his face. The pleasure grows as he puts the metal bit to her lips and as she opens to it. He fits it, carefully ensuring the leather strap and buckle don't catch in her hair and asks, "Is that comfortable?"

It isn't comfortable, so she shakes her head, but it is something she wants, so her eyes smile up at him.

"But not more uncomfortable than is appropriate?" he confirms.

She nods at that.

"Now, I think it's time for us to have a little talk." He takes her answering grunt as acceptance. "Am I right in thinking that you were being cheeky while I was giving you your massage?"

She nods unhappily.

"But that you thoroughly enjoyed the massage and the orgasm I gave you at its conclusion?"

Her next nod is enthusiastic.

"Do you understand that giving you that massage took a great deal of effort and was something I wanted you to accept and enjoy as a gift to you?"

Ella Jane lets her head fall. He'd spend three hours giving her pleasure and then capped that pleasure off with the longest orgasm of her life. The nod that she eventually conjures up is truly miserable.

"Therefore, some form of punishment is due?" Another nod. "But so far as I have been able to determine, a spanking or a whipping isn't something you necessarily regard as undesirable?"

Her answer to this is a garbled series of syllables that make no sense to his ears.

"I'll take that as a yes. I'd thought you might apologise by putting this rather interesting device to use, but I suspect its opening might not be wide enough. Let's put that to the test before we move on to punishing you, shall we?"

She nods, and a first narrow string of drool escapes her lips. He stands, and her hands go to his belt, and fly, lower his trousers and underpants, takes his already hard cock and brings its tip to the ring-gag's opening. Just as he'd thought, she can get no more than the end of his foreskin and its very tip through the hole.

"That's a shame." He rearranges his clothes and offers her his hand to help her rise. "We'd best get straight on with doing something about your behaviour then, and save your apologies for later."

She nods miserably, and a second strand spills onto her chin.

"Let me see? Ah-yes." He goes to the printer, opens its tray and takes out a sheet. "Better idea." He takes two more and arranges them together then folds them it two. "I'm going to have you hold these against the wall with your nose for ten minutes. If you let them fall, I'll start the time again."

She does all she can to pout, but the gag's presence spoils the effect.

"While you're standing, I'm going to set a timer to chime every two minutes, after each of the first four chimes I'm going to strike you across your buttocks with my belt, after the fifth I'm going to release you from your positions and then your sin will be forgotten. Do you understand?"

She nods again, her eyes blinking her regret for her earlier fun.

"And do you want to safeword?"

The gag frustrates her effort to explain that her desire to safeword and escape the punishment is less than her desire to show her contrition in a way that has meaning to him.

"Do you accept this punishment rather than choosing to use your safeword?"

It's a more complicated question but it allows the gagged Ella Jane to give a complete answer with a nod of her head, so she gives it.

"Good girl."

He guides her to the wall directly opposite his desk and has her stand with her toes six inches from the skirting and her feet over shoulder width apart, far enough that she knows from experience that her lower lips will be visible to him from his chair. Satisfied with that he commands, "Up on the balls of your feet please."

She looks around with a plea in her eyes, a plea he answers with nothing more than a raised eyebrow, so she turns her face back to the wall with a resigned sigh and another strand of drool and does as bidden. As soon as she lifts her weight from her heels, her muscles tell her they're going to have to work to hold her up. This is not going to be an easy or a short ten minutes, especially once...

"Now hold this with your nose."

She tries to swallow and manages to get some of it down her throat. Then she leans forward, touches her forehead to the wall and her nose to the wad of paper.

"Just your nose please."

A sob of misery escapes her lips, but she adjusts her head and her nose squashes uncomfortably against the wall her in her effort to maintain balance.

"And place your hands behind your neck." She does this too. "Good girl. I'm starting the timer now."

Having started it he presses a small ball into each of her hands. "Left is yellow, right is red." With that, he pats her bare bum and returns to his work.

The first two minutes are interminable. There's nothing to do other than count seconds, try to keep the paper in place and try to ignore the discomfort in her calf muscles. There's also no way to clear the saliva from her mouth without allowing the papers to fall other than by letting it spill out and run down her chin and fall.

She's almost relieved when she hears the first chime. The sound is followed by that of him pushing his chair back and undoing and removing his belt. She senses him moving close, sees him position himself to her left out of the corner of her eye and hears his, "Are you ready?" He takes the sound she makes as a yes, and a moment later she sees movement, then hears the belt move through the air.

Then comes the impact and the blaze on the right side of her bum as the belt's tip wraps and bites. She presses her head hard against the wall and lets out a garbled cry then a sob as she resets herself so only her nose is pressing.

He returns to his work with nothing more than a matter-of-factly spoken, "Good girl, that's one." And a brief touch of a hand to her back.

The second two minutes are harder for her as her legs grow sore and her neck feels stiffer. The only comfort she's afforded is knowing she won't have to wait for him to take his belt off again. This time, he positions himself to her right and the belt wraps to her left butt cheek, but the pain is as great. At least he says, "Good girl, that's two," before he returns to his work leaving her to her suffering and the contemplation of her sins.

In the next two minutes the soreness in her legs grows to a burning, and her mind sets itself to the moments as she was lying on her back trying to coax a smack or an orgasm from him while he worked. At last, the sound of the third chime interrupts her misery. She hears him rise. Sees him from the corner of her left eye, braces herself to endure the pain she knows is coming without allowing the wad of paper to fall. He strikes and she succeeds. This time she snivels for longer, and when she hears him leave the room rather than going to his desk, she lets out a sob. He returns before the next chime, and when he does, he comes back to where she is, kneels behind her and does something she cannot see on the floor between her feet.

He's still doing it when the fourth chime sounds and he has to go to his desk to fetch the belt. This time he goes back to her right, and the pain explodes on her left side His, "Good girl." is followed by, "That's all with the belt." And a gentle kiss to her shoulder.

The comfort of his words carries her through the next minute, but in the last, the aching in her calves grows into such a pain that she's shaking and sobbing by the time the final chime signals the end of her punishment. Ella Jane still holds her position though, right up until his hand touches her, and she hears his warm, "It's over now."

She turns and tries to set her heels down, but yelps at the complaint from her tortured muscles and allows him to carry her back to his desk.

He sits her on the desk, and has her lean back while he stretches out her calves. As he stretches, his hands perform a brief reprise of the massage she had treated so lightly earlier, and her muscles melt in gratitude even as her sense of guilt rises. As always when they are together, time seems to have no meaning and he indulges in his soothing until long after the pain is eased. He then goes to the place where she'd been standing and bends. She sees him lift the hand towel from between where her feet had been and brings it back, uses the parts of it that aren't already wet from her drooling to clean her face of tears and drool then dries the patches of wet from her breasts and body.

Ella Jane gives him a pitiful, "Hang-hoo," through the gag and his lips curl up.

"Would you like me to take that off now?"

"Eff-eese."

He chuckles as he unbuckles the gag, eases it from her mouth and carries on as she stretches her jaw muscles. Then he hushes her as she pours out a stream of apologies. Hearing the distress in her voice, he lifts her and lowers her into his lap and holds her close while he fills her ears with *it's overs* and *good girls*.

She wraps her arms around him and lets him cradle her there for an age. She feels his warm and his forgiveness and processes her first true experience of punishment at his hands, "May I speak?"

"Yes."

"It's about the massage."

"About you being naughty?"

"Yes, sort of."

"That's over, but so long as you understand that, you're free to speak."

"I didn't realise..." his arms remain around her, and his eyes remain patient, "Not how much it meant to you or..."

His eyes blink slowly as he waits for her to continue.

"Or how nice it would be..." he smiles at that and a first sign of cheering after her unhappiness and catharsis makes itself known in a barely audible squeak of laughter. She then colours, "Or how long I could cum for."

He lets out a laugh and then so does she. Tears follow her laughter and blushes, and kisses and smiles follow the tears.

"I'll be good if you massage me again. If you want to, that is."

"Oh, Ella Jane!" He smiles at that with a trace of wetness in his eyes, and blinks the wetness away. "Yes, if you stay with me a while longer, I'll massage you again. And now that I know your body better, it will be better."

"Can it be better?"

He bends to her upturned face and kisses her lightly, "Yes, a lot." then deeply, before breaking off to chuckle in his wicked way, "I might even manage to give you a better orgasm."

She nuzzles into him unsure whether she can manage to bear a more intense orgasm as she does. "You're never satisfied, are you?"

"Au contraire." He kisses the top of her head. "With you, I'm always satisfied; I just always want to see if there's more."

She kisses him. "You're always so you."

"And you aren't?"

Her immediate reaction is to suck her lips into her mouth, but doing so doesn't stop her eyes creasing in mirth, or the butterflies in her stomach doing their will he laugh or am I in trouble flutter. "Are you going to spank me again if I say *I'm not you*?"

One of his cheeks twitches and the butterflies take flight. Then his more expressive right eyebrow rises, and they perform aerial acrobatics.

"Yes, spank and kiss. You'll be teasing like that in private."

"And in public?"

"We don't do each other down, even in jest. That's right up there on the hard limit list."

"Even though this is only a New York thing?"

"We fought in each other's corners on the first day of the conference. I liked that. I think it's simpler and better to keep things on that basis."

"Wasn't that just because I was right?"

"It was *also* because we were both right, but once two people cross certain lines they're vulnerable to one another, it works best if from then on they keep any mutual criticism private.." He grins. "Now, which would you want first, the punishment or the reward."

Ella Jane makes to rise from his lap and he allows her to stand. "Given the choice? Punishment, then you can make me feel better." And she holds a hand out to him.

He lets her lead him into the bedroom then pulls her to face him when they're standing by the foot of the bed. "Regretting telling me everything when we were message-pals an ocean apart?"

She sits, then lies back looking up at him with need filled eyes. "I'll tell you after."

"After this, after the punishment, or after the reward?"

"That would be telling." He growls, but all she does is hum, roll over, pull her knees under her body, spread her legs and press her face into the bed. "Is this how you want me for my punishment, Sir?"

"You haven't actually earned another one yet." She may not have, but he still moves behind her and starts stroking the parts of her body she's offering up.

Ella Jane cranes her head around so she can see him. "Can't you just pretend I have?"

"We can just play, you know?"

She bites her lip. "I wasn't sure you'd have the energy?" then yelps and joins in with his laughter when the flat of his hand lands on each of her buttocks in turn with just enough force to send a pleasing shockwave through her.

He reaches up to her mouth with his left hand. "You might want to lick."

"Yes, Sir." She takes his fingers into her mouth and, guessing his intention, she edges her knees even further apart when he withdraws them."

"Good girl." He slips the slick fingers between her outer and inner labia.

She wriggles against his fingers, and chuckles at his growl, "You know me as well as I do."

He sandwiches her hood and presses his palm against her pubic bone in that way only he ever has. "Hmm, physically perhaps, but still not well enough even there."

"Well, you did used to teach."

"I did, and I still study, there's more than just the physical though, I don't know *you* as well as I'd like." He sweeps her tumbling locks from her back and kisses along the top of her shoulders. "But I'm trying. Now, do you want a spanking or shall we try something a little more calming?"

"Calming?"

He continues to stroke her skin. "Yes."

She colours and buries her face against him. "Like the massage was supposed to be?"

"Hmm," he chides, "you know well enough that punishment and forgiveness draw a line under an infraction."

"I do, yes, something more calm."

So he does something more calm. No toys, no extended bouts of edging. He just kisses and caresses and brings her to a long, sweet orgasm with his tongue, enters her and makes slow love to her until he does and finishes by bringing her to a second orgasm with his fingers while the spoon.

Her Friends

Having agreed to stay in New York with him, Ella Jane uses the excuse of having to let people know to get some alone time, so she can order enough things to wear to cover her extended break and to speak with her *I'm a bit tied up* friend. He swallows the white lie and, having kissed her lips, he disappears into the suite's office to immerse himself in music and work, leaving her free to go online and order some things to carry her through. Her initial look at the bargain store that kept her going through her college years triggers a, 'what am I doing' moment. Instead, she goes to PrettyLittleThing where she finds some underwear she likes and thinks he will too, a spare pair of jeans and a couple of casual tops. She looks at nightwear too, and then smiles at the thought of seeing the horror on his face that anyone in his arms could be cold or that any his submissive should dare try to deny him her nakedness.

Ella Jane sits with that smile for a time, issues up a prayer that her publisher and agent's promises that her sales will allow her to afford such extravagances, and clicks buy.

Having done that, she thinks about her protagonist Abigail. To get herself in the mood, she pads from the bed and sneaks one of his casual shirts to wrap herself in. Abigail most definitely isn't a girl who lounges around naked in the day. With her mind a little more in the Abigail mode, she sketches out some ideas she thinks will match up to what will be protagonist's first impressions of the city. She then messages her mother to say she's staying longer in New York in order to avoid explaining why.

Next she phones her university friend Louise to makes good on her promise made while *tied up* to tell her a less edited version of her adventures so far than she'd feel comfortable telling anyone else she knows

Louise is naturally curious. "Are you still *not going out* with him?"

"Um, sort of," she swallows, "I've moved in with him in the hotel."

"That was fast!"

"It's only for a few days while we're both here in New York."

"Aren't you a cramped?"

Ella Jane laughs into her phone, "So cramped, let me show you!" and switches to video, "He's got a suite, it's incredible." And pans the phone around the bedroom then gives a tour of the bathroom before going out camera-phone in hand to show her the rest of their cramped room.

He's in the office, working at his laptop with headphones on, but with the door open, so she pokes her head in. He looks up, works out what she's doing, and makes an 'on the phone' signal with his hand.

She nods.

He mouths "With your mother?"

She shakes her head and mouths 'a friend'.

His response is a laugh, and a mouthed, *phew*. However, it takes him a couple of tries to convey 'the same friend?' without signalling tied up.

After she nods her confirmation, he speaks aloud, "Hello again, Ella Jane's friend."

She points the phone towards him.

He calls, "I still haven't murdered her."

Ella's face drops but she hears Louise's laugh on the phone, and seeing her, she laughs too.

As she leaves she says, "He thinks he's so clever," with a look over her shoulder as she goes. Knowing she's going to pay for that later.

She then goes on to give an almost complete tour only omitting the second bedroom because as her hand approaches the door-handle, she remembers them having left the shackles and toys out in there, so she hastily explains, "Just another bedroom." She also does a couple of rapid turns to avoid facing any mirrors directly and giving Louise a more complete view of herself than necessary. Having given her friend the tour she shuts off the camera and talks into the phone as she goes back to the bedroom, and carries on chatting with her now even more intrigued friend.

Shortly after she rings off from Louise, Ella Jane's phone chimes, and she checks the newly arrived message. It reads:

Too bad you don't read the glossies.

It comes from Haley, her oldest friend, who most certainly does read them.

Ella Jane has absolutely no idea what her she's going on about, so she messages back,

Have you been drinking?

Haley's in the next message is more cryptic still,

Authors hit the write note at The Met.

It's followed shortly afterwards by a third

Can I call?

The confused Ella Jane decides to cut to the chase and makes the call herself.

Haley answers before she hears the phone ring and her voice bursts excitedly from it. “Can we switch to video?”

“Why?”

“I’m not saying till you agree.”

Ella Jane grumbles, but borrows his discarded dress shirt and switches. “Happy now?”

“Yes, ecstatic!”

“Why are you happy now?”

“Because I want to see your face when you see this.” She aims her phone’s camera at her computer screen. The screen shows a page from a gossip website dominated by a photograph of them standing outside the Metropolitan Opera House. Ella Jane is in all her rented finery; He is looking every bit the tycoon. Neither is remotely resembles any stereotype of a writer.

“Oh my God! What does it say?”

Haley reads through the text. “There isn’t much but they describe him as notoriously reclusive English author. Ooh! I like this, ‘the young beauty has been identified as up and coming writer Ella Jane Tyler.”

Ella Jane just stares at her phone.

“You really didn’t know, did you?”

“No, he just took me to the opera and there was a paparazzo.”

“Your *not-a-date* must have been pretty good if he bought you that dress!”

Ella Jane finds herself falling back on his defence. “It’s only rented.”

“It looks amazing. You still look amazing. Do you want me to send you a link so you can pass it on to your folks?”

“Please!”

He emerges from the office in search of coffee and pops his head around the bedroom door when he hears Ella Jane talking excitedly into her phone. She wave at him and mouths *Oh My God*.

Unsure of her meaning he frowns first, then chuckles and holds his arms out to his sides as he performs a courtly bow and polishes his knuckles.

A narrowing of her eyes confirms that she wasn't just OMG-ing his existence, but that expression is immediately replaced by the return of her excitement. She waves him over and tells whoever is on the phone, "He's come out. Hang on; I'm going to show him. Thanks bae," before aiming her phone's screen at him.

The screen shows a picture of them outside the Met Opera House. It's on the Instagram account of a gossip magazine.

"Gosh."

"Is that all you have to say?"

"Did they spell your name and the title of your book right?"

Her face clearly doesn't think that's the most important thing about her first brush with social media fame, but she checks anyway. "Yes."

"Fantastic. Are you telling a friend about it?"

"No, she's telling me."

"Same friend?"

"No, this is Haley."

"Hello Haley." Curiosity sated, he fetches his coffee and goes back to work.

Ella Jane has not long finished talking when a woman from the butler service knocks on the door to their bedroom and announces that lunch is served in the dining room. She thanks her and, when asked, says they won't need further help while they eat. Then she waits for the sound of the butler leaving and slips his shirt off and back into his wardrobe before heading to the office to find him.

He may have said he'd be working but he hadn't just been doing that. He's a man who listens and who, having listened, is happy to either act or arrange for someone else to. He'd heard Ella Jane say she only brought enough things for a few days, and now she's agreed to stay longer. He's arranged for going out clothes for her since she brought regular ones with her. Simple logic dictated his course of action.

While he's taking advantage of being five time zones west to talk to some people he normally has few regular hours in common with, he does a quick search for designer lingerie and New York. His preference being both for women having things they find attractive and for sourcing locally. One supplier catches his attention, the company's name, God Save Queens couldn't be more appropriate to either the location or to an Englishman shopping there so he clicks.

Their garments are neither garish nor appear flimsy, and he has her sizes thoughtfully supplied by the dress hire shop. This makes getting her a couple of sets as simple as a few instantly-forgotten clicks.

Then there are the bits of work that have stacked up too. He may be on holiday but there are summaries of minutes to meetings, documents and emails relating to the visits he's due to make. There's also the possibility of travelling with Ella Jane. That prompts him to request someone finds more elaborate lodgings than just the Gulfstream.

Those things out of the way he turns his mind to his writing projects and the mind-farm. He sketches plot passages, fills out a scene, 'fires and forgets' a half dozen ideas into the mind farm and comments on another several threads, all the while the music flows through him and thoughts of things to do, for and with the baffling young woman who's fallen into his life.

He's just paused for a moment to think about her when there's a timid knock at the door and she peeps in.

His eyes light up, then he glances at the time on his computer screen. "Lunch?"

"Yes, they said it's served."

"Oh. Good, I didn't realise the time."

"Have you been miles away too?"

"Yes, we can have the rest of the day to ourselves if you'd like?"

"Yes, of course. Only I've got to pop out to a store after we eat."

Over lunch Ella Jane asks the question that's been bubbling up ever since Haley told her about the pictures. "Did you know?"

"About the article?"

She nods.

"No, I just gave the guy my card; he must have called Roger's or my office and got our details."

His answer reminds her that, he isn't just him, and prompts her to ask, "Does that mean your office knows who I am?"

He confides, "They have a little file with your dress size and a note saying to pay for anything you order on room service."

"Just like that?"

"You needed a dress, and you're staying in my room." He shrugs and then winks, "Just please don't disappoint me by buying their Bentley. I doubt I can sneak it into my luggage allowance."

She smiles at his joke, so he presumes the matter is closed. "Now, we've got that out of the way, is there something you'd like to try?"

"You aren't going to say anything else about our picture?"

"It's a lovely picture, and you look stunning in that dress and out of it. If Cynthia complains about you doing publicity without telling her, blame me."

"Will she complain?"

"No, but she might mention it, just as you might have missed a more immediate point."

"What?"

"The chance to tell me something you'd like to try."

"Er..." she licks her lips, then brightens. "Can I look in your collection of toys, or are they a state secret?"

He counters, "You can look at what I've brought. May I look at yours?"

Ella Jane twists a foot awkwardly. "I only brought one vibrator with me." It's the first time she's ever been embarrassed by not having more toys.

His tone is pitying when he observers, "Some men would regard you bringing a vibrator as showing a lack of faith." And as he speaks his face assumes a positively lascivious expression.

Having learnt not to mention bringing a vibe to meet men after facing reactions far more extreme than, *are you showing a lack of faith,* Ella Jane winces, then sucks her lips into her mouth while her eyes start to smile, "Several have, but you've brought a battery of them. Men never bring anything except maybe a favourite whip, let alone however many toys you have with you, and they mostly don't know how to use mine properly." She leans forward and touches a palm to the material of his shirt and squeezes her thighs tight around her now seemingly ever tingly entrance. "I'm not sure I knew how to use some of them a week ago."

He holds his right hand up, looks at it, and then smiles into her eyes. "Why would I bother learning to use my hands but not bother with the simpler skill of how to use a vibe?"

"That makes me feel worse." Her fingers trace the lines of his learned, and now familiar, fingers.

"Is that a compliment?"

"So modest again? Ouch!" She pouts as the equally adept fingers of his other hand exploit the sensitivity of each of her bare breasts in turn to chastise her for her barbed comment. "I might ask you not to do that – Oh, ow! – if I didn't sort of like you doing it."

He shrugs smugly. "I'm fascinated by the this-is-going-to-hurt look in your eyes combined with the then-it's-going-to-feel-good feeling in your soul." Then he gives her his devil smile again and rumbles, "How could a man resist?"

"You might be surprised how few men can see..." Her lips part, expecting his kiss, but he evades them and busies himself gentling her outraged flesh.

As he caresses, he muses, "Now, where were we? Ah, yes. What is a vibrator?"

Ella Jane makes to answer, but he holds up a hand. "Is it, A) a gadget; B) a way to give a woman pleasure; C) a way to control a woman's pleasure; or, D) all of the above?" When he finishes, he starts kissing circles around her chest.

She laughs, "Is that one of the questions you used to ask at your salons?"

"It is."

"A and B for me, and D for you because you're a wicked man."

Then he pulls her shoulders back, making her breasts stick out further.

She expects his fingers to chastise her for her teasing. When he leans towards the tips of her breasts, she holds her breath, expecting to him to bite. Instead, he gently sucks each bud into his mouth in turn and lightly grazes his teeth against them until they are as stiff as they've ever been rather than sinking his teeth hard into their tips.

That accomplished, he lifts his head away and gives a boyish smile as his fingertips take over. "And there are three things a man should like more than a gadget, giving a woman pleasure and controlling that pleasure."

"That's only two."

"Bacon."

"Bacon?"

"Yes, that or music."

"Are you teasing me?"

"Yes, but a man should have a second interest as well if he doesn't want to become dull."

Ella Jane chuckles and leans her head against him. "Funny too, and you do that massage thing. Can you cook more than just eggs and bacon?"

He raises an eyebrow as if questioning whether his not being able to were a possibility.

She chews at her lip and shakes her head slowly as a hint of a smile begins to light up her eyes. "Of course, you can. Where have you been all my life?"

A voice in his head shouts that things are moving beyond his comfort zone and urges him to say something about having been being a grown up while she was at school, but he tells it to shut the fuck up. He's enjoying being with her, and she seems to be having fun too. "England mostly."

"Always an answer."

"Yes," His expression becomes even more smug. "Even if the answer's *I don't know*."

She pokes her tongue out, though she does so more in response to his expression than his answer.

"If you're going to keep teasing, I could phone down to the kitchen for a bag of brown rice and a bag of white rice..."

She swallows. "You would too, wouldn't you?"

"Yes, but I'd rather not." Another kiss. "Toys or room service?"

Ella Jane blurts, "Toys, please, Sir!" and then grins. After all, she thinks to herself, I can always enjoy imagining being made to kneel on the floor, sorting out rice grains, but the chance to explore his toy collection is real and immediate.

He takes her to their bedroom and starts going through drawers, retrieving additional whips and sets of cuffs. There are more butt plugs and a glass and a steel dildo too. The thing that surprises her most, however, is the vibrator collection. She's already met the two wands, but there are several others as well. "You were meeting me for a night?"

"A fellow has to be prepared."

"The vibrating plug and the rabbit aren't even opened. Nor's this?" She holds up a third cellophane wrapped box.

"It's a G-spot vibe. I don't share anything plastic and internal between partners."

"So you just throw them away?"

"Think more sort of gifty."

Ella Jane can't help it. She really can't. First her cheeks tighten, then her shoulders shake, and finally she bursts out, "I'm bored of you, but you can keep the vibrator! That's a hell of a dumping present!" before erupting in gales of hysterics.

Fortunately for her, he sees the funny side and joins in. Also fortunately, he waits for her to stop before explaining. "I tend to make the gift at time of using. That way it doesn't result in me getting them thrown at me."

He then waits until they've both stopped laughing again before quite ceremoniously unwrapping the rabbit and offering it to her. "Happy un-birthday."

She chuckles, "Why thank you, kind Sir. Should I knight you with it?"

"You could. Though I might crown you if you tried."

"Sir Cumalot?"

He raises an eyebrow and fetches out a simple desk chair. "Come here."

She tightens the line of her mouth and curls one arm protectively over her breasts while tucking the other behind her to cover as much of her bum as she's able as she approaches him. "Have I done something wrong, Sir?"

The eyebrow rises further. "Are you going to pretend you don't know?"

"Only if that's the best way to get you to put me over your knee and use this on me."

"Did it come charged?"

"Um..." she examines it and finds the subtle plus sign of the on button on the unbroken silky smooth material covering it. Button found, she presses it, after a couple of seconds it bursts into life. "Yes!"

He lowers his head, allows his lips to curl into a cruel smile, and hardens his voice. "Then I suggest confessing and throwing yourself on my mercy."

The voice, the bloody voice, Ella Jane's insides tighten and her heart speeds up. "Do you actually have any mercy?"

He sits on the chair and pretends to think. "No, but if you want a spanking and to have me make you cum, that's the way to do it."

Taking her cue, and hamming her response up outrageously she kneels in front of the chair. "Oh cruel and terrible, but beloved Master, your worthless slave humbly apologises for being insolent on receiving your generous gift and begs to be punished terribly, so she may earn your forgiveness."

She then blinks up at him with pride in her impromptu speech and expectant that he's both going to really let her bum have it and enjoy trying the vibe on her.

He harrumphs, "Don't push your luck," and sets about testing out the vibrator's functions. He finds how to control which of the toy's little motors is running, how to change the pattern of the vibrations and finally how to change their intensity while she hums contentedly and expectantly as she watches him enjoy his tinkering.

Satisfied that he has mastered the gadget he returns his attention the errant, but unrepentant Ella Jane. "Very well, get in position."

The little squeal of delight Ella Jane lets out as she rises doesn't do anything to create an impression that she's submitting to some form of punishment. But then neither does the way he pulls her into his lap or the long slow kiss he gives her before telling her to roll over and bend over his knees.

He has her spread her legs and holds her lower lips open. Then he checks to see if they'll need any lube, and on finding out they won't, has her clean one if his fingers while saving the other for himself. Tasting complete, he slides the longer, internal tip into herself, bends the external part of the vibrator up against the line of her slit and lets go. It stays bent against her with its head over her clit. "Is that in the right place?"

She lies, "Um, I don't know," and gets a whack for doing so.

"Ha-ha, yes, I think so." She wiggles her bum. "There's one way to find out."

He smacks her bum again, but he also turns the vibe on. The first setting makes the piece over her clit start vibrating.

"Yes!"

A second stops it but starts the one pressed against the front wall of her vagina.

"Oh, ooh!"

The third makes both work at the same time.

"Fuck, yes," her breathing immediately catches.

"Bugger." A click of another button replaces the continuous buzzing with an undulating pattern and two on the minus reduce the intensity. "Better?"

"Ha, no."

He whacks her again.

"But yes, I can hold on for a while."

His hand strokes the offered curves of her bum. "Good girl. Are you ready for me to begin?"

"No, yes." Not knowing whether to laugh or sigh, she wraps her arms around his calf and presses her lips to his skin, then signals her hesitant readiness. "Never, but always."

The spanking he gives her is long and slow, not especially hard, but her body still remembers both her earlier funishment and her punishment, so it's certainly hard enough. The vibrations aren't strong enough to send her rushing towards orgasm either, at least not to begin with.

He spanks, strokes, toys with her breasts, and slowly, one level at a time sets the toy working harder. When she gets close sooner than he wants he asks, "Are you feeling repentant yet, young lady?"

It makes Ella Jane giggle, and her amusement resets her body back to a lower level of arousal. She answers with, "Bastard, Sir." and lets out a low sigh when the series of spanks that follow land hard and square on her upturned cheeks.

When he pauses to caress her reddened skin she, allows her mind to sink into the scene and breathes out, "Sorry, Sir." Her voice sufficiently softened by desire to sound apologetic.

"Really?"

"Mostly, yes."

He bends so close to her that she can feel vibrations from his low chuckle in her skin, and turns the rabbit up a notch.

"C-can you slow it down?"

"Everything okay?"

"Yes," she giggles. "But I want to do something for you too."

His hand runs down her back and through the valley between her buttocks to the vibe. "There might not be enough room."

Ella Jane lifts her bum higher and closes her eyes. "I'm sure there is somewhere." She then lets out an involuntary squeak of laugher when he places the vibrating tip of his thumb against her rosebud. "You must be a mind reader."

She doesn't wait for him to take the initiative. When he helps her to her feet she uses one hand to hold the rabbit in place, and her other to lead him into their bedroom. Once there, she goes to his bedside drawers, touches the one he keeps the lube in and looks at him asking permission.

He nods, but smiles too, and opines, "It might be easier if I you took your new vibrator out, or let me do some of the arranging.

"I..." but he's right, she does want to do something for him, but she doesn't want to stop the buzz she has going. "What would you like me to do when you're arranging?"

He pulls a chair close to the bed and spreads a towel in its seat. "Show me how you'd use that thing if I weren't here."

She colours. "Are you sure?"

That brings a smile to his face and his eyes scan appreciatively down the length of her body and back up. "You're already holding it."

He moves to within inches of where she's standing and trace the lines of her should her and arm following down to her fingers and the bright pink toy she's holding. "I'd love you to show me if you feel brave enough, but don't cum just yet."

Her eyes ask him to let her escape, her body asks her to go ahead, and a voice in the back of her mind reads from passages in which her fictional heroines have done as he's asking her to.

His eyes neither plead nor fill with anger, and rather than force, his hands keep up their artful caresses.

That's what catches her. His sensuous her wrist starts to move in sympathy with his hands and, having begun to pleasure herself, she lets her lips smile. "That's cheating."

He kisses her cheek and murmurs, "Think of O." Then lets out another chuckle when the way her eyes lower tell him she has been.

She arranges herself in the chair, and makes a face when he signals for her to move her hips forward and spread her legs further, but she does as he asks, and can't help smiling at the way his eyes focus on her. "I thought you were arranging things!"

"Sorry, got distracted." Neither his voice, nor his expression indicates the least trace of remorse.

Ella Jane somewhat self consciously moves her free hand to her chest and strokes the undercurves of her breasts teasing slowly closer to their tips.

After a while of watching though, he does set about laying pillows and a towel in the centre of the bed. He then gets the lube out, sits on the side of the mattress facing her and squeezes a dollop into his palm.

When he sets the tube aside he draws his foreskin back and applies some to his glans then slides it forward again to spread more over his sheath and shaft with one hand. He watches her and she watches him, each seeking signs the other is as flush with anticipation.

He leans forward as he works and his free hand joins her in caressing her breasts and then caresses her hand. Taking a hold of her wrist he draw it away from circling her areolas and guides it to his cock where he has her replace his slowly stroking fingers. He then adds more lube to his hands and to hers and applies his fingers to her, first coating her rosebud and ring with the lube's slickness and then her breasts and their erect tips.

They carry on until both are rocking in a shared rhythm. Then he slides his hands to her sides and eases her to her feet.

Ella Jane doesn't let go of his cock until she's lying face down over the pillows, and when she does it is to pull herself further open for him.

Their hands spread her and guide him to her back door, and he presses against her there. With the rabbit inside her she's tighter.

They take it slowly. When he stops against her inner ring she turns the vibe up and presses it against the back wall of her entrance squeezing the sensitive tissue there against the tip of his cock then lets out a low groan which she follows with a chuckle when he rumbles, "*Oh!* Do you like that too?"

"Oh yes!" They both laugh and during the lulls between laughter and thrills of pleasure he makes his way into her.

Filled and stroked in both of her openings, and with the rabbit's two electric motors and their four hands on her, Ella Jane's body rushes towards and through a first climax. The orgasm's waves rush her breasts where their kneading hands catch and hold them and to flood to her muscular rings which spasm frenetically around his shaft.

Despite turning the toy down as her private eruption subsides his rhythmic stroking inside her tightness sets another building. Her breathing becomes urgent again spurring him on and his longer, faster and more forceful thrusts hasten them both onwards.

Their bodies heat up and their sweat mingles binding them together with its salty sweetness. On feeling his hardness surge she turns the rabbit up to its highest setting and clings on to his arm as his hands crush her breasts and he buries his full length into her and starts to shake. Her second orgasm begins moments after and carries on until they are both quite spent apart from the slow pulsing of his cock inside her and her body's response to it.

They Eat in the Bar

Ella Jane stretches and sighs.

He strokes her hair away from her face. “What’s wrong?”

“Nothing, not a thing, but we’re going to have to move soon, aren’t we.”

“Oh, why’s that?”

“You’re going to want to go somewhere exotic to eat, aren’t you?”

“We’re eating at Table 55 tonight.”

“Can’t we stay at the hotel?”

“We are. It’s here, just in the bar, not the suite.”

“The bar?”

“The King Cole bar. They have a special menu for two. I’ve been told it’s quite the thing. A friend insisted I try it so I can report back.”

She frowns. “So, you’re taking me for your friend, not me?”

“I’m taking you because I’m with you. It’s supposed to be a wonderful experience. Besides, housekeeping probably wants to change our sheets and run a duster over.”

“Okay, Will there be wine?”

“Lots of wines, each married to a dish, all of them quite something.”

Ella Jane makes a face, knowing how he feels about play after more than a couple of drinks.

"That's one reason we're having a day of fun beforehand, the..." he checks his phone, "Nine hours of kinkiness should satisfy even you."

Used to wanting more than others could give Ella Jane sucks her lips into her mouth to save herself from making a dishonest claim to appetites more modest than they seem to share.

"Besides," he grins and kisses her delicately, as though they hadn't even had nine minutes of snogging in the time they've known one another, "There's no reason we can't be vanilla-ish after dinner, it isn't as if either of us is bad at that."

"Hmm, okay." She reaches up and touches her lips to his. "Should I wear my dress?"

"It's only in the bar. I was thinking we could go casual."

"When's dinner booked?"

"Not for a while, and it isn't as if we're going to get stuck in traffic.

"Do you have anything planned?"

He stretches out. "Might have, I was thinking a spot of DIY might be fun."

Remembering his previous efforts to make things she smiles and asks, "Are you going to tie me up while you make things again?"

"This time I've found you some things to make too."

He's printed out the instructions for making a two coloured flogger, and a bondage belt and wand holder out of paracord.

Her mouth opens. "You're serious, aren't you?"

"Yes."

She muses wistfully, "My gran loves crafting."

"Excellent, it must run in the blood. Just don't show her these if you ever plan on introducing us!"

Ella Jane is rather less confident of her abilities than he is. "Are you sure you trust me to make these?"

"You should be the one who's concerned, I don't plan to use them on myself."

"Was that supposed to reassure me?"

He furrows his brow. "Um..." and then brightens. "That depends if it did."

Ella Jane's eyes narrow and she answers him slowly, as if speaking to someone both less intelligent, and less intimidating. "It's not supposed to work that way."

"Oh? I suppose not."

"No. What happens if I make a mess of it?"

He shrugs. "There's a lot of paracord. *Someone* once told me there are hardware stores that don't get through as much as we've got in a month."

Petite, and naked though she is, Ella Jane's instinct to put her hands on her hips and set her chin wins out. "I know! That was me."

He beams at her delightedly. "Then you are very wise."

Despite the printed instructions, her first effort to make a flogger is unsuccessful, but fortunately it is so unsuccessful that she's easily able to unravel its too loosely bound cords with the intention of trying again, once she's looked up a YouTube video. However, what he's doing attracts her attention; he has his tablet and laptop out and has collected some pipe and tools. "Aren't you doing some DIY?"

He holds up the hot wire cutter and winks with a grin. "No."

Ella Jane's mouth scrunches up as though she'd just bitten into a lime, but she holds her tongue.

"Yes, had an idea." He turns the laptop so she can see the screen then takes a length of wide PVC and cuts three pieces one, two, and three feet in length each of which he drills through at one inch intervals. That done, he cuts two one-foot and two two-foot sections of a thinner pipe that fits snuggly inside and drills these.

Ella Jane frowns as he works but doesn't ask what he's doing, preferring to guess what sort of bondage equipment he's constructing.

She doesn't have to wait long, and her face lights up in realisation when he inserts the two thinner sections into the ends of a wider tube, threads a length of rope through, and then bolts the pieces of piping together. When he looks up, she declares, "Another spreader bar!"

"Good girl. Got it in one." He goes to her, strokes her face and kisses her lips. "Do you want your reward now?"

It had been an easy guess, but she still glows, both at his praise and in anticipation of him using it on her. She has another question to ask though. "Why do you need another spreader bar?"

"Because this one's better." He thread a rope through the middle sections and then adds the narrow extension pieces and bolts them in place. "See, I can do this." And he fashions bars ranging from shoulder-width, to longer than Ella Jane is tall. Then he shows her how he can fit eye-bolts through the drilled holes to allow him to tie her, and secure the bar in place, in a variety of ways.

Satisfied with his work, he sets his tools aside.

She watches him, how he meticulously clears the tools away, and the moment the last is back in its place she floats, "I suppose you want to try it out now?"

He isn't even facing her way, but he turns on hearing, and there's a wolf-smile on his face. "Well, if you aren't too busy?"

Ella Jane giggles, "I think I can fit you into my busy schedule. Where do you want me?"

"Hmm, the cuffs are in our bedroom, so we may as well start there."

The bar is even more rigid than his first. His new design has another advantage as well; he's able to adjust the bar's length to enable him to restrain her in place more precisely. So when he binds Ella Jane, she has less freedom to wriggle. "How did you get the idea for your new design?"

"I thought of it while I was helping you with your morning stretches."

Ella Jane smiles at his oblique reference to the way he ties her up in ever closer to a splits every morning. "Can I see?"

"Of course." He holds up a mirror.

"It is prettier, I suppose."

"More adjustable too, and easier to set-up and transport."

"Does that mean it's coming with us?"

He leans over and kisses her lips while his hand strokes her neck. “It’s all coming with us, though I’ll grant you, I’m going to need to alter a few of the frames a bit.”

The kiss and caresses are nice, and so’s the bondage, but being tied in a way that draws her mind to her inner thighs and wide open entrance stokes her desire for more, and her voice is thick with need when she asks, “Do you want to make sure it doesn’t break when you make me cum or fuck me?”

It doesn’t break when he does either, nor when he teases her to distraction. He even gives her a few good licks with a crop while encouraging her to try and break free. However, she isn’t even about damage it when he tickles her mercilessly or when he uses a wand on her while fucking her.

During an interlude he unties her and compares the two spreaders, then allows her to do so. While she’s looking at his newer design he has another idea. “I could use this as a yoke as well, couldn’t I?”

“Yoke?”

“Yes, put a ring-bold through the middle and lock it to a collar then secure your wrists to the ends.”

“I see, and why would you want to do that?”

“Did we just move into a much duller parallel universe where either of us needs a reason for me to tie you up?”

“Ha, no, I suppose not.”

“Good, I’ll have to make another one so we can use a yoke and spreader at the same time.”

“Do you have to do that now?”

“No,” he grins, “I have other plans for now.”

Just as in their room and in the restaurant, the staff in the bar move around them with an almost choreographic precision.

Ella Jane leans forwards with a smile and whispers. "They're treating us as though I was in my dress and you were in your tuxedo."

He lets out a low chuckle. "They're very good, you're very lovely, and I expect doing this set menu is something they get a kick out of." He doesn't say a word about his exquisite manners or the obscene amount he's paying, but he privately suspects they aren't hurting the level of service any too much either.

Several starters arrive in choreographed succession, are eaten and their empty plates and glasses are whisked away, and are followed by a sharp, delicate sorbet that Ella Jane tastes with caution at first, but scrapes every trace she can from the glass it is served in. "Mmm, that was interesting!"

"I'm glad you thought so." He gives her a squeeze. "Tell me, do you have any plans after the weekend?"

"No, just see my folks and arrange moving out of my apartment at Duke." She looks down, so he can't see her nervous smile. "Not unless your idea is now an invitation?"

He locks down his expression "It is."

Ella Jane shows no such reticence and allows her face to light up with a grin that melts his stern countenance. "What shall we do if I stay?"

"I'm sure we can amuse ourselves, he grins. "And as the native, I'm sure you have some ideas."

"I'm not a native of New York."

He blinks and his voice lightens. "Aren't all Americans familiar with everywhere in your country?"

"I hope you're teasing."

"Yes, sort of." He kisses her and beams. "More an old joke." He kisses again and explains, "I've had a few of your countrymen assume that I must know everyone and everywhere in England."

"Not even at your age?" she asks innocently, then laughs at the narrowing of his eyes she'd been seeking. "Am I always going to be able to get in trouble that way?"

"Hmph, do it at the wrong moment, and it won't be so much fun."

She strokes her calf against his under the table. "So I always have to pay attention to your mood?"

"That, where we are, and who we're with." He takes her hand and punctuates his requirements with strokes of his thumb along her palm.

"And do the same rules apply to you?"

"Sort of, I plan on not getting either of us arrested, thrown out of anywhere we might want to visit again."

"Mmm, that's considerate of you."

"I was thinking you might want to travel with me. Roger hinted at getting you some signings arranged, and hotels are no more expensive for two."

"Where are you going?"

"A few cities around the US and a couple in Canada, some work, some signings and I've got a few days footloose before I have to head back home."

"I'll never be able to get flights. I haven't even got my passport with me."

"You can travel with me, and I'm sure can get your passport sent."

Ella Jane dissects and devours a meticulous little plate of seafood and washes it down with a mellow, oaky chardonnay. "I'm not sure they'll let me sit on your lap on airlines."

"Between Roger's people, your publisher and my office, flights won't be a problem."

She winces and thinks of her modest advance. "Is this where you say, *in first class*?"

He frowns and pours authority into his voice, depth, crisp consonants, clear vowels, and all. "You're invited as my guest. I'm not in the habit of giving my guests bills any more than I am of sitting in different parts of a plane to them."

Next comes a serving entitles beef five ways which comes with two glasses, a rioja and a grand Chateaux Lafitte. During which her efforts to engage him in conversation fail, first because he's enamoured, and then because all she can think of is savouring the varied textures and tastes.

Another miniscule course and another glass of wine arrive and he tells her a story about his calamitous experiences with the education system in his country and how one in particular was entirely his own fault.

The meal reaches its climax with three exquisite and elaborate desserts, a detail which sets the by now tipsy Ella Jane off in a fit of giggles.

They have the lift to themselves on their way up, and he takes advantage of the brief period of privacy and the lift's mirrored walls, though he declares his regret that, owing to the prudishness of the establishment's proprietors he isn't able to keep her naked and lead her on a chain.

The suggestion sets Ella Jane's imagination running wild and she spends the whole journey up to their top floor imagining herself naked in the multiple reflected images of herself with his hands on her.

When they step into the foyer outside their suite she stops and looks around. There really are no other rooms on this floor.

"Are you expecting butler service?"

He shakes his head, "No."

"Oh, good." She starts unbuttoning her shirt.

"What are you doing?"

She continues undressing. "Are you okay with using your belt instead of a chain?"

So he leads her naked for the final few steps, and she kneels and takes him into her mouth the moment he closes their door behind them, though he doesn't allow her to continue her dainty ministrations for long. Hot, hard, and in need of a fiercer intimacy he lifts her, carries her through to the dining room where he sets her down and makes to bend her over the long table.

She pleads, "No, your office."

But he insists, "Here first, so you can look along the table."

Ella Jane looks at him and then at the table and the fine window at its far end, and bends over it of her own accord.

Her Shopping, His Shopping

With Ella Jane becoming more familiar with the exercises, he devotes more time to his own. This gives her a chance to watch him and to watch his body as he labours. He sweats and grimaces and gasps for air as much as she imagines himself doing.

"How long have you been training like this?"

"Donkey's years."

"And it still hurts?"

"Every time, yes, but it's okay. It's the right kind of pain." He sets the heavy steel clubs he'd been swinging down and gives her a sheepish look. "Well, mostly."

She touches the curves of his upper arm. The muscles there are still pumped, hot and full of blood. "I like it."

"What?"

"That you understand the right kind of pain." She presses her mons against his hip and touches her lips to the round muscle of his shoulder. "That it's positive."

He turns into her embrace and lowers his face towards hers, curses, and wipes a drop of his fallen sweat from her cheek. "Each different kind of pain is like the edge of a cliff. Some people are drawn to stand at it, and are brave enough to go on their own, other are, but need to be coaxed or forced to experience the thrill, while others still take one look at the drop, and think *fuck that for a game of soldiers*."

"I'd have said that about lifting weights a few days ago."

She ignores his sweatiness to kiss him and taste the salt and feel the energy of him.

Ella Jane is expecting a delivery, while he only made his order as a way of solving a problem. He doesn't remember that he has one coming.

She's ordered her things to be delivered any time, because that was the cheaper option. His forgotten delivery however is due early, because when rush delivery comes to a fraction of a percent of the value of an order, why not?

When reception phones, he says to send the delivery up and put it in the sitting room. It's she who responds. She pops a morsel of pastry into her mouth, checks her teeth and lips are clean using her phone's camera as a mirror, slips into her robe, and bounces into the suite's reception room expecting to see packages labelled PrettyLittleThing containing the pretty little things she's ordered.

However, the neatly wrapped packages that arrive are all labelled, God Save Queens.

She's looking at them in confusion when he emerges from the dining room coffee cup in hand, "Anything nice?"

Ella Jane looks at him and demands, "What's this?"

"What?"

She tears open the tape on the first neatly packed box and lifts out an elegantly packaged plunge bra and holds it out towards him without even looking at it. "This?"

Taking in her agitation, he manages to not say, *a bra* and searches his memory instead. "Oh, you said you were short of underthings, so I Googled while I was working." His enthusiasm then kicks in. "Did you know there are companies in New York that make underwear?"

"I didn't, but it's the biggest city in America, so there was bound to be!"

"That one's called Queens, after the borough, but being English, it made me smile. Their things looked quite nice, so I got you a couple of sets."

She continues to look through the contents. His idea of *quite nice* is, as usual, a world away from simply quite nice. The first box contains more than two bras and two pairs of panties, and there's a second similarly sized one she hasn't touched yet. "A couple?"

"Yes."

A quick inventory reveals a corset, two styles of bra, a suspender belt, two thongs and two pairs of panties. She draws in a breath and, "Did you cancel my shopping from PrettyLittleThing and order these instead?"

He blinks. "I didn't know you'd ordered anything. I was just trying to help."

She remains stony faced, but his lips begin to twitch.

He reasons, "I might seem quite influential, but I don't think I'd be able to magically change other people's shopping. Even if I could, that'd be a fairly serious step beyond any limits we've discussed."

And there it is, he's wearing helpful smile, but he's presumed again. The things are lovely. And they're all in her size. "So, you just?"

"Just thought they'd be fun. God Save Queens underwear instead of an 'I heart NY' t-shirt, and they'll look nice on you."

Her mouth opens and something pithy on the subject of the differences between a stash of designer lingerie and a *ten freaking dollar T shirt* doesn't come out. Instead she says, "This lot must have cost a fortune."

He shrugs innocently but in the situation annoyingly. "I don't really know."

"How can you not know?"

"I was in a bit of a hurry, so I just clicked on some things. They had sets so I picked two and got one of each."

Ella Jane half turns her head to the side, partly so she can draw his attention to the large quantity and partly so she can look at him sideways. "Can-may I ask what you think constitutes a set of underwear?"

"Couple of tops, a few bottoms, and one each of any accessories. Like when I get a suit."

"Like a suit?"

"Yes, that's what my tailor starts out at one jacket each with plain and coloured lining, though I normally add a couple of extra pairs of trousers and a few waist-coats. Only I wasn't sure where to get ladies under-things made over here."

"Get them made?"

"Well, yes, I presume people do. There are designers in London who do that."

"You really just clicked on a couple of things?"

"Only things I thought wouldn't be too frumpy or tarty."

Ella Jane sucks her lips into her mouth and bites, then counts to three and consciously releases them. He's certainly avoided those pitfalls. It's not as if she'd committed to seeing him beyond him leaving New York, and he's even said she can use the spare room in the suite. And the things are just so nice. She plays the idea of refusing them through, then the reactions she might get if she told anyone – *you broke up because he bought you underwear you like, the sort you stop and look at the ads for when you're browsing?* It doesn't work.

She can't quite let it go either though. "You can't just keep spending money on me."

"I've hardly spent a penny. I couldn't really expect you to go to the theatre with me and not make sure you had a dress, could I? And everyone needs clean undies."

"Undies?" She looks at the stack of tastefully gorgeous black designer lingerie and then at his puzzled face, and asks herself if it's worth the argument. A second voice in her head asks her what the things would look and feel like on. Then again, there are a hundred other things. She's trialling being submissive to him, she *likes* being submissive to him and she may not be the most experienced sub in the world, but it strikes her as pretty certain that turning down something so thoughtful doesn't go with the territory, particularly as he can obviously afford it. There's her sense of the ridiculous, too. "You got me all this because you wanted to make sure I had a pair of clean panties?"

"Yes."

"There's a store five minutes' walk away you could have gone to."

"Not while I was working. I'm sure the hotel would have sent someone out for me if I'd asked, but I was on the phone, and I was browsing."

"Do you want me to try them on?"

"Better that than have you wear dirty underwear."

"I –."

"You deserved that. Of course I want you to try them on unless this is a Red moment."

Say red or try the beautiful lingerie and carry on dreaming? She finally lets her lips curl in response to his generosity and his enthusiasm. "I'm not ready to wake up yet."

He wanders to his favourite armchair and his eyes wander from Ella Jane in her robe to the neat boxes. "Well?"

She looks at him looking at her, and then makes to pick up boxes to take to their bedroom.

With her eyes on him already she sees his brow twist in displeasure, and stops. Then, with a slow warmth spreading from her centre, she asks the question she thinks she knows the answer to. "You want me to try them on here, don't you?"

"That would save time."

"And let you perv on me?"

"I was only thinking of your exhibitionist kink."

They exchange complicit smiles, each knowing the other has been well and truly busted.

Ella Jane is still smiling as she chooses the set and items to try first. She lips the robe from her shoulders and lays it across the arm of a chair.

"I've never got dressed for anyone like this before."

"If you'd like I can help unbox?"

Taking his offer at face value, without considering the implications, she answers, "Okay."

He collects each of the boxes she's chosen with him to his preferred armchair and sits, ready to watch her with his hungry eyes, and to hand her the filmy wisps of lace one at a time while she waits, naked, or nearly so, within easy reach of his hands.

The first garment he chooses to unpackage is the garter belt, and her skin glows her understanding as he slowly and deliberately unwraps and inspects it before holding it out not quite far enough for her to reach.

Her tongue moistens her lips in anticipation of further teasing as she takes it from his hand with a shake of her head at his audacity and a, "Yes, Sir," to signify that she's getting into role and enjoying doing so.

Next come her stockings, one at a time. She's certain she gets their seams and the garter-straps perfectly aligned but he encourages her forward so he can make imaginary adjustments and in doing so allow himself to apply his deft hands to her willing flesh.

He opens both the thong and demi-bra, then holds one in either hand, inspecting each as well as her near naked form and musing aloud at the difficulty of his decision while she shift from foot to foot and struggles with her own urge to either cover or touch herself.

Eventually he makes a decision. "The bra, I think."

Ella Jane swallows and licks her lips working up courage to compete with his teasing, breathes out with a whoosh and brushes he fingertips over the achingly stiff tips of her breasts.

She continues until he holds his breath, and on until she feels the muscles around her opening clench involuntarily right there, inches from his hand, then pours all the insincerity she can muster into her voice, "Is that because my chest looks cold, Sir?"

They both stifle the urge to laugh, and she carries on with the game by taking her time putting the bra on cups and shoulders and before reaching behind her back to do up the eye-hooks rather than simply wrapping it around her waist and doing them up in the front then turning it around and pulling it up.

For his part he expresses his concern that it may not be comfortable and insists that she move closer still and allows him to manually make certain the soft lace isn't unduly constricting her.

Once satisfied, he asks, "You seem a little flushed, is everything okay?" while his hands trace the lines of the fine black material of the bra and belt against her skin.

"Yes, Sir, just eager for you to see the whole ensemble together."

He makes to pick up her thong, then feigns a sudden thought. "I'd best make sure you aren't wet first. It would be a shame if these didn't fit but we couldn't send them back."

Everything else fits perfectly, just as she'd expected when she learned he got the sizes from Amberlee's meticulously taken measurements, but she plays along in expectation of the pleasure she expect to receive as he checks and that his eyes tell her he anticipates taking in doing so.

It takes his fingers no time at all to find the dew on her nether lips, and little more for him to verify what it is from its delicate taste and have her confirm his analysis. However it takes longer to address the *problem*. Eventually he resolves that he will have to like her as well as using his hands to get her sufficiently clean and has her set on knee on either arm of his chair.

Even after her experiences of being stretched with his bar every morning she can barely maintain position. He finds he has to slide down in his chair to go about his task, but does so without grumbling, and sets about his self-appointed duty.

Her first orgasm, he complains, only makes things worse, but he persists and when the shaking induced by her second subsides he declares her as dry as she's likely to get.

Ella Jane climbs unsteadily back to her feet and flexes and twists to work her stiffness out, as she does, she decides that if she is dryer now it must be due to the time she's spend uncomfortably stretched and further decides not to voice that opinion. Instead she thanks him when he hands her her thong and croons as she pulls the soft lace up her legs and smoothes it against her still tingling skin.

Her Day of Tourism

Having finally been allowed to dress, Ella Jane looks out over Central Park. The cloud is low, well below the tops of the skyscrapers. "We won't be able to see a thing from the Empire State Building, will we?"

"Not a thing. The One World Observatory and the Edge will be even worse. To be honest, even the Statue of Liberty's going to be a bit of a bust." He wraps his arms around her from behind. "Unless we're big fans of grey."

She rubs the back of her head into his chest and looks up over her shoulder. "Are you?"

"I am, but I'm English. We have a plentiful supply at home. It seems a bit wasteful to come all this way to study yours."

"So, you aren't a true connoisseur then?"

"Not really."

"I hope you didn't bring it with you?"

"The grey?"

"Yes."

"Not deliberately, New York has its own variety, so I didn't feel the need. We can still do the rest of your bits and save the classics for another day."

"So you don't mind me and Abigail being tourists?"

"Not at all, you and your central character are both most welcome. Just don't forget we've accepted my agent's hospitality for dinner, and that we may have to be there to pour him into a taxi before we can head back to the hotel to try out some of my new, home-made toys.

He dons a soft cotton workman's shirt and jeans then scruffs up his hair before applying gel. "Dressed down enough?"

They're still alone in his suite when he asks, so she gives her unfiltered opinion. "Are you trying to pass for a mere millionaire?" She brushes a palm down the soft material of his sleeve and the firm muscle beneath. "I like you in a work-shirt."

He glances at the nearest mirror checking how the shirt hangs from his broad shoulders. "As much as in a suit?"

"I think so, they're different." And she smiles at the thought that he's vain in either.

As they can't do her big ticket items, they enjoy a day of small galleries and large New York deli sandwiches. Ella Jane learns that he likes glass and ceramics in classical styles. She then looks at him with relief when he walks past those exhibiting works with no apparent craft but is happy to indulge her lingering in front of art photography. That's just as well. Not only does she enjoy photography, but Abigail is passionate about it, so she explains, he's outnumbered two to one.

He raises an eyebrow "Are you really going to go with that?"

Unsure whether it's a good idea to stick to her guns, she takes her lower lip between her teeth, but, as he seems more amused than angry she tries, "Uh-huh."

"Ha, good for you, just remember that when we do my day of touristing."

They also find quirky shops, in one he picks up a pair of floggers and passes one to her. It's heavier than any she's ever felt, and its falls are of a thicker, softer leather. "Wow!"

"Moose-hide, it's the best if you want to go long and heavy. I didn't bring mine."

"You'd know. *May* I ask why you want two?"

He answers, "You *may*," but doesn't actually answer her implied question.

"Very funny!"

"I thought so." He holds out his hand for her to return the second flogger and looks around, while she runs the thick soft suede through her fingers for a last time. "Is there anything else you like?"

"No, I was just browsing."

However, on their way to the till he sees a slash fronted dress. He stops and ruffles through the hangers, finds one that looks small enough and holds it up in front of her. He makes an approving face. "Do you like this?"

She answers, "It's nice, but I'm never sure anything's going to fit." Rather than responding with the hoped for, *oh, okay*, he asks the nearest member of staff if they have a changing room.

Having admitted that she likes the dress, Ella Jane allows the purple-haired woman to guide her to the back of the store. The woman returns and collects the dress in a size up and, after searching to the back of the rack, a size down. On her way she looks at the floggers in his hand and drawls in an impeccable Bronx accent, "Good call."

He favours her with a warm deep, "Yes, I know."

"You *are* naughty."

"I couldn't possibly comment. You'll have to ask my friend."

"I might just do that." She looks over her shoulder as she makes her way back to the changing room.

A few minutes later, Ella Jane messages him a photograph of herself in the dress. He answers with an emoji of a suggestive nature and asks her if she's going to show him in person.

Her reply reads,

Not while you're standing out by the front window, I'm not.

With no alternative he makes his way to the back of the store.

The dress was indeed something that he could imagine Ella Jane not wanting to wear to the front of the store. It's slashed down the front and back and only held together by its halter-neck, at the lower end it hugged her hips, and the longer side went halfway down her right thigh. It wouldn't get her arrested on the street, but it might cause a few accidents and would certainly get her stared at at this time of day, even in New York.

He admires her, and she awkwardly practices coquettish poses. For her part the assistant drawls, "I told ya he'd like it," and gives her a wink. "Anyone'd like it." She looks Ella Jane up and down. "An' they'd like you in it more, even if they ain't as naughty as him." Having said this, she looks him up and down too, paying particular attention to the two floggers in his hand and then going back to his eyes before returning her focus to Ella Jane, whose eyes are set on Him.

He observes, "It would go down well at a party." He wets his lips as he looks at her in the dress. "So much more subtle than your bodywhisp."

Ella Jane gives him a look, then walks around the back of the store turning and bending as she checks that the Lycra weave material doesn't ride up her thighs or drop away from her breasts.

"Do you like it enough to want it?"

To Ella Jane, it sounds very much like him preparing to buy her yet another thing. She looks in the mirror again, then to the assistant who either likes how it looks or is really good at her job, and to him. "Yes, I do. I'm going to buy it." She keeps her eyes on his, daring him to say anything.

His features show no sign of objection, not even when she focuses on the little muscles at the sides of his jaw. "I'll just pay for these while you change back, shall I?"

She makes her way to the changing room but not without a swish of her hips and a backward look, one she maintains until she's sure she has his attention. Having secured it, she gives him a triumphant smile.

He pays while Ella Jane changes back into her jeans and top, but not before picking up a pair of fur mittens. "I have a suspicion I might need one of these too."

The purple haired assistant grins as she gives him another appraising look from his eyes down to his waist and then back. "Ya sure know how to give a girl the nicest and naughtiest of times."

"Ah, a fellow tries, but you'll still have to ask my beautiful companion about that."

He's chatting to the assistant when Ella Jane gets to the till. As they go to leave, the assistant calls after them. "You have a nice day, you naughty people."

Once outside and a few doors away, Ella Jane says, "She was so flirty!"

"Outrageously! She's either bored, professional, or has excellent taste. It's a big improvement on have a nice day though."

She squeezes his arm and bumps against him. "You wouldn't mind if she fancied me?"

"That kind of attitude would lead to constant paranoia or only being with women I couldn't imagine anyone else desiring." He makes a face, and she grins at the expression of what he thinks of that prospect. "As we're shopping, would you like to get some keep fit things?"

"What?"

"Um, gymwear?"

"Oh." Ella Jane stops still and frowns; they've never really discussed her interest in clothed dominant, naked submissive play. She'd always just assumed he'd share it. There'd been no suggestion in any of their conversations prior to meeting that he didn't. And well, after all, what Dominant doesn't like having their submissive naked? "Why?"

He answers, "We might train somewhere less private."

Her eyebrows furrow and her lips tighten. "But not for our morning sessions?"

His face softens, "No."

"And we aren't going to stop them?"

The corners of his mouth tilt upwards, "Not if you don't want to." His eyes flick down the length of her body and back to hers, "I wasn't certain you were as fond of them as I am."

She suppresses a smile. "I'm not. That's why you need your whips." And she sets off again with a swish of her hips, leaving him to catch up.

When he does, he swishes the bag with his news floggers in it against her backside, an action which has absolutely no calming effect on her mood.

Following his suggestion, they stop into a sports store and look at things for her. Each picks out something clingy and a couple of less attention-grabbing items. She frowns at him for doing it, but he ignores her.

"How would you like it if I bought you clothes?"

He shrugs and wanders over to the men's section, where he selects a baggy tie-dyed white and pink stringer top, "Fine if you don't expect me to wear something like this." Then he makes a face before returning it to the rack.

Ella Jane narrows her eyes. "What size are you?"

"2XL tops and large bottoms."

"Just like that?"

He shrugs. "If you want a fight, try and get me to wear the pink top." Then lowers his head and his voice and quietly adds, "But do it in private," while enunciating every consonant crisply.

She smiles.

"Did I say something funny?"

"No."

"But you're smiling."

"Yes."

He lifts his hands palms up, lowers his eyebrows and pushes his lower lip out.

"It's not *that* kind of smile." She touches her lips to his. "Are we going to pay for these things? Then we can go back to the hotel, so your favourite call girl can spend the whole night finding out what a man does to a girl who turns up wearing that sexy dress she bought herself with the money her favourite client paid her."

"That's a wonderful idea, but not yet. If you hadn't forgotten, Roger's going to spend some of the obscene amount of money he charges me on buying me dinner at Gabriel Kreuther. You, my dear, are invited."

"Really? And why's that?"

"Because Cynthia's coming too, and by happy coincidence, they work for the same company."

When they step out of the shop, it's raining. He curses, turns, grabs a golf size umbrella and pays for it. "Do you want to take a break from touristing?"

"We could go back to the hotel for a little while first."

Ella Jane pulls at his arm. "You and me, or you and that hooker?"

He tilts his head an looks at her face, "I'll let you surprise me." then sees a patisserie that takes his fancy and drags her in despite her protests that there hadn't been much point buying fitness clothes.

They cab back to the hotel. The car is clean, but not as sumptuously comfortable as the various limousines they've taken. He leans close to her and murmurs, "Now you know why I take cars everywhere."

"Meanie."

"You know it." Still with his lips close to her ear in the back of the car he enquires. "Have you decided who I'm entertaining?"

"Only me, if that's alright. I have something special in mind for the other thing."

He takes her chin in one hand and tilts her head back. "You are never only you."

"No, Sir."

"Good girl."

The cab draws up outside the hotel and he pays the driver off. As they make their way up the steps he suggests. "How about we do something to get us hungry enough to enjoy these cream cakes?"

"You should make up your mind how you're going to kill me."

"Hey?" They're half way across the grand marbled lobby by the time he works it out "Oh! I see. We're not quite sure just how she died, but it must have been a helluva ride."

She lets out a burst of laughter and hurries on to the lifts, there's already someone waiting. He holds back, but, when the woman presses the doors open button to make sure they can get in Ella Jane tugs at his arm and he follows her into the car.

On seeing that the other woman has pressed the third floor, Ella Jane asks for the tenth so he doesn't have to use his room key card and thanks the woman, then mouths, "See," to him and moves to the back. She edges against him and casts a glance in his direction as the other woman steps out of the lift car leaving them to make alone on their way up to the penthouse.

He presses the top button and taps his card on the panel, then turns his attention to the now smiling Ella Jane. "Is that mischief I see in your eyes?"

She looks away again. "I'm not sure a person who's just bought whips and cake gets to accuse others of planning *mischief*."

The lift doors open to their own floor and he signals for her to step out first. As she passes him he swats her rear and reminds her of her omission. "Ahem?"

She twists around as he joins her in the lobby and blinks. "*Sir*!" The word at odds with her expression and the tone of her voice both of which hint more at *make me* than dutiful submission to his will.

He inserts a finger into one of the belt hoops on her jeans and drags her to a halt and warns her. "One of these days you'll wind up in trouble, you know that?"

That has more effect on the young American, and she turns and moistens her lips. This time her voice and expression are sweet and soft as her words defy. "I've been in trouble at least once a day since I met you, *Sir*."

"Ha, so you have." He touches his lips to hers and opens the door to their private space.

She sashays past him as he holds the door for her and laughs as he delivers the invited swat to her bum.

"Are you going to try your new dress on so I can see you in it properly?"

Looking over her shoulder as she passes into the reception room she teases, "You saw it properly in the shop."

He follows and takes her arm his iron strength while applying little pressure. She stops, and he waits until she turns to face him before speaking. "Not properly." He releases his hold, gestures caressing her and his eyes brim with a shallow pretence of innocence.

Ella Jane scoffs, "You mean not improperly," but misses in her attempt to sound matronly.

"I suppose, I didn't think it would have been appropriate."

"No," she chuckles. "But I don't think that assistant would have minded in the least."

He puts on a half decent impression of the woman's accent. "You gawgeous people are sooo nawdie!" Then he switches back to his own as they exchange amused looks. "Now, about trying on and showing off your new dress."

"Hmm," she trails a fingertip down the soft cotton of his shirt and the dip between the heavy muscles of his chest beneath it. "That depends."

"On?"

"On whether you're going to demonstrate why you wanted two of the same floggers."

"Are you topping from the bottom?"

On seeing the opportunity to circle back to her earlier evasion, Ella Jane challenges him. "That depends too." His eyebrow rises. "Are you going to punish me for it with those two floggers?"

He glares at her.

And she beams back at him, delighted at her self-serving offer.

For the first time in their brief acquaintance he caves first in a staring contest, allowing the corners of his eyes to crease.

"Or you can think of it as an act of service. I know you want to try them on me."

"Now who's a bloody lawyer?"

"I will be if that gets you to..." she looks at the bag with the floggers in it and dances away from him laughing.

"I'm not going to get a moment's peace until I use them on you, am I?"

She pours triumphant satisfaction into her voice as she declares, "Nope!"

He stalks towards her. "I could tie you up and put you in the spare room until you calm down, you know."

Ella Jane glances over her shoulder, and backs further away; there are two doorways she could try to escape through. "Mhm, you could, but..." she lets her voice fade away as she quite deliberately backs herself up against a wall.

"But?" He closes the distance between them and sets his hands against the wall either side of her, the bag containing the floggers still hanging from his left.

She lifts her hand to the dangling bag and strokes it. "You want to use them on me as much as I want you to, Sir." With that, she swallows and looks down, toe to heels her sneakers off, and her hand goes to the top button of her shirt.

He doesn't move, not even when she slips it from her shoulders, and she looks around for somewhere to put it.

Given the choice between the two sins of dropping it on the floor and hanging it over his arm she opts for the cheekier and more intimate one. After all, he's going to whip her anyway, and his eyes are already smiling down at her more decorated than covered breasts. Ella Jane's eyes double down on her tease by looking up at him insolently as she hangs the shirt over his arm but her skin is less cocky and develops a rosy glow. Next, she unzips her jeans, and as she peels them down her legs, she makes sure to give him a clear view of her décolletage. She straightens and drapes them over her shirt with as suggestive a wink as she can muster.

Down to just her underwear she glances to the mirror and pauses as she reaches behind her back and undoes her bra.

"Shy all of a sudden?"

His question causes her cheeks to glow more brightly. "No, yes. It's the way you look at me!" When she glances up her teeth have a hold of her bottom lip.

"Do tell."

"I can cope with it when I'm wearing clothes or when I'm naked. It's just..." she looks down again.

He brushes the tip of a thumb along the line of her cheekbone. "Just?"

Ella Jane had hoped he'd save her, but he hasn't, and she struggles. "When-when I'm undressing."

His caressing hand moves to the underside of her chin and gently tilts her head up to face him. His eyes are more kind than lust-filled and his lips descend to hers with slow tenderness. "Then finish undressing and you'll be fine."

She pouts. "Practical and mean."

"I'm not using them on you through your new underwear. Not the first time anyway."

Undoing the clasp and sliding the straps from her shoulder she passes an invisible threshold. Only her hands are preventing the lacy bra from falling away and other than that her body's only covering is the fabric of her delicate panties. His enthusiastic expectation helps too. Along with that clear look in his eyes, telling her he wants to see her naked, and go to bed with her when they only broke off their lovemaking and play a few hours before.

Her lips and the tips of her breasts tingle, and her pelvic muscles flex of their own will and her face returns his smile as she lowers her hands. The bra joins the rest of her clothes over his arm and she bounces on her heels.

His body remains impassive, though he his eyes burn and his mouth moves as if he were tasting something sweet as her hands go to her hips. She bends and lowers her panties and steps out of them, and when she stands, she does so with impish delight. "There. I'm ready!"

"You'd best take these somewhere then." He gestures with his clothing laden arm.

Ella Jane takes them and scampers past him, looks around and chooses one of the chairs neither uses to lay them on. "Now, where do you want me?"

He moves slowly to the chair, reaches into his bag and lifts the heavy whips from it. "You know, I fondly imagined when I started that this sort of thing would strike delicious fear into the hearts of submissives."

"It does. It just makes me want to play too."

"Hmph!" He sets the still-far-from empty bag down, takes one whip in each hand and experimentally swirls them swinging faster and faster until they whir through the air. Satisfied with his control, he moves closer to her until they pass so near to her that the wind of their passage moves her hair as they pass.

She swallows and dares, "Where do you want me, Sir?"

His eyes rove down and back up again. "Everywhere."

"That's flattering but unhelpful."

Stilling the whips, he considers the different rooms, then nods to himself. "I think the bathroom works."

"Really?"

"I want you to see yourself in the mirrors."

She bites her lip, but follows him. When he stops in their bedroom, she allows him to fit a wide leather collar about her neck and cuffs around her wrists. "Put your hair into a ponytail, please." He waits for her to do so, then clips the cuffs to her collar.

His eyes sparkle with mischief as he strokes her shoulders and back with the whips heavy falls. "Feeling vulnerable enough?"

Her smile and nod answer him and he threads a finger through the eye ring set in the front of her collar and leads her into the bathroom.

She positions herself in the centre of the room facing the mirror setting her feet apart and looks to him in their reflection.

"A little further please."

She edges her legs still wider until he nods.

He opens his mouth, and she answers the question he hasn't asked. "Red, yellow and I'm looking forward to this, Sir."

He shakes his head slowly and flicks her ponytail over her shoulder and positions it falling between her breasts "Don't you ever get enough?"

"I didn't know what enough was until a week ago, so I'm trying to get it while I can."

"Hmm." He starts the two whips twirling again.

The first impact is more a caress, the tips of dozens of soft thick strands brushing downwards against her back and then her buttocks. After a few brushes, he moves his hands closer, and then she feels the first slaps. The blows are sharper where they first impact and soften as the falls move over her skin.

He rains these blows onto her from shoulders to thighs down the back of her body, only avoiding her spine and lower back, and then up again. The hardest lashes fall on muscular curve of her bum but even these aren't hard enough to hurt hurt. Rather he builds a slow kindling warmth in her skin and the flesh and bones beneath.

She watches him, watches his concentration, sees his eyes on hers and feels a surge of connection pull her towards the mirror's glass. The whum of the floggers, the rhythm of the whipping and the echoing pulsing in her core soothe her mind with their hypnotic music.

Moving to one side he sends the blows against her thighs. Ella Jane gasps when he works upwards and yelps when he strikes the side of her breast She chuckles when it doesn't hurt as such and lets out a long, slow moan when that light impact is repeated a dozen times.

Continuing to move around her, he whips the upper curves of her breasts until they turn a rosy shade, and their treacherous buds are as hard as they've ever been, as hard and as sensitive. Her flesh is more concerned with its arousal than with any pain she might feel in consequence.

He whips until her lips begin to emit a low groaning and the muscles of her abdomen clench in time with the blows, then pulls back, reverses the rotation of his wrists and starts sending blows upwards against the undersides of her mounds. When they strike here the heavy floggers send deeper, richer vibrations through her body and soon her hips are rocking to the beat of the whipping.

A wider circling of his right hand sends the falls of the whip it holds lashing against her opening and she cries out at the impact. Once again there's not sharp sensation of agony. Rather, what she experiences is something more akin to the impact of a lover's hips, though the falls curve against her exposed vulva striking her everywhere all at once.

Her breathing and her eyes, like the tips of her breasts are traitors to any desire to save herself that might remain, ragged breaths and imploring looks tempt the devil in him on and the devil obliges.

He sends one blow in six and then one in four up against her yoni, and each impact stokes the fire in her centre.

She begins nodding her head in time and he transfers both whips to one hand and then sends every blow up between the V of her legs.

Her knees shake, but she fights to keep herself standing, she's so close and the fire is so bright.

She stares at her body as he whips and she quakes, and at long last convulses.

Her eyes seek his, urge him to continue, and he does until her knees buckle.

He catches her, and holds her against himself. His hardness as urgent as her imploring eyes had been just moments beforehand.

He leads her from the bathroom and swathes her in their duvet while he strips and in their bed still in the wild time after the whipping when her animal soul possesses her utterly. His heat reaches inside her and finds her own.

She croons as she lies next to him. "So is that why you wanted two?"

"Mm-might be. Did you like it?"

"Ha, it was, um, intense, yes, intense."

He questions her further, "Good intense?" his voice an amused rumble.

"Very, I didn't..."

"Didn't what?"

"Didn't think I'd ever experience that. I've heard about it, but then I've heard about dragons. I just never thought I'd get to ride either of them."

"Keep paying me compliments like that and I might just have to try and find you a dragon."

"You madman. Do you do that to all your submissives?"

"Sadly, it only works for some."

"Oh? Poor others." And she kisses him.

Her phone the suite's phone interrupts them. He answers, listens, and hands it to her. "It's for you."

"Who?" But her phone chimes, and he laughs at the sight of her simultaneously reaching for two phones. The voice at the other end tells her there's a package, and asks if she wants it brought up at about the same time she reads the delivery notification.

He puts two and two together. "See, I told you I didn't cancel your stuff. Now you can do me a whole private fashion show not just show me your dress."

"Do I have to?"

"Yes you do, if you want to see what else I bought?"

"Not more whips?"

"No. Something a little gentler."

"If I promise, can I have a cake now? I'm going to have to shower before I try anything on anyway."

"Oh, very well."

So they share the prettily packaged creations from the patisserie and save a little for later when Ella Jane declares that she couldn't eat another thing. They then shower, and she studies body in the mirror in wonder that, once again, he's whipped her but not left a mark. While she does she also notes that despite his constantly plying her with delicacies her figure is if anything trimmer than it had been before she came to New York.

Having failed to find any evidence that his feeder habits have harmed her figure, she allows herself to be chivvied into trying on her dress, the remaining combinations from God Save Queens and her PrettyLittleThing emergency clothing delivery.

Her initial reluctance melts when he proves an appreciative audience. Although she finds it an inconvenience when he finds one set sufficiently enticing to ambush her, causing another get-cleaned-up break.

Finally thinking she's finished, as she assumes he won't want to see her try on anything as mundane as her new jeans she gives a bow. "Did I get the modelling job?

"I don't know, I was hoping to find a girl who can put jeans on."

She complains at the thought of having to get dressed rather than playing. "Oh!"

But he insists, explaining, "Well, you'd better put something on. Johnson's picking us up to take us to dinner with Roger and Cynthia in half an hour."

She frowns, and then when that doesn't deter him, she sidles close and strokes her fingertips across the buckle of his belt. "There's a lot we can do in half an hour."

Their Agents' Gambit

The agents arrive early, and Roger lays out his intentions to his junior colleague over pre-dinner drinks. He gestures expansively, "Look at it this way. The agency makes a great deal of money out of our relationship with Him, but he's difficult to work with sometimes. He has everything he wants, and that can make a writer lazy. Also he has a hundred other calls on his time. A busy man sometimes focuses elsewhere."

Cynthia's brow furrows. "What's that got to do with Ella?"

The older agent leans back. "He likes her, and He's a draw. If I can tell him people will give her publicity, if he's included in the deal, I can probably get him to go along with it. We win, Miss Tyler wins, and it won't hurt the old boy any."

The corners of her mouth turn downwards. "Isn't that unethical?"

"It might be if she doesn't like Him." He drains his glass. "If it bothers you, you can ask her next time you call."

"I –"

"That wasn't a request, Cynthia. He's our most profitable client, and you yourself told me she's going to be a star turn. Your job is to make her more successful. If you can get her to do signings and publicity with him, at least while he's over this side of the pond, then that's your job."

Ella Jane watches the sun emerge through the trees in Bryant Park as Johnson drops them off outside the restaurant.

His eyes follow hers, and he leans down to her. "If you were a cynical Brit, you'd mutter something like 'typical' or 'just my luck'."

"Hmm, fortunately I'm not."

"The view at night's not bad. We could use that as an excuse to leave early unless it's open all night." He consults his phone as they go. "Closes at eleven, the upper gallery is supposed to be quieter."

"Something you didn't know?"

"Knowing when you just look things up is a skill."

"I know, it's my generation's speciality."

Roger and Cynthia are already there when they arrive. Cynthia in particular observes the couple intently as they continue their flirtatious verbal sparring on their way into the restaurant and across to the table.

Cynthia greets her client. "I have some good news for you. Your publisher would like to arrange some book signings and interviews."

"Oh, when?"

"Over the next few weeks while your book's still new. They wanted me find out if you're interested before lining anything up."

Ella Jane looks at Him, and He nods His encouragement, so she turns back to her agent. "Where would they be? I might have plans for the next week or two?"

"Nothing too far afield, just here in the States and maybe one or two in Canada."

He takes a sip of water then interjects, "I've got a few things lined up. Maybe you could look at some of the same locations?"

Cynthia clears her throat and begins. "Actually, that's something I'd like to ask you about." She looks across at Roger who nods sternly reminding her of their conversation before their guests arrived. "Um, are you two sort of...? Only I noticed you arriving together and...?"

He glances at the now blushing Ella Jane, then at the smirking Roger and raises an eyebrow. "Are us two, what?"

Cynthia swallows and bites the bullet. "I saw the pictures of you together outside the Met. Um, are you an item?"

Ella Jane's eyes go to his and she holds her breath. Watching her he places a hand on the table palm up, close to her and waits as she edges hers towards it. He only looks back at the agents once her fingers touch his.

"Nothing either of you are to make any press statements about. We're still, ah, getting to know one another."

"Does that mean you might be travelling together?"

This time he defers to Ella Jane who squeezes his hand and answers, "That or meeting up. We haven't decided which." without taking her eyes from his.

He hedges, "If we can, we're travelling together," while keeping his eyes on Ella Jane, rather than either of the agents.

Ella Jane smiles at that and a silence drags out until Roger clears his throat. "Ah, um, I think it will be easier to persuade Miss Tyler's publisher and local broadcasters to cooperate if we arrange things in the same locations. Um, if that's alright with you both?"

They agree to look into the possibilities and then move on to ordering and less formal matters.

With the business of the evening dealt with, Roger is on fine form and happy to have the two younger women to regale with his stories of his career and his illustrious client. "He used to wonder why the world didn't see how talented he is, just like you probably didn't. For the same reason."

Ella Jane leans fowards. "What's that?"

"You didn't get around to letting it be known." Roger sips and gestures to himself and his colleague, "That's your agent's job, or you have to do some smart marketing yourself." He then fixes his client with a hard look. "Things like arranging publicity photographs outside opera houses and circulating them for example."

"Sorry old chap, it really did just happen."

His agent harrumphs at that, but otherwise lets his calculating, but usually publicity shy friend's reply pass.

Given the opportunity to talk to someone who's known Him for a long time, Ella Jane asks Roger about Him. "Has he always been so decisive?"

He casts a sidelong look at his agent, who returns his look and raises an eyebrow questioningly, but doesn't reply to her until he sees his old friend shrug his permission. "That's something he seems to have developed over the years."

She leans forward sensing that her lover's friend might be more forthcoming than he himself has proven. "Is there a story there?"

"Ha, several." Roger begins slowly after looking across at Him. "I think it's fair to say we've come a long way together, we first met in a flat in –."

He chuckles, "Crappy flat. I couldn't afford to eat in places like this, and Roger's expenses budget wouldn't have covered the cost either in those days. It was certainly not enough for taking me out."

"Back then he had six half finished manuscripts, and he'd cooked something wonderful with pork he bought at an end-of-day discount. His writing was good, and we haggled our way through his book ideas and found a couple we both thought might be ready for editing. Then we worked at hoodwinking a tame publisher into putting out." The tale drags on through the early part of His career with good natured interjections from Him and further questions from Ella Jane.

When Roger asks if they fancy going somewhere for drinks afterwards, Ella Jane touches His arm. "You asked me to remind you about your early meeting."

"Thank you. I'd forgotten."

Roger tries to persuade them, but Cynthia suggests they get a cab.

"Actually I think we'll walk. Now the weather's cleared up, there's a chance we can make viewing the gallery at the Empire State before we slope off for an early night."

Ella Jane smiles at the agents. "Sorry. It's my first time in New York." That convinces Roger to subside.

They make their farewells, and he consoles his agent. "Never mind old chap. I won't rat you out if you tell them I drank a couple more Armagnacs."

Ella Jane kisses Cynthia's cheek for real rather than air-kissing it, and then hugs her. "Thank you again for signing me. It's a dream come true." And then smiles at the older agent. "Good night, Uncle Roger." The pained look on His agent's face sets him laughing as they make their way to the door.

Once outside he takes Ella Jane's hand and leads her to the curb looking for a gap in the traffic and asks, "Didn't you want to get drinking again?"

She looks at him as they cross the road. "Not unless you're going to be less strict about drinking and playing."

"Then that's a no. There's a decent Laphroaig at the hotel for after, anyway."

"My hero." They walk through the trees in the little park. "Aren't you going to check the map on your phone?"

"Not tonight. It's just through here, left and then right down 5th Avenue." He winks. "I thought all Americans knew that." Then he starts laughing before she has time to protest about being new to the city and state for the dozenth time.

"How do you know New York so well?"

"To be honest, I vaguely know a small patch of midtown Manhattan."

He buys their tickets for the higher gallery as they walk north along Fifth Avenue. By doing so, they avoid the queue, and make it in time to have some fun admiring the city's ocean of lights below them and those of the scattering of similarly tall skyscrapers around. It's quiet enough for them to avoid others and beyond looks exchanged with other couples also looking to set down a memory being together in the city at night. Having got in first by needlessly directing his attention to the brightly lit pinnacle of the Chrysler building, she teases him for not knowing every single building. He mutters a dire threat that sets her giggling, kissing and asking if they can go back to the hotel yet.

They stay a little longer, and both cheat by looking up the names of buildings on the overhead guide and, for lesser landmarks, their phones and pretending to know them. The game finally comes to an end when she points out the plaza hotel. She gets the rough direction right, but he's sure they have no clear line of sight to it and calls her bluff. A quick check on an online map confirms the Rockefeller Center is in the way.

She grins, and leans close to him. "You'll just have to put me over your knee for being naughty, then take me to dinner in its restaurant as aftercare."

"Hmm, why do I get the feeling you might secretly regard that as getting two rewards?"

After that they make their way down to see if they get to the lower deck to have a quick look from outside before it closes. The staff are initially adamant that it's too late, but his honey smooth Englishness and her outrages flirting with her eyelashes buy the pair access on swearing that they will be quick and won't tell a soul.

"It feels higher out in the open, doesn't it?"

"Yes, it probably felt higher still before they put up the jumper resistant railings."

She laughs, but hushes him. "Don't! Some people are scared of heights."

He confides, "I know, I'm one of them, but whatever you don't fall off makes you stronger."

Their extra few minutes mean they avoid enduring a crowded elevator car, though they don't have it to themselves. The company means he's unable to do more than make her blush with whispered suggestions as to what they might be able to get up to during the eighty-floor descent if they were alone.

As they pass 42nd Street, he looks east towards the foot of the building they'd admired from up high. "There used to be a club or in the upper floors of the Chrysler building."

"Do you remember it?"

He seems far away, "No, I just like the idea."

Ella Jane leans her head against him, and looks up. "The world not being perfect really does offend you, doesn't it?"

"Bit." He gives her a rueful smile.

"One of these days you're going to have to settle on one favourite word."

"Bit, is probably up there."

She touches hands with him. "Just like probably."

"Of course, if," and he drops his voice to its deepest and enunciates every consonant, "*Turn around and bend over young lady*, was one word..." Just like that the sadness has passed.

When they emerge, he turns left up Fifth Avenue without thinking.

"Did anyone ever tell you Americans don't walk anywhere?"

"As you keep telling me, you're from West Virginia, not New York."

"Just as well I came out in sneakers, not heels."

He stops to admire St Patrick's first and then St Thomas on their way back. While he's looking up at St Thomas, he suggests they might pop back and look inside if they get time.

Ella Jane hugs him even as she teases, "Half atheist and half devil and more fond of churches than anyone else I know."

Which gets her another of his shrugs. "I'm a connoisseur of beauty."

This in turn earns him a kiss, though she teases, "Am I just another beautiful thing to you?"

"Of course not, you're a wicked little fuck-bunny, too."

They're still laughing about that when they reach the hotel.

They have the elevator on the way up, and Ella Jane seizes the opportunity presented by the semi-privacy. She moves in front of him and takes a hold of his hands. "May I do something when we get back upstairs?"

He quips, "That depends what." Then registers her seriousness and nuzzles her. "Of course, if it's important to you."

"I want to do something to say sorry for fooling around while you were giving me my massage."

"That's dealt with."

Her eyes plead. "I know. Maybe I put it wrong. You did something that made me feel special. I want to try to do that for you."

"Then yes, of course."

When he opens the door to their suite, she takes his hand and leads him into the reception room where she arranges him facing the tall mirror before fetching a cushion and setting it on the floor at his feet. She then steps back between him and the mirror, and starts to undress.

He makes to unbutton his shirt, but she shakes her head. So he just watches her as she slips the blouse from her slender shoulders and sets it aside. Her shoes come next, then her pop socks. She turns away to peel her jeans down her legs and bends, making certain he has a clear view of her arse. She lowers them to her ankles. Rather than try to balance awkwardly on one leg, she then straightens and treads herself out of them before picking them up and laying them by her blouse.

Down to her underwear, the corset bra and one of the matching thongs he'd bought her, she steps up to him, puts her arms around his shoulder and lifts herself onto tiptoes to kiss his lips.

"May I please you, Sir?"

He smiles, looks down at her and then at their reflection before he answers, "You do please me."

"No," she casts her eyes down to below his waist. "Please you."

"Of course." He touches his lips to hers and waits to see exactly what she has planned.

Permission granted, she presses the tip of her tongue to her teeth and strokes her hands down from his neck to the first done up button of his shirt. She doesn't undo it though, just runs her hands over his skin before lowering them to his fly.

When she kneels she finds she can't easily get his erection out of his briefs and through his fly, so she edits the fantasy and undoes his belt as well. With him standing she doesn't have to take his trousers all the way down, and she takes advantage by leaning her bare breasts against their fine woollen cloth.

Whether it's knowing that, with the conference over they don't have anything to get up for, or something else, she takes her time even more than usual. *Usual* she muses, usual after a few nights? Well, and a few days. As she does, her mind plays back the way he combines words with sensations, taste, and scent, how it impacts her, how intense the combinations with his words are, and she promises to try to please him as well. She kisses him, caresses him with her hands, lips and tongue, first through his foreskin and then having pulled it back and absorbs the sense of absolute physical and familiarity that rises in her.

It's something akin to a sense of belonging and after such a short time is unnerving. Yet taking him into herself each of her openings remembers him. She pulses her tongue against his frenum and feels his glans swell further against the roof of her mouth the words, and the idea add to the warmth that spreads from the contact between his silkiness and the inside of her mouth. It may be that what happens in New York stays here, but for now in this time away from reality, belonging is a word that fits.

He lets out a gasp and she pulls back, sliding his foreskin forward as she does. "Sorry."

That makes him chuckle. "It wasn't a complaining sound. That's sensitive but good."

She purrs and places a kiss on his shaft then takes him into her mouth again, this time with his foreskin advanced.

It takes an age for the muscles behind his perineum to start pulsing and then a moment for her to get over the horrified thought that his legs might buckle sending his great weight down onto her petite frame. But his shuddering breaths filled with words of praise, and the way the head of his cock swells inside her mouth under the seductive rhythm of her suction are seductive to her. At length she feels his essence spill into her mouth and clenches her thighs tight together, to share as little of the pleasure she's giving. It isn't quite a mutual orgasm but the thrill is as real as her sense of achievement and her pride at being the one orchestrating his pleasure for a change.

Of course, he repays her indulgence, and when she tiredly asks about what else he bought, he introduces her to the delight of fur mittens.

His Telephone Call and Her Eavesdropping

Ella Jane doesn't know what wakes her, but when she reaches to his side of the bed for the comfort of his warmth, the sheets are cool, and he's gone. She looks around in the darkness and strains her hearing. He's in the suite's small smart office when she finds him, but he's talking on the speakerphone, so she doesn't interrupt.

The other voice is English too. Not as deep as his, but every bit as much the upper class or film actor. She doesn't mean to eavesdrop, but she hesitates to move away when she hears to person on the other end of the line say. "This was supposed to be a business trip."

From her position, she can only see a small portion of his face, but even just that reveals the tell-tale hardening of his eyes that she's learned to associate with him putting his foot down. Though he keeps his voice even. "It was supposed to include site visits, glad handing, a bit of publicity for the Magnate, and negotiations with studios and production companies. It was *also* supposed to be my first holiday in three years."

"You don't do holidays."

"I thought I'd try one. So I can write about them better."

"You –"

His jaw muscles tighten too, and he adds an edge to his voice. "I know I don't have to write, but writing is creating, and when I'm creating is when I get my ideas." A shadow passes across his half visible face and his voice hardens further still, "The ideas that feed you."

"Then there's this girl you're with outside The Met."

"How did you know her?"

"You really should check up on your media folders. We and your agents both keep it updated."

He clicks away at his keyboard, sure enough there's a portfolio of links from his agent, together with a suggestion that Ella Jane is good publicity. He mouths a silent curse as he looks at the pictures of the lovely young redhead on his arm. "Rather witty and very bright. She's a writer. Roger's company discovered her. They're quite excited."

The voice on the phone accuses, "So it said, but she doesn't look like a writer."

His, "There are people who say *I* don't look like a writer, Mark," is delivered so abruptly that she finds her insides clenching out in the hallway.

"So you just hooked up with her at the conference, and now she's hanging around?"

"We've known each other a while. We met up. We went to The Met. She may going to be accompanying me around the states while I do all those site visits you've been nagging me about and some book signings Roger has." He leans back, frowns then smiles. "I'm just giving in to both my consciences at once."

"Was this Roger's idea?"

"You seem awfully interested."

"You make an important trip and a mysterious beauty appears? Of course I'm interested."

"We chatted online for months before she even knew who I was, Mark."

"Maybe, you haven't been putting in the hours you usually do. Changes in your behaviour make me nervous."

Ella Jane sneaks back to bed and pulls up a web browser. It only takes a second to find the pictures she's already seen. There's nothing more than there had been on the gossip site and magazines her friend Haley had found. But now there are thousands of results, and hundreds when she searches her own name, most of which are actually about her rather than other random people with similar given name. She browses through some. A few name-check her book Abigail Leaving Home, most just gush about her dress. Sleep finds her while she's still browsing and before he returns.

They talk a few minutes longer. He uses that time to remind Walters of his position, and of the value he places on him. He also promises to review the outstanding projects and his messages. Having got off the phone, he opens the mind farm and picks at a couple of threads, then sends an email and reads, and, where appropriate replies to a few with his two-cents-worths.

He decides to make another call while he browses. This time, he selects his director of agricultural technology reasoning that if anyone if likely to feel in need of love during his absence from the UK, it's likely to be the research chief he sees most often in the flesh when he's at home. "Alistair, are you feeling ignored with me out of the country?"

"No, why do you ask?"

"Mark's been fretting. I wondered if anyone had been telling tales."

"No." His colleague hums, "To be honest, if anything, you haven't been sticking your nose in too much."

"Thanks!"

"You do tend to worry at things."

"And I'm not?"

"No, it's like when you get stuck into something, one of your books or when you pushed through your body armour project or the float glass acquisitions."

"I thought I was the one who was supposed to be cryptic."

"You are, Boss. It's good. Whatever project you've got your head into, it's got you in my happy place; do you want me to ask the Hammonds to snoop?"

"No, thanks. I'll give Lucy a bell later to see if she can find anyone unhappy, or if it's just Mark."

He rings off and continues to read, think, and contribute until his head begins to nod. Then, pleased with his contributions' elegance, he returns to bed and the sleeping Ella Jane.

She mumbles when he kisses her shoulder, so he gently wakes her, as a reward to himself for his cleverness. Once awake enough to respond she returns his kisses enthusiastically and brings to a series of orgasms, first with his fingertips, and then with his mouth. . She's fading by the time he enters her, and after his long day and night his humanity is making him painfully aware of itself, so he spoons her and joins her in sleep.

When she wakes, she asks, "Did I hear you on the phone?"

"Yes, sorry. I can't have shut the doors properly."

"That's okay. I like hearing your voice. It's like having my very own Alan Rickman."

"Really?"

"Mhm, yes, only with more booming and laughter."

"Is that so?"

"It is." She smiles at her cleverness in turning around their use of phrases. "Who were you talking to?"

"That was Mark Walters."

"What was it so important that you spoke to him at this time?"

"He's in London, so it's not still this time any more. He wanted me to work more."

"Oh, do you work for him?"

"No, he's more or less my business Roger."

"What does that mean?"

"It means he works for me, but I wouldn't have got to be anywhere near so successful without him."

She recalls "Are your businesses as successful as your books then?"

"They do quite well, yes. That's why I have to go and visit people and tell them how clever they are and how hard they work."

"Oh, okay."

She Reprises Her Role-play

The next morning at the end of their exercise session, and her time stretched by the spreader bar, the sweat rimed Ella Jane jokingly poses and flexes in the bathroom mirror. Then she squeaks with delight, "I've got a new muscle!"

"Where?"

She points at her shoulder and at the faint line between two of the sections of her deltoid muscle.

"You had shoulders before."

"But not like this!" She bounces and throws her arms around his neck.

Her ecstatic mood continues through breakfast and she works up to making a suggestion. "You know I said I had something special in mind?"

"Yes."

"Of course, you do. You never forget anything, do you?"

"I don't seem to forget much about you."

"Could you pretend you're coming home?"

"Pardon?"

"I want to try something, but it needs you to be coming home."

He scrunches one eye up, but her enthusiasm infects him and he nods. "Just so long as that something isn't wedging a chair against the front door. I'd hate to have to sleep in the lobby."

"I promise not to wedge the door shut, but I might ask you to pretend I had, and that you're cross about it some time."

"Okay, how long do you want me to be out, and what do you want me to wear?"

"Mmm, one of your suits would be nice."

He asks her to join him in the shower, but she begs off. "If I do we're not going to get as far as starting my game."

"Would that be such a bad thing?"

"You know it wouldn't, but please?"

"Hmm, very well."

He showers and she watches until he raises an eyebrow at her, then laughs and leaves him to his ablutions. When he emerges she helps him dry then hurries him along and makes him promise to give her fifteen minutes to get ready before she goes into the bathroom and locks the door.

It gives him enough time to dress in a leisurely fashion, selecting a charcoal two three piece suit, plain grey silk tie and a simple platinum tie-clip and cufflink set. He then heads down to the bar to order a whisky and muse as to what she has in mind.

Ella Jane arranges herself on the floor of the suite's hallway, having slipped a robe under the little table opposite the door just in case anyone from the butler or room service arrives.

At the sound of the lock, she presses her forehead down onto the marble, the footsteps outside had been so quiet she's sure it's him and not one of the hotel maids. She waits anticipating the sense of him, of his presence, and prays she's guessed right.

The door swings open, a near silent footfall...

The rumble of his voice comes to her bringing with it a wave of relief. "Oh, what a pleasant surprise." There's a hint in it of his serious and comic sides battling for control.

She keeps her head low as she replies, "I hope you don't mind. The cleaner let me in." It matches her assumed role and helps her not spoil it too soon.

"Stand up. Let me get another look at you." She stands and as soon as she has, he commands, "Hands behind your neck, legs apart. Good, now turn for me."

She does, and her nerves play a hundred tricks on her even though, having indulged in so many twisted fantasies with him, there's surely a little more they can have to fear.

His voice and manner are curt, "Still as lovely. That's good. I must say, I hadn't been sure you'd be brave enough to volunteer to come a second time after all the things I did to you and promised to do if I saw you again. Come through." And he walks past her as if expecting her to follow.

Ella Jane trails after him as she trips out the explanation she'd prepared. "Please Sir. They said they'd pay me extra if I came, and do worse than I could imagine if I refused and..."

"And?"

"And I was scared, Sir, but..."

"But?"

"But I wanted to come, wanted you to do those other things you said, mark me so you have to keep me and keep doing those things."

"You want all that?"

"Yes, Sir."

"And the things I did to you last time?"

"Sir?"

"What about those?"

"I've thought about them every day since, Sir, even when I've been with the other men they sent me to. I thought of you to get me hot."

"Is that so?"

"Uh-huh. Even my boyfriend." She smiles slyly. "May I ask something, Sir?"

He frowns. "You may."

"O-other clients, the other men they send me to, they don't always want me again. They say...."

"They say you're too much, and that you're too cold."

"Sir!"

"They warned me about you, you know. And they suggested I order another girl this time, but I asked for you."

"Wh-why, Sir?"

"Because I wanted the best. I wanted a woman with untapped passions, a woman who can be trained with pleasure and with pain to be the perfect vessel for my enjoyment of both." He moves close and growls into her ear in his deepest rumble, "I want to break you, so you will jump to perform the least act just to be near me, so your body will quiver in fear and need at the very thought of me."

When he goes to pull away her lips turn to his and open to him. She arches back and his arm goes around her slender body, supports her as he lowers her to the carpet while her hands go to his belt and fly.

She pushes his trousers and underwear down past his hips, spreads her legs and looks up at him with hunger in her eyes. "Don't you want to hurt me first?"

"No, I'm going to fuck you now, then take my time giving you more pleasure and more pain than you've ever imagined."

She takes a hold of his cock and guides it to her ready entrance, "Oh, Sir, you already gave me that and more. That's why I wanted to come back."

The talking ends there. He fucks her, and turns her over, and fucks her some more, uses his hands on her to make her cum, and has her use her hands on him as her orgasm crests. Then he fucks her once more. The next time she goes into a spasm and cries out, he joins her in her primal celebration pleasure and then collapses on top of her in panting, sweat-soaked exhaustion.

"Wow."

"Mmm-hmm." She twists under him and smiles up, "You're as full of shit as I am. You know that?" Then buries her head in the thick carpet and howls with laughter.

"Yup." He lowers his head to her shoulder and gives her a friendly bit. "It was fun though."

"So much fun."

"How are your knees?"

"Not good. Hopefully I haven't got much carpet burn there or on my ass."

"That's something. I think mine are fucked."

She smiles impishly. "Serves you right for all those evil things you whispered."

"You liked me whispering them!"

"I know, I'm not sure how you kept a straight face."

He chuckles, "I practice."

Ella Jane flushes and her voice is thick with passion. "They were hot!"

"Thank you."

"I'd like you to do that again." She kisses him fiercely and when she pulls back for air she floats, "But best not to lead with any of them on a vanilla first date."

"So no! If I were you, I'd stay away from the showing up naked and saying you're a hooker trick too."

"Really?"

"Yea, think of all the guys who'd pay you every penny they had and never be able to afford a second date."

He runs a fingertip along her lips and she nips it and pouts. "So kind, yet so mean!"

"Isn't that what you like about me?"

"It is." She wriggles her bum against him. He's still inside her, and it feels nice, so she does it again.

"Is that your way of saying you don't want to get up?"

"No, we should. I don't want to get my hips carpet burned."

"Good, I don't want to get my knees more..." And he kisses the back of her neck. "Go on then. Get up."

Obviously, she can't. She's half his weight and less that than of his strength. She tries though, and calls him a dick then yelps and laughs when he swats the sides of her bum and thigh before laughing more. When he withdraws, he curses on finding out that, though his knees are less damaged than he feared, the tops of his feet are worse.

On learning this Ella Jane does her best to hide her smirk.

He helps her up despite her lack of charity however he does so partly in order to get her to lower her guard so he can land a resounding whack on her bum when she least expects it.

She pouts as she rubs her stinging butt. "So do you like the courtesan that much?"

"She's welcome to visit whenever you want a night off."

Ella Jane straightens and frowns in an effort to seem offended. "Hmm, I'm not sure how I should take that."

He doesn't bite though preferring to remain coolly dispassionate. "Permission to play a role you enjoy or my terrible unfaithfulness?"

"Either!" She tilts her head and hedges, "How about if I only want an hour off?"

"In that case you can either return or she could have a family emergency."

"And you wouldn't mind?"

He shrugs. "No, not so long as you're willing to accept similar changes of tempo on my part."

"You are such a slut!" The words are out of Ella Jane's mouth before she realises. She laughs through the tickling he gives her, and the spanking she's earned and keeps going until his soothing hands awake something still stronger than laughter. At long last she pleads that her ribs hurt and a minute later she begs, "Please stop, I don't want to say red."

He finally relents, and she kisses her thanks. "I'm sorry, Sir. You're not a slut." Then laughs and winces.

"Might I suggest a shower and something to eat?"

"I don't think I've ever been half as clean or well fed."

"I should hope not, nor half so well fucked or whipped?"

She shakes her head. "Nope."

"Am I reading this wrong, or have we sort of dropped out of the role playing?"

"Er, yes, sorry."

He shrugs and kisses her cheek. "That's okay, I like you almost as much as my mysterious businessman likes his little harlot."

Ella Jane whacks his shoulder with a fist and stares at him with narrowed eyes.

He protests, "That was payback!" as he stands, but also grins and offers her a hand up, "but I definitely deserved the punch!"

She lets him help her and confirms, "You so did."

"Yup, do you want to have lunch here or go out?"

"You and your stomach!"

"I can't help it. You're hard work. An old man needs sustenance to keep up."

Ella Jane's eyes narrow at the reminder of the difference between their ages. "You aren't an old man."

He looks at her and wishes he weren't, but he doesn't say anything. Well, nothing more than getting her to say what she wants for lunch.

Roger calls him while they're waiting, "Just thought I'd let you know I've managed to get Miss Tyler added to your signings in Dallas and Detroit, unless you want me to get her de-added, that is?"

"Great, no, that's perfect; do you want to give her the good news yourself?"

"No! That would be Cyn's job, but we thought you might like to tell her."

So he hangs up and tells her, and she frets that nobody might come, but doesn't tell him she's scared of sitting there alone while a legion of fans ask him about his many books.

He says something and she doesn't hear. "Pardon?"

"I asked if you have you got your passport with you?"

"No."

"Oh, that's a shame. Can you get someone to send them?"

"I could. Why would I need them?"

"I was thinking of popping up to Canada, so a passport would help."

"It's not that you're thinking of kidnapping me and selling me into slavery then?"

"I've pondered the notion, kidnapping you and keeping you in slavery. But selling? No. Not unless you want me to."

"Really?"

"No, I gather they disapprove of that sort of thing in Canada, but it might be a fun game."

"Who for?"

"That would depend on the rules."

His Bathroom

After they eat Ella Jane asks if it's okay for her to bathe alone, and he agrees and takes the time to go online and set his drone flying over his beloved estate.

With time to spend, Ella Jane sorts out her things in the bathroom and investigates his. They'd been too busy playing and fucking the night she moved into his suite, and have been ever since. Nothing's that out of the ordinary, discounting the set of handcuffs and bath friendly rechargeable want. But she can't help noticing something she doesn't expect, and she calls out, "You have a body brush?"

A minute later, having set the autopilot to return the drone to its base station he saunters in and leans nonchalantly against the doorframe. "I have several body brushes, but I only brought two."

"Why do you have them?"

He smiles, "I have several reasons." Then his smile turns devilish, "But right now I can only think of two."

Ella Jane tests the back of the brush by slapping it on the palm of her hand, then does the same with the bristled side.

"Still just one reason."

"May I ask what the other one is?"

"Hmm, what do you know about my tastes?"

"Pain… and, pleasure?"

"Have you ever had anyone use one of those on you?"

"No, I've used one on myself though."

"For?" he asks archly, smirking as he does.

She pouts and replies, "Brushing!" to which he raises an eyebrow. "Okay! I tried spanking too."

"And you like both?"

"They're okay."

"Only, okay?"

"Uh-huh." With that dismissal, she holds the brush out to him.

He lifts it from her unresisting fingers and swishes it experimentally through the air, "Then, I hope you're in for two treats," and his eyes slide all the way down her body and then all the way back up before settling on hers and reaching inside.

She draws a breath in to gather herself and challenges him, "Are you always so smug?"

"I don't know."

"Liar!"

"Are you trying to provoke me, young lady?"

She gives a little giggle, "No."

"Then don't accuse me of being a liar. I've always been this smug up until now, but I won't promise for the future."

His defence amuses and exasperates Ella Jane and her hands make their way to her hips. "You're incorrigible!"

Her posture doesn't dissuade him though. "And also, encourageable?"

"Hmm, can I answer that if they turn out to be treats?"

"Is that consent?"

"It might be." She waits for his face to respond to the missing word, and then for her insides to tighten in their own response to his change of expression before adding, "Sir."

"Then I suggest bathing and a demonstration."

"Bathing?"

"Trust me."

"Another trick you picked up?"

"Something like that."

She narrows her eyes as she assesses his playful expression. "Or do you just want us to get in the bath together so you can do filthy things to me?"

"Ha, something like that too."

Ella Jane chews her lip and tilts her head, "All those people at the seminar listening to you speak."

"What about them?"

"I bet they don't know you're the naughtiest man alive."

"*The* naughtiest?"

"Well, the naughtiest one I know."

"And you've met so many men?"

"I have."

He oils her skin as the huge tub fills. Ella Jane revels in his touch, but complains just enough of his using the whole exercise to get his hands on her to earn herself a few good natured spanks and tweaks. She apologises after each with the kind of mock contrition only a submissive contentedly offering body to her laughing lover and cheerfully willing to accept his physical chastisement can get away with.

The water is deep and hot and, he bathes her with an indulgence very much at odds his stated aim for this to be a precursor to showing her the body brushes uses.

She leans back against him as he works up a lather in her hair while making sure to also gently but powerfully massage her neck and shoulders as well as her scalp. "Aren't you in a hurry?"

"No, why should I be?"

More keen in teasing him than on having him cut their soak short she muses, "Oh, I just thought you had something you wanted to do after." While playing at seeing how many bubbles she can collect on one leg and how high she can raise it out of the water.

"I do, but there's no sense cutting one pleasure short to get to the next one."

"Is this really a pleasure for you?"

He flexes his pelvic muscles making the hardness against her bum surge. "Can't you feel?"

"The only other person who's ever bathed me was my mom."

"Hopefully this is a little different."

She humphs and tries to bite him, and he laughs as he admits to deserving to be bitten. "It's *very* different."

"Good different."

"Good anyway." She kisses the hand she'd tried to bite. "What do you get out of it?"

"So many things, including the favour being returned."

"Oh, have you finished?"

"Nearly." He eases her forwards and slips around her to take hold of the nylon brush. "You're getting part one of the demonstration first."

"Mmm, lucky me?"

"I'll let you decide."

He uses the brush on her body in long sweeping strokes starting with just enough force to not quite tickle and build up to not quite enough to hurt. His strokes start at her neck, skirt her folds and stop just short of her hands and feet.

She allows stretches out in the hot water and allows him to lift and turn her body and limbs as he pleases, abandoning herself the latest sensuous experience. "Are you exfoliating me?"

"I wouldn't put it like that. Isn't it nice?"

"Do I get into trouble if I say you know it's nice?"

"Hmm, let me think..." He occupies himself while he thinks by sliding an arm under her back while is brushes slow light strokes around her breasts and down to her mons. As he continues, his strokes progress, turning the deeply sensual experience into an intensely sexual one and graze their areoles causing the buds at their tips to stiffen. At last he sighs, "Ah, yes!"

Ella Jane rubs her head against his supporting shoulder. "Are you finished thinking?"

His *I am* is a happy rumble, and he continues with his ministrations.

She chuckles at combination of pleasing actions and unhelpful words, "And?"

"Yes, but only a little." He smiles and bends to touch his lips to hers, then runs the bristles across each of her nipples in turn. "Nothing much more than you'll get anyway in the demonstration."

"Is that so?"

"It is."

"In that case," she lays her head back and looks him in his eyes. "You know it is."

His *Hmm* is long and drawn out as he manoeuvres his legs under her and lifts her hips enough to raise her mons out of the water. "Do you know what you're letting yourself in for?"

"Ha-ha, no."

He taps the knobbly back of the brush against each of her swollen buds and her mons then goes back to his stroking. "Are you sure?"

"I think I can guess, Sir."

"How clever you are."

He adds the smacks in a pattern rather than mixing them in randomly. Two of the slow caressing circuits, then one swat to the tip of each breast, another two and then a harder one to her mons just above her entrance. None are so hard that an individual blow is too much, but all with enough force to build and maintain an increasing heat and set it sinking deeper into her flesh and bones.

After a few rounds her nipples start sending messages of pain up to her head, while simultaneously sending entirely different ones down to her centre, and her breasts develop an overfull swollen aching. The smacks to her mons though have no ambiguity in their effect and Ella Jane moves her legs father apart, plants the soles of her feet down and raises herself further, angling her hips so as to encourage him to strike lower.

He sees, fixes his eyes on hers, reads, waits for the moment her focus shifts, in which her world becomes first the room, and then just the two of them. Then he reaches his supporting arm around to take the tip of her far breast while his lips take the near. With her breasts no longer available to brush or strike he circles and strikes her mons.

Her hips begin to rock upwards to meet every blow, and he strikes lower.

She whimpers, and he ceases his stroking.

There's only the rhythmic beat of wet slaps as the back of the brush impacts her outer lips and mons those of her building crescendo and the water in the tub.

He rouses her with a rumbled. "Can we get out now?"

"Hmm?"

"Our toes are bound to have gone wrinkly."

"Okay." Ella Jane kisses his chest. "Thank you for showing me how to use a body brush."

His deep chuckle goes right through her. "I've only demonstrated one of them so far."

"You really are going to kill me."

"Just la petite mort."

"A thousand little deaths can add up, you know."

"That's why I'm dividing them between different sorts."

"Ha-ha, you're a poet as well?"

Her chuckle may not echo in his bones in the same way, but it does make him laugh and want; and he kisses the top of her head. "Come on, time to get you dry and finish your lesson."

"Poor Sir."

"Huh?"

She kisses his chest and lightly sucks his nearer nipple. "After all that, you didn't get to have me bathe you."

"I'm sure I'll live."

They get out and dry one another and he insists on being even more thorough than usual, though he doesn't oil her body as usual preferring to gather the body brushes and lead her to the massage table.

Unsure whether to climb on face down or face up, Ella Jane asks, "How do you want me?"

He grins his wickedest grin.

She clarifies, "Other than orally vaginally and anally!"

"Oh!" He feigns innocence. "Face down to start."

He begins with the natural fibre brush by applying the same long, slow strokes only more softly still, so light she barely feels them.

Ella Jane screws up her face expecting the brush to tickle, then giggles and squirms for a different reason when it doesn't. "Are you demonstrating or just trying to get me in the mood again?"

His answer begins with a low, wicked chuckle and continues with a laconic, "Or?"

With her body laid out and supported he's able to stroke from her shoulders down to the soles of her feet in uninterrupted sweeps and with a hypnotic and slowly developing intensity. After a time she state purring and he begins to hum. Already drifting and daydreaming about what might happen as she does, she asks, "Is this all there is to it?"

"Do you want it to be?"

She chuckles, lifts her head from the bed's face-hole and lets her eyes challenge him.

It's all the provocation he needs. This body brush is heavier. Its reverse side is highly polished beech wood, and her upturned backside is the perfect target.

The blow to her right cheek makes her buck and forces a screech from her lips and the one to her left makes her shriek the word fuck.

He bends, kisses the middle of each glowing mark and resumes his stroking as if nothing had happened.

Over the next half hour he repeats the cycle, brushing her skin until she falls into a reverie and then whacking her bum with blows so heavy they set her insides pulsing. Unlike the whipping with his new floggers it doesn't make her cum, but the combination definitely sets her simmering and when he asks her to roll over the tips her breasts stand out like matching cairns. She spreads her legs to the sides of the bed in invitation.

When he brushes the front of her body he has more targets to aim at, but he doesn't strike any so hard, limiting himself to light slaps to the outer and under sides of her breasts and lighter ones still to their tips and to per pussy. He smacks her mons harder but none of the blows come close to causing her to match her earlier cries of outrage.

She's so close that the sounds she makes barely change between when he's stroking and when he's smacking. By the time he sets the brush aside, she cries out and convulses within moments of him reaching two fingers into her and clamping his thumb down over her hooded clit.

The bed is only feet from the table, and it's a far more comfortable place for aftercare and shared bodily warmth so he carries her there. Ella Jane, though, is interested in more than warmth and the long play session has left him just as keen. With her body still buzzing, she crests again quite easily when he enters and caresses her, and he doesn't last long after.

Still in carer mode, he gets chilled waters from the kitchen and brings them back. Ella Jane greets him enthusiastically. Though softened, his cock still has its thickness and length, is still engorged with blood, and, as she knows from past experience with men, it's doubtlessly still sensitive, ready for pleasure, so long as she's gentle.

Ella Jane doesn't know him though. He's still new to her, still fresh, even though her body knows him well already, both inside and out. As she lies curled up against his strength and her body revels in the sense memories of his caresses, of his torments, and of their passionate couplings. She wonders if she dares take it into her mouth without asking permission. His silky soft foreskin seems to call to her, and though she knows she might be earning some chastisement for her boldness, she reaches out a hand. She doesn't aim directly for her target. Instead, she lightly brushes her fingers down the far side of his broad chest.

Her fingers attract his eyes to her. With that connection established, she allows her touch to drift toward his V and away again while she searches his face for signs of encouragement or admonishment. Her fingers dance towards and away until he comes to full hardness and until she sees a trace of a smile. On seeing that sign, she brushes her palm against the silken fullness and then away.

Despite his smiled consent and her own desire, she takes her time anticipating, and getting into position. Ella Jane applies feather-light touches and kisses, trails her tongue up the spongy line on the underside of his cock, draws his stiffness away from the flat muscular wall of his stomach and opens her mouth to its head. She opens wide and takes its fullness as far into her mouth as she can without touching and copies his breathing warmth against intimacy. Then she seals her lips around his shaft and presses her tongue against the underside his foreskin over the underside of the head of his cock.

Their Electrifying Evening

They spend the rest of the afternoon in bed and dine in the suite too. Eventually he suggests they at least poke their noses outside, she reluctantly agrees to a turn in the park. He elects to remind her of the nature of their relationship by having her wear a small steel plug while they walk. Being plugged does nothing to make her less excitable, but he hadn't really expected it to.

On returning to the suite, he has her take off everything but the plug and asks, "Do you want to play tonight?" with a look that says he does.

I've wanted to play all day, and we have!"

"Oh good, but would you consent to me trying something new?"

"That might depend. Which thing?"

"Electricity."

She sucks her lip lower into her mouth. "You have before."

"And I will again. There are so many different ways and places to apply it, just as there are with impact. And this is a new one."

"I'm intrigued."

"Ha, that's my cunning plan. You were supposed to be."

She lets him lead her to his strange looking bondage frame and arrange her on it.

Despite the enormous difference in strength, he goes about securing her limbs methodically. And despite her increasing vulnerability and impending torture, her eyes tease him mercilessly.

Having secured her and tested her bonds, he takes a hold of her by the tip of a breast and by her entrance, and holds her with enough force to draw a long sigh from her lips. "Anyone would think you were at the start of a new rollercoaster."

Her tongue snakes between her teeth to moisten her lips. "Aren't I?"

He raises an eyebrow. "Not scared?"

She shakes briefly. "Scared."

The eyebrow rises further.

And she briefly takes each of her lips between her teeth, then allows he mouth to smile a little. "But..."

His grin spreads. "You're going to love this." Then his voice turns demonic. "Or at least I will."

He takes out a neat rectangular case and sits on the floor by the frame. The case contains three neat matching TENS units and an assortment of electrodes, clamps, and other devices.

He applies stick-on electrodes to the ends of each of her outer labia and applies a clamp over her hood. It pinches firmly enough that it doesn't fall off when he swats her bum, but not hard as to be painful. He then attaches another clamp to the base of her butt plug and two different looking ones to the tips of her breasts. He then tests the clamps, and taunts her with his eyes as he does. Then he attaches the wires and tests each connection with a little jolt of electricity, enough to make her react but not to yelp or sigh. Satisfied, he stands and smiles, looks down, leans over her, traces every line of her bound body with loving caresses of his hands, touches her entrance, and finds her receptive. Smiles more widely, he raises a finger to his mouth, and tastes her, then presents another of his wet fingers to her lips and watches her welcome it.

"Ready?"

She half nods and looks up with nervous anticipation, as he moves behind her, kneels, and enters her.

The first wave starts in the tips of her breasts. The voltage builds slowly as his hands skilfully knead the tender flesh beneath, rising from a subtle accent to his touch to a consuming rush. By this time, the second set of electrodes has begun to send their impulses through the lengths of her swollen outer lips; he's flexing the muscles of his thigh against her there. She's undulating against him, and her body is rushing towards a crest when the electrodes on her breasts approach their maximum intensity, and a wave of pain through their buds overrides all other sensations.

The agony is so intense that she fancies the clamps are actually piercing her flesh. But the pain doesn't last long. It fades as electricity begins to make the presence of the little clamps on her clitoris and hood feel more urgent. This new stimulation is accompanied by his deft touch as the wave strengthens, and her body rushes to the point of mewling ecstasy before the previous set sends their greatest current through her in a bolt of pain. And so it continues, the tingling starting in her breasts again as her pearl and its covering are taken through heaven and hell.

She parts her lips and let out sighs and cries, and her eyes join them, adding a silent plea which his lips answer. When his kiss is still not enough for either of them, he thrusts inside her, giving her muscles something to clamp down on as each wave flows through her. Something familiar and something that fills her and touches her in yet more places. He moves slowly, rises from the kiss to focus his eyes on her and her responses. Then he buries himself deep in her as the ecstasy turns to agony, his presence inside helping to transform the pain into something beyond. She sees and feels his heavy muscles move, and her bound limbs strain uselessly to reach them, hold him. Instead, the ropes and cuffs hold her captive, and she's unable to do anything but feel what he and his electricity are doing to her.

The waves surge, recede, and overlap with one part of her body anticipating while another delights and wicked flames of pain consume another. And all the while she feels his hands, his eyes, and his presence inside her. Prayers, promises, and pleas pour from her lips.

She thinks she cums, rather, she thinks she starts cumming. Just as she thinks she starts to scream at the way lightning jolts pierce her most tender flesh. Her body peaks, and does so again and again, as wave after wave cycles through her straining nakedness. Similarly, her body and mind tell her that he tenses, shudders, releases his essence into the tranquil core of the storm her body has become. And then he cums again, as her world begins to fade into exhaustion.

The next thing she's sure of is his warmth and that her limbs are free. She feels his solidity against her and his readiness against her thigh and presses against him. Her hand takes a hold of him and the thickness and the extra heat there tells her what her memory says her mind and body did and that he too is half spent and drifting.

"Back with us?" His voice is a barely audible rumble and accompanied by a squeeze from his arm.

She buries her head in his side. "I'm not sure." Then she looks up at him and grins.

"Still tingling?"

"Uh-huh." She clings to him and presses her lips to his skin and falls quiet.

They lie there in silence for an age, his arm protectively around her and the covers and his warmth comforting, connecting.

She murmurs, "How did you come up with that?"

"Hmm?" His hand strokes her shoulder. "You said you were interested, and a few simple electro toys are easy to fit into a travel bag. Add a little experience, a dash of improvisation," he leans down and kisses her, "and a lot of inspiration." He then smiles cockily. "Did it work?"

The flash in her eyes and the blush in her cheeks would have made lying impossible even if she'd wanted to. "You know it did."

"Nice change from impact?"

"Nice, certainly." Her hands touch her body where the electrodes had been, half expecting to feel painful after-effects but instead finding nothing more than additional sensitivity. "Wild."

"You'll be tingly for a couple of days." His hands touch her, press, squeeze, and awaken vivid nerve memories, and his eyes smoulder as if to say he knows exactly what she's feeling. "And it doesn't do any damage so..."

"You like that, don't you?"

"Hmm?"

"Being able to torture me without leaving a mark."

"I can mark you if you want, but this way we both know, and nobody else ever will." He slides two fingers into her, places the tip of his thumb over her hood, and presses down her hypersensitised flesh. "And we both know I can do it again whenever we wish."

The rush of sensation at his words, his voice, and the electrifying contact spills out of her eyes.

He murmurs, "Yes," and she rocks her hips. "But don't close your eyes."

It takes only a moment for her to begin tensing against and around him. She struggles to keep her eyes open and feels his release spill out of them.

He doesn't force her to a second orgasm, just relaxes his grip and brushes his lips against hers and then the tip of each of her breasts.

"That was insane."

"Told you you'd feel tingly."

Her hand strokes his thick forearm, tracing all the way down to where his fingers enter her opening. "So sure of yourself."

"With the right partner." His thumb circles. "You're passionate, and responsive, and..." His grip tightens again.

She closes her eyes and rocks against his grip, and his free hand guides hers to his hardness. Then he takes her there, slower this time, but with the same easy confidence, slowing twice as she gets close and reading her easily, the tightening of her grip around him turning her body's already transparent communication into a virtual neon light.

He lets her cum again eventually though, and her frantic grip as her body convulses sends a quivering orgasm through his, even though it doesn't draw forth his essence.

While they're recovering Ella Jane asks "So that was a few simple electro toys?"

"Just three vanilla TENS units and some clamps and electrodes. I've got some fancy ones and a couple of wands, but they aren't quite as travel friendly, and I didn't know how well we'd get on." His touch roams lazily as he speaks, and her hand slowly eases up and down. "We do get on, don't we?"

With the offhanded comment and his manner, that he asks while she's got his hard-on in her grip and while her body is still glowing, Ella Jane can't help laughing. "Maybe." She rolls onto her side and faces him. "Would you like a clue?"

"That would be helpful." His deadpan voice contrasts with the mischief in his eyes.

"Let me see. Ah..." She kisses his lips and pulls back.

"Was that the clue?"

She shakes her head and kisses the underside of his chin as she continues to stroke his hardness.

"That?"

This time she chuckles, "Nope," and presses her lips to where his throat meets his chest. "I'll tell you when I've given it to you."

"Ah, then I shall be patient." Then he lets out a sigh as she trails her tongue in a spiral around one pectoral and then suckles gently as the circling reaches a point.

A surging of the hardness in her grip tells her to hurry, but she has no intention of allowing its urgency to deny her a languorous enjoyment of him or of repaying his patience with haste. She suckles long and slowly, feeling echoes of her ministrations in her breasts as she moves between his eager little buds, but teases herself and him by not continuing down his body until her need for something inside her becomes too strong to resist. Even then, she kisses along the thick slashes of muscle over his ribs and the lines of his obliques and abs. She teases a warm breath along his V and past her slowly stroking hand, which she then slides up his shaft, pushing his foreskin forward. “I like this. I haven’t met one before.” Her tongue and lips play at kissing the soft silky skin. “Is it as sensitive as my folds?”

He chuckles in his turn. “I can’t quite be certain, but it’s very sensitive. It’s supposed to be like your inner lips and hood.”

“Mmm.” She takes his tip into her mouth, rubs it against her palate, and swirls her tongue around it. She plays at flicking her tongues tip over the opening in his foreskin as she pulls it back. “And this?” She lifts her head and pulls the protective sheath back to reveal the gleaming eagerness beneath.

“That’s sensitive too.”

Her laughter tinkles. “Oh good.” She eases herself between his legs and scoots her knees up so she can use both of her hands as well as her mouth in comfort.

He strokes her hair and reaches down to cup a breast beneath her, then lies back with a sigh. “At moments like this, I understand ceiling mirrors. Have I had my clue yet?”

Ella Jane curves the fingers and thumb of one hand around his cock, moulds her other to the shaft behind his balls, and murmurs, “Not quite,” in a faraway voice as she settles into enjoying him and the way that having him in her hands, in her mouth, and up close reminds her of the feeling of him elsewhere.

She takes her time and then takes more time when he too has trouble holding still. She looks up for permission and, having received it, takes more time. She chuckles to herself as his curses and prayers mingle with the sounds of his pleasure. In the end, she takes pity on him and on her aching jaw and burning forearms.

She sucks, milks his full measure with her hand and tongue, drinks him down and then gentles his sensitivity against the roof of her mouth.

When she moves to kiss his mouth and to lie against him, she too curses as her legs complain at having to straighten.

He teases. “Was that it?”

And she settles contentedly rubbing her head against him and gives him he smug, “Uh-huh?” of a woman who’s always been told she gives great head, then chuckles.

His laughter joins hers, and his arm holds her close.

“So, we sort of get on?”

“A bit.”

Their Midnight Feast

“However well we get on, I’m going to need something to eat before bed.” She clings to him for closeness but he unpeels her arms and gets up. She sits up, and when she does, a wave of light-headedness catches her.

“Peckish?”

She complains, “We only ate a couple of hours ago.”

“A couple of hours is *ages* ago.”

“But we ate so much! Well, you did.”

“I’ve been working since, and you seemed to expend a certain amount of energy too. I don’t want you getting hangry.”

Her protests fade though as the suggestion of food works its way to her stomach. “Yes, those things you do to me are hard work, you know?”

His *Poor you* drips with sarcasm.

But she tries, “That’s why I shouldn’t have to do your training sessions in the mornings.”

That suggestion results in a darkening of his expression and a hardening of his voice. “They’re good for you, and you’ve started making progress.”

She mumbles, “I know, but they’re hard.” And she pushes her lower lip out in a slight pout.

He kisses her protruding lip, and leads her in search of the makings of a meal. "There's supposed to be the makings of something fun in the kitchen."

"Supposed to be?"

"I gave them a couple of recipes to leave the kitchen stocked up for."

"You stay in the best hotels and get them to stock the fridge so you can create?"

The fridge yields up noodles, baseball steaks, onions, mushrooms, ginger, and chillies. "I should be able to rustle something up in a few minutes."

Ella Jane doesn't know why she says it, but she does. "Only one kind of mushrooms?"

"Ha," he holds up the neat bags, "Just the two, and two of chillies. You can't expect the full comforts of home when you're travelling."

"My poor Sir, slumming it in five star luxury."

"It's just the kitch – very funny," He raises an eyebrow and lowers his head as he archly adds, "I suppose you want me to address that?"

The still-naked Ella Jane insinuates herself up against him and twines her arms around his waist. "I've waitressed in a restaurant with a kitchen that wasn't this impressive. Even if it isn't as perfect as you want everything to be. If you want you can use me for another perfect play session after you create your culinary wonders and I tell you what a good cook you are." She rubs her body against his and kisses his chest and she speaks, smiling up at him all the while.

He looks down at her with the seriousness that takes over his face when he works or cooks or does something complicatedly delicious to her, but tonight her animated glee is more powerful still and he grins back. "Are you trying to bait me or just over excited?"

"I don't know." She turns her head sideways and pressed it to his chest. "I don't mean to be bratty. I never have been before."

His fingertips trace down from her temple to under her chin and exert the lightest of upward pressures.

Ella Jane lets him tilt his face up to his, and opens her lips to his kiss. "We'll get back to your sub-frenzy when we've dealt with my food frenzy and staved off the hunger crash you're going to hit if I don't feed you."

"Yes, Sir."

He directs her to hunt for crocks and cutlery while he hunts out chopping boards and kitchen knives. Having found the knives he selects two, tests their edges and nods his appreciation.

"Sharp enough for you?" She bites her lip and her eyes dare him.

"You are a very bad girl," he accuses.

She swallows, folds her arms behind her back and waits, wondering if he will.

"You know I don't generally play with knives, don't you?"

She tries to speak, fails, touches the tip of her tongue to her lips, and tries again. This time when her voice fails to make words she settles for giving a tentative nod.

"But you trust me to?"

Her tongue passes over her lower lip again and the smile spreads across her face.

All the playfulness drains from his face as he places the point of the almost invisibly thin filleting knife at the hollow of her neck. "Don't blame me if I nick you."

Ella Jane swallows but holds her nerve.

His eyes darken further, "Remember, red. You say it if you want. I'll say it if I see it."

Her teeth take a hold of her lip and he begins to move the knife down her sternum.

The knife moves slowly. His eyes stay on hers. His hand remains steady. As steady as when he shoots. As steady as when he holds her on the edge.

At first, she fights the urge to look down, but then the intoxication of holding his gaze while her skin tells her where the lethal blade is moving.

It traces the lines of her ribs and the curves of her breasts and he reminds her to breathe.

She draws in a long slow breath as he runs the needle sharp point up the undercurve of her breast and holds it as he pressed the bright cool steel into the centre of its rosy bud.

He holds the knife still as he leans forward and brushes his lips against her cheek. "That's enough for now. We need to eat."

Ella Jane lets out a sigh of regret as her insides knot and twist, but she surrenders to his decision without protest despite the voice of complaint that rises in her mind. After offering herself to him so absolutely doing anything else, would be a betrayal of her essence, and of theirs.

He straightens, smiles, sets the knife aside and holds her.

She blinks, sniffs, feels a tear rise and blinks again. Then she tenses the muscles of her thighs and pelvic floor and allows herself to sink into the feelings. Doing so, and feeling him against her nakedness, consumes her.

One of his hands moves up to cradle the back of her head. The other drifts down her arm. Relieved of the tension of holding the knife against her skin, he takes a turn and enjoying the sensation of his teeth and tongue against his lip as his eyes drink her in, and his hand moves lower.

He knows where it's going, and so does her body.

When it reaches her hip they both twist a fraction to allow it to get there, and she pulls herself against him, burying her face and crushing her breasts against his warm solidity.

His deft fingertips make their way down the line of her V to her now rhythmically clenching vulva, move lower, cup without pressing, and hold still for a timeless time as the heat of his body reflects and adds to that of her need.

At length she rubs her face against him, and her throat produces a gentle mewling.

Her gesture and that sound are the signal he hadn't realised he was waiting for.

He doesn't do much.

But he doesn't have to.

He moves his hand upwards drawing her outer lips away from her hood and presses the tip of his middle finger over her centre and her body begins to shake.

She clings, and he holds until long after her quaking subsides. Only then does he guide her back to their bed to gather the duvet and wrap her in it before taking her back to the kitchen. Once there he sets her down on a chair within touching distance of the space he has chosen to work in.

First, he sets a skillet heating. Then he sets about dressing the already beautifully cut steaks to his taste. He cuts wafer thin slices from the curved edges of each until he has two large squared blocks and then sections each into four near perfect cubes.

The ease with which the knife that had been pressed against her skin slices through the dark red meat sets her imagination running and insides clenching. So does the mastery with which he works.

He places the cubes into a bowl and grinds salt and black pepper over them tossing and turning until every face of each cube is covered. Satisfied with his work, he cuts butter into the pan before turning his attention to the other ingredients. He cubes the large Portobello mushrooms, and trims and halves the strand-like enokis, peels and slices two small white onions and a bright yellow pepper.

Last of all, he puts a disposable glove on his left hand before he peels and slices the ginger and ring cuts both the fleshy sweet chillies and their fierier slender pale red cousins.

By this time Ella Jane has recovered enough to ask him why.

The devil rises in his eyes, and he unwinds the comforter from around her. He moves his gloved fingertips tantalisingly close to her skin.

"Do you really want to know?"

Her eyes blink, and she eases her knees further apart. "No, but I do."

"I'll show you if you promise never to play this game with anyone who doesn't know their chillies."

"Why's that?"

"Because there are places you really don't want a chemical burn."

"Ouch! What will these ones do?"

"With the ginger they'll hurt for a couple of minutes, then tingle for another ten or fifteen. Still want to try?"

Her teeth whiten her lower lip while she thinks, but her fears are fighting a losing battle with her curiosity. "No, but yes."

He anoints the tips of her breast, then her outer folds before touching the fiery blend to her entrance, up and around her hood. After each new area he waits, studies, makes certain her delicate flesh hasn't had too strong a reaction and moves on. Next, he peels back her hood and coats her tiny pearl. Finally, he has her lean back as he circles her rosebud and presses a gloved fingertip within.

She's squirming by the time he peels the glove from his hand and wraps her in the duvet once more and kisses her lips. "That should keep you amused while I cook."

"May I ask a question?"

"Of course."

"Why did you use the glove if you were going to do that?"

"I hadn't been. I was just improvising because you're buzzing."

She squeezes her thighs together to try to relieve the tingling. It helps at first but the pressure she exerts works the spices further into her most intimate flesh causing her to perform a wriggling dance. "And you thought this might calm me down?"

He chuckles at that and touches his lips to hers. "Right now I don't think anything you've earned or that I want to give you's going to calm you down. So I'll settle for distracting and getting you to help with the meal."

"What do you want me to do?"

He guides her through turning the cubes of steak to sear all of their surfaces and cooking the noodles with encouraging words and touches. The burning sensations caused by her first experience of chemical play fade, or else her concentration distracts her from them.

He cooks the onions, ginger and peppers in a wok. His final touch is to add the Portobello mushrooms to the steak and turning it down. Meanwhile, he flash-fries the chillies, then adds thin strips of beef and enoki mushrooms and folds the noodles in.

The results are the prettiest meal Ella Jane has ever participated in cooking. A fact which she emphasises by racing off to their bedroom to get her phone. She photographs the appetising plates and gets him to take some of her with them, then, realising she can hardly send those to her friends or post them online, she puts a robe on so he can take some she can share.

As he hands her phone back to her, he wryly observes, "I hope it's as good as you think it looks."

"It will be, won't it?"

"Provided you really do like your steak on the pinker end of medium rare, it should be okay."

By the time they sit down to eat Ella Jane is, much to her relief, feeling sufficiently recovered from his application of chilli and ginger to her most sensitive places to sit in comfort and enjoy her meal. His *okay* turns out to another of his English understatements. "Oh wow! You could cook in one of the restaurants you go to!"

He smiles his delight at the compliment, but shakes his head. "I wish. My presentation skills aren't in the same league."

Ella Jane cuts herself a piece of beef, bites and chews the tender meat, her eyelids half closing in appreciation for the flavour. "The two cooking methods are so different."

"Both good though?"

She answers with a chuckle and by snaring a spicy strip, popping into her mouth, and consuming it with a relish. "Horrible."

He takes her to bed after their meal and doesn't make any further use of restraints or toys. Despite their spiced meal, neither's mouth causes any burning sensations beyond a pleasantly mild tingling as they sate the hungers the rich food has rekindled.

They Move "Home"

Ella Jane pushes her chair back and rises after finishing her second post-breakfast pastry. "What are the plans for today?"

"Ideally we'd hang around and carry on playing, but we have to be out of the suite, so I thought we could do a viewing platform and visit the Statue of Liberty today."

"Not yours things?"

He confides, "We can hit mine easier from the new hotel." Then he looks away. "We can also pick up one of your bucket list items there."

Ella Jane looks at him with a furrowed brow until she works his hint out. "We're going to the Plaza?"

"We are."

"Just for me?"

He hedges. "This suite wasn't available for the whole of my stay."

"That's shocking!" She puts a hand in front of her mouth. "Did some president want the President's Suite?"

"No, I think some crown prince got in first for next week. Fortunately, the Plaza has a suite."

She sidles up to him. "Is it the biggest suite they have?"

"No, just the Grand Penthouse."

"Just the Penthouse?" He misses her teasing, or appears to, so she tries, "Do you stay in their proper-sized suite often?"

He shrugs but doesn't bite, or bite back. "Just once, I'm assured the penthouse is quite nice too, even if it hasn't got a kitchen. It has a nice terrace."

Ella Jane casts her eyes around the palatial room they're in and observes, "So long as it's *quite nice too*," while studiously looking away from him.

It's possible that she might have got away with this final tease. Her voice had been even, and her tone, though light, hadn't betrayed a trace of incredulity, but the urge to look and see his reaction is too strong. Being with him is like tight rope walking – it's exciting when you stay on, but even more exciting when you fall off. She glances and sees and senses the metaphorical rope under her feet and the abyss below it.

His cheeks are tensed with mirth, but the sternness in his eyebrows is winning the fight for control of his face, albeit they're doing so slowly.

She has a choice to make. She knows that, and that she has a limited time to make it before he decides to do *something* to correct her attitude. The question is whether to meekly accept what's coming or set off on a mad race around the suite's many rooms before they have to move out.

It doesn't take her long to decide, and she does so just in the nick of time. He starts edging towards her and sets off in pursuit in the moment between her feet starting to fly and the laughter erupting from her lips. She manages to lead him twice around the dining table and once around the main reception room. But when she attempts to weave her way around the massage bed and back out of the second bedroom, he gets close enough while at the same time having somewhere to shove her without harming her. Ella Jane lands with considerable force but does so onto the emperor-sized mattress and suffers no injury.

He's on her in a flash, pinning her. She kicks and does her best to cover her bum with her hands. But he's bigger, stronger, and heavier, and he's also not averse to cheating by tickling in order to get his way when they're playing. In no more than a minute, he has her wrists secured at the small of her back and her upturned cheeks are at his mercy.

Ella Jane is fully aware of just how precarious her situation is. She knows he can deliver a painful whacking, having received a number at his hands. But the thrill of the chase and his tickling, have left her with an uncontrollable attack of the giggles. Her fit of hilarity is so intense it doesn't even relinquish its hold for long enough to let out her first yelp until the sixth heavy swat has landed on her bare behind.

He doesn't go easy on her, and she doesn't cry *red,* not even when her bottom is that colour all over.

The duration and hardness of the spanking doesn't deter her from kissing him when he finally decides he's made his point and lets go of her. It certainly doesn't stop her welcoming the way he applies his soothing skin cream to her glowing flesh.

She turns and kisses him again when he has.

He notices her wet eyes, and kisses away one tear then brushes another with the tip of a thumb, "Did I hurt you too much?"

Ella Jane shakes her head.

"Pain?"

She nods. "Laughter, too." And kisses the salt of her tear from his lips. "And release, it's been -"

"Intense?"

She nods again and tears rise. "Good, though."

His hands begin to sooth, but soon the way she is rising against them is anything but in search of soothing and her eyes fill with a fierier need.

He responds with an intensity of his own, and when she crests, he enters her with a slowness that has her clawing at his haunches.

His fingers stroke a stray curl from her face. "Are you always this cheeky?"

"No!"

"So it's just me you wind up?"

"No... I don't mean to... It's the way you look serious and like you're going to laugh at the same time." She reaches a hand over to his far hip and strokes the line of his V. "There's this too. He's always as keen as you are."

"So it's just me and my cock you wind up?"

"I don't mean to wind you up, it's just..."

He kisses her forehead, then opens his mouth to speak, but changes his mind. Instead, he kisses her lips and pulls her closer.

She lets him draw her close to his mass and his maleness, soaking in the heat of his presence against her and revelling in the memory of it inside her. "I'm not used to everything at once the way it is with you. One minute we're laughing, the next you're spanking me or tying me up. Then before I know it, you're doing things with your hands."

Unable to read what she wants him to say, and unable to put together words he's willing to say, he does some of those things with his hands and when they finish, he hurries her to get ready to go if she wishes to see the Statue of Liberty.

They find a spot by the ferry's bow on their way, and he leans close and picks up their earlier conversation. "Any particular things?"

"Pardon?"

He reaches his hand up to the side of her neck and strokes her skin. "Things I do with my hands."

Her fist bats ineffectually against his heavy thigh. "You *know* which things! You cheat too."

"We haven't made any commitments, and we haven't been out of each other's sight long enough."

"Not on me. You cheat at everything else."

He frowns in puzzlement. "Do tell."

"Like at the conference; being the joker and the serious one, then taking over."

"When did I take over?"

"You do it when you speak. It's like the room isn't big enough for you. Then you and Johnson, and this!" She waves at his body. "And this!" She indicates the two of them. "You stay in the president's suites, and you talk to the doorman and the receptionist." She shakes her head. "You even bring enough toys for us to spend all week trying different things. Then you get more here, and just to make a point, you buy up half of Home Depot and know how to make even more."

"I like making things, and Craig and I are sort of friends. We just do us, and it's not my fault your microphone broke."

"Does *anything* bother you?"

"Lots, but it doesn't help to show it."

"Just when we're alone, and I tease."

"Is that your way of saying you don't want me to let you get away with too much teasing?"

"It might be."

"Mmm, very well." He allows his fingers to skate gentle circles on her bum. "Oh, I forget. Do you play piano?"

"No, why?"

"Some hotels will put a piano in your room if you want."

"Oh, I've never stayed in a hotel where they did that before."

"If you like piano music, they can arrange for someone to play it."

"Is that better?"

"It is if you want to see them play, yes."

"You just don't..." Ella Jane lets her voice face and squeezes his hand instead. Of course he doesn't get it. Why would he?

Fortunately the ferry approaches Bedloe's Island before he has the chance to press her further, and she seizes the opportunity for a change of subject that presents itself by drawing his attention to the way the statue rises above them.

Johnson is waiting for them when their ferry gets them back to the mainland, and for once isn't certain of their destination. "Where to boss?"

He passes the question on to Ella Jane. "Would you rather go straight to the new hotel or pick a viewing gallery and get the full daytime experience?"

It doesn't take her long to decide. The thought of seeing the city from on high by daylight is tempting, but the call of the Plaza is stronger, and the city will be here for the rest of her life, but the invitation to stay in the iconic hotel might prove a one-time thing.

They Arrive

She pauses, looks up and draws in a deep breath when she steps onto the sidewalk outside the gleaming white building and remains staring even after He takes her arm.

He gives her a moment, and savours one of his own, as he drinks in the happiness he's giving this remarkable young woman, but moments come to an end and he leans down to her. "I could pinch you if that helps?"

His voice drags her eyes from the view and onto his expecting to see mockery on his face, but she reads nothing of the kind on his smiling features.

She nods, "Mom's going to be *so* jealous."

Her arrival at the St Regis may have been marked by her own nervous state of being overawed, but, a week on, and on His arm, she has the confidence to take her time appreciating the palatial foyer, while keeping her jaw muscles under control.

He leans close and breathes, "I said this place was okay." and she lets out a laugh and blinks up at him.

Here he's Mr Sabre, and they are both greeted as if they were royalty even though surely the staff must have already gossiped about the strange and elaborate luggage that will have preceded them.

When they emerge from the lifts they have to walk down a corridor to their suite, and he mutters, "Shocking, isn't it, we haven't even got the whole floor."

Ella Jane hisses, "Stop it." As she follows him, in an effort not to let his light heartedness dilute the experience, but in the end it doesn't, the way he walks as if he owns every place his feet touches becomes a part of it, and she finds herself watching him as closely as she does their surroundings.

When they get to their door he turns to her, "Ready?"

She nods and he opens the door.

Like at the St Regis the door opens onto an entry hall. "Want to close your eyes we get to the cooler bits?"

A smile, another nod, the closing of her eyes and the offer of her outstretched hand answer him and he leads her through.

On stepping into the grand reception room with its elegant staircase and regency style furniture he casts his eyes around and then sets them on Ella Jane. He drinks in her appreciation before making his way to the windows to look out over Central Park. The view is impressive, but he supposes nothing like it will be in daylight.

For her part, Ella Jane stares at the room and then at him. As she does so his *I'm assured the grand penthouse suite is quite nice* plays over in her head.

There's no physical comparison between them, none at all. His age, size, and strength are all so much greater than hers. There's his wealth too. She doesn't know *how* rich he is, but she does know how successful a writer he's been, and his room, *suite*, is far bigger than the apartments she's shared at college for the last five years.

She only feels herself as close to his equal in their exchanges, both of humour and amorously. Those similarities are in many ways more surprising than the differences. After all, almost all men are bigger than she is, and she'd known he must be well-off as soon as he'd told her his real identity–well, as soon as he'd convinced her of it. However, even the youngest and most athletic of her previous lovers and dominants have never approached the energy he pours into their kinky or sexual play.

After a time he turns and sees her still staring, "What's up?"

She shakes her head without moving her gaze and allows a flicker of a smile to reach her lips despite her desire not to seem impressed. "You don't know, do you?"

"I was expecting you to bounce on the sofa or look at the view; the long odds were on running up the stairs or doing something suggestive by the banister. I hadn't even considered you staring at me." He reaches out and gently strokes her upper arm. "It's flattering but unexpected."

"All of those are because of you. Before we met, I thought all of those were further away than you, and you were on the other side of the Atlantic."

"We're all within a few feet."

She eases across the room to stand next to him and touches the window frame in front of them as she sighs, "Physically within a few inches," Then she leans her head against him. "But I'm not sure you're within a few worlds."

He kisses the top of her head. "Same world, same Central Park, and just up there you can see the same Met Museum."

"Did you arrange to move here just so you could have a shorter walk there?"

Having lived with less in his past life he puts his arm around her shoulder and silently kisses the top of her head. He also makes a mental not to write down that, *it's only money* strikes one of his characters as a crass line.

Mistaking the reason for his silence Ella Jane ventures, "Or because I said I liked this building?"

"Ha, there's a thought. Fancy looking upstairs?"

"I have to, if they've creased my dress, you won't get the deposit back."

As they make their way up he notes. "It's a nice staircase."

"It is, and yes, these banisters definitely have potential."

"If you like those then you'll love the other interesting feature."

"What is it?"

"Ah, that would be telling."

It doesn't take her long to discover the roof terrace, nor to step out and look around. No other rooms in the hotel appear to overlook it.

He joins her under the stars a few seconds later, and she stares up at the scattering of lit windows in the towering buildings within sight. "Are you thinking what I am?"

"That depends on whether you're suddenly wondering if you might be overdressed."

She leans back into his strength. "You're as wicked as I am, aren't you?"

"Possibly more so, a little discrete outdoor nudity strikes me as more along the lines of sweetly innocent."

Despite his complaint about the lack of a kitchen, and his enthusiasm for the roof terrace, he settles into the two-story suite as if he'd been born there rather than arriving a scant few minutes earlier.

The suite at the plaza is different, split over two floors, and with fewer living rooms, more like a hotel suite than a luxury apartment. But it's just as ridiculously opulent, and the staff have the same combination of practiced and professional self-effacement. "Do they have combined theatre, dance and hotel staff schools?"

"Say what?"

"The way they move around. It's like they're the cast of a huge production, like something from back in the thirties. They dance around and make you feel like the star even when you don't know your lines or where you're supposed to stand."

"If you don't want to put that in a story, may I?"

"I'm being serious!"

"So am I. I've never quite worked out how to describe their behaviour before, but that's it. The restaurant we're going to tonight is like that too."

"You're certainly teaching me how the other half live."

"The other tiny fraction of a percent. And most of us only live this life on high days and holidays."

"However often, I'm thoroughly enjoying my education. You've got me started on a new story as well as my sequel." She climbs into his lap and leans up against him.

"Good, just don't tell Roger and Cynthia if you finish the wrong story first. They'll blame me."

He Trusts Her to Choose Her Own Dresses

They usually discuss their plans for the day over the latter part of breakfast, and their first day in their new hotel is no different. He mops up the last of the egg yolk from his plate and floats, "If you're coming with me, I have a favour to ask if that's not taking too much of a liberty?"

Ella Jane gives him a look as old as the stars and fills it with reminders of the hundred liberties she's allowed and even encouraged him to take.

"Nothing like that. Well, everything like that, but this is extra."

Unsure what extra he could possible expect of her that their extensive discussion of limits hasn't ruled out, she bursts out laughing.

He takes a full half-minute controlling his own amusement and allowing her time to stop.

"Am I going to have to put you over my knee, young lady, or are you going to take this seriously?"

Her cheeks start twitching again, and his eyebrows go into overdrive.

"Um, hmm, can I take it seriously, then laugh some more and get spanked for it?" This time her smile is winsome and entirely in control.

He blinks, she counts his count of three seconds, sees him roll his lidded eyes skywards and his lips mouth *and breathe* and is still smiling when he opens them again. "Can you pop back to that store, see your friend, and arrange to borrow up a couple day dresses and another for the evenings?"

"Friend?"

"Yes. You and the assistant were thick as thieves."

Ella Jane gasps. The thought of them being friends is ridiculous. "Hardly friends. She was just being professional."

"You can see another assistant or try another store, but I'm told that's the best."

"No, that's alright. You don't want to choose what I wear this time?"

His brows knit. "Don't you like the blue one?"

Mention of the gown still makes her want to race to the wardrobe and look at it again. "I love the blue one."

"Well then?" He grins. "We both have good taste, and you did say you wanted to choose anything else yourself."

Ella Jane shifts her weight from foot to foot. "Why do you want me to have more dresses?"

"Outfits. They don't have to be dresses. So you can wear them."

"I might not have space in my luggage for them."

"That's okay; I have bags, I'm happy to pay any excess fares they result in if it comes to that."

She sets her mouth into a disapproving line. "Hmm, that's very generous of you. Can I ride in the Bentley again?"

"Afraid that came with the St Regis. I'll get you something else fun. I'm taking Johnson with me."

"Are you being mysterious?"

"Moi?" he asks, failing to even try to sell the lie.

She narrows her eyes but backs down in the face of his eyebrows.

"And don't forget to take a signed copy of your book for your friend."

"She's not my..."

But he's already turning away with a twinkle in his eyes.

As rush hour winds down, he walks her out of the hotel's front doors. Two limousines are waiting, and he kisses her cheek before they part company. He heads off on his mysterious errand with his even more mysterious giant after seeing her, with a copy of her book clutched in her hand into the back of a Rolls Royce.

As soon as she sits down Ella Jane registers the driver's scarred features. Her sister had tried to annoy her by showing her pictures of burn victims, so she has an idea what the man has been through. She bites down on her instinctive horror, looks away and then back to him. His scars, and knowing Mr Johnson used to be in the army, give her an obvious question. "Do you work with Mr Johnson?"

"Yes, Ma'am. Well we work for the same company. Oh, and Ma'am, I can't stay outside the store to wait for you. Would it be okay if you called a minute before you're ready to leave?"

He smiles his relief when she agrees, gives her his number and insists that she message it to confirm she has it down right. Then he drops her off with the same exaggerated courtesy and observant eyes as Johnson always does.

Amberlee smiles as Ella Jane slips the blouse from her shoulders. "Nice lingerie!"

Ella Jane half smiles. She's wearing some of the things he bought her. "He went online shopping."

"He used the measurements I sent him! I like that."

Ella Jane winces as she takes her jeans off. "Hmm, I'm not so sure."

"What's to not be sure about? That's gorgeous." Amberlee sips his wine while Ella Jane twists a foot on the carpet. "Not sure if he's being pushy?"

"Yes."

"Don't you like what he bought?"

Ella Jane can't help a glance towards her reflections in the changing room's mirrored walls, and seeing herself in her guiltily received finery she can't keep her lips from twitching with hints of delight at what she sees. "I love it."

"And did he tell you we can choose what we want today?"

"Uh-huh." Ella Jane frowns. "It's not fair! I know it makes me sound ungrateful, but everything feels too much."

The tall Amberlee straightens to the imposing height her heels allow her and speaks firmly. "Life seldom is fair, but today it's not fair because it's been too good, not because it's crappy." She smiles, and goes to lay a comforting palm on the back of Ella Jane's hand but stops when the shorter woman's shoulders stiffen. Amberlee pulls back, smiles and tops up their glasses, hoping to get her client to relax. "Why not just try the things on and enjoy a glass of wine?"

"Um..."

"You wouldn't want to upset me would you?" Amberlee wheedles while smiling at herself for doing so.

Ella Jane frowns. "What do you mean?"

"There must be something you don't like? It can't be our beautiful clothes, or your boyfriend's gorgeous wine, so that just leaves your highly sensitive fake friend..."

"No, it's not that. It's too much, and he's not my boyfriend!"

Amberlee shrugs. "Then send it all back when you stop enjoying not being his girlfriend." She leans forward and confides, "But seriously, I'd keep the underwear if I were you. You never know if you'll ever have anything like it again."

Ella Jane chews her lip. "It is nice."

"Nicer than I wear most days, and I work here." Having secured her customer's renewed cooperation, Amberlee changes the topic of conversation in what she hopes will be a more fruitful direction. "So where's he taking you?"

"I know we've got signings in Dallas, Detroit, and a couple in California. Also he says there are some businesses he needs to drop in on and some *fun surprises*."

"A man of mystery?"

Ella Jane clamps down on her facial muscles to avoid showing excitement. "He seems to be. Our agents are finding more cities for book signings, too."

"Are you going anywhere you haven't been?"

"It feels like everywhere I haven't been!"

Amberlee smiles, and indicates towards the copy of Abigail she's just been given. "It'll do you good. Just think of all the places you'll be able to write about with first-hand knowledge."

They try more things. The fair-haired woman instantly dismisses any garment, piece of lingerie or accessory she or Ella Jane has the slightest hesitation over. "We're only getting you a few things, so they have to be just right."

By the time they finish the list and the wine, Ella Jane has a modest collection of immodestly fabulous clothes, and a soft spot for the tall assistant, but she is most definitely shopped out. There's just one problem, deciding which of the two black cocktail dresses she wants. She thinks she knows the stylish bare shouldered cut-out number would fit in better with the kind of people and events he has in mind. The more beach-chic strapless one with a subtle semi-see-through lace skirt and embroidery sections at the waist is more her though, and she loves it more.

Amberlee, working partly on commission, aware of the eyewatering budget she's been given to dress her client, and also fond of her, has a simple answer. "If you can't decide, why not take both?"

"That's easy for you to say."

"It's easy for you to do, too. I'm sure I can fix a small discount for my favourite pretend friend. If you tell him why you have both like you told me why you want them, he'll be delighted."

Ella Jane doesn't know whether it's the wine and girlie company, the magic of beautiful clothes or if it's just a good idea. In any case, he'd made it quite clear that she and Amberlee were to choose. "Are you sure he won't mind?"

"Rich men never mind a bargain."

The redhead flares. "He's not like that!"

The fair haired assistant hides her amusement at fierceness with which Ella Jane defends her not boyfriend, and makes an excuse to depart for a minute. "I'll just ask my boss."

Amberlee returns to the changing room after a minute to find Ella Jane looking at the two little black dresses with a pensive expression.

"It's okay. The account he set up won't let you charge more than he budgeted, and I've kept it under."

"Thanks."

"You can even manage an extra pair of shoes if you want."

"No!"

Amberlee grins. "It's good to be of service, and to have a customer who worries about saving her not-a-boyfriend money."

"He's..."

"I know." The tall woman air kisses her. "You now have an outfit for every occasion."

"Thanks, I think."

"Hey, you'll have a great time and see some new places. Have a wonderful trip, and if he's still not your boyfriend by the end of it, I hope you find one who looks at you the way he does."

With Ella Jane safely seen on her way, he and Johnson head to their meeting. It's with the representatives of Sig and Billings Medical & Military and a representative from the Department of Defence. It may be routine, but like many routine things, it's important and signing off on the next stages of the testing and acceptance process takes a weight from His shoulders.

After the meeting, they hit the gym and make another quick visit to the range. While they're there he receives a call letting him know that Ella Jane is nearly done.

* * *

The car draws up outside the dress store to collect her within a moment of her stepping out onto the sidewalk.

Seeing the driver for the second time, Ella Jane finds his scarring less of a shock and manages a smile as he makes his way around the car and opens the kerbside door. "Thank you. I must say, you're as professional as Mr Johnson.""Why thank you Ma'am, that's saying a lot."

When he gets back into the driver's seat she asks, "Are you not just a driver too?"

His grin is lopsided, but nonetheless full of amusement. "You could say that Ma'am."

"But you're a bit more subtle than he is?"

"Ha!" He gestures at his face. "Not that much less. But yea, he has an impressive presence."

"Is that a disadvantage?"

"Not really, he's so obvious nobody notices the rest of a protection team at all. You and the boss are highly valued clients."

Ella Jane hadn't even considered the possibility of other people looking after Him or them and she forces a smile. "You certainly make me feel safe and well cared for."

The car delivers her to yet another restaurant for a late lunch. This time the cuisine is Thai, and his decision that they'll be sticking to alcohol free beverages makes her want to race back to their suite after they finish.

"Did you and your friend have fun?" he asks.

After enjoying the morning with Amberlee, she lets his *your friend* slide. "So much. Until today, I didn't understand what any woman could see in being a princess or a model."

"Enjoyed being pampered?"

"It's not that I wanted to be Barbie when I grew up. I knew I was never going to be tall enough to be a catwalk model, and I was always too shy and more interested in other things than clothes. But I'm glad I got to experience it for a while."

"Did you snap pictures of what you got?"

"No, she said I should make you wait until they've been adjusted."

"Hmm. Like I said, thick as thieves."

She suggests skipping dessert, but he has other ideas and whisks her to a nearby patisserie and then a chocolatier where they pick up delectable looking creations. He claims to have had each recommended to him. Only when they're well laden does Johnson's BMW sweep up to the curb to collect them.

His Day of Touristing

After their morning rituals of exercises, play and a breakfast to shame many a dinner table Johnson whisks them up New York 9A along the green, wooded bank of the Hudson River to the Museum's Cloisters site.

He has no particular plan. They simply wander the grounds and galleries, both pausing when and where either's eye takes a fancy. When she asks how it all came to America he tells her the little he knows about George Grey Barnard and how Rockerfeller, JP Morgan and others acquired collections and donated them.

She threads her arm through his. "Is this where you come when you visit New York?"

"I've mostly come on business; I usually fit in an opera or a concert."

"Is that all?"

"I like the botanical garden."

"Can we go there?"

"Now?"

Her arm squeezes his. "I'd like to see what you like."

His brow furrows, but she's looking up at him with her eyes wide, and he does love the garden. "Okay, if you wish." Without further hesitation he phones Johnson, and before long they're on their way.

Their route takes them through the Inward Hill and Van Courtland Parks, then down the Mosholu Parkway, and Ella Jane can't help commenting on the amount of green space in the city as she looks out of the car.

He touches her hand. "Is that you or Abigail?"

She looks around, expecting to see mockery in his eyes, but there's nothing but warmth. "I – both of us I suppose."

"Do you both like it?" she nods, "I'm glad."

It's Johnson who breaks the silence. "The city bought up a lot of land as it was growing, to keep some green, and some was gifted, then I expect they built some of the best roads through it. I think you'll both enjoy the gardens."

"Both?" Ella Jane asks and turns to Him. "I thought you'd been to the gardens before?"

The big man's eyes flick from the road to the rear view mirror and focus on Ella Jane. "He has Miss; I was referring to you and Miss Abigail. You aren't the first writing with a story in their mind I've driven."

Unlike at the Cloisters, the driver accompanies them. He leads the way though, with Johnson bringing up the rear a little adrift of the couple. His route takes them to and around the huge greenhouses and decorative ponds of the conservatory, which he admires with a wistful eye. Ella Jane doesn't know much about botany, and asks a him a number of questions, a few of which he answers without referring to the garden's labelling and some of which he candidly admits to now knowing the answer to.

He moves around the garden's paths and trails with a purpose to his stride, and before each new view his face and voice become animated. When the subject of his excitement comes into view he slows and looks in her direction.

She stops when he does, takes in what she sees, and mostly doesn't have to force enthusiasm into her expression or feign interest.

Several times while they stand, Johnson meanders into view. She glows with embarrassment when she realises the giant is watching her as half dances through the blossoming trees of the cherry collection, and when they stop at the waterfall, He looks across at the giant and then down to her, "Hungry?"

Ella Jane realises she is, nods, and then, when the three have watch the river for a minute longer, she takes her phone out to take a picture and checks the time. "You must be starving; I've never known you go so long without food."

His eyes go to the now approaching Johnson, "Fancy a bite?"

"Always boss, I'm nearly as bad as you."

"The Hudson Grill's closest, the food's okay."

Ella Jane doesn't resist the temptation, but does put a twist on it by asking Johnson, "Is that a Him okay?"

The big man's responding laugh comes suddenly and attracts the eyes of those passing. "She knows you well, boss. Yes, it's good."

When they return to the suite, he leads her into the second bedroom.

She looks at the obvious item in the room and asks, "What's this for?"

"It's a massage table. We used it at the St. Regis too."

"I know that." She smiles and dodges out of his reach. Then, when he raises an eyebrow, she moves closer again, blinks slowly, runs her lower lip between her teeth, and turns away from him again, so he can't see her face when she reminds him that he hasn't answered. "I asked what it's for."

It isn't fair he has the right to respond with what she's sure he would in his English way call, *the bleeding obvious*, but that's the point. He doesn't have to be fair.

The sound and sensation of the flat of his hand striking her offered backside interrupts Ella Jane's train of thought, "One, Sir." Then comes the caressing before he lifts his hand away again, and the silence before it strikes her other bum cheek. Her breath catches again, and she breathes out the words, "Two, Sir."

This time, the caress is followed by hair stroking and a whispered, "Good girl."

She turns back to him, puts her arms around his waist and looks up. "Thank you, Sir." The fire in his eyes suggests to Ella Jane that he too regrets making it such a mild and brief spanking. "May I ask what the massage table is for, Sir?"

"For massages." One corner of his mouth creases into a lopsided smile.

"I thought they brought the table with them when you get a massage in a hotel?"

"I might want to give you another massage."

The table is thickly padded and adjustable, and its legs look sturdy. "And may I ask if there's any other reason for it being here?"

"You may guess." By now, his smile is a full-on grin.

Her lip finds its way between her teeth again. "Might it be for tying me to?"

He feigns delighted surprise. "What a very good idea!"

"Is that the reason?"

"It might be one of them."

"Ooh! Are you going to tell me?"

"We've got a while before we have to get ready for dinner. Would you rather have a demonstration?"

"You know I would."

"I do now." He touches a hand to her cheek and his lips to hers. "Until you said, I was just guessing." Then he grins. "It's part of the fun of getting to know one another."

She puzzles, "We didn't get to know each other while we were chatting online?"

"We did, but it's hard to do the whole body-language thing in chat."

Ella Jane raises a sceptical eyebrow. "Even with the suggestive way you use emojis?"

He smile and shakes his head. "Still not the same."

She lowers her voice and presses her head against him. "No, it isn't."

"So, you want us to get to know each other?"

He squints his eyes, searching for any sign as to whether her question is a green light or a red one, but gets nothing. "I think so, yes. You?" Ella Jane nods, and he enfolds her with his arms, kisses the top of her head, and murmurs, "Funny old world," in a faraway voice.

Unsure of his meaning, and unable to think how to answer, and with her arms around him at the level they are, she squeezes. "And a sexy old bum." She chuckles as she feels him absentmindedly swat her own and nestles into his chest.

They stand in silence for a while, neither breaking the spell until he kisses the top of her head again. "Time to undress if you want that demonstration before dinner."

She tightens her eyes and answers back with a note of defiance, "And if I don't?" She does so more to see what he does than out of any lack of desire to play.

The serious lowering of his head and tilting of one eyebrow give her a clue, and the hardened consonants with which he speaks brook no objection. "Then it's time to undress because now that you've gone on about it, *I* want to give you that demonstration."

"So considerate, *Sir.*"

"Aren't I just though."

She gets another swat and, when she turns her face up toward his, another kiss and a rumbled, "Would you prefer me to undress for you, or would you like to strip me?"

His fingertips brush her cheek, and he softly rumbles, "Such a pleasant choice." As she leans her head into his touch, his lips twitch. She tilts her head in inquiry, and he breathes, "I'll tell you later," in an almost laugh as he answers her by moving his hands to the zipper at the back of her dress.

Ella Jane stands, passively allowing him to undress her and raises a smile of her own when he lifts the cotton fabric over her head. When his eyes ask, her lips open to say, "I'll tell you later." But she closes them again at the warning shadow that passes across his face. "I just haven't had anyone take my clothes off for me since I was a child."

He drapes the dress over the back of a sofa and turns to her with sadness in his eyes. "That's a shame. It's a pleasure a person, and especially a woman, should experience." Then he returns to her, traces the lines of her fine lingerie with his fingertips follows them with his lips at the places where his touch makes her sigh or laugh. He kisses and caresses as she stands in her underwear and shoes, his eyes full of urgency he denies and her body screaming for him to take her now. "But sadly, I'm going to have to rush this." His fingers go to the clasp of her bra.

She breathes, "You're good at that."

"I've practiced."

"Eugh."

"No, I've literally practiced, getting it right, getting it wrong, finding out if you can get a stray thread from a buttonhole caught on one of the hooks."

Ella Jane tenses her lips to hold back her amusement at the thought of him attached to a half-undone bra.

He protests, "Research is important." Having managed to half derail the seduction long after it was complete he picks up something in her expression. "You're smiling."

"I'm imagining you with a row of tailor's dummies and an assortment of bras, practicing failing to undo bras." Then she bites her lips. "Does that happen often in real life?"

He folds her bra, sets it aside, and returns his attention to her. "That would be telling."

Having uncovered her breasts, he proceeds to tease his them with caresses that promise to become more intimate but slide by as though she weren't already eager. "It's just the one tailor's dummy, and it doubles for pick-pocketing practice and dressing as well as undressing."

Ella Jane lets her body lean towards his touch as one hand passes over the upper curve of a breast and then towards her ribs. Meanwhile his eyes tell her that he knows what he's doing, and not doing. "Do you practice many things?"

He murmurs, "You'd be surprised."

"I'd have been more surprised a few days ago."

"Really?"

"No." She laughs and pulls herself against him. Despite his mind having headed off in a seemingly non-sexual direction his body is as ready as her own. "Of course really!" and she kisses him with a passion.

Her Interesting Walk

He takes her to the edge and stops, with the tip of his tongue still pressed lightly against her clit and looking up at her, he asks, "Are you hungwy?"

The silliness of his failed attempt to say *hungry* is enough to break Ella Jane's progress towards what was building up to be another highly satisfying orgasm. She mutters a silent curse, looks at his mirth-filled face, stifles another, and then lets herself smile before letting out an exasperated, "I'm *never* hungry before you are!"

"So I should finish?"

"Yes!"

"Or sort of start again?"

"*Yes!*"

"Oh, alright." He takes himself back to the start, lightly kissing each of her dusting of freckles, starting with those furthest from her centre. As he does he makes frequent pauses to make theatrical efforts to compare their relative distances during which his hands caress her while his eyes tease.

At one point, she attempts a good-natured complaint between her mewls and giggles. She watches with fascination as he goes about the frivolous task with contentment painted on his focused features. However, in complaining, she accepts an element of risk. He might defer letting her cum again or make her take a turn at pleasuring him. He might even choose to switch to a more exotic enjoyment of her body to punish her.

After their languorous afternoon of mutual enjoyment, these *risks* strike Ella Jane as being more accents to the pleasure she takes, though she abandons her teasing while he's still smiling.

He raises a serious eyebrow while battling to control that smile. "Am I going to have to tie you up?"

She responds with a bite of her lip and a batting of her lashes. "If you think that would be best, Sir."

The unconscious flexing of his shoulders and narrowing of his eyes might well have cowed a room full of people less willing to submit to their declaration of innate power and implied threat of force, but Ella Jane is already offering her wrists up to him.

"Speaking of dinner."

"Hmm?" she looks up at him sleepily through her tumble of locks.

His face softens, and he enunciates more precisely, "Speaking of dinner..."

Ella Jane chuckles. "You frequently do."

"Would you like to go somewhere fancy?"

"Fancier than the places you usually take me?"

"Different, but that sort of thing."

"A surprise?"

He evades with a *possibly* and a hint of a smile as he casts his eyes away from her.

A tensing of excitement grips her cheeks, drawing the corners of her mouth upwards. "Have you got something wicked planned?"

He looks back to her and places the flat of his hand not at all earnestly over his heart. "Would I?"

Ella Jane shakes her head slowly from side to side. "Yes! Have I got anything to wear?"

His features begin to develop a terribly-pleased-with-myself expression before he opens his mouth. "Mm-might have."

She narrows her eyes, “When did I get something to wear?”

“They left the things you and Amberlee picked out in the reception room about ten minutes ago.”

“You’re a bad influence.” She keeps strict control of the muscles around her eyes, but those controlling the corners of her mouth start to act independently and draw her lips into a smile because they are taking their orders from the subconscious part of her brain that likes pretty things.

“I’m having a fun, and I’m doing my best to have it with you.”

She slips the covers from over her slender frame. “Then we *could* eat in the room.”

His eyes rove slowly down her body and his hands follow. He runs a finger along her opening, then touches it to the tip of his tongue. “We both already have.”

“You are so filthy.”

He raises an eyebrow. “Am I though?” He kisses her, then guides her head downwards.

It doesn’t take much thought to gather his intention, though she deliberately takes her time about getting to her destination and casts teasing glances on the way. When she arrives, she opens to him, tastes, and explores him with her tongue before letting him slip out of her mouth and giving her verdict. “Mmm, no. You’re clean.” Then she plants a kiss on his shaft and adds, “Clean, and you taste of me,” before resuming her attentions. “What time’s the table booked?”

“Nine.”

Assured she has no need to hurry, she grins up at him and sets to exacting a small measure of revenge for all the times he’s taken her to the edge.

When she eventually emerges in search of her dress for the evening, there's a jewellery box on the table it's hanging by. "For me?"

"You might want to open it before thanking me."

Her eyes narrow, but her teeth take a hold of her lower lip. "Can..." she remembers before his expression changes, "*May* I?"

"Of course."

She opens the box, which contains three differently sized porcelain eggs. "And these are?"

"Exactly what you think they are."

"You already bought me one!"

"I did, but these are a set."

"And you bought them for tonight?"

"I brought them from England as a just in case. Do you have any opinion as to which you'd like to try first?"

The middle egg is roughly the same size as her jade one, so Ella Jane picks it up from its satin bed and tests its weight. "This one I suppose. I'll put it in just before we leave."

"I thought I'd insert it."

She smiles. "Are you planning to make us late?"

"No, I just thought it might be fun."

"Fun for who?"

He tilts his head to one side and does his best to say without smiling, "You, of course."

"Hmph! What is it with you and putting things into me?"

On hearing her question he allows his grin to spread. "I can't think." The way his gaze roves down from her eyes and then back confirms his bare-faced lying, he clearly not only can think but is doing so.

His second effort at self justification is more plausible, and even sexier. "This is more about you letting me put things into you and surrendering control of your body to me." He runs his fingers up either side of her opening as he speaks and sandwiches the head of her clit and its little hood between them, then circles.

She breathes, "Fuck..." then looks up at him smokily. "So long as I agree?"

"Of course."

Her hand offers up the bauble. Once he has accepted it, she interlaces her fingers behind her neck and edges her feet further apart to allow him better access to her entrance all the while looking him in the eyes and poking out her tongue.

His answer is to take his time about inserting the egg and to tease and torment. As ready as she is, he *could* slip the little thing into her in a second. He certainly has no *need* to caress or inflict pain on her or to get her any more aroused. However, her display of impish defiance prompts him to do both, and, having done each, her body's responses, the sound of her voice and the misting of her eyes, seduce him into doing more. He inserts the porcelain egg into her far enough to rub in the front wall of her vagina. As he does so, he watches her until her face betrays that he's found the places where its smooth hardness has the most effect. He runs the egg's polished surface between her folds, and his fingers tantalise her body inside and out.

Her breasts don't escape his attentions either as his lips, fingers, teeth, and nails ensure that she receives full measure of payment for both her cooperation and her defiance.

The release his touch promises though is something he does not grant her before he makes a show of checking the time and finally sets the egg deep inside her. "Time to get dressed."

Her eyes beg, and he raises an eyebrow. Then she curses in the silence of her soul and smiles. "I deserved that."

His face tries to join in with her amusement while he tries to make it stay serious. "You did indeed, and I'm going make sure you remember that all evening."

Ella Jane has the good grace to try to look abashed, before flashing her eyes back up to his and answering, "Yes, I'm sure you will," with a grin.

Having always gone out by car before, Ella Jane expects to see Johnson and his BMW waiting for them, but the kerb is empty.

He holds his crooked arm out for her to take. "I thought we might walk. It isn't far, and it's a lovely evening." His eyes dance with mirth, and she stares up at him with daggers. Walking across the lobby and down the steps had been bad enough.

If she hadn't been so hungry...

If it hadn't been so much fun so far...

If their play before leaving hadn't left her eager to get back to the suite and deal with their *unfinished business...*

She takes his arm, though the smile she aims up at him is icy.

He carries on as though he hasn't seen, but they both know he has. "It's not far. The walk will do us good." And, taking the outside as he always does, he leads her the few blocks to the restaurant.

The ceramic egg presses against the muscles inside her every step. And every step she offers up her silent gratitude that she chose the middle, just-right egg.

He looks down when they're almost there. "Are you warm, darling?"

Ella Jane's brow furrows in puzzlement.

"Only your cheeks are a little flushed. Would you like me to take your coat?"

"Thank you. I'll be *fine*, Sir."

"Excellent. I wouldn't want you to be uncomfortable."

She tries to give him another murderous look, but his sadistically good-humoured smile defeats it. They walk the last few steps arm in arm with the petite American walking slowly and him solicitous of the tender condition he is entirely responsible for.

When they arrive he asks the Maitre D, "I don't suppose there's a private dining room, is there?"

"I'm afraid not, sir. We've remodelled since your last visit."

"Oh, that's a shame."

There may be no private dining rooms, but their table is in a quiet corner, away from the windows and kitchen. It's perfect for a discrete dinner. The setting puts Ella Jane's creative mind in motion, and she can't help imagining characters meeting here, perhaps a clandestine assignation. That thought makes her smile, and smiling makes her muscles clench around the secret hidden inside her.

She snaps herself out of her reverie though. All the fooling around and then the walk from the hotel have left her flustered and in need of a trip to the rest room. So she makes her excuses as the waiter shows them her table and asks for directions.

Once she's departed, he orders a half bottle of Krug Grande Cuvee and surveys the menu, making his choices. Then he admires the decor and checks his phone.

By the time she returns, he's sipping water. He smiles as he sits there, watching her as she crosses the room. It's a knowing smile, one that speaks to her on a level that his voice does, but words have trouble reaching. Walking with the egg inside her has made her more vulnerable to this, and sitting causes it to moves again. She tries to look away, tries to ignore her heat, but it doesn't work. All she can manage is to look back as she feels the heat rise slowly inside her, knowing it's going to reach her cheeks.

She wants to ask him what he's planning, or planned, but she can't muster the courage. Instead, she draws her lower lip between her teeth as the blush takes control of her face.

"Mmm." He rumbles his appreciation as if tasting her, and he places the box for the eggs on the white linen tablecloth. "Tell me, is the rest room nice?"

"I'd say opulent. It's not quite your hotel suite, but still bordering on the palatial." She can't keep the amusement from her voice. "The cubicles are as big as the bathroom in my university flat."

"And clean?"

"Yes." She gives him a quizzical look. "Spotless." She finds his strange curiosity amusing, and it piques her own as to what he's up to. "Why do you ask?"

"I was wondering if you were wet?" They're in a public restaurant, but he speaks as quietly as he does confidently.

Ella Jane blinks at him. He was inside her just minutes ago, and then he put the egg into her. He must know the answer, but he waits, so she confesses, "Yes, soaking." Then she conveys her embarrassment, "And you're making it worse." It's a mistake, of course, and she regrets the moment the words leave her mouth. His look just grows more lascivious. She looks at the box. Surely he can't expect her to retrieve the egg at the table.

"I'd like you to choose another egg. Then go to the rest room again, and swap them over."

"Now?"

The waiter returns with the wine, shows it to Him before unwinding the cage and easing the cork out with a soft phut, rather than a loud pop, just like the way He opens champagne.

"You can wait until after we've had our starters if you wish." He tastes and nods his approval.

On seeing His nod, the waiter pours a glass for Ella Jane and then tops His up. "Can I get you anything else, sir?"

He cocks his head. "Are you ready to order, my dear?"

Their early evening activities have left her hungry, and she wants to order but hasn't seen the menu, so she asks the waiter, "Can you wait here just a minute?" She feels self-conscious about asking him to wait, but he smiles his willingness. The ludicrously expensive half bottle ordered without even asking for the wine list suggests strongly that providing the best service he can to this couple will be worth his while, and that of the restaurant.

"Shall I go first?" He offers, not keen to break convention, but wishing to make her feel comfortable. She smiles her gratitude. By the time he's drawn out ordering a starter, first course, and main, she's settled on her choices. That done, he orders a domestic Tempranillo, priced to rival some of the imported wines, to accompany their mains, and the waiter departs with a look of appreciation.

"Where was I?" He asks, though his face confirms her suspicion that he knows precisely where.

"You were sending me to the bathroom, Sir."

"Oh, yes. I'd like you to go into a cubicle, undress to just your heels, and change eggs."

The idea strikes her as wicked, discrete, but then not. "Is that all?"

"Hmm, almost." He ponders, or pretends to. "You'd best lubricate the new egg in your mouth if you need to, and you should certainly clean the one you're taking out that way." He pauses, "Oh, and don't forget to record it on your phone."

Now her cheeks really do flame. Her mouth feels dry, so she takes a sip of champagne to moisten it and fortify her nerves, and despite herself, she exclaims. "Wow, that's good!"

"It is, isn't it?" He takes a sip and deliberately misinterprets her. "I rather like the champagne too."

Ella Jane looks at him as he sits there, smiling. He's so damn cocky! That's it -- *cocky*! That's him all over.

"Yes, very." She doesn't ask how much the wine is, though the rich vanilla undertone to the taste hints at a lot. Another sip and she dares the question, "Any other instructions, Sir?"

"I think that's about as much as would be discrete, unless you'd like to edge yourself while you're in there?"

"Um," she hesitates. It's tempting, but the walk here has left her hot with distraction. "I'd rather not."

"No, that's sensible." What he's asking her to do is far from sensible, but that might well be a foolishness too far. They exchange a private smile. The entire conversation is carried out with the tips of their fingers forming an intimate bridge between them and in voices barely above a murmur but still within sight of the other diners and staff. If one were to be a lip reader, or to have especially acute hearing.

Ella Jane swallows, and breathes, "I think I'd better go now." Hunger is one thing, but she wants to do this before her courage fails her. Besides, she wants to enjoy the fine food without the distraction of anticipation. She opens the box, selects the large-sized egg, puts it into her purse, then rises, and makes her way back across the restaurant. She is certain in her heart that every person here knows exactly what she's doing. It feels good, decadent, and extremely naughty. It sets her submissive heart beating.

The movement inside her and the anticipation of what she's about to do have her close by the time she locks the cubicle door behind her, and she leans against it to gather her wits and decide how to proceed.

Annoyingly like so many clubs, bars and restaurants, there's no convenient flat surface. Presumably it's to discourage any diners who wish to indulge chemically. But the inconvenience frustrates her in her desire to carry out his instructions erotically. Instead, she closes the lid over the seat and sets her phone carefully leaning back on the close lid of the lavatory, taking all the time she needs to get the least awkward angle. That done, she takes a deep breath, starts the phone recording, and peels off her dress as suggestively as her ability and the surroundings permit.

Her efforts to put on a show for him and to work quietly enough to remain undiscovered make undressing slower than it might have. She hears another woman enter the rest-room while wearing nothing but her lovely new matching bra and thong, and her heels. She doesn't chicken out though; despite a rosy blush rising all over her body. The sound of the other woman using the facilities for their intended purpose almost forces her to laugh aloud, but she catches herself and proceeds to reach behind her back and undo her bra eases its straps from her shoulders. Slowly she lowers its cups away from her breasts revealing their excited buds to the camera.

She lays it down in front of her phone and then waits, idly toying with her breasts and rolling her eyes with impatience for the other customer to leave before sliding her panties down her legs and stepping out of them.

Once naked, she slips the new egg into her mouth and spreads her legs to give a clear view to the camera as she retrieves the one inside her.

The egg is the temperature of her core and feels hot in her hand. She even feels it's warm when she swaps it for the one in her mouth and tastes herself. She fancies she's also able to taste him on its smooth surface. By way of contrast, the new one is cool as it slides into her. It's heavier too, and oh my, she catches her breath again before she dresses and stops the camera phone.

Task completed, she runs her hands under cooling water and touches up her sparse makeup before gathering her will once more to return to the table. The time she takes in the restroom gives her mind the chance to process, to appreciate how she's coming to accept his control of her body, and to consider how it affects her – erotic and intense. It's less than an hour since he had her and edged her in their hotel, and she wants him again with a fierce intensity. She shakes her head slowly and takes one more steadying breath. Then she straightens and leaves the rest room.

Being larger, the new egg fills her more and presses more intimately inside her as she walks back to him. As she moves back across the restaurant, she muses, *Edge herself? There had been little need!* She wonders if he knew there wouldn't be and guesses that he's such a bastard that he knew the likelihood.

Ella Jane is breathing deeply again by the time she reaches the table, and her blush deepens as she sits and the larger egg settles.

"Well?" he enquires, his voice giving no hint that he appreciates what she's done, or how she feels, though his eyes.

She glows her pride at completing the task and carefully puts her purse on her lap out of sight before taking the egg from it into the palm of her hand, and reaching her hand towards him, she opens her fingers just enough that he can see.

His pleasure with her shines in his eyes as he holds his hand out palm up, and she places her own hand palm down over it and discretely passes the brightly coloured glass egg to him.

"Mmm, still warm."

She tenses at his words, and her muscles clench on the still cool one inside her. "Yes, Sir. It is. It was quite hot when I took it out."

"It will have been." He passes his tongue around his mouth and swallows, congratulates her with a, *Good girl* and squeezes her hand before pulling back and returning the egg to the satin-lined box. He takes a sip of champagne and indicates her glass to her. "And the recording?"

Ella Jane gulps. She hasn't even watched it herself yet. She sips too, first water and then champagne, before unlocking her phone and passing it to him. The returning waiter interrupts before He can play, and much to her relief He puts the phone down while the young man serves their starters. She sips while he serves, and her eyes widen again.

His lips twitch. "It's still not bad." Then He looks into the past, and His smile carries on spreading.

The waiter's eyes snap to Him at hearing the words not bad.

But Ella Jane translates into American. "He's English. He's saying it's very good, and it is." Then she raises her glass to Him. "It's as wonderful as you said it would be."

Her words drag His attention back to her till his focus returns to her. "I still remember the first time I drank Krug. It's not something you forget."

By the time the waiter leaves, Ella Jane's phone has gone back to sleep, so he has her unlock it again. He then watches her performance with obvious pleasure on his face while she squirms. There's no risk of anyone else seeing, but she still knows what he's doing and hasn't seen it herself. He shifts on his chair as he watches, and she hopes she knows the reason. Her imagination is forming an idea when he speaks. "It's a shame we aren't somewhere a bit more private..."

He doesn't finish the sentence, but then, he doesn't have to. Ella Jane is thinking the same thing, of kneeling and taking him in her mouth while the egg and her fingers... that or some variation on the theme. "Definitely!" Then she takes another bite of to-die-for ravioli and waits until he has a mouthful. "If the food wasn't so good, I might risk it anyway."

Much to her delight, he laughs, and it catches him by surprise. Once he's recovered his composure, he watches her closely as he replies, "We could arrange something if you'd like?"

"Um, I might like that, I'm not sure." He holds his silence, and she continues after a time, "I like the idea of it."

They touch hands and play footsie as they eat. He expresses his regret that the table's too wide for him to see how close he can get her, and she pretends to be disappointed. Then privately she rues the missed opportunity, especially when he returns her phone and offers her the chance to watch herself. The sight of her performance and the memory of it at the same time almost send her over the edge on their own.

The conversation, and the touch they can manage, keeps them warm and connected. The waiter takes the plates for their mains and asks if they'd like to see the dessert menu.

Her first instinct is to say just an espresso, but the thought of the walk back to the hotel with the larger egg stops her. Instead she says yes, and jokes about the dessert game he made her play on their first night together.

She looks around taking in the restaurant's magnificent Belle Époque décor as they eat. Its high ceilings and her finery truly making her feel every inch fairytale princess, or they might if it weren't for the constant pressure at the top of her vaginal canal. Though, given the travails of many a fairytale heroine, perhaps the various sweet torments and harsh demands he makes of her are as fitting as the palatial settings and haute couture he introduces her to.

While they choose, she leans forward. "Can I take it out before we go back?"

He gives her a wicked look as his voice feigns innocence. "Why would you want to do that?"

"Because otherwise I'm going to cum on the way to the hotel."

"I recall you saying you were good at hiding your orgasms." He has more innocence on his lips and more devilment in his eyes. When she doesn't answer, he offers, "If you wish, you can change back to the smaller one, but if you do, you'll be making another video."

The idea of making another video is tempting, so is that of getting back to the hotel without having an orgasm in public. Her pride stands in the way though, so she politely turns down his *kind* offer, and steels herself for the walk.

"Okay, but can I ask one thing if we do this?"

"You *may* ask."

"I'd like to choose my own clothes if you plan on taking me anywhere else."

His eyes rove across her suddenly self-conscious form. "Don't you like the ones I've picked?"

"They've been beautiful, but I'd like to choose."

"Very well, it's a deal. So long as you promise me one thing in return." Her expression asks what. "No clashing primary colours."

She coughs back a laugh, then assumes a business-like manner. "In that case, I want you to promise to look after me if I cum on the sidewalk on our way back to the hotel."

He seals the deal with a wolfish smile and a kiss on the back of her hand.

Seeing a conclusion being reached the waiter returns. However, that conclusion has had nothing to do with the menu.

Wanting to get Ella Jane back to the hotel, he quickly chooses a tasting platter for two, then tosses a mental coin and opts for ristrettos instead of espressos.

Ella Jane manages a taste of every artfully crafted creation on the platter, and has a second of the tiny, intense coffees. As she sips, she watches him indulge his taste buds in the culinary delights and his eyes in hers, and then, with nothing more to put off the delicious torment of the walk she takes his offered arm and does her best...

She makes it to within a block before she pauses, nestling more closely into his bulk and his strength as she does. She doesn't say a thing, and he doesn't ask. He holds her for as long as her shuddering goes on, and then a little longer, then responds to her kiss. A kiss she lingers in until she feels renewed stirrings before breaking off and asking him to take her to bed.

Her Chance to go to the Ball

Waking and finding himself smiling at the sense of Ella Jane next to him, he watches her blink herself awake. He bites the bullet about his promise. "Do you remember me mentioning a scene party?"

Ella Jane hesitates, and nods cautiously.

"Only there's one tomorrow night."

"Are we going?"

"I'd like to. It's organised by a friend of mine."

She narrows her eyes, "A lover?"

"No, she's a Domme."

As far as she's concerned that might not preclude a liaison. "And you couldn't possibly?"

"No, not for either of us anyway." He steers the conversation away from that line. "Would you like me to get you something to wear?"

"You've really taken to that dress hire place haven't you?"

"I was only thinking of you."

"Hmm, aren't any of the dresses I've got from there suitable?"

"Not really. You're welcome to get something else, or to wear the Bodywhisp."

"Do people really go to those things dressed like that?"

"Some do."

Ella Jane decides to set down a marker. "I'd like to wear my new dress." Then realises she doesn't know for certain what would be appropriate. "Unless it won't fit in, that is?"

He leers down at her nakedness remembering her in the clinging garment. "Oh, it'll do quite nicely."

"Good. What are you going to wear?"

"I thought I'd wear a tuxedo."

"You've got more than one?"

"Yes, but I only *brought* a couple."

"Is that because you were only going to two black tie events this trip, or because not even your luggage allowance is infinite?"

His fingers trace the length of her neck and skirt around the curves of her breasts. "Are you teasing me, Miss Tyler?"

"No, I just don't think I've ever met anyone with more than one."

"I don't have many." He diverts again. "Have you ever been to a *scene* party?"

"A couple, but nothing fancy. What's this one going to be like?"

"Don't you want to experience it first fresh?"

Ella Jane humphs. "You're getting to know me too well."

He leans down and kisses her throat. "Isn't that what a good dominant is supposed to do?"

"I suppose it is."

"Well then."

She bites her lip and smiles. "But I want to know, too."

He checks his phone conspicuously, "You will tomorrow, unless you really want me to answer."

"Hmm. Have other subs you've known get so excited they got into trouble before going to one?"

He laughs and her cheeks colour. "I think one or two might have, but I don't think I've heard of anyone putting it quite so charmingly."

"Can I have a clue so I'll know and not know?"

"Very well. Every event is different, but I think you'll like this one. Madam Alexandra likes everyone at hers to have what she considers the right look, and her friends know how to put on a show."

"Will *I* fit in?"

"Yes, very much so."

"Is it like Eyes Wide Shut?"

"No, that was more a swinger's thing. This is a party, so everyone has a bit more of a sense of fun."

She opens her mouth, then closes it again. "Are you going to keep me entertained, so I stay out of trouble?"

"I was thinking tomorrow morning we could start with some light play. Then we could visit St Patrick's Cathedral and St Thomas's church."

"Are you planning to get pre-forgiven for lots of sins?"

"You know, I hadn't really thought of it like that, but then I don't think of any of the things we've done or plan to do as sinful."

Ella Jane's lips twitch. "I'm not sure you can have paid much attention in bible class."

"Ha, I never went, and I'm not religious. I have read the bible, and a few other religious texts. If there's a god or gods they created us with a capacity for pleasure and pain, and they made us curious."

"Isn't that a –" She cuts herself off, but dammit he could have walked out of a courtroom drama.

"Lawyer's defence? Possibly, but I've never seen you do anything to harm anyone, nor heard you take the lord's name in vain except when you were feeling, um, close to God."

"I'm not worried anyway; I can tell St Peter my Dom made me do it all."

"Thanks."

She grins, "So what do you want to make me do before we go to churches?"

"This and that?"

"Don't you have anything planned to keep us out of trouble before you take me to your party?"

"I've got to send a few emails and make a call or two. Then I have a few things lined up for us."

"Can't we just do the things you have lined up?"

"I've got some things that won't wait until people in England have gone home from work." He touches her cheek. "You should keep in touch with people, too."

"I don't want to take time away from being together."

His eyebrows do that thing where one goes down in the middle and the other goes up. "No, you're so excited about the party that you want to spend the whole of today playing. If we do that, we'll be too knackered to enjoy it."

"I'm not... maybe."

His lips twitch with amusement at her confession. "Maybe a bit?"

She grins at his insistence on including one of his favourite words and apes his accent in response. "A tad."

"Then what are we going to do?"

"If we're going to be in each other's pockets for the next few weeks, you need to keep in touch with your life outside of us."

Ella Jane leans her head against him.

He kisses the top of her head. "How about I go and make a couple of calls to finalise a few details, and you get in touch with one or two friends. Then we'll go for a walk?"

Her cheeks flush at the memory of the night before. "A walk doesn't sound all that exciting."

His eyes meet hers causing her blush to deepen. "You might be even more surprised by a walk one of these days."

She grins hopefully. "Today?"

"Not this morning."

"So mean!"

"Ha!" He cuts a piece of bacon, egg, and maple syrup laden toast. "Still not going to spank you yet but still counting reasons." Then he puts the morsel into his mouth and chews slowly and appreciatively.

Ella Jane narrows her eyes at him, but all he does is cut another piece and offer it to her lips. Her first instinct is to refuse it to express her independence, and her second is to do so in an effort to provoke him. But when he makes to withdraw the offered delicacy, she snatches it from his fork.

When he finishes his second plate, he chooses a pastry and makes to rise.

She pushes her own chair back. "I can get more coffee."

He counters, "I'll get us some while you put some cuffs on and fetch a coil of rope."

"Can I phone Louise first, so I don't have to tell her I'm a bit tied up again first?"

"Ha, okay, then."

She kisses his cheek. "Can I call from our room?"

"Sure."

"Hi, Louise."

"Hey, famous girl."

"I'm not famous."

"Would you rather I said *heya, kept woman*?"

Ella Jane protests, "Don't!"

Having hit the wrong note with her attempt at levity, Louise rows back. "Sorry, just jealous. It's nice to hear from you again."

"We're friends!"

"But some people don't remember their friends when they're living the high life. Are you still playing at being first lady?"

"Wha –"

Her friend's laugh pours out of phone. "Presidential Suite! You're usually the one with the quick humour"

Ella Jane catches on. "Oh, yes, good one. No, we've moved to the Plaza."

"Wasn't the other place fantastic enough?"

"No, not that. It was just as nice–" She pauses, struck by her own use of his phrase, and not wanting to seem like him while she's talking to her friend from what she still considers the real world she corrects herself, "as wonderful. He said he couldn't get one suite for the whole time."

Louise can't see much more than Ella Jane's face, and, much though she loves her, the rare chance to have another glimpse into the other-worldly life her friend is experiencing is too much to resist. "Do I get a tour here too?"

"Okay. So long as you promise not to say I'm a kept woman in front of him."

She walks Louise around the upstairs first, and shows her the views from the roof terrace and over Central Park. When she goes down to the reception room, he's seated by the windows and also on a call.

Judging from her voice, the woman He's talking to is possibly even more aristocratically English than He is. "Antonia said to say thank you for your notes on Table 55 and Gabriel Kreuther."

He turns his laptop. "I'd like you to meet Ella Jane Tyler, the lovely and talented new writer I told you about, Ella Jane, this is Lucy Hammond, the wonderful woman who makes sure everything runs smoothly from back in England, but still has time to look after us on the other side of the pond."

The woman on the screen is striking and looks as upper class as she sounds. Ella Jane says an awkward hello and continues her tour then takes her conversation back upstairs.

When Ella Jane gets back upstairs her friend asks, "What's it like living in the lap of luxury?

Ella Jane shrugs and smiles. "Weird."

"Good weird?"

"Weird weird, I'm still trying to work everything out. Everyone's so nice, like best friend's mom nice."

"That's good isn't it?"

"But I don't know if it's him. If he's the reason everyone's so nice to me, they and goes out of their way to make everything." Having broached the subject her mouth gushes on. "I don't know if they're doing because they're nice, or they like me, or if it's all to impress him or to get me to make him like them or of he makes them do it because he likes me."

"Are you ever going home?"

"I am, but in a few weeks, we're doing some signings and he's invited me on his holiday."

Louise's eyes widen. "Wow, that was fast!"

"Not really, we've been chatting for months online, so it's not like we only just met."

The conversation drifts through Ella Jane's experiences in New York, and Louise's back on campus in Durham until he knocks on the bedroom door to ask when she's likely to be ready for lunch.

Downstairs he's ordered snacks for before they go, and the hotel has delivered. His memory of her tastes as expressed over the time they've known one another has once again informed his choices for her. That, or he's scrolled up through their long thread of messages. A thought strikes her that the aristocratic Englishwoman could even have ordered for her.

"Who's Lucy Hammond?"

"She does some management work for me."

"And she's brilliant as well as pretty?"

"She is, as are you, but she's also married."

"Who's Antonia?"

"She's the chef friend who suggested I eat at table 55, and I have the strong impression that she thinks of herself as a surrogate mother to me."

"Let me guess, she's brilliant too, or is she talented?"

His eyebrows knit, but he doesn't speak.

"Everyone around you is, or they're a giant, or a Wall Street billionaire."

"I know some interesting people, you're one of them."

"Am I really?"

He takes her by the shoulders with gentle hands but half flexes the muscles of his upper body as he does so, and when he speaks it's in a basso rumble. "Yes, either that or you have me fooled, which I suppose is its own kind of interesting." Then he leans in and brushes kisses against her cheeks and then her lips.

They Stay Home at the Plaza

Despite her attempts at reticence, his deep voice, his artful touch, and being praised by a man who surrounds himself with the exceptional work their magic on her. "Hmm. What adventures do you have planned for the rest of today?"

His lips twitch and slowly curl into a smile. "Are you standing quite properly to be asking a question?" He asks the question lightly, more as if it were a joke from a friend than an instruction from a man she's been submitting to.

"We haven't discussed positions."

"Quite right, so the answer would be yes, or you could choose to play along."

She doesn't respond at first, but when he still doesn't answer, she smiles in response to his levity. The amusement doesn't leave his face, but he does raise an eyebrow, doing so with that same glacial slowness with which his hands tease. Unable to think of anything else to do, she turns to face him, eases her feet further apart, and folds her arms behind her back. "May this girl ask a question?"

"Yes, you may."

"What adventures do you have planned today, Sir?"

"Not a thing." He stretches contentedly. "I thought we could slob around in the suite and see what we can get up to with the various bits and bobs we have here."

She blurts, "All day?" with her good girl act having survived a bare few seconds.

His eyes and mouth tighten in response to the implicit challenge. "If you're not busy, that is."

"You mean you could have let me sleep in and beasted me through my exercises later?"

"I could." He answers in a tone of pure self-satisfaction, and he allows his expression to soften. "Though I'd foolishly imagined you might be emotionally ready to try out some of those high protocol things you mentioned only."

Ella Jane looks at him, then down, with her face glowing. "Sorry."

"No biggie, those are things you have to be in the right headspace for, we can keep today less formal."

"What if I'm still sore from last night and this morning?"

"There are still a hundred things we can do, but I'm guessing that in playing with full protocol you're trying to initiate something *full on*."

She opens her mouth and closes it again without trying to lie her way around his understanding. Her mind plays through the long list of items from Home Depot and those they'd both brought. Given her experiences with his imagination over the last few days, a hundred is probably just a starting point. "I'd like that."

He moves close as she thinks, and her body accommodates his hands as he lightly brushes the skin of her shoulders and arms and whispers, "You do know this was going to be a play session anyway, don't you?" The contact is somehow as intimate as if he were touching her outthrust breasts or between her parted thighs.

"I hoped, but I'm still learning to read when you're teasing."

The touch of his voice is more intimate still. "We're both at a loose end, and we have a hotel room with a staircase and a roof garden. There are so many possibilities." His hands continue to caress and continue to deny her the specific caresses her eyes invite and her pose makes so freely available. "You are having fun, aren't you?"

Ella Jane doesn't want to keep feeding his ego, but she can't see a way of getting what she wants without being honest. "Maybe a bit."

His obvious erection betrays the truth that she isn't the only one in need, but he still draws the moment. Her eyes lock on his cock and her pelvic muscles flex of their own accord. Her tongue plays over the surfaces of the inside of her mouth in remembrance and anticipation of that silky hardness. And behind her back, her hands clasp her arms more tightly before releasing their hold and moving towards him

She touches the flat of her hand the slashes of muscle over his ribs. "You haven't put your robe on."

He places a hand over hers, maintaining and extended their physical contact. "There's no reason to. There's only the two of us, and you've already seen me naked." He stops in mid-preen and turns to her, tilting his head and consciously posing his impressive frame just a little more without actively tensing any muscles. "Or don't you like seeing me naked?"

"I do!" Given the excuse, Ella Jane lets her eyes take in his body. The way he looks is still a surprise. It isn't what she'd expected when she found out their age difference, not even what she fantasised about before then, and it is definitely a bonus. "It's nice being with a man who's a pleasure to look at."

The compliment puts him back in full preen mode. "Well then?"

After the excitement of the last few days, Ella Jane can't help adding a tease about his arrogance to balance her compliment and doesn't even try. "Even one who knows it?" She doesn't hold herself back from letting out a delighted squeal as he goes to swat her behind, though she does let him catch her. The spank and the way he holds her after delivering it makes it easier to speak. "It's just..."

He strokes her rosy bum cheek and kisses the top of her head. "Just?"

"It's just sometimes..." She moulds herself more closely against him.

"Hmm?"

"Sometimes I like not having clothes on when you're dressed."

His initial, "Oh?" is curious, but once his brain and ears fully connect. He follows it with an, "Ohh!" and a wicked smile. And when he speaks, he does so with the lowered pitch and hardened consonants of command, "Is that so, young lady? Do you like the being-more-exposed feeling?"

His affectation of seriousness sets butterflies dancing in her stomach. "Yes, Sir." She presses her lips to his chest. "It's the way your clothes feel against me too."

"Well, in that case, would you be so good as to fetch me a robe?"

He has Ella Jane kneel on the glass topped coffee table and face the armchair he has adopted for when he sits alone. Then he secures her ankles and knees to the table's legs at either end. That done, he has her sit erect and binds her arms behind her back in a box tie.

She settles and looks down at how he's arranged her. The bind makes her breasts stand out, and her anticipation and the tension it applies has caused the buds at their tips to stiffen achingly. "Are you going to whip me again?

"What a good idea!" He brushes his palms across her skin. "Later perhaps, but not now. That's not what I have you in this position for." He bends, kisses her mouth, and shows her her ring gag.

She swallows nervously. "I could almost wish I hadn't brought that."

"But you did, and you told me you had."

She looks down as he says this.

He cups her face in one hand and strokes her cheekbone with his thumb. "You brought it because you want me to use it on you, and you told me because you trust me to use it on you."

Ella Jane swallows; both are true, but...

He touches her cheek and assures her, "It only takes her a word to change your mind."

Making up her mind to try, she shakes her head. "How do I use my safeword once you've put it on?"

"Ah!" he goes to the row of cupboards and retrieves something which he hides behind his back. "Funny you should ask that. I was about to show you." With that he brings his hand in front of him.

She can't help but smile. "Those are dog's squeaky toys!"

"Correct." He squeezes each in turn. The red one makes a higher pitched sound than the yellow does. "Which hand do you want for red?"

The bound Ella Jane shakes her head. "You're crazy. You think of everything, but you are crazy."

"I try. Now, left or right?"

She shrugs as best as she can in a box tie. "Right, I suppose."

He reaches behind the balls swapped to compensate for the bind. "Test squeeze."

Two squeaks and an accidental giggle later, Ella Jane is as ready to be fitted with a spider gag as she's ever going to be.

He holds up the gag. "Ready?" She nods, "Open wide." That's what her dentist says to her, so it's a poor choice of words and provokes another giggle. "I can't put it in while you're laughing, you know."

She tries to stop herself and complains, "You're not helping!"

"Would you like me to help?"

Ella Jane answers, "Yes please." proving that he isn't the only one capable of choosing their words unwisely.

He makes another trip to the cupboards, and returns another 'surprise'. This time a pair of nipple clamps linked by a chain, "These might help you see the serious side."

Her eyes shoot daggers at him even while her lips say, "Thank you."

"You really should learn to control your facial expressions a little better young lady." Despite his warning he's still considerate in the way he coaxes the tips of her breasts to full hardness, even if he isn't in how he applies the clamps. Once he has them on her he pulls on them to make sure they don't come free easily, then because of how her breasts stretch, and again because he likes the way doing so makes her groan through the gag.

As he continues to play with her breasts, he muses, “I think your defiance earns you a little stricter bondage, don’t you?”

She shakes her head, but doesn’t drop either ball, so he pulls harder on the clamps until a wave of pain passes over her face.

“I asked if your defiance earns you stricter bondage.”

This time the bound Ella Jane nods, and instead of tormenting her he caresses.

“Such a good girl.” He leaves her again and this time he returns with his hands behind his back.

“One nod for right, two nods for left.”

She studies the way he’s standing, but divines no clue as to what might be in either of his hands, so she nods once. He brings his right hand out with her anal hook in it.

Knowing there’s only one more of her toys he hasn’t used on her, Ella Jane moans through her gag.

“Ready to see what’s in my left hand?”

She isn’t but, unwilling to end the scene before it’s properly got started, she nods anyway.

Much to her relief, rather than her nose hook, his hand holds a black tube of lubricant. The relief must have shown in her eyes, because he chuckles as he unscrews the lid. “You didn’t think I’d forget to prepare my second, or is it third favourite entrance, did you?”

His hands take their time seducing her body, into letting him ease a lubricated finger into her rear, and he continues stroking in and out until she starts to rise and fall against his movement in order to increase her pleasure.

Her eagerness earns her another chuckle and he runs two fingers through her folds to gather her moisture, then slides them through the hole in her ring gag. With widening of his smile he starts to move both hands in time and continues until she finds a matching rhythm of her own.

Using the little freedom of movement her bondage allows her to fuck her own mouth and arse lets her build up a pleasant wellspring of pressure, one that she's sure will eventually lead her to orgasm. And he lets her carry on until her breathing becomes ragged and pupils start to dilate.

"So wanton, and so beautiful, but..." and he takes his hands away from her.

Ella Jane howls her loss and her impotence through the gag.

He picks up the hook. It's not a huge one, it's inch wide, rounded head is far narrower than the shaft of his cock. He knows he's lubed her well enough that it will easily slide into place, but where's the fun in simple? "I think this needs to be a little slipperier."

Rather than go to the tube he chooses to apply her own lubrication. The hook enters her easily, but he elects to rub its head against the front wall of her vagina until she starts to groan again, *just to make sure.*

Lubrication applied he removes it, once again leaving her body feeling empty, but the sensation doesn't last. Soon she feels it against her rosebud and his free hand on her breasts. His teasing of their swells and rocking of the hook coax her tight muscular rings into allowing its hardness into her.

"Are you comfortable?" She nods. "Look down, further, good girl."

He has her lean far enough forward that she can see the reflection of her waiting entrance, and t steel hook passing into her rear and stay in that position while he slides two fingers into her and presses the tip of his thumb against her clit.

"You love this, don't you?" she nods again, and he kisses delicately around her wide spread lips. Then tells her she's a good girl again before securing the hook to her box tie and leaving her again to go and fetch yet more toys.

There's no choice when he returns, just a blindfold, and, knowing his preference for seeing her eyes, she grins at his willingness to indulge her taste for imposed sightlessness.

Once she's blind he announces that he'll be back soon. Ella Jane knows he can't have been gone for more than a minute or two, but time does funny things when a submissive is bound and blindfolded, and the fear is rises when she hears him ask, “Left of right?”

This time there’s no hope of visual clues so she simply nods once.

Ella Jane’s ears tell her roughly what she’s chosen a moment before the soft heavy falls of one of his new floggers curve around her outthrust breasts. The sensation of the falls on her skin and through her flesh is as delightful as before, but the way their impact catches the clamps sends accompanying spikes of pain through her.

The whipping he gives her is long, and slow, and most of the blows strike her buttocks and wide spread thighs, though he does make sure to heat he breasts, mons and vulva too. Through it all he only occasionally strikes with great for, just often enough to slow her passage into a trance like state.

“Nod twice. Nod Twice. NOD-TWICE.” She has no idea how many times he’s repeated the words but eventually she registers and understands and nods and he wraps an arm around her and presses the tip of a wand to over her clit. The orgasms begin before he removes the clamps from her breasts and starts tenderly kneading their sore buds.

Time looses all meaning though at some point he must have moved her because she’s kneeling on soft folded towels in front of the long mirror in their bath. He’s naked, behind and inside her and the blindfold is gone.

The mirror tells a story. Having been ring gagged through a series of orgasms and while he took her, Ella Jane’s drool and their mingling flow from her. She feels them on her thighs and spilling onto her chin and from there to her breasts and down her smooth flat belly to her mons and on to mingle further.

The rest of their day and evening is gentler. He unties her and eases the hook from her, then bathes her long and slowly in steaming heat in the huge tub. They dine in the restaurant like a regular couple. He wears a dinner suit, and she takes the opportunity to show off her finery, and they talk. In their suite afterwards he pours port and serves cheeses and seduces her body as if it were a temple.

As they lie together Ella Jane strokes his skin, and muses, “It’s interesting.”

"Are you picking up my terrible habit of starting conversations half-way through?"

"Not intentionally, but that's an idea."

"It's a terrible idea. However now you've started, would you mind telling me what interesting thing you're referring to?

"It didn't feel like you were my dominant when we were talking online. No, that's not quite it. It felt like I had a mysterious dominant I was playing and in negotiation with."

"Only safer?"

"You were taller and younger, but you weren't quite as..."

"As?"

"As domly."

"Can I take it we're keeping that word?"

"I like it."

"So do I."

Ella Jane touches the tip of her tongue to her lips and their corners start turning upwards. "Does that make me subly?"

"Sometimes, subtly subly but occasionally brattishly bratty."

"I don't mean to be."

He Humphs. "Not always, anyway." He narrows his eyes and tightens his jaw but the fire in his eyes has something else alongside its menace. Ella Jane's instincts calculate faster than her conscious mind, and before she knows what she's doing she repeats the tease about his being younger and taller in her early imaginings despite his darkening expression.

"You are in so much trouble young lady..." His words threaten, but his tone is close to laughter.

This early in their in-person relationship, Ella Jane has little to base her estimation of his intent on other than their online exchanges. That provides two contrasting, but to her tantalising possibilities, she shies away from his eyes in response, "No fair!"

He tightens his jaw further, "In what way?" Then he pauses before adding, "It isn't as if you haven't been warned."

The way his already bass baritone voice keeps getting deeper, and how he focuses his eyes inside her he must know... "You can't expect me to behave when you say that!"

He slowly and quite deliberately he caresses her already sensitised breasts, "Why not?"

"It works!"

He raises an eyebrow.

"It works SOO well." She nibbles her lip, "And I just can't help wondering how...Ooh! I can't explain!"

"I'm sure you can, young lady." He pours growling and honey into his voice and Ella Jane nostrils flare in response. She takes her lip between her teeth, but her cheeks rosy and the corners of her mouth twitch.

"No." Then she glances away for a moment. "I've never met anyone who enjoys everything so much! I get carried away, and we start laughing and then you put on your stern voice and..."

"And before you know it, you're being sweetly bratty?"

"Yes, sorry."

"Don't worry." He chuckles wryly. "It took me a long time to learn to be unimpressed by anything." Then he winces. "And even longer to unlearn it."

"What do you mean?"

He sets his face at its most serious as he confides, "It's very important to a certain kind of man to be able to appear unmoved by the world no matter how much its wonders strike awe into us." Then lets his expression soften into a smile and continues with the warmth restored to his voice, "But as a writer and a lover one benefits immeasurably from the opposite."

Their Religious Interlude

On the morning of the party, he makes a point of edging her during her spreader bar time, rather than letting her cum. That, combined with her anticipation, sets her to teasing in the hope of provoking a scene or persuading him to take her. She tries squeezing her thighs together and touches her hand to his when he massages her aching inner thighs

At breakfast, she sits closer to him as they eat and takes the initiative in telling the butler they don't need any further assistance once the dishes are laid out.

Once they're alone, she fusses over making sure he has enough on his plate and mixing his fruit just the way he likes it. "What are your plans for us today?"

His hand rises instinctively to resist being pampered, but he restrains himself and allows her to continue. "I told you. Churches."

Having served him Ella Jane dishes her own meal and sits, all the while smiling until, unable to hold her amusement in. "Have we done so many wicked things we need three confessions?"

Her humour causes a crack in the seriousness of his expression, and he smiles and bends to touch his lips to hers. “Very clever, but I’m not going to rise to that sort of thing until at the party or after it.”

The he then clicks his fingers as if remembering something “Oh, and outfits.”

“For the party?”

“No, to visit churches in, you’ve got your new dress for the party, but jeans will fit in better in a cathedral.”

“Very funny.”

Their first stop is the furthest, St Patrick’s Cathedral. He pays for the VIP tour; there are two others on the tour with them so there’s plenty of opportunity to chat with their well-informed guide. The guide points out the best places to take photographs from. He seems to know almost as much about the amazing old building as the historian, does, frequently asking informed but open questions about the next point of interest on the tour as they leave the last. Soon the two are talking like old friends.

They spend a little time in the walking around the church with the historian after the official tour finishes. Then they say their farewells and walk back northwards.

St Thomas has a tour too, and he rounds up his donation to the same value he had in the Roman Catholic Cathedral. While they’re admiring the church organ and the row of high stained glass windows behind, it an elderly cleric approaches and asks Him about his camera. He turns out to be semi-retired and only really still working at all because of his love for the church and its congregation. He’s well-versed in the church’s history, and discovering that He is English and that the couple share a fascination with fine architecture, he waxes lyrical about the Cathedrals in England urging Ella Jane to visit if she gets the chance.

Looking up sunlit stained glass the old man breathes, “It’s so very peaceful here, and the sun through the windows brings me a little closer to God.”

He smiles ruefully.

“Certainly to the divine.”

“Yes, a person may not believe in any kind of a god, but there is certainly a sense of the divine here.”

The old man apologetically tells them they’ll all have to stay quiet for a time if they wish to stay as the choir are due to practice. It’s the first time Ella Jane has heard a full choir in a large church. Yet another emotive first for her. She stands close against him, feels his hand squeeze hers, and sees his face. She watches him as the voices fill her, sees him being without doing, and, sure that he must shared other intimacies with many women, wonders if this is a rarely seen window into his private self. He listen to some passages with his eyes closed, others with them on the singers and drinking in the building’s beauty. The rest of the time he focuses them on hers.

When they leave, she hugs his arm against herself. In all their long conversations, Ella Jane never had a sense of him as a spiritual man. In their few days together while she's connected his ways, it’s been with his hedonism, not with him seeing something sacred in the world around him. It gives her a new perspective of him, and of his music, his wines, his fine food, his eye for beauty.

A thought strikes her like a blow. Is that what he sees in herself, in the way he looks at and touches her, how he holds her, even the ways he tortures her? She stops, her insides tangle and twist.

"Are you okay?" His eyes are full of concern.

“Y-er-yes. They remind me of the chapel at Duke.”

“Yes?”

“The sense of wonder is quite something. That building is what made me decide to study there.”

"You'll have to show me some time. Before electricity and recorded music it must have seemed even more impressive."

She smiles. "Duke isn't that old, but it is English Gothic. That old priest was right; I should visit England and see for myself."

They continue walking and stop at the Presbyterian church as well. They take their time here too, drinking in the detail and scale of the stonework, glass, and ceilings. Though, like that faith, the church is less ostentatiously magnificent. Ella Jane stays close by his side. His eyes show the same delight as they walk around it. She studies what he does, but her mind is on him.

They lunch in the main restaurant at the hotel. She jokes that he's finally fulfilled his promise. Then she laughs at his stony expression and slowly rising eyebrow until her mirth infects him.

When he regains full control, he suggests they go out in the afternoon.

"Not upstairs?"

"I thought we might wait for the party?"

"Do you want to do a scene there?"

"I don't know. Maybe we'll just enjoy the performances and play when we get home?"

After lunch they set off for the Metropolitan Museum. There's a most New York-ly unreality to stepping out of from the Plaza's grand entrance and crossing the road into the semi manicured beauty of Central Park.

At the museum he shows a fascination with the Ancient Greek, Roman and Medieval exhibits, in particular picking out examples of period armour and weapons.

"One more thing you have a passion for?"

"Partly, partly research; I have a couple of pre-industrial series."

"I love that."

"What?"

"How you don't assume that I know you've written books *everyone* has seen the movie adaptations of."

"Oh, well, probably not everyone has."

When he walks past a row of suits of armour without stopping to examine them or take photographs she nudges his side. "Didn't you like those ones?"

"They were on display the last time I was here."

"What if I want to look at them?"

"Do you?"

She considers, "Um, yes."

He shrugs, and makes to turn back.

"You'd really do that?"

"Of course, we're here together, not with you as my secretary."

She steps in front of him and slips her arms around his waist. "Not even as Edward Grey's secretary?"

He places his hands on either side of her head and a kiss on her lips then murmurs, "Now, now Miss Holloway."

Her eyes smile up, "Only you aren't shy and weak at all are you?"

"And you are far from the lost and broken Miss Holloway." He clears his throat. "Now, hmm, what would you like to know about these exhibits?"

He knows, or seems to know a lot, of course he does, and he even manages to make them interesting to her, though it's his passion for the progression in design the display shows she truly enjoys.

Despite his focus on the historical arms and armour, but he also picks out halls and displays Ella Jane's choice of galleries on her day suggest may be of interest to her, and allows her to draw him into others.

All in all, it isn't the same as spending the afternoon rehearsing a hundred things Ella Jane imagines might occur at the party, but it is serene, and connecting and they return across the park arm in arm and head on shoulder.

They smooch once they have the elevator to themselves, and she sets her bag down and kicks her tennis shoes off as soon as he shuts the door to his suite behind her.

Ella Jane follows him through the entry-hall and by the he reaches the reception room and turns to ask her if she'd like something to drink, she's taken her shirt off entirely.

"You do remember you aren't going to cum yet, don't you?"

She pouts as she moves to him, with her eyes focused in his, and strokes her fingers down the side of his chest. "Ow, does that mean I can't make you cum either?"

"I was planning on saving myself for later too, yes."

She asks, "Really?" and the straps slide down her arms, and her teeth whiten her lip, as she reaches behind her back to unclip her bra.

He knows he should probably put a stop to her shenanigans, but he's sure he'll have the self control to after a little more fun. "Really," he brushes a thumb down the length of her now exposed arm, "But if you can bear it, we can have a bit of fun without cumming."

They've only been together for a short while, but Ella Jane can recognise the dare in his eyes. And a dare is something she's always had trouble resisting...

Her insides clench in anticipation, and she moves to the sofa and lays her shirt and bra out, then her fingers go to the buttons of her jeans.

He lets her finish undressing completely without consciously moving a muscle, but also without hiding the appreciation on his face, or in his body's reaction.

When she's completely naked Ella Jane moves to him, and kisses the underside of his jaw as she traces the outline of the bulge in his trousers.

There's no way he's going to make this that easy though, so he takes her wrist and, despite his enjoyment of her touch, he pulls her hand away. "First I'd like a glass of water."

Ella Jane gives him an appraising look, but still turns to go to the fridge. She makes sure to wiggle her bum as she moves and casts a glance back at him to make sure he's watching as she opens the door. Not wishing to be out-done in teasing she bends unnecessarily to reach the bottles of water, shifts her feet further apart, and looks over her shoulder again to ask, "Still or sparkling?" though, like him, she fails to keep a straight face.

"Definitely sparkling."

"Very good, Sir." She straightens, and makes to open the usual glass cupboard, but changes her mind, puts the bottle down, and reaches up on tiptoes to the higher one. There's no need, there are plenty of glasses, but by doing so she gives him a profile view of her stretching up.

"I should tan your hide, you know."

She licks her lips as she puts the glasses down and pours. "Whatever you think is best, Sir."

"And I'm going to. *After* the party, or possibly at it."

Ella Jane's eyes light up and she hands him his glass. "I submit myself to your judgement, Sir." She then picks her drink up in both hands and lowers her face to sip and to hide her smile from him.

He doesn't drink straight away. Instead, he holds the passes his glass below the undercurves of her breasts close enough that the spray from the icy bubbles bursting lands there.

The smattering of chill droplets send tingling rivulets through Ella Jane and the corners of her mouth curl upwards. "If there anything you can't make kinky and fun?"

"Not that I've found yet."

She smiles at his confidence, and strokes a fingertip across her ribs. "You've made my tits all wet."

"Only your tits?" His smile says he knows the answer...

And her insides respond to his cock sureness with a reflexive pulse. "Ha, no, not just them, no."

He teases her with seemingly casual caresses, "Does that mean I'm going to have to tie you up to keep you out of trouble?"

She looks over her shoulder in search either of somewhere to run, or of somewhere that might be fun to get caught...

The banisters look fun, so she edges that way as she asks, "Has tying me up ever managed to keep me out of trouble?"

Her route of non-escape makes trapping her easy, though, not having cuffs or a hank of rope to hand he has to make do by attaching her by looping his belt around her neck and one of the balusters just tightly enough that she can't get her head free while he goes and fetches something more suitable.

Left alone, Ella Jane has the opportunity to use her hands to undo the buckle and escape, but she doesn't do that. If she did, she reasons, then she wouldn't be tied up any more.

When he returns he has cuffs, rope, a bottle of oil and a towel. She pouts at the lack of anything more exotic, but smiles at the memories times he's done more than exotic to her with just the tools nature gave him.

Over the next hour, he keeps to his intention of neither torturing her, more allowing either of them to cum, and she manages to hold herself back from biting, scratching, or kicking, though she does curse occasionally.

When it nearly gets too much for him he enters her half way and holds still, she tries to fuck him but her bind and his hushing and calm embrace persuade her to become still herself. In that stillness, with the heat of him inside her she finds a measure of comfort and smiles and allows him to hold her in silence. He stays in her unmoving for a time, she doesn't know for how long, but she does realise that her body and his both begin to flex in their union.

He takes that flexing as his signal to withdraw though he joins in with her exasperated sigh when he does, and promises that before long he will do all they both wish in the moments before he unties her.

While he's working the life back into her shoulders he enquires, "What do you fancy for dinner?" as though nothing had happened or was planned.

"Can we not eat first? I don't want to look fat in my new dress."

He takes her by the shoulders, then waits until she looks into his eyes before slowly enunciating, "You don't, and you won't, and I'm not having my companion fainting because I didn't look after her in front of my friend."

With that he sends her to begin bathing and phones down to room service.

He's already changed into his dress shirt and done up his bow tie when the selection of light delicacies for them, and a steak sandwich for him arrive.

Ella Jane is in still doing her hair despite his mild protestations that she looks edible, and he has to order her downstairs.

As they eat Ella Jane asks, "Do you live in the country? Somehow I always imagined you in some city apartment."

He looks around them, conspicuously pausing with his eyes on the room's opulent features and then the view before returning to her.

She narrows her eyes. "Before I met you!"

"Oh! I moved out of town a few years ago. It's a house in a nice little village, not too far from London, but not too close either, with plenty of space for me and the occasional guest." Technically it isn't a lie, there's certainly plenty of space for the occasional guest.

There's a momentary pause in conversation during which Ella Jane imagines herself joking about him putting the gold in goldilocks zone, and she finds herself saying, "Goldilocks, not too near, not too far."

He tilts his head, and looks at her, lips twitching, but eyes level. "Blonde curls aren't really my thing." And goldilocks would probably not have chosen the daddy house.

Being uncertain whether he's going to laugh, chastise her or both saves her from stepping further down the road into provoking him. Instead she moves her chair next to him and leans her head against him, looking towards the park. "No, you're more a more papa-bear or mister wolf."

"Are you trying to get me to play some more before the party?"

His hand glides up her arm and along her shoulder to cup her chin and tilt her head up to face him.

Her cheeks take on a light colour once he eyes meet his, and she allows a half confession. "Not consciously."

He growls his answer slowly, “Hmm, that’s good.” then drops the subject and wistfully observes. “We should probably finish getting ready.”

Their Kink Party Experience

He calls on Johnson's services once more to deliver them to the party, and for once, Johnson does the full chauffeur and bodyguard act, making sure to appear every bit as professional and dangerous as he undoubtedly is. There's no queuing at the club. It's strictly by invitation, and the thin stream of arrivals make their way past the suited door staff. The suited doormen are formidable looking, but would have seemed more so to Ella Jane if she hadn't just been helped out of their limousine by a giant and escorted by her supremely confident companion.

The entryway is grand in the New York style and suits the opulence with which the guests are dressed, though its classicism contrasts sharply with how some have dressed. The guests chosen attire falls into four categories: formalwear, fetish outfits, and those wearing nothing or nothing more than body paint or bondage. The fourth group, comprising some of the younger women, are dressed as if to attract attention in an exclusive vanilla nightclub, which, Ella Jane supposes, this is on other nights. Some of this fourth group however are giving wide-eyed attention to everyone else. The guests, dungeon monitors, and staff are all, to a man and woman, lovely to look at. She allows herself to look around until she worries she might be taken for one of the wide eyed novices, and then fixes him with a face splitting grin.

His eyes glitter wickedly back at her. "What do you think?"

Ella Jane had chosen to wear the slash fronted dress she bought in Greenwich Village and the heels that came with her gown. Her clingy new slash fronted dress is the most revealing thing she's ever worn out, and it, and the eyes that pause on her make her half flush, but despite that, she's distinctly modest by comparison to some. "I'm not sure. Am I underdressed or overdressed?"

"If you decide you want to join the funsters, I've got your bodysuit, and a collar and cuffs set in my pockets."

She frowns until she guesses what he's referring to, then raises an eyebrow at his description. "My bodysuit?"

"Your bodywhisp."

"The one you bought me for a joke?"

"The one I bought you for a rather bad joke that backfired somewhat pleasingly when it turned out that you look fabulous in what there is of it."

Ella Jane widens her eyes and puts it more plainly to him. "The one that frames everything without covering any of it?"

"Yes, that's the one. Just as well. If it were any bigger, it would spoil the lines of my suit."

"If it were any smaller, you might not be able to find it among all the other wicked things you've probably brought with you."

He blinks innocence. "Would I carry a wicked thing?"

"Yes, Sir. You know you would."

He takes her hand and air kisses it. "Quite right."

"I wasn't sure if you were going to punish me for saying it."

"You were right, so I can only funnish you for it. I'll do that later if either of us like."

He's so matter of fact about it that she can't help but play along. "That's so generous of you."

"I suppose it is. Generous to a fault, that's me."

A statuesque woman in an outlandish body covering Lycra suit sweeps towards them. Ella Jane guesses her to be in her forties and can tell from the way the suit clings to her that she takes pride in her appearance and athleticism.

The woman smiles at Him and spreads her arms inviting an embrace. "So pleased you could come. And, my, what a beautiful creature you've found to bring with you!"

He accepts her invitation. "Alexandra, how could I be in New York for one of your gatherings and miss it?"

"Quite. The whole of New York would never forgive you." She turns to Ella Jane and confides, "I'd never let them."

"Madame Alexandra, I'd like you to meet the beautiful and talented..." He pauses and looks at Ella Jane, realising they haven't discussed whether she wishes to use her real name.

She saves him. "Ella Jane Tyler." And offers her hand with a little bob of a curtsey.

"I'm delighted to meet you. My spies assure me you're quite the wordsmith yourself."

Ella Jane sees and hears the years of friendship in the way he and Alexandra interact and feels a pang of regret, but the woman speaks to her with such warmth. "Here, let me look at you!" She appraises Ella Jane from head to foot. "You're going to break the heart of every sub tonight and every Dom if he doesn't let someone steal you away." Then she laughs and air kisses her. "How do you like my little gathering so far?"

"It's amazing! But it's so warm in here!"

Their hostess casts her eyes around. "It has to be warm enough for all the naughty naked people."

Ella Jane's eyes make their way around the room taking in some of those encased from head to foot in elaborate costumes. "I suppose so, but it must be hard for the ones in latex and leather."

His follow. "It is, but those who dress in those materials are usually willing to suffer in the name of beauty."

Madam Alexandra touches Ella Jane's arm lightly. "Let me show you around and introduce you to *all* the interesting people." Then she shifts her pointed finger toward Him and add, "And I show introducė you to the *new* interesting people."

He obviously recognises some of those they're introduced to, and Ella Jane equally obviously doesn't. There are too many for her to remember, but either he or Madam Alexandra makes sure that each learns, rightly or wrongly, that she's the next big thing in women's coming of age literature.

Those who are naked, or nearly so save for restraints, appear the most at ease with themselves and their surroundings. Two tall slender women dressed in nothing more than elaborately stylised pony harnesses and heels race up to him but stop short on seeing Ella Jane at his side. They then smile, lightly hug, air kiss them both, giggle, and do to the same to Madam Alexandra before turning *admire-me* pirouettes.

For Ella Jane, the air kisses would have been more comfortable if, when standing their full heights and heel heights the bare tips of their breasts were a little further below her eye level.

When the two pony-girls return to facing the little party, they soak in the praise they receive and then look expectantly. He responds with a boom of a laugh and spreads his arms to turn while the pair clap. Left with little alternative, Ella Jane then accepts his hand and allows him to hold her while she does her own three-sixty.

He and Madam Alexandra do the introductions to Princess and Fancy, and everyone agrees that everyone else is beautiful and that Alexandra throws the most wonderful parties. Everyone looks and appreciates, but no-one comes too close, despite a number of implied requests to play with one or more of their glamorous little group.

Having completed a circuit, Alexandra takes a deep breath. "I hope you don't mind; only I've been a little presumptuous."

"Yes?"

"I didn't know you were bringing a plus one, and I sort of promised you'd top a scene on one of our demonstration stages."

He looks at Ella Jane.

And she looks at him.

It isn't something they've discussed.

Alexandra touches each of them lightly on the arm with an open hand. "Would that be okay? Or do I have to make my apologies find someone less talented."

"Well..." He focuses on Ella Jane, "If it's just a demonstration."

Ella Jane agrees. It isn't the first time she's been with someone who's topped a scene with someone else, and she genuinely doesn't mind... not until she sees the ravishing young woman who approaches Madam Alexandra.

By then, it's too late.

His Scene

Madam Alexandra leaves the two of them and steps up onto the stage to announce the performance. She's effusive in her praise, and she mentions things that tug at Ella Jane's memories of her time with him, his skill with a flogger and the way he keeps a woman teetering on the edge of orgasm before gifting her a world-shattering release.

With him having been introduced, it really is far too late.

He bends and kisses Ella Jane's cheek, takes the Nordic beauty by the hand, and leads her to the stage. He takes his jacket off, hangs it, and methodically undoes his cufflinks and rolls up his sleeves. Then he helps the fair-haired woman up onto the stage and waits patiently for her to remove her clothing. She does this with a dancer's grace and sureness, clearly familiar with being nude, if not in public, then certainly in select company, and entirely confident in her own beauty. Ella Jane can see no reason why the lovely woman on stage might lack such confidence with her height, figure, all over tan, the fullness of her breasts and hips, and the slender athletic waist between.

At his direction, she turns, given everyone in the room ample opportunity to admire her, and then positions herself ready to be bound into the frame. He takes his time securing her, and, as he does so, he uses the firmness of touch that Ella Jane recognises and yearns towards, assured, strong, and gentle. She can see from the way this other woman melts that his sure hands work as surely as on this other woman as they do on her.

Alexandra takes His place at Ella Jane's side and watches with her as much as she watches the stage. "May I ask how long you've been with the old reprobate?"

"He's not a...," Ella Jane's denial dies on her lips. He most certainly is a reprobate. "He's not old."

"That was neatly avoided, my dear."

Whether it's her warmth, and her being the first woman in the scene she's spoken to since they started, or that she knows Him, Ella Jane decides to tell the whole truth. "We've known each other online for a while, and we were both a the writing conference last week, so –,"

"So you've been together since then?"

"I'm not sure if we're together exactly. We're friends, but I think it's more a situationship."

Next to Ella Jane, a willowy brunette croons, "Watching someone who knows what they're doing is fascinating, isn't it?"

She answers hesitantly, "I suppose so." Fascinating or not, the person who knows what he's doing in this case is the one she'd expected to be doing something like this to her.

"Liselle is so lucky. She's so beautiful, and wow is he..."

"Who's Liselle?" Then realisation dawns that she must be the woman currently being whipped by the man who brought her to the party. "Oh! Yes."

"He's a fuck monster, isn't he?"

"Pardon?"

The woman lightly nudges Ella Jane's shoulder. "You know, your Dom. I saw you arrive all over each other." She then leans close, "Some of the more irritating women will be gutted. He *never* brings anyone unless he plans on going home with her."

Ella Jane half frowns. "He's... we're just getting to know each other."

"Lucky you, discovering all his wicked tricks for the first time."

Ella Jane colours.

The woman's eyes take her in from head to foot and back and surely see Ella Jane's flush, and gives her a conspiratorial smile as she leans close. "Or should that be for the first, second, third..."

"I'm sure I don't know what you mean. We only met in real a few days ago."

"Really?"

"Yes, really."

From Ella Jane's other side, his lycra-suited friend interjects. "Are you sure you're okay with this?" Her eyes go towards the little stage where he's just finished securing the lovely woman into an elaborate bondage frame. He's now stroking her skin with the flogger's long falls he's holding in one hand and periodically tapping her bum and thighs with the crop in his other.

Ella Jane responds hastily. "It's okay; we aren't... not really, just getting to know one another."

Madam Alexandra tilts her head. "You're sure?"

She nods but looks away.

On the dais, he may have tuned in with the emotions of the beauty under his hands, but he's also been mindful of the audience, and one particular person in it. The tension he sees in Ella Jane unexpectedly creates a matching knot in his stomach causing him to take his time before moving on to the next stage of his scene while he decides how to proceed.

He stops, steps on something that allows him to rotate the frame, and with it the naked woman. He places a reassuring hand on Liselle's shoulder as he does so. "Close your eyes, please."

He takes the woman's blindfold from her, steps behind her, and strokes her. "Now open them slowly. Look at each of your fans, all the people who will be with you or be you in the privacy of their minds when they cum tonight, whether it's alone or with their lovers. Seek out that connection in their eyes."

He continues to stroke the fair-haired woman's back, keeping her grounded in her body. He applies the occasional pinch with his right hand to the tips of her proudly outthrust breasts when she starts to drift on the pleasure of his touch and watches her eyes as they adjust to the return of light, sees where they settle, where they pause.

His eyes flicker back to Ella Jane, see her moving closer in to Madame Alexandra's side, and read the tightness of her lips and shoulders. When he drags them away again he sees what he's looking for when Liselle's eyes stop, lock with those of a man in the audience, and the man rocks forward on his feet as if drawn to her. He allows the pair a moment for their mutual attraction to take hold and issues up a silent prayer of thanks to the gods of pleasure that they have provided him with a suitable sacrifice. He then directs Liselle to carry on looking around the crowd by swatting her rear with his riding crop. "Look at each of them. Remember their hunger, the hunger you're creating, feeding." Her eyes move on, and his return to Ella Jane. He whispers, "Now look back around the room."

Liselle's eyes stop on the same face on the way back, and He inflicts pain on her by tweaking one of her nipples and then caresses it away in a way that sharply reminds Ella Jane of the way he seduces her body as He studies the tall, fair-haired thirty something, reads the burning in his eyes, smiles to Himself, casts Ella Jane a glance, and gives her a relieved half wink. "All the way back to the start, not just as far as the one you think is pretty."

The woman does as commanded, looking into each face in the crowd one at a time.

"Will you remember them all without seeing when you cum?"

Her voice is half lost when she breathes, "Yes, Sir," in answer.

He murmurs, "Good girl," as he re-applies the blindfold speaking with his lips against her ear and his face hidden from the audience. Once she's blind again, he gives a hand signal to the audience. It only takes a few exchanged gestures to persuade the fair-haired man to step forward. As he does, He casts another glance towards Ella Jane and Madam Alexandra who nods to him and acknowledges the gesture in her direction. She steps to the extensive toy rack, selects a wand vibrator, and fits a condom over it. Then she hands it to the man, leans close to him, and whispers her instructions.

Madam Alexandra then leads him up onto the stage with silent footsteps, and whispers, "I'm sorry I upset your little friend. I hope the hand-off works." Before kissing his cheek and returning to the audience.

Back at Ella Jane's side the dominatrix threads an arm through hers and enthuses. "This should be fun."

All the while, He applies careful, confident touches to the bound woman's body. "Are you ready to continue?"

She nods. "Yes, Sir."

The 'Sir' is barely out of her mouth when his flogger lands on her far hip, sending the tips of its falls wrapping around her and biting her in the crevice between the rounds of her buttocks.

He whips her with a slow rhythm, adding occasional sharp slaps with the stiff crop to the softer blows with the flogger, and has his assistant apply the wand to her at regular intervals, stimulating but not allowing her release, until, save her lower back, her skin is reddened from her shoulders to just above her knees.

Once he has her prepared, he changes up, at times folding the flogger's falls to deliver heavily duller sensations at others sending their tips wrapping around her either to bite and sting or to land harmlessly against their own leather creating the impression of a sudden enfolding embrace. He even goes back to his stroking for a while as his assistant touches the wand to the tips of each of her breasts and to the points just above and just below her opening.

She goes through pleading and tears of frustration and release and still the whipping and application of the vibrator continue. He has his assistant deny her. Then, as she begs to be allowed to cum, He strikes along the length of her opening.

Only when her responses blend into one tell-tale sign that she's drifting does he allow the fair-haired man to bring her to her long-denied orgasm and have the younger man hold and comfort her while He takes His bow from the assembled company. Show over, He releases her bonds and lifts the covering from her eyes, kisses her cheek, places the pseudo-couple's hands together, and directs them to the recovery area.

He holds his posture until they've left the stage. Then he rolls his sleeves back down, casually drapes his jacket over one shoulder, steps down, draws a deep breath and moves to where Ella Jane and Madam Alexandra are standing. The taller woman waits for Ella Jane to embrace Him first, but when the petite red-head holds back, she opens her arms. "Magnificent as ever. I loved the twists you applied."

"I try to add something and please those involved either physically or personally." He directs this comment towards the still reticent Ella Jane.

The willowy brunette woman congratulates him too. "That was wonderful. It's almost as good watching you as being involved. If you and your gorgeous girl are interested, I'd love to do another scene with you later."

"Thanks, lovely to see you again. Maybe not tonight. We're still working things out between us."

She half turns away as she replies, "Okay. Well, if you do decide you're interested, you know all the best people, and they know where to find me." She then blows a kiss at a point half way between them and mouths, "So lucky. Enjoy him," to Ella Jane before she heads off in search of further entertainment.

He turns his full focus onto Ella Jane. "Ready for our *one drink limit*?"

Ella Jane creases her forehead and looks first at him and then at his friend.

Madam Alexandra explains by holding up her right hand, which has a single black star on the palm. "No drinking before arrival, or no playing. One star per drink, and no playing after your second star. Get emotional with anyone and have too many stars as well, and a person can get banned. Strict rule."

Ella Jane nods her understanding and allows him to take her to the bar. Once she has her drink and her star, she draws him to a quiet-seeming corner. In that semi-privacy she folds her arms in front of her chest and asks, "Have you had *all* of the beautiful women at this party?"

His enunciation begins to become more precise, "Not all. Just you, and in the past, a select few others."

"The ponies?"

A flicker of a smile starts to grow on his lips before her darkening expression stifles its spread. "Yes."

"And the tall one with dark hair who was standing next to me?"

"Yes, we had a couple of play sessions and a weekend."

"She's hot."

"She is. So are you. She's fun as well. Though, she and I have less in common than you and I."

"Such as?"

"Writing, insatiability, getting my English jokes."

"And Liselle?"

"What about her?"

"You gave her to that man!"

"Not exactly. I let them choose each other because you weren't interested in her. There's always a dungeon monitor in the recovery area for if she changes her mind, and Alexandra filters her guest list very carefully. Liselle needed someone, and I wasn't available. She wanted him, and he wanted her." He reaches his hands to her upper arms, but sensing resistance, he doesn't pull her towards him. "Didn't you see how they both reacted when I spanked her while they were looking at each other? All I did was add him to the scene and sent them off together for aftercare."

"You didn't need any aftercare?"

His hand tightens on her shoulder. "I did, and so did you, so I came over to you."

Her *Sorry* is drawn out with regret.

"There's nothing to be sorry for. If you and she had been interested in one another, it would have been you I invited up, but you weren't, so..."

Ella Jane's face forms the beginnings of a pout, and she makes to begin a second apology, but he touches his lips to hers.

"I see." Her frown deepens. "Did you teach one of your salons here?"

"Yes. Two years ago. It was a great success, though I'd like to think I know a bit more now."

She looks around, her eyes taking in the elegantly dressed and elegantly undressed all about them. "So, they all know..."

"You've read my stories, and I write under my own name. It's hardly a secret that I'm a student of pleasure."

"I suppose so."

"Hey. Anyone who looks at us together will conclude that one or both of us is fortunate in the extreme."

"That was your," she tries out her version of his North London accent, "*the bleedin' obvious* voice. Wasn't it?"

"Of course. Rumour has it that I use it to say things that are bleedin' obvious." He slips an arm around her shoulders, and, though they stay stiff, he kisses the top of her head.

"And we're 'fortunate in the extreme'?" Ella Jane sniffs.

"Hey, what's wrong?"

"N-nothing." She drains her drink. "Um, do you want to stay much longer?"

"Not if you don't, but we should at least do a lap and find Alexandra again to say goodbye."

"Sure?"

"Yes. You said you wanted to come, and I promised I would. We can say our farewells, and I can invent a work emergency and make my apologies."

"You don't mind?"

"Not at all. That's one of the blessings of having half a dozen boring jobs. Nobody questions the disappearing act. I warn you though, if I do that, she'll ask if you want to stay."

“That’s okay. I can play the good little sub and tell her my duty is to be at your side.”

“Come on. Let’s see what else is going on and find out if there are any decent nibbles before we go.”

“You and your stomach!”

Ella Jane lets him lead her but winces at the sight of the scene going on in the second viewing area and looks up at him, her shoulders tightening.

A half smile makes its way across his face before he turns away, using his mass to steer her. When she doesn’t resist, the way his movement guides her in a sedate turn away. Neither speaks or looks at the other until they’re out of sight and earshot.

She looks up at him with her lips sucked into her mouth.

He speaks first. “Busy not yucking?”

Ella Jane nods.

“Essentially, this is a good sign.” She frowns without letting go of her lips.

“Both turning green at the same time.”

She finally lets go of her lips and a short cough of laughter escapes.

He grins in triumph at winning a laugh from her. “There’s nowt so queer as folk.”

The expression is unfamiliar to Ella Jane, but the context of people enjoying an act both instinctively turn away from makes its meaning clear to her. “Apparently not.”

“And anyone who’s planning to do that really does need proper instruction.”

“Ha! Yes, I suppose so.”

“Shall we go and find Alexandra and say goodnight, maybe go for a walk or get a drink somewhere else?”

“Please.”

Madam Alexandra is indisposed when they find her. The first stage has been reorganised, and she’s on it conducting a scene with a strikingly lovely couple.

Both are in their twenties and naked, hairless from their necks down, collared, and cuffed, though initially neither is bound.

Ella Jane's eyes plead with Him, but his look is firm, and the dominatrix had been so sweet to her. Besides, a little voice in the back of her mind whispers that it, for one, wants to know what's going to happen.

For the next hour, Madam Alexandra binds and releases one or the other, playing fire tricks and dry ice tricks on their skin under the artful lighting. While she displays her skill with each, she has the other worship at her feet. The show concludes with her arranging the pair together and sending first a ripple of flame and then one of the icy vapour over their orgasming bodies.

The applause is rapturous as the dominatrix steps down from the stage, and two of the dungeon monitors step up to free her subjects.

She makes her way to Him with a gleeful smile.

He inclines His head. "You are a true artist my friend, and just to think you said you were worried I might upstage you!"

"Hmm, you might have if you'd had this lovely creature to work on." With that, she turns her attention to Ella Jane. "Come, can I find some devilish entertainment to make up for my earlier faux pas?"

After giving Ella Jane a quick glance and seeing her still adamant he winces and explains. "I'm afraid work calls."

Their hostess lets out a puff of air and focuses on Ella Jane. "It may, but I'm sure it can wait until you've enjoyed a scene?"

Ella Jane's eyes tense.

Madam Alexandra purses her lips and offers, "Even if it's with this devil in a private room?"

The petite redhead shrinks back.

He raises his hands palms up in apology. "Sorry, it really isn't something that can wait."

The dominatrix's eyes don't believe him. However, she doesn't allow the rest of her face to show it. "Very well. It was still lovely seeing you, even if you have turned into a terrible and terribly gallant liar." That said, she bends, touches her lips to Ella Jane's cheek, and softly whispers, "Next time I'll save any scene I ask him to do for you."

There's not a trace of regretful emotion left on her face when she straightens. Instead, she cheerily bids them goodnight and reminds them that the party doesn't end until four if they've the time to return. She then announces that she must go because two very beautiful young people owe her their worship and their gratitude and disappears to receive further congratulations and those thanks.

Their Awkward Conversation

Ella Jane waits until they're standing on the kerb outside the club to ask the question that's been repeating in her head since he started the scene with Liselle. She tentatively asks, "How do other women react?"

He tilts his head. "That depends when and to what?"

She leans closer, drops her voice, and, keeping the movement of her lips to a minimum, she expands. "To the things you do and meeting the other women you play with? To seeing you do scenes with them?"

He sways his head. "They're usually surprised and pleased. Some seem to regard me as a one-off special time. Others want to do it again." He raises an eyebrow, and lowering his head, he looks her straight in the eyes. "Some of them want to see if we can go even further. Some want others to see us playing. Others prefer to play with me alone in private. Some want to see me play with third parties." And here he touches Ella Jane's arm lightly, and his expression softens. "And others don't."

Ella Jane quietly mumbles, "That's all the possibilities."

He shrugs uncomfortably. "Who'd have thought that women could be as varied and unique as men?"

"Are you making fun of me?"

"No, I'm being uncharacteristically open and comfortable. Don't let anyone know I do this consideration shit with you, or they'll all want me to."

"Is that true?" she looks up and studies his face, then leans her head against him. "Thank you."

He tentatively wraps his arms around her shoulders and holds her until she eases away.

She worries at her lip. "The woman you whipped was beautiful."

"She was," he agrees. Then he confides, "I suspect they choose the prettiest subs for the performance areas at most events."

"And the handsomest Doms?"

"Possibly, but I think they're more focused on skill for those on my side of the slash."

"You were going to sleep with her, weren't you?"

"We went together. I was rather hoping to sleep with you."

"If I hadn't stayed in New York."

"I was invited to the club, and said yes. When you agreed to stay over a few extra days with me, I took you as my plus one. Madame Alexandra arranged the scene intending it to be a nice surprise for me."

"Oh!" They walk on a little further.

"What if I liked girls as well?"

He shrugs. "Then I would have asked you if you were interested, and if you were, I'd have asked her if she was."

Ella Jane's chin tucks in and her lip curls. "Aren't I keeping you satisfied?"

"If you weren't," he bumps up against her, "I wouldn't have invited you to stay." He's all reasonableness. "But if you were bi, I'd accept that I don't have a right to expect you to deny yourself."

She gives him a stepped-into-a-social-minefield look. "Sorry, I've got no right. I know we aren't together like that, it's just—."

"Complicated?"

"Yes."

He rumbles. "Everything's complicated these days." A few steps later, he floats, "It felt a bit weird doing the scene to be honest." His voice sounds far away.

Ella Jane looks up at him. "It did?"

The arm around her shoulder tightens. "Yes, we hadn't talked about that eventuality." His arm squeezes again, and the corners of his mouth turn down. "Which was remiss of me."

With an effort to see the other side and a memory of how his friend had stayed by her while he worked, Ella Jane notes, "Madame Alexandra was sweet."

"She is. She reads people quite well, too. I think that's one of the things that makes her good at what she does." The petite redhead gives him a querying look. "Not with me. Just in general. People speak highly of her, and you saw her performance."

"I did. It's fascinating watching a dominatrix at work."

"Oh! Why?"

"Because it's hot, and I like the idea, even though I don't have any interest in women."

"I feel the same when she works with a man. *So hot*, but..."

She joins in with his, "So not." And they each lean more heavily against the other.

"Want to do something about that hot?"

Ella Jane's face creases up. "Is it okay if we don't?" Then she squeezes his hand. "Not yet, anyway."

"Sure. We can walk if you want?"

She mouths *thank you* and touches her head to his shoulder, "Not eat?" and tries a smile up at his rueful rumble.

"Are you being cheeky, young lady?"

"Just trying it out."

The swat he gives her backside is almost as light as the kiss he plants on top of her head. "How about we walk until one of us is hungry?"

Ella Jane crosses her feet the next step to sway against him and glances slyly up through her tumbling curls. "So half a block?"

He gives a "Humph!" then mutters, "Maybe even three quarters, if you can behave for that long."

They walk further than that until they reach the west side of Central Park. He stops there and asks, "Cut across?"

"Is it safe?"

"I won't break it if you don't."

Her eyes narrow, but she holds herself back from a verbal barb. "You know what I mean."

"I'm told it's pretty safe, provided you don't get lost or fall in one of the lakes." He takes out his mobile. "Seventy five percent charge, so we can rely on satnav if we aren't home in twenty minutes." He looks down at her, studying her face for signs of a further softening in her attitude.

She looks up, fighting his effort to be the one setting the pace, controlling the twitch of a cheek, the mirthful tightening at the corners of her eyes. "Isn't that dangerously close to asking directions?"

His eyebrow rises, the right one, the one that goes up instinctively rather than ironically.

"Still just trying it out."

He stands stone still, and while he does so, Ella Jane tries to make him change his expression, moving away and back close, smiling, frowning, even when she makes to walk into the park alone.

She stops, ponders defiantly telling him she's got his spare key and his suite has a spare room just to see what happens. She doesn't, though she savours the thought of herself doing just that after he finished playing with Liselle.

He waits until she becomes still. "This is a moment. Isn't it?"

Ella Jane shifts her feet but doesn't take a step forwards or back.

He starts cautiously, "That was crass and awkward, and–."

"And I'd always wanted to go to a party like that. Just..."

He answers slowly, with none of his usual three moves ahead bravura. "Just maybe not in the first few days of finding out if you're in a new dynamic or just having a bit of fun?"

The muscles of her neck tighten and so do those in her forehead. They look at one another until her chest and then her shoulder twitch. The movement spreads to her lips and finally her eyes before she speaks. "Is 'crasser' a word? Or should I stick with more crass?"

He raises an arm and allows himself to return her smile. "Crassest might be a word too."

Ella Jane steps back to him. "It was a fantastic party."

"It was, and it will be until 4 a.m."

She hasn't forgiven him, his friend, or the cruelty of the world in general, but being up against him provides a physical comfort. And right now, she needs that more than she needs to hold onto her anger. "And thank you for not making me watch that other scene."

"Thank you for not embarrassing me about it, or making me watch."

They speak in unison, "Don't yuck someone else's..." then try again.

This time Ella Jane begins, "But so no."

While his opening is, "But do have a stiff drink and pray to forget it exists."

Ella Jane approaches her concern from an oblique angle. "Madame Alexandra with that couple was super hot though. So was your whipping."

He squeezes her up against his side. "It got more relaxed for some people once I pulled that guy out of the audience."

Ella Jane blinks, but then smirks at the memory. "He almost fell over his feet when you did that."

"He did. You almost smiled too."

She stiffens at that and looks up, searching for a trace of mockery. "Mhm."

His eyes crease at their corners. "Still fancy that walk in the park?"

"Yes." She says it firmly, determined not to let the evening be completely spoilt. "I fancy a drink too."

They cross the road and enter the park with his arm around her, even if, unlike their steps, they still aren't entirely in synch. Anxious to allow things to cool before sitting with her, he asks, "In a hurry to get that drink?" in what he hopes is a light-hearted voice.

"Not, if you aren't."

"Then we'll give the tavern on the green a miss and take you somewhere. If you were telling the truth about liking Scotch?"

Relieved at having something else to talk about, she lets out, "I love whisky!"

"You never did say how you got into it."

"My granddaddy."

"He introduced you?"

"No, he didn't mean to anyway. He drinks it. I love the smell." Ella Jane leans against him as she looks into the past. "The first time I tasted it was a shock, but I still liked the smell, and..." she lets out a little chuckle, "I quite like shocking sensations."

"That burning sensation as it runs down your throat?"

"Uh-huh."

"Well in that case, I'm more or less obliged to take you to the Caledonian Bar." He stops, turns one way, then another, and comes to a decision. "West Side's closer, and it's a nicer walk back."

He guides her up the pathways and along the lake, taking a detour to Cherry Hill with its stonework where he points out the roof of their hotel and on to the Ladies Pavilion to show her the views over the water.

Ella Jane's hands are drawn to the old pavilion's ironwork. "Wow, fantastic binding points! Imagine a party here? The view, the open air, lots of convenient places to tie people to."

Her eyes dare him, and he backs her against the railing. She reaches out to the sides and up as high as she can in emulation of a bound captive and lets out a shuddering breath as he presses his strength against her and softly rumbles, "You have a filthily creative mind."

She bats her lashes. "Why thank you, Sir."

He draws her towards him and has her turn to face the lake. "Better still if a submissive were positioned diagonally here. Arms high and wide, free access to every part of their body."

"Are you thinking of their body?"

"I'm thinking of your body." He bends, kisses her, straightens and traces her wide spread arms. His eyes look around, and he frowns. "I *might* not have anything with me to tie you like that." With those words, he winks and one hand goes inside his jacket pocket. One at time, and with a magician's smile, he pulls out two slim leather wrist cuffs. His eyes are on her. "Seeing as how you missed out on playing earlier, we could..."

"Where did you get those from?" He guides her hand to a row of slim pockets built into its lining; three of the five still contain leather strips, which she assumes must be for her neck and ankles.

"This is one of my party jackets."

"You have suits made just to go to parties?"

"I have basic suits with several pairs of trousers each and a small selection of jackets and waistcoats."

Having allowed him to take hold of her hand, she makes no move to reclaim its freedom, instead preferring to adopt the tones of a southern belle. "Why, Sir, that shows uncommon dedication."

He answers, "Yes, ma'am, ah take pride in my art," without missing a beat.

There follows a brief silence, which she breaks with, "Aren't you afraid of getting caught?" Though, she's already half made up her mind.

His mind seems entirely made up. "Not if we don't go as far as full nudity."

Ella Jane pouts, "Spoil sport!" and follows it with her start-of-a-rollercoaster smile on her face.

He shrugs and raises an eyebrow. "You're the one who'd be naked when they led us off to the local cop shop." That thought wipes the smile from her face. "As the D, I'm responsible for making sure that doesn't happen."

"What am I responsible for?"

He finishes applying the cuff. "Using your safeword if you have to." Then he checks her bondage is neither too tight nor too loose. "And not screaming for help unless I ignore it."

She seals the deal by offering up her other wrist. "I think I can manage that, and I can look out for passing cops, unless you distract me too much, that is." The simmering look he gives her at the suggestion that he might not do so makes her catch her breath.

"Good. Fortunately, your attire should allow me enough access for a little amusement at least."

The next things to emerge from his coat of many pockets are two neatly wound lengths of nylon cord. "I did say you were right about the wicked contents of my pockets." He bends and kisses. "Now, where shall we arrange you? Ah, yes!" He loops them through the pavilion's ornate ironwork and threads them through her cuffs, raising and spreading her arms as he does and ensuring she has little room to wriggle. When he's finished, she's facing the moonlit lake. He then lowers his lips to hers and kisses his captive while his hands trace the edges of her dress. The kiss is long and slow. After all, she isn't going anywhere, and she's breathless by the time he breaks away, and his eyes look down at her. He then kneels and eases her feet further apart. "Can I trust you to keep your feet like this?"

"Yes, Sir."

"Good girl." He takes each of her feet in turn and removes her heels. Once he's done so, she has to stand on the balls of her feet to avoid the cuffs digging into her wrists. Ella Jane's immediate reaction is to edge her legs closer together. She stops herself, but not before he notices the movement.

Having detected it, he tuts his disappointment and carefully repositions the errant foot. He then stands and slowly raises the dress's narrow skirt until her garters, thong, and garter belt are fully exposed.

He stands there, having done this, looking into her eyes. "Do you deserve to be spanked for that, young lady?"

She swallows, chews her lip, knows she does and yet doesn't, and knows this is as ridiculous as it is hot. "Yes, sir."

His left hand holds the dress up while the palm of his right circles on her almost bare bum in the cooling air. "You do, indeed." He bends again, kisses the side of her neck, murmurs, "Good girl," and lifts his right hand away. When his hand falls, his palm strikes her with an impact that shakes her body to the core and produces a sharp crack that sounds out across the still water and returns to them.

A second spank to her other cheek has the same outward effect and an additive inward one. Having delivered it, his now warmer hand resumes its circling on her now warmed bum, and his left hand traces the lines of her thong. "Oh, that might be a problem." His lips touch that exact spot half way down the side of her neck, just behind her ear. "If I carry on with that, the whole of New York will hear and come and investigate."

She looks at him, her eyes hungry enough to make him wish he'd only been kidding.

"I'll just have to find some other ways to punish your sin and reward your honesty." His brow furrows as he takes time to think, seemingly oblivious of the bound and eager woman in from of him in this not exactly private spot. "I'll have to see what else I can find." With that, his hands go back to his numerous pockets.

In addition to the cuffs and cord, his pockets yield up a small vibrator, a Wartenberg wheel, a wicked looking little lock knife, and a set of clamps joined by a chain that fit over the nipples and clit. He shows her each with a boyish delight while her eyes widen. He takes his jacket off and lays it out on the neat wooden bench in front of her and sets his collection of wicked treasures out in a row on it. Then, in a final flourish, he undoes his belt, pulls it free, and lays it with the rest.

The dress's plunging décolletage makes it easy for him to slip his hands inside, and her excitement makes the tips of her breasts ready victims for the little clamps. He toys with the screws until they're tight enough that a light tug draws a gasp from her lips without pulling them free. Satisfied he holds the third clamp up. He knows she knows where it's supposed to go, but he still muses, "I wonder where..." before slipping it under her thong.

She mutters, "Fuck!" as his fingers find the top of her slit and gasps as the little jaws close around the hooded tip of her clit.

With the clamps applied to her most sensitive flesh, he takes his time playing with them and with her. His clever hands, artful lips, and praiseful words, set her on a path he has no intention of letting her reach the end of so soon. When he decides she's close enough for the next step, he runs a finger along her wet, ready opening one last time, and raises it between them so the glistening of her arousal catches in the pale light. "It seems you're enjoying your punishment just a little too much." He then tastes her essence with the tip of his tongue and presents his finger to her lips. "Don't you agree, my dear?" She suckles and smiles as she does so, drawing an appreciative rumble from his lips. "What have you got to say for yourself?"

"I'm sorry, Sir. I don't know what's come over me." Her words are as sincere as her eyes remain insolent as her tongue touches her lips, wetting them invitingly.

"Hmm." He goes to the neat row of toys and selects the Wartenberg wheel. "Let me see if you find this as amusing?"

The close-fitting dress presents some impediment to his use of this particular toy, but his imagination and her already aroused state compensate. The needle-sharp spurs tantalise and sting her neck, arms, and thighs. He rolls it down the dress's slash cleavage aside, and they find the inner curves of her breasts. When he pulls back and looks into her eyes, Ella Jane nods her consent.

He eases the dress's material aside exposing the clamped buds at their tips to his caresses and the spiked wheels sweet and not so sweet touch.

Between the pricking of the wheel's gleaming spikes and the clever touches of his free hand he tugs the network of chains linking the clamps biting her flesh excite her ever further Soon Ella Jane is no longer watching out for passers-by.

Once again, her response is more lustful than penitent, and as a result, he feigns disappointment once more. He repeats his routine with her nectar, she her act of false contrition, and he concludes that he will assay one more attempt at correction.

With this resolution made, he sets the wheel aside and takes up the vibrator. "One imagines that, with your naughty pearl so clamped, the effect of this will be most painful." It's a lie, and an outrageous one, but Ella Jane has absolutely no intention of calling it out.

After a few experimental attempts, he finds a way of setting the little toy along the length of her slit with its head against her clamped centre, and, with a couple of clicks, he manages to set it buzzing at a low setting, just intense enough that, left alone, it will take her a long while to crest.

"Does that hurt, little one?" The twinkle in his eyes tells her he knows damned well it doesn't.

She pleads, "Agony, master." Though her only discomforts, from the way she's bound and from biting the inside of her mouth to help her keep a straight face, are mild. "Take pity on me!"

"What should I do to punish you instead?"

Her mind goes to the belt. She likes them, and she's sure he set it in view because he knows she does, and her eyes settle on it.

His voice is slow caramel as he asks, "The belt?"

"Yes, Sir."

"You want me to whip you with it instead?"

"Please master! This hurts too much!"

"Very well." He lifts the belt and flexes it. "But first." He reaches down and turns the vibe up to maximum. The effect is immediate, and her breathing becomes urgent within moments.

She registers his, *Count for me* feels him raise her dress once more and hears the heavy leather strap move through the air. She only manages a count of three, and that's as well because the sounds of leather on flesh and her cries of ecstasy echo across the water and around the park.

After she crests, he rearranges and smoothes her dress, snatches up the knife, and slices through the nylon cords starting with those holding her legs apart. He supports her as he frees her arms, catches her weight, wraps her in his jacket, and sits her down. That done, he retrieves and hides the cord in a trouser pocket and returns the belt to his waistband before joining her on the bench.

He then stills and retrieves the vibe, unclamps her, hides these last pieces of evidence away in the pockets of the jacket around Ella Jane's shoulders, and holds her while she recovers, hoping all the while that no one will come before she has time to compose herself.

However, their luck having held this long, runs out. Two of New York's finest approach at a swift walk with torches out and their hands on the butts of their holstered weapons. A voice with a Brooklyn accent demands, "Is everything okay, ma'am."

Ella Jane looks up at Him, so He answers in his best I'm-in-charge voice. "I'm terribly sorry, officer. A bat flew into my companion's face, and it gave her such a shock."

"Is that so, ma'am?" The voice is a little cowed by His confidence, but the officer is still quietly determined.

"Yes, Officer. I'm so sorry to have disturbed you. You were wonderful arriving so quickly."

"Hmm. Well, that's okay, ma'am." The officer smiles and relaxes.

His partner meanwhile is already relaxed, and his torch and his eyes are focused down by Ella Jane's feet. More precisely, they note the neatly laid pair of shoes by her feet.

The couple both follow his gaze and register his smile.

The cop who'd found the situation amusing touches his cap, "Well, you folks best head off once the lady's recovered, and don't go disturbing any more of the park's wildlife tonight if you can avoid it." He turns off his torch and leads his less worldly colleague away.

Once they've left, Ella Jane puts her shoes back on, and they wait in silence avoiding one another's eyes like a pair of naughty children who've almost got away with something and only need to avoid a bout of collecting giggles to be in the clear. They hang on hoping the two cops will move out of earshot before they erupt. Just when they think they may be safe, they hear the sound of laughter coming from the direction in which the policemen had departed, and they allow themselves to laugh long and hard themselves.

He shakes his head slowly with relief. "That was a close call."

"It was, wasn't it?"

"Still fancy a whisky before *bed*?"

"I do, but you've taken the edge off for me, so I don't mind if you want to go straight back."

He pulls her close up against him, making his hardness still more obvious to her. "I think I can manage to hold off for an hour or so yet." As he lets her go, his hands brush down her sides. "Just about."

The rest of the walk to the bar is relaxed, and even a little playful despite the pair not encountering any more bats.

The bar is somewhere between an old Scottish pub and pure old New York from the happy time after prohibition was finally abandoned. They make their way to the long counter and peruse the rows of whiskies.

"Would you like me to order?"

Ella Jane nudges him with her shoulder. "Don't you trust me?"

One corner of his mouth curls upwards. "There's a method to my madness."

"Oh, is there?"

"Yes." His eyes flicker down and back to hers, before he continues with words intended to remind her of other things. "Start light, something like a Talisker or a Dalwhinnie. Then work your way up in strength and peating till it stops feeling as though it'll be fun to go heavier."

She moistens her lips and smiles her appreciation of his innuendo. "Is that so?"

His eyes are the devil's own as he assures her. "It is."

"And you know this because?"

"Because I've been drinking whisky for a little while." His words about whisky but...

She blinks, hearing what his voice says but his words don't. "You were going to let me anyway, weren't you?"

"Mhm."

He leans close. "And there was I thinking I'd disciplined you enough for the evening."

"Not till you've done more to me than you did to Liselle."

"Is that so?"

Her voice is thick with emotion as she borrows his phrase. "It is. I don't want you to dream about whipping anyone else tonight."

He places his hand on her upper arm in the way that puts the inside of his forearm close to her breast, and he allows her to turn just enough to press against him."

"I've had Talisker."

"I remember you saying. That's why we're starting with a Dalwhinnie."

"Did you really? Or did you scroll back through our messages while I was recovering?"

"The latter. The only reason I did that session with you at the pavilion was so I could distract you while I looked up your whisky drinking history."

"You're a very devious man!"

"I am, and you're letting me ply you with strong drink."

The barman pours one glass, and He raises two fingers, so the barman pours a second.

"I believe the traditional toast is *Slàinte.*"

"And how is Slàinte spelt?"

"Not S-L-A-N-J. If you want me to pretend I know the right way though, I'll have to do something else to distract you while I Google it.

"I like the way you distract me, but I don't want to get thrown out before we finish, so Slàinte." She goes to drink, but he raises a finger just as she's about to tilt her glass.

"Remember to sip, but make sure you have enough that the fragrant trail of amber fire trickles all the way down your throat and sends curls warmth up to your ears."

"You should be a writer."

"Someone told me that once. So should you. Slàinte, here's to writers."

She drinks her first taste of the new whisky, and he watches with eyes that remember his and appreciate it again.

Once she's savoured her sip, Ella Jane looks at him, sees his unstarted drink and the fascinated attention of his eyes on her. She grins her appreciation even as she flushes under the intensity of his gaze. "It's good."

"It is." He drinks, and his eyes half close with the simple pleasure.

Ella Jane's eyes linger on his smile as she runs a finger down the side of her glass. "I bet you've had this a hundred times."

"Maybe not a hundred. There are a lot of whiskies, but it's a lovely one."

"And you still enjoy it?"

"I do."

They talk, and their conversation strays to things they can't imagine trying and things that didn't work out. When their glasses are empty he asks, "Friends again?" and she sniffs and nods. "Just a Macallan for the road then."

The bar has an eighteen-year-old cask strength. This time he drinks first and half-bares his teeth as he appreciates the primal aroma and heat. It takes Ella Jane's breath away with its intensity, though it stops short of making her cough.

"Good?"

"Hah, wow, yes! It's a good thing I like a little pain!"

"It's a good pain."

"It is."

They savour the rest of their second drams in silence and make their way back across the park without stopping at the pavilion or encountering her two would-be saviours. As they walk, she asks, "Did your friend think I had the right look?"

"Ha, yes, she did. Why do you ask?"

"What would have happened if she didn't?"

"For a start she wouldn't have tried to persuade you to stay or to play. Other than that she would have been terribly polite."

"Just that?"

"For you? Yes. For Me? I'd have been in receipt of a sternly worded communication explaining the rules and explaining that regrettably not even our long friendship allows me to break them."

He pauses on the Gapstow Bridge though, to kiss her and point out the windows of their suite.

Ella Jane leans against him as she looks up at their hotel's illuminated white stonework. "The Plaza does look like something out of a fairytale in real life, doesn't it?"

"Yes, ready to go back?"

She nods and squeezes his hand.

Her Night

Ella Jane floats across the magnificent foyer's marble floor on a carpet woven from the heat from their play session and the warmth from the whiskies.

They have the lift car to themselves on the way up to his suite, and Ella Jane's glance of encouragement finds him already moving close. The hours of teasing her have him where she wants him, and he pins her to the mirrored wall and kisses her fiercely until the doors open on the top floor.

He then drags her, unresisting, from the lift and along to his suite.

Once inside she fervently promises, "Now you can do a proper scene without worrying about nudity or anyone getting upset watching. I promise I won't act jealous this time," while he undresses her.

"Want to see what I was planning as a finish earlier?"

"Yes."

"Good, but I'm going to have to fuck you first."

"Better."

He slips one arm under her shoulders and places the other at her entrance. Before she realises what he's doing, his index finger is inside her. She barely has time to register how nice it feels when he withdraws it and places its now slick tip against her rosebud. Moments later, his finger begins to penetrate her, and his thumb is sliding into her. He takes his time getting both fully inside her, and bends his thumb so the knuckle presses against the inside of her pubic bone. Once his hand is in position he applies a finger and thumb grip her through the thin layers separating her openings. Then he lifts her and grins evilly down at her look of surprise. "Bed."

Ella Jane wraps her arms around his neck, clamps her legs around his invading hand, and stares hungrily up at him as he strides across the large room to the elaborate staircase.

When he gets to the master bedroom, he throws her onto the bed so enthusiastically that he has to catch her by an ankle to save her from bouncing off the other side. He then shrugs himself out of his jacket and discards it even as he's kicking his shoes off.

After taking a moment to get over the near disaster, she pulls herself close to him, her hands going to his belt and fly while he concentrates on his cufflinks and black tie. Once she has them undone, he kisses her mouth fiercely and pushes her onto her back again. Then he lowers his mouth to her breasts, suckles, and rakes his teeth over their tips. He bends further, breathes a long slow growl over her mons and lips, kisses again, draws her hood and clit into his mouth, and flutters his grooved tongue over them as he kicks his clothes below the waist off.

Once his legs are free, he lifts his face with hungry eyes and drives into her. Her hands work at his shirt's upper buttons and lift it up and over his head. She then clamps around his broad shoulders as she abandons herself to him and to her need.

For the first time, he takes her as though her pleasure is nothing but a consequence of his taking his own and that her body and each of its openings are his to do with as he pleases. In doing so, however, he forgets none of his artistry.

An age later, they lie together with his initial desire sated. Ella Jane allows her lips and tongue to explore his chest and play with his eternally eager nips while she presses herself against his renewing hardness. She looks up. "Did you need that?"

He answers with a lopsided smile and a kiss to the top of her head. "Maybe a bit."

She pulls herself up and kisses his mouth. "Me too. Just a bit."

They laugh and kiss. He rolls her onto her back and starts to kiss his way down her body again, but after a while, he glances to the floor by the door. He continues down but looks back, and her eyes follow his.

Ella Jane laughs again. "It's bugging you that your jacket's not on a hanger, isn't it?"

"Yes." He lets out a sudden guffaw.

She kisses him. "Then I'll be a good little slave girl and hang in up for you, Sir." She slips out from under him and hops out of bed, her petite derriere white in the dimly lit room. Bending at the waist, she picks up the heavy garment, giving him a full view of herself, then stands, and goes to the wall of capacious wardrobes. She has to reach up to hang it, and her pale figure stretching upwards is a vision.

"Dammit. When you strut around like that, I don't know whether to spank that bum of yours or fuck it."

Hearing his words, she holds her pose a second longer than she needs to and replies, "Whichever you wish, Sir." She can't see him from her position but imagines her words having their effect on him just as they are on her. She holds for another moment to savour that feeling and imaging both the spanking and the fucking before she turns and approaches the bed again.

When she arrives, he's sat up on the bed. She half turns, proffering her rear to him. "Which would Sir like to do first?"

She knows she should have lowered her eyes as she said this if she were playing the perfect little slave girl, but seeing his desire rise and feeling it resonate with her own is worth any punishment. And if it makes the spanking or the fucking all the harder, so much the better. Her game of seducing and teasing him is as much foreplay for her as his of doing the same to her.

He seizes her, and she lets out a squeal of delight as he throws her over his legs. The first swat is heavy and loud and fills the room, the second just as hard. The heat of reddening suffuses her buttock and the soothing warmth of his caress to them. "Raise yourself up on your elbows. Push put bum out. That's right."

It's impossible not to imagine how she must seem, moving marionette-like to his words, exposing her most intimate places. She's offering them up to his lust and his cruelty, and it's impossible not to allow that imagining to kindle the heat of both shame and desire in her.

"There's a good girl."

It's something he's often said to Ella Jane in their few days together. Break off from inflicting pain or bondage to talk with her while applying the trance-inducingly skilful touch of his hands. He never explains why he does this; whether it is to remind her that he can give her all the pleasure a woman could need without resorting to the cruelty she has always before required, for the simple joy of giving that pleasure.

Ella Jane reasons through possibilities as she lies there spread and open awaiting his resumption of the spanking or his decision that it is over. *Does he do it to deepen her submission, or to enjoy that submission*? She doesn't ask though, and her curiosity doesn't compel her to. In truth each possibility excites her, the play, the letting go, the sense that she is offering and yet at the same time being compelled.

"Now, tell me why I'm spanking you."

Under his touch and in the intimacy of the moment Ella Jane gives no thought to lying, though she does embellish. "Because I teased you, Sir, and because I failed to lower my eyes."

His left hand teases the curves of her breasts while the fingers of his right skirt around her freely offered openings with the lightest of caresses. She fights and defeats her body urging to press herself into his hands in search of more instantly satisfying contact.

"You're such a good girl once you're getting what you want, aren't you?" He circles her upturned bum cheeks. It's an action she knows well he delights in following with one or more blows of his hand or whichever instrument of torture he is presently using. "Or is it once you're getting what you think I want to give you?" As he speaks this second sentence, he at last begins to focus his attention on the tips of her breasts.

So it is that Ella Jane lets out a low purring sound before she answers, "S-sometimes, each Sir, sometimes both and..."

His right hand slides down between her buttocks to gently cup her sex. "And?" Having asked her to elaborate his thumb presses lightly on her rosebud and the tips of his middle and ring fingers ease their way between her outer lips to sandwich her hooded clit.

"Agh, and sometimes I don't know. I get excited, and the next thing I know, we're doing something."

He rumbles out a laugh as his hands continue to take their time about her pleasure. "That's a good answer. Now I have another question for you."

She purrs again resting her head on the soft covers. "Yes, Sir."

"Would you like me to demonstrate the proper conclusion to the scene I started at the club now, or after I finish attending to the twin needs of this cute little bottom of yours?"

The question is a challenge for Ella Jane, doubly so with her buttocks waiting and his hands pleasuring her, the pad of his thumb pressed against the tight little opening he intends to take again. She wants to overwrite the memory of his whipping and caressing the beautiful Liselle by outshining her submission and her cries of pleasure and pain too, but she knows the correct answer, and gives it. "Whichever pleases you most, Sir."

His grip on her tightens as she speaks confirming the rightness of her decision.

He leans close and murmurs, "Are you feeling brave and adventurous..."

And she leans into him. "And?"

"Just the tiniest bit turned on?"

She buries her head further into the sheets and lets out a low laugh, after all he has one hand toying with her erect nipples and another holding her wet, eager sex. "Might be."

"I'll just go and see how warm it is out."

"Out?"

"Yes, if it's warm enough I thought you might enjoy a session under the stars."

"Outside again?"

"Outside naked. It's a scene that doesn't really work well with clothes on."

Ella Jane emerges onto the roof terrace still wrapped in the warm glow of after.

His voice draws her from her reverie. "Are you sure you want to do this?"

"More than sure, I want to feel you perform your party piece on me."

He smiles and touches his lips to hers and then to her cheek. "This will be more like at home than at the party. I'll be using my own toys." He brushes his thumb down the side of her neck. "And I'm using them on someone I know, not just putting on a show."

"Good."

The frame is less elaborate than the one on Madame Alexandra's little stage, but then they have no audience other than the night sky.

Her lips part, but she doesn't speak, though her eyes follow him hungrily and her head cranes after him as he straightens. With his mouth beyond her reach, she kisses his hand as it traces the lines of her face.

"I'm looking forward to this, to having the whole night to explore your darkness."He has his own whips and toys which he knows intimately, and, in Ella Jane, he has a woman whose body and submissive soul he already knows and delights in. He also has the whole rest of the night.

For her part, Ella Jane brings a need to outshine Liselle in her submission, to symbolically reclaim him with her absolute and intimate surrender.

Having positioned mirrors so that she can see behind and to the side, he binds her in as close to the same pose used in the club earlier. Just as he did with Liselle in the club, he first takes her freedom and her power to defend herself in any way other than by calling out her safeword. The bind he applies is as close to that he used earlier as he can achieve. That done he positions mirrors so she can behind and to the side. He then confuses her by depriving her of the sense of sight with a soft, velvet blindfold.

With her world in darkness he uses the subtle power of caresses and rumbled words. His voice, hands and the floggers' heavy falls to seduce her body into a trance-like state of submission. Unlike in the club though, there's no-one watching who the scene might upset or not be able to see, and there's no need for distraction, or to reach a timely conclusion.

As far as he can, he applies same touches of his hands, the same stroking of the flogger's falls as he had with the fair-haired Liselle, but inevitably there are differences. Not all women are the same, and neither are all whips. Knowing Ella Jane as he does, and already having begun to learn the pair of moose-hide floggers the instincts and pride which guide him to excel kick in. He trails their falls over her skin with agonising slowness.

After a while, he lifts the covering from her eyes. "No blindfold tonight, for Liselle it was so she didn't get distracted by the audience. I want you to see the stars and the city's lights. To imagine a thousand eyes seeing you in the distance, unrecognisable except as a beautiful, bound, naked woman enduring pain and ecstasy for her lover's pleasure."

When he goes from stroking to striking, the thick, soft falls impact and wrap, transferring his energy into her with such vigour that her flesh transmits it into her bones.

As the floggers strike again and again the strange sensation of being at once beaten and embraced takes Ella Jane's awareness and tries to lead her into the warm waters of subspace.

She holds back, wanting to see him, watch his joy in all he does to her, read the responses of his body and the lust in his eyes, but the falls curl around her with their bite and comfort; breasts, thighs, belly, mons, even her opening, and she follows. In his hands the whips are lovers and masters and in her bondage her mind releases herself to them as both.

Memories of the great churches they visited that morning rise in Ella Jane's mind. The bondage frames serve as cross and altar. The night and the city's lights are vaulted ceilings and stained glass. Her suffering is crucifixion, and her ecstasy becomes rebirth.

But this is something primal, transported from a time long before. The city's night looks down on them as they play out what could be a ritual from some long dead pagan faith.

Ella Jane pictures herself as the human sacrifice and him as the high priest. His caresses and tortures, and the sounds of her voice and body in her rapture and suffering become the prayers.

There comes a brief time in which she registers him arranging the wand so its head is held against her, and in which her half awareness mourns the absence of the falls impacting on her skin, but that time is brief indeed. The buzzing starts and a moment later the whipping resumes. He whips her as she takes flight, and continues until he has drawn all but the last pitiful whimpering from her and then frees her, holds her, enters her and does nothing more until she kisses him.

As she does, she pours out a tumble of words and tears. Tears which he does his best to kiss away until she laughs at his efforts and complaints. Her laughter brings his, and his makes her self-conscious. She colours, attempts an apology which he hushes away and then kisses him again, this time and she rises up on his hardness.

The sex is the gentlest kind, and ends with whispered words and him pulling a blanket around her.

Ella Jane croons, and her fingertips idly circle on his shoulder, as she muses, "Is that all you had planned?"

His basso chuckle fills the night, "Well, there is another way to do something like that we could try."

"Yes, please, I want to."

He kisses the top of her head and asks, "Are you sure?"

"Please!" there's need in her voice, so he takes her to the frame he build to set her kneeling over.

Having set cushions for her feet, knees and elbows, he arranges her kneeling over the frame before attaching the wand bracket to it and fits the wand. He adjusts the position of the wand's head and asks her to strain against her bondage to reach it. She can't quite do so, so he edges it a fraction closer and has her try again. After a third adjustment he has it where he wishes. Able to hold her centre against it firmly for a few seconds or barely touching for a longer time.

Satisfied, he sets it to a low steady humming and fans the falls of one flogger across her back then strikes with the other with his full power over their protective blanket.

In her elevated state this latest twist makes Ella Jane cry out long and loud. He strikes again and again. The impacts echo through her body through the armouring blanket of soft, thick leather strands protect her. With the flick of a wrist, he lifts away her shield. And with a slight of hand, he transfers the second flogger, so that he's holding both in his right hand.

It gives him double the weight to strike the blows are spread between twice as many thick, soft strands of soft warming leather.

This next phase of her beating transports Ella Jane back to their first night, to the wet towel within the dry, then carries her forward. Her tears rise and flow though she doesn't know their cause, and her body glows.

No matter how hard his lashes strike her, nor how intense and drawn out the ecstasy he inflicts, not one of her cries contains any of the simple words that would make him stop. Instead she howls her true soul to the ancient stars hidden by the city's lights and the modern architecture that surrounds them.

He impales her with tender cruelty, kneels and worships at her centre, denies her, and then forces her to beg both for him to continue and for him to stop. As the night progresses, she makes wild offers, if only he will allow her to cum. And then she begs for him to stop making her cum, for him to cease her sweet torture.

Ella Jane looks up at his reflections from her bondage as he lavishes his skills on her. The effect of his focus on her is a thing above and beyond even that of his skills. Here, now, in her ecstasy and her suffering she has him. No matter how many Liselles there may have been or may yet be, she's the centre of their private world. His eyes, his hands, his strength, and his hunger are on her and for her alone.

He draws the scene out through more cycles of pleasure and pain than she can truthfully bear, so many more that he only relents when her whimpering barely ceases between caresses and whipping. When he goes to release her bonds, he fucks her long and hard belabouring and cumming in each of her body's openings. He finishes in her rear, while using yet another of his vibrators on her clit and the swollen flesh around her opening to bring her to yet another crashing orgasm.

Stillness comes to them both, he above and about Ella Jane, she below and in her turn about him, supported by the frame she's bound to. He releases her in the fullness of time, though he has to support her when he does so. By then she, isn't sighing, crying, or calling out. Her capacity to do all of these things is utterly exhausted. Only the heat lamps and his body keep her from shivering as he carries her inside. He bears her to their huge bed and wraps her in its soft covers.

When he makes to leave her there her fingers clutch at him, "Please..."

He stops and sits. "Hey," his hand strokes her arm and her hair, and his lips brush her cheek. "I'm just going to shut the French windows.

After getting back into bed, she holds onto him. He responds by gently wrapping an arm around her, but that isn't enough for her, and her embrace becomes more urgent. "Please."

"Aren't you sore?"

"Not too sore? Are you?"

He chuckles, "No, not quite." Then he rolls over her. There are winces, giggles and ouches as they arrange their tired bodies. He enters her as he works up a rhythm, but every time he asks if she's okay she urges him on. She complains that her clit can't take any more when he reaches down to work her over the edge and manages a tired sort of orgasm when the tips of his fingers press her rosebud and perineum against his penetrating cock.

She kisses him fiercely in its aftermath and pleads, "Fuck me."

Despite the hour and his earlier exertions, he builds up to a frantic pace. She does all she can with her internal muscles and whenever exhaustion makes him slacken her hold on his haunches tightens urging him on. Eventually his drained body stiffens, and he lets out a stream of guttural sounds while she kisses his shoulders and neck.

They lie together afterwards once again, this time on their sides and facing one another, he on his left, she on her right. "Do you really prefer this to play and sex?"

His brow furrows, and he brushes an imaginary curl from her cheek. "Maybe not prefer as such."

"You said it was your favourite thing."

"We can't do aftercare without the play before, and aftercare is the thing some people don't get. It's the complete intimacy that follows on after an intense scene. So in that way, it's my favourite."

"Don't receive or don't understand?"

"Yes." He grins.

"That's a sneaky answer."

"I'm a sneaky person. I meant understand, but both now you mention it."

She evaluates him through her curls. "You aren't really sneaky. Maybe crafty?"

"I'll take crafty." He touches his head to hers.

"Speaking of things, we've talked about..."

"Yes?"

"You said you'd tell me your thoughts about dominance and submission properly if we met in real life."

"Dominance is about freedom used responsibly and about the enjoyment of that freedom within that limit."

"And submission?"

"Submission is about exploring your fantasies, your hopes and fears, pleasure, pain, surrender. It's about giving yourself over to the desires and wishes of another, having the choice, and revelling in the illusion of having that choice taken away." As he speaks, he slips an arm behind her to take hold of her left arm, pinning it and, in so doing, trapping her right arm beneath her body and her body against his.

"Is that so?"

"It is. Though, there are many things that are important on both sides of the slash."

"Such as?"

"The ability to accept the absolute attention of a partner." He chuckles. "Of course, sometimes a submissive gets to cheat on these by blissing out or their D wanting them to take a passive role."

"And how do you know that if you've never been a submissive?"

"Study, asking, reading. Every submissive is their own unique blend, but there is a common core that unites every pet, brat, good girl, bad girl, prey, and primal. It brings together the eager slave, the home submissive, and the bedroom player."

"So you know everything?" Her face glows with the kind of mock innocence she's used in the past to signal her need for a partner to go harder.

His fingertips take a hold of Ella Jane by the tip of a breast. He toys with it, letting go of its bud and stroking around her areole without quite inflicting the torture she thought she'd earned. "More a case of knowing enough to realise I'm never going to know everything or read everyone perfectly."

She twists her torso a fraction, making as if to pull her tender bud from his grip, but in reality, only moving far enough to cause his hold on her to stretch it and the sensitive tissue behind it in the way she adores.

"Hmm!" His voice rumbles. His eyes make a stern enquiry, one that makes her pause her breath and tentatively bite her lower lip. "Let me see."

He shifts, rises above her, and rolls her onto her back, allowing him to use both arms.

The change in positions also frees Ella Jane's arms. Rather than use that freedom to try to protect herself, she reaches towards to the sides of the bed, abandoning her breasts and their tender tips to whatever fate he has in stall for them.

"One thing I think I do know though."

"Yes?"

"Is how to judge whether a submissive is interesting enough to put in this much effort."

He makes her laugh, and then responds to her laughter, and he makes her cry out both in pain and pleasure, and she embraces both rather than merely submitting to them, and both surrender themselves to the act on union which comes before the fading of their awareness.

Their Morning After

He wakes her gently and gives her coffee in bed without any chiding about who should be serving who. She accepts with a sleepy smile, though when she tries to sit up to enjoy it, she winces and lets out a low hiss at the way her body complains.

Unperturbed, he slides under the duvet next to her, places a coffee scented kiss on her lips. Then he eases one arm beneath her thighs and his other under her shoulders.

Ella Jane lets out a soft *ouch,* but he manages to get her wedged up against the pillows and headboard and presents her with her cup. Lifting her arms to accept it forces a second complaint from her lips, and a giggle follows. "That was intense!"

"You did ask for it."

She sips and holds her cup in one hand while she reaches down to his morning enthusiasm. "I did. I wanted him to go to sleep thinking of me." She tightens her grip and as he makes an appreciative sound she grins and draws his foreskin back.

His face tightens, and he murmurs, "Sorry, still a bit sensitive from last night."

"Have I broken my insatiable Sir?" Her voice is laced with sympathy but her eyes light up.

He answers her by licking the tips of his fore and middle fingers and setting them above her hood.

She lets out a little squeaked, "Owh!"

"Would you like me to diddle you?" His eyebrow rises and one corner of his mouth curly up in a cocky smile.

"No, not yet. He seems to have broken me too." She reaches across and touches his cock. It's hot to the touch, and his foreskin feels swollen. "And I might have broken him a bit."

His teeth take a hold of his lower him to stifle a smile, but they give up and he chuckles, "But it was worth it!" Then he leans in to kiss her.

Ella Jane manages to answer, "So worth it." Between kisses and giggles. "We should tidy..."

She turns toward the French windows that lead to the roof terrace and she sees the restraints, toys, and whips have all been brought inside and are laid out neatly. At some point in the night, he must have got up and collected them.

"You've already done it."

"I brought them in once you were sleeping. I didn't want the dew to get on them."

She pouts her disappointment. "I'm sorry. I was dead to the world."

He cups her shoulder with a comforting palm. "You were. So was I a few minutes later. I'll help you clean them up and put them away when you're ready to get out of bed."

"Are you going easy on me after last night?"

"Yes." He brushes the backs of his fingers against her cheek. "Think of it as the aftercare we fell asleep before we could share."

She takes a hold of his hand and brings it to her lips. "More like passed out."

For the first time since he started putting her through her morning exercise routine, he doesn't demand that she do more than the previous day. He still makes sure he has a whip with him, but he breaks from his habit and only uses his voice and guiding hands to *encourage* her.

It's just as well. Her body is still aching, and her mind still fogged. Though Ella Jane's spirit is willing, her limbs fail to do more than plod through the regime. He even eases up on her spreader bar stretching, and in deference to her soreness, there's no teasing and no edging. He just uses his fingers on her perineum, a vibe against her g-spot and the palm of his other hand on the top of her pubic bone to grant her a simple, tender orgasm before releasing her.

He works her shoulders and hips through their ranges of motion while she's still in her post orgasmic haze and sinks his strong fingers into the places where her body's aches are most intense. Then he bathes her in the shower. They dry one another, and he slathers her from knees to neck in a soothing concoction from his aftercare box. As he does, she examines her body in the bathroom's mirrors.

Her fingers trail across her breasts, buttocks and thigh awakening memories of her whipping, and she breathes, "There isn't a single mark!"

"Did you want there to be?"

"Maybe, I'm not sure. Wearing reminders might be nice, but there's still the feeling, so it's like wearing them inside. That's..."

He pauses in his ministrations and touches his lips to hers. "More intimate?"

"Sort of, yes. I like that." And she kisses him back.

They've only just emerged from their post exercise shower when Ella Jane's phone rings. She looks at the screen and mouths, "Sorry." But he just shrugs, wraps the towel he's been drying her with around her shoulders and takes his own into the bedroom.

When she emerges, she's grinning from ear to ear.

He asks, "Who was that?"

"Cynthia." The word almost explodes from her mouth.

Although he guesses, he wants to draw the story out of her. "Your agent?"

"Yes! She's arranged an interview with The Washington Post for me tomorrow."

He chuckles. "Lucky old you."

"Be nice. I'm not used to this sort of thing."

"I am being nice." He rises and goes to her, puts a hand on her shoulder and kissed her cheek. "Well done. They didn't ask me. You can use the room for your interview if you like."

"I love the way you call this palace a room."

"Hotel room. It's a generic term."

"It's hardly a generic room though." She gives him a sidelong look. "Six hardly generic rooms."

"Well, the offer stands. It's comfortable, and I can hide upstairs while you and the butler service play host."

"Will they mind?"

He scoffs. "I've never met a journalist who minded swanking around in the lap of luxury."

"Isn't that just a bit mean?"

"Are you meeting a journalist?"

"Yes."

"And are journalists people?"

"Yes."

"Well, sort of. They're a kind of writer, so it's debateable. But have you ever met a person who didn't like the lap of luxury even if they were too proud to admit it?"

“I’m not sure. Maybe not.”

“Well then.”

“You should have been a lawyer.”

His face hardens. “I’d rather be a journalist.”

They breakfast in the suite, dressed in robes and with service. The weary Ella Jane is grateful for the attentive butler’s care, and for the mountain of food He’s ordered, and He is both careful to ensure she eats well and keen to satisfy his prodigious appetite.

When they finally finish, she’s of a mind to curl up and doze, but he insists they take a turn in Central Park to clear out the cobwebs after sleeping late. Ella Jane is initially reluctant, but he mentions the bat and maybe being able to visit the Ladies Pavilion without it scaring her.

“Do you mean visiting the scene of our crime?”

“It wasn’t a crime. Nobody saw. The law’s funky like that.”

“By about sixty seconds.”

He shrugs. “I’m a man. Sixty seconds can be important.”

“You only said that to get me to say how much more than sixty seconds worth you are, didn’t you?”

“Maybe. Now get dressed and we can take an innocent photograph of you by the lake as a memento.”

Unwilling to simply accept his decision no matter how appealing the idea is, Ella Jane carries on complaining. But her heart isn’t in it. For his part, he’s already decided her curiosity’s going to win out, so he heads upstairs to change.

She watches him go with her hands on her hips, and allows him a minute to come back and listen. She then waits another while, determined not to meekly follow. Her feet edge to the foot of the sweeping staircase though, and from there she hears him whistling cheerfully.

Her sense of triumph is short lived though. He may be coming down, but he’s dressed and has clothes and sneakers for her in his hand.

“You just left while I was talking!”

"That's because we're going." She sets her jaw ready to start arguing again, and he holds out her thong and smiles. "You want to go, we're going to go. You can argue about it all you want, but you aren't going to safeword, so you might as well get dressed.

"I..." her voice fades as a sheepish smile starts forming on her face, and her hand takes the thong.

"Good girl." He lays the rest of her clothes down draws a chair out and settles down to watch her dress.

"It's a good thing I'm not self-conscious."

He raises one eyebrow while lowering his other and hardens his voice. "It's a better one I'm not biting. However, I am getting close to the point at which my patience might start to interfere with my appetite for fun."

After that, Ella Jane keeps her complaining comments to herself. She doesn't even say anything about the fact he didn't bring down a bra for her.

As she dresses, the magic of touch awakens works its spell on her. Each contact with the soft fabrics of her clothes awakens the sweetness of a caress or cruelty she suffered and was seduced by in the night, and sends a rush through her skin that melts into her well loved body. All the while he watches her with eyes hungry to tear or peel her clothes from her again.

She shifts, squirming under his gaze, as it warms her from the inside. "You make me so self-conscious!"

Her protest only makes his smile more wolfish though. "Judging from your blush and the way you're smiling, that's a good thing."

She tries to glare at this man whose bed she wishes she were back in, while half-dressed just makes her glow brighter, so she finishes dressing in silence and tries to ignore the pulsing in her body.

They cross 59th Street arm-in-arm and he guides her to turn right towards Fifth Avenue, to the same entrance they'd used the night before.

The day is just on the cusp between warm and cool, but the walk is short, her stomach still full from their oh-so-late breakfast, and his solidity is by her side. It's very much a walk-of-shame feeling, only without the sense of shame. It's well into the day, and she's with her lover. She looks up at him. Her glowing lover whose eyes are on her. His feet take them to back to the Gapstow Bridge first.

She leans her head against his shoulder as they walk. "Do you ever forget anything?" He lets out an amused rumble and she jokes. "Is that you not saying you don't remember forgetting anything?"

The rumble repeats, and he presses his lips to the top of her head. "Am I that obvious? Or haven't I sifted through those negatives?"

"No, it's just..." she lets her voice drift. Revelling in the moment is easier than face chasing down rabbit holes.

His arm squeezes briefly, but he doesn't answer, or ask her to complete her thought.

The park doesn't have the same vibe on a grey lunchtime as it had when they entered in the starlit night of a few hours and a few lifetimes before. For starters there are the people. An elderly couple's labradoodle uses the length of its spring leash to approach them, and they exchange brief greetings while the dog enjoys both their attention.

As they move on she nudges against him. "I didn't know you liked dogs."

"I suppose not. We haven't really had time to talk about much at all, except..."

"But we've been talking for months!"

"True, online," he chuckles with a slow sly look, "and almost exclusively about sex or writing. Since then other things have always come up."

Her hand teases as far towards his hips as she feels the well peopled pathway allows and she chuckles. "I'm sure."

They continue to chirp at one another and exchange shoulder nudges until Ella Jane can see the lake to their right. Then she stops, draws him to a halt and tilts her head upwards in the hope of a kiss.

He obliges. When they part, he slides his arm around her shoulders, and they make the rest of the way to the little pavilion in silence.

She draws him to a halt when they get close and stands, squeezing him tightly, before disengaging and approaching it alone. He allows her a moment of silent contemplation before joining her, when he does, she's running her fingers along the structure's cool cast iron. He touches her shoulder lightly and she takes his hand and ascends the steps.

The bench where they'd been sitting when her would-be rescuers arrived is vacant, so they sit and exchange foolish smiles. He glances down and notices a scrap of cord on the ground, and comments, "I'll just re-tie my lace." Then bends and fiddles with his training shoe as camouflage for palming his accidental litter.

Ella Jane sees what he's doing, and her cheeks flare. "Is that what I think it is?"

Even his face flushes as he nods in confirmation and slips the piece of evidence into a pocket. "It is unless we aren't the only bat spotters who've been in the park lately."

She puts her palm against his cheek as he speaks and angles her face up to his. Their kiss begins tenderly but deepens and he puts his arms around her. Ella Jane sighs and abandons herself to it and to her body's memories.

When they eventually part there are tears in her eyes, and embarrassed looks from the strangers around them. He ahems, straightens himself, gives her a second, more chaste kiss, then stands and takes her by the hand.

Unsettled by the surge in Ella Jane's emotions, he doesn't take her straight back to the hotel, instead he leads her by a different route, around the north of the lake and through the rambles.

His choice softens the rawness as they pass through the wooded area and past olde-worlde features, which set them light heartedly plotting future bat encounters. There are people at a faux-rustic shelter, but she plays up to their scheme by stretching her arms over her head against one of its rough columns and making eyes at him outrageously as he takes her picture. She then asks which way they need to go and races off along the path he indicates, so she doesn't have to face any possible looks of realisation.

His cut across the park takes them to the Conservatory Pond where he wants her to see the view south from by the Alice in Wonderland Sculpture.

Ella Jane admires it with him for a few moments, but she's more interested in sculpture.

"Like it?"

"I do. I know I'm a grown-up Alice, but I'm not sure if you're the Mad Hatter, the Cheshire Cat or the White Rabbit leading me on."

He draws her into his arms and lowers his lips to hers. "Well, it always teatime."

Her arms tighten around his waist, and she presses her head against his chest. "Hmm, just don't smile and disappear."

It's another book it seems they have in common, and the banter is too good to let it go. "Ha, I'll tell you a secret. I may be mad, but I'm not that mad."

Wrapped in his arms and with her face tucked against his warmth Ella Jane's, mind drifts to Lewis Carroll's whimsical exchange. "All the best people are." She clings and blinks until the sudden welling abates, and he holds her in silence.

When his sense of awkwardness passes, he suggests, "Literary walk?"

Ella Jane sniffs and blinks again before braving looking up. "To pick out your spot?"

"Ha, *our spots*. Come on." He takes her hand and leads her back West towards the lake, this time heading south along the shore path to Bethesda Terrace.

The angel of the water fountain is surrounded by a mix of office workers and tourists sitting on the stone and eating their lunch. They don't linger, though Ella Jane asks him to take her take photograph by the steps.

He snaps a dozen while she tries different poses and sends them to her as they make their way through the terrace. "You didn't ask me to do this last night."

Ella Jane grins back. "No, I should have though."

"You do know I'll remember that?"

In answer she steps away from him until their outstretched hands are all that connect them. "Why do you think I told you?"

He pulls her close again with a laugh. "So playful."

Her Lesson

When they return to their suite, there are two, three-way vanity mirrors and a table in the hallway. He expresses his satisfaction with an *Excellent!* then turns to face her without explaining further.

Ella Jane sets down her purse and raises her eyebrows, hoping against hope that he won't make her ask. When he volunteers nothing, she purses her lips and asks, "What did you get the mirrors for?"

He reaches out a hand and brushes his knuckles along her cheek, and his face slides into a lopsided grin. "So you can see things in them."

"I see." She sets her eyes on his and holds his gaze until her insides clench. "And what do you want me to see in your mirrors?"

"Guess."

She knows him well enough by now to make an educated guess. "Me or us."

His eyes rove down the length of her body and back to hers. "Close."

A flush rises to her cheeks. There's only one way her answer can have been close. "Me *and* us."

"Such a clever girl." He leans forward and touches his lips to hers. "I think that earns you a reward."

"Thank you." No matter how manufactured his praise is, it still warms her. Of course, praise has another side to him, and to their play, and the warmth spreads further as she takes the opportunity to poke the bear. "Now all you need to do is invent a reason to punish me as well, and your evening is set up."

"Hmph, if I were being picky, I could choose that little touch of sassiness."

Ella Jane opens her mouth and eyes wide and holds her hand to her lips in feigned surprise. "Oh no!"

"However, I think it might be a good idea if you sat down and spent a few minutes writing out the thoughts you had about how Abigail would feel about the park."

She takes her time telling him how the park's curated imitation of nineteenth century countryside would initially offend and then charm Abigail. Then she describes how her character's imagination would see weddings at the Ladies Pavilion, like in the photographs online, rather than innocent young women encountering bats.

Having got her writing, he leaves her for a short while. When he returns, he takes her feet onto his lap and massages their soles. When she pauses, he asks her more questions and encourages her to set down her, and Abigail's, thoughts. Eventually, feeling she has done enough, he asks, "Did you have a productive writing sprint?"

Her eyes look away, but his *ahem* draws them back to him, and she confesses, "I did."

Crow's feet of happiness spread from the corners of his eyes, and he continues to lovingly soothe the foot under his thumbs. "And are you now feeling tremendously grateful?"

There's so much she wants to say, and to ask, about how he seeps into every aspect of her life, demanding she cares for and works on herself, and supports her in doing so. About how he's there, larger and more real than the world around, outside the bedroom as well as inside it. But those are hard questions and hard things to admit out loud, and she's with him and he's teasing and his eyes are on her and filled with desire and... "Have any of your submissives ever told you you make a graceless winner when you want to provoke them into deserving to be tied up and taught a lesson?"

He nods. "One or two, yes. Why do you ask?"

"Wouldn't it be simpler just to say playtime?"

"I suppose I could, or I could ask if you've looked in the spare room."

She jumps up. "Am I getting another massage?"

"Not exactly. I think a class would be appropriate." He grins at his own cleverness and her puzzled expression. "Your comment about being tied up and taught a lesson was too good to pass up."

"You said you didn't like the naughty schoolgirl thing."

The devilish doesn't leave his eyes. "This is more a case of adult education."

He leads her into the downstairs bedroom. "Ideally I'd have an examination chair, cameras, and screens, but seeing as how you're the only student, this will do."

Her eyes take in the details of his latest kinky DIY creation. They may not have a chair, but he does have the massage bed, two spreader bars, the mirrors, and a selection of toys. He's tilted the top section of the massage bed up to its highest setting and tied his homemade adjustable spreader bar and a board to the lower one. It's enough to support her upper body at a forty-five-degree angle. She tests how firmly the spreader bar is attached and gives him a sideways smile when she finds she can't move it at all. "Very clever. I'd wondered what you'd snuck out to do."

"Now you know."

"I do. I suppose you're going to want me to undress again?"

"Yes, if you wouldn't mind that is?"

Her eyes dare him. "And if I would?" And his face turns to stone as he rolls up the sleeves of his shirt without taking his eyes from her. Left with a choice between cooperating and not playing, she slowly raises her hands and begins to unbutton her shirt. She's always been comfortable with her body, whether clothed or unclothed, but usually when she's been with someone they've both just taken their clothes off. The ritual of undressing while the gaze of a man, who knows her body as well as she knows it herself, burns into her is still new and still exciting. Expectant tingles flow across her skin as she slides her shirt off. She then faces him to bend and pull her pop-socks off. Doing so exposes her décolletage to his hungry gaze. It challenges her transitional shyness, but also stokes her passions. When she straightens, his eyes linger on her chest before returning to her needful eyes and flushed face.

Her flush deepens as she undoes her jeans and pushes them down over her hips. Her insides pulse as she wriggles them the rest of the way down and kicks her legs free. She turns as she folds them conscious of her matching underwear and of his eager gaze.

"You're always so prettily dressed."

She twists and poses. "Thank you, and for once a change I'm wearing my own, not yours."

Once she's naked, he has her climb onto the impromptu doctor's couch, guides her feet up level with her hips, and allows her to shift to make herself more comfortable. He sets an open hand above her openings until a slow flush and a shy smile communicate her understanding of how she has opened herself up to him before he secures her ankles to the ends of the bar. Next, he adjusts the bar stretching her feet further apart until they're perhaps six inches beyond the edges of the bed.

Having got her into position, he binds her upper body to the raised section, cross tying soft ropes from her shoulders to below her ribs framing her breasts. He completes her bondage by drawing her knees wide, looping ropes under the bed and securing her legs at the knees as well.

Contentment fills his face as he secures her, and when he's satisfied with his work, he arches an eyebrow enquiringly.

"Can you move?"

She understands exactly what he means, but waves her unfettered arms nonetheless. Then she grins at his frown and tries to close her legs and move her body. After a few efforts, they're both satisfied that all she can manage is a little wriggling and hold her legs a fraction wider for a short time.

He strokes a palm along the ropes framing her breasts and asks, "How does this bind feel?"

Her teeth worry at her lip; he's already so pleased with himself about his relationship with her breasts. "You know!"

"I think I do, but I want you to tell me."

"I like the pressure. It makes my breasts feel as though they're waiting to be touched."

"And here?" He strokes the insides of her thighs out to where the ropes hold them wide.

The muscles of her inner thighs and around her opening flex in response. "Open, exposed."

Warm?" She nods, and he declares, "Excellent," and sets about arranging one of the three-way-mirrors to give her a triple view of her own folds and openings...

The bound Ella Jane tries to snipe back, but after the sensual joy of surrendering to his bondage, anticipation leaks into her voice as she chides, "You would say that."

"I would and did. Good job you like this sort of thing too."

"It is, isn't it? You could get in trouble otherwise."

Leaning down next to her, he checks the angles of the mirror's three panes. "Feeling exposed?"

She looks down at her intimate reflections, then gives him a raised eyebrowed look. "What do you think?"

He chuckles as he reaches to his stash of equipment without taking his eyes off her and picks up a jar.

"Coconut oil, not lube?"

"We aren't using anything it might affect today, so yes." He opens the jar. "Do you want me to do the honours?"

She sighs. "Are you sure this isn't just an excuse to grope me again?"

His eyebrow rises as she asks, but the amusement doesn't leave his eyes. "I could just do that, couldn't I?"

"Yes, but you men do like to overcomplicate things."

He lets that bounce off his impassive expression and continues coating her thighs, stomach, breasts, and vulva with the sweet oil.

When he presses the slickness against her rosebud, she lets out a squeak, then smiles. "You still haven't told me what kind of adult education you had planned."

"You seemed curious about my salons, so I thought I'd give you a quick run through of my basic female pleasure one."

Taking her bondage and his liberal use of oil into account Ella Jane enquires, "Basic?"

"Basic for us, anyway."

He tries beginning with a low-level anatomy lesson and starts that lesson with some ice-breakingly basic points.

"This is your left breast, and this..." he pauses for effect while she tries to work out whether to laugh or be offended, "is your right breast." He bends and places a solemn kiss on it. "Though I imagine right now you're thinking of me and the phrase, *Right tit*."

At this point, his perfect poker face cracks, and Ella Jane laughs her relief.

The buds atop her breasts begin to stiffen, and he teases each in turn as he patiently says, "Left nipple," and, "Right nipple."

She snipes, "Nipple is the word." Then she grins as he winks in response.

"I thought you might have waited till I got around to asking about this." His fingertips graze across her rosebud.

Her lips part in a sigh of pleasure that soon turns into a smile of mischief, and she mimics his schoolroom enunciation. "Ass-hole."

"Arse-hole."

"No, I'm American. It's my ass-hole. You're English, so you're my arse-hole." When he swats her inner thigh, she yelps but doesn't stop giggling. "If you keep this up, you're going to have to let me go to the bathroom before I've learned anything."

He places his index finger and thumb onto her outer labia close to the top of her slit and gently presses up causing the pearl of her clitoris to peek out from under its hood. Then he, quite deliberately, straightens the mirror between her legs and licks his right thumb before touching it to her centre. "And what's this?"

Ella Jane savours the slight stretching of her intimate flesh and the pressure and warmth of his hand, but his comment is so ridiculous. "Why, Sir! I believe you may have finally found my clitoris!" She knows exactly what she's doing and what that result is going to be. She is both laughing and begging before he has time to start preparing his inevitable retribution.

With her legs already bound far apart, he doesn't have to worry about them, so he goes for her wrists. There's not much she can do to keep them out of his grasp, but she makes the effort nonetheless and adds a token struggle when he tries to pin them together in one hand. She doesn't succeed, and he soon has then stretched over her head.

Once he has her where he wants, he looks her sternly in the eyes. "Do you accept that you deserve to be funished?"

She attempts to pout without a smile spoiling the effect. "Isn't this a bit unfair that when you make jokes I just laugh, but when I make them, you laugh *and* whack me?"

"It's desperately unfair, but you like being funished almost as much as you like teasing me."

Ella Jane bites her lips until she can be sure of not smiling as she answers, "That isn't the point."

He strokes the index finger of his right hand through her slick folds and holds it up glistening in front of her eyes. "Do you believe that?"

"No." She moves her lips close to his fingertip and takes it into her mouth.

"Well then," he observes and slides the finger in and out and observes, while she swirls her tongue around it.

When he withdraws his finger, she licks her lips and strains her legs wider still than her bonds hold them.

That, and the way she holds her breath, tempt him to spank her right away. But he strokes down the length of her body to savour her submission first. He takes the time to circle her breasts and trace the lines of her eager swollen outer lip then cups her vulva and bends to breathe in her ear, "Ready?"

It's not as if she can escape. He has her where he wants her. Even if she weren't holding her thighs as far apart as she's able, she couldn't close them enough to protect herself from him. Of course, she doesn't want to.

Ella Jane draws a slow breath, licks her lips and answers *yes* in a low voice thick with emotion.

He raises his hand and strikes.

The slap is hard, and loud, but he keeps his had cupped to the curve of her body, so it strikes the whole of her vulva.

She bucks and cries out as the shockwave surges through her being. Her reflexes try to free her hand to protect and comfort her outraged flesh, but the strength of his left hand holds them. Meanwhile, his right hand turns from torturer to carer and applies light caresses and caring warmth as the pleasure that follows spreads outwards.

He dreamily trails his hand along her inner thigh as he watches the muscles around her opening pulse. "I really want to do this properly, but I promised you your lesson."

Looking up at him with dilated eyes, she tempts him. "I'm sure the lesson can wait."

"Hmm. Lesson first. I might have to chastise you properly if you prove a poor student."

Ella Jane tilts her head to one side. "And if I call you a spoil sport?"

"Then I'll address that after your class and might not let you cum during it."

That stops her in her tracks.

He raises a stern eyebrow and hardens his voice. "So you won't be doing that, will you?"

Her cheeks twitch with amusement. "Um, no."

The devil peeks through in the depths of his eyes as he rumbles, "Good girl. Now first of all, I want you to show me how you touch yourself."

Ella Jane swallows and knits her brow. "Is that strictly necessary?"

"In a salon I'd normally have my assistants demonstrate for the group, but it's just you and me. So this is more so I can see what you know and what you enjoy."

She colours and smiles. "I don't know why this makes me self-conscious."

He gently takes her hands in his and guides her favoured right hand to rest over her mons and opening and lays her left over her right breast. "Rest, breathe, and feel. There's no hurry to start."

"I still feel self-conscious."

He calmly lays a hand on her shoulder. "Take your time. If you prefer, you can close your eyes while you start, or I could blindfold you."

The notion is tempting – to not have to see him seeing her. But it strikes her as something she shouldn't do; it's better to face her embarrassment and use it to fuel her arousal. "The idea is that I watch though?"

The way his eyes light up is a reward in itself. "That's right."

With a swallow, and a silent rosary to her unsaintly heroine O, Ella Jane resolves to continue. "No, thank you."

It takes her a further minute to begin. She starts with her left hand. First, she strokes the side of her breast and then its undercurve, before moving on trailing a single fingernail around her areola. All the while her eyes study his face for signs of approval. His nod brings a flush to her cheeks and a smile to her lips. She continues her experimental caress. The tip of her breast swells and hardens in response to her touch and their communion.

Ella Jane pinches it lightly from the sides and kneads its sensitivity, and as she does, she presses her curved hand more firmly over her opening. The fluttering comes quickly, but she knows there's more beyond that. He's already shown her he has the patience, so she carries on until the flares of connection flicker out from her breasts, and down to her centre.

He lays a hand over hers and nods his encouragement again. "Tell me how you feel here?"

"Full. Ready." She lets her mouth stay open and touches her tongue to her teeth. "Though that may have something to do with being tied up."

"Then start when you wish."

She moves her left hand to her left breast and stokes herself there until its bud stiffens before letting her right hand begin.

Wanting to show off what she's seen and learnt not just show him her usual, *quick cum* routine she starts with a pulsing of her whole hand, then slides her ring and index fingers up along the length of her outer labia. The slickness he applied allows them to glide over her skin in a delicious, but unfamiliar, way. As they do, her lips curl upwards. "I like the oil."

He gives her a wink, and she bites her tongue to stop herself sticking it out. The oil is nice after all. After a second pass along her outer lips, she slips her fore and middle fingers into her folds and around her hood and squeezes a little.

It's what she usually does – trap her clit but not too hard, then press and circle until she cums. But showing her exotic lover that isn't something she's prepared to do, so she breaks off when the pulsing sensation starts to build in her. Instead, she pushes her hand further down and curls her middle finger into her opening. She can't press her thighs together, but she still gets something by tensing against her bondage as she reaches in rubs.

This is the other half of her *I've got some time*, technique, though not her full *I don't care how much noise I make* method. On those occasions when she has both time and a place to herself, she uses her vibe on her clit and either her nJoy inside, or a plug to finish.

"Is that what you do?"

"Um, when I have time, I swap between the two until I cum."

"Very good. What about toys?"

Ella Jane tells him it all, the words coming out in a rush and continues her self-touch. She adds something she rarely tries by lightly stroking a fingernail along her folds. Then she appropriates the pinching of her perineum that he introduced her to on their first night in an effort to impress him.

He lets her talk herself out and watches as, having done so, her focus returns to what she's doing. He observes how her hips begin to rock against her hand and her breathing quickens. "How are you feeling now?"

"Fuck, so good, so naughty."

Her flush, breathing and the ways she's moving are all dead giveaways, but he asks. "Are you getting close?"

She closes her eyes and nods. "Uh-hum"

"If you hadn't been talking, would you have cum by now?"

"Ha," she stops speaking, pants and lets out a sigh. "Oh-God, probably." And just then, he takes a firm hold of her by her wrists. Ella Jane resists for a moment, then subsides with a whimper.

He pins her wrists together in one hand, and stretches her arms above her head again while he strokes her face and neck with his other. "Do you think you'd have had a bigger orgasm after?"

She pouts, "I would if –"

"If I'd let you, you'd also have been too fuzzy headed to concentrate."

Ella Jane doesn't answer. She doesn't care about concentrating, but she also doesn't want to disappoint him. "In a salon, two or three volunteers would be invited to show the group their techniques, and we'd have a discussion. Then I'd take work how best to proceed depending on what was said."

"And with me?"

"You've shown you know the basics."

He returns his hand to her mons and draws her hood back again and touches the tip of the pearl under it. Then he waits for her body to respond and for her to recover enough to focus on him. "You called this your clit. The anatomical term is clitoral glans, very like the male one only cuter and with even more nerve endings.

It sometimes gets unbearably sensitive after one or more orgasms are caused by stimulating it. This is particularly true when doing so directly." He presses and circles then commands her to touch herself there.

Ella Jane sighs as he strokes her. Then she tentatively reaches her middle finger down and mimics his caress. "I saw a video saying the clitoris is more than people think. I had a lot of fun trying to find the different parts."

He grins and allows her hood to cover her centre again then slides it back. "And this is your prepuce, very like my foreskin –"

"Only smaller."

Her interruption was well timed for his intention. "Yes, it's sensitive and flexible, nice to caress, stretch, pinch and apply electricity or clamps to." With those words of warning, he pinches it sharply between his nails, and as she pants to process the sudden outrage, he adds, "Quite a common place to pierce in the community."

Ella Jane bites her lower lip as she waits for the stab of pain to pass and the warm flood of sexual heat to follow. Piercings are on her list of hard noes, but talking and thinking about them isn't. "With a piercing it only hurts once, but you can do that again as often as you want."

"As long as you agree to it, yes."

He allows her hood to cover her clit again and strokes over its opening. "Stimulating the clitoral glans through the prepuce provides a less intense sensation, but it's easier for a woman to bear to experience multiple orgasms when touching indirectly."

Once again, he strokes her until her breathing accelerates. Then he has her copy his caress until he's satisfied. "My hand feels different to yours."

"I should hope so." He holds his hand and forearm up. "Put yours against mine." Every part of her hand and arm is smaller and more delicate.

"I know you're bigger."

"For the purpose of this, just different." He strokes his fingers against hers. "Your skin is softer, and your fingers and hands can get places mine can't. But I can apply more force for things like that heavy press on your mons."

"I like that."

He chuckles, "I've noticed. Several times." He kisses her taste from her still raised fingertips. "I rather like it myself. Now back to class. What comes below a man's glans?"

"Man's glans." She repeats the rhyme. "His shaft."

"Good girl. This is where yours is." He places his fore and index fingers side by side with their tips over her hood and presses the top joints against the little section of engorged flesh above her clit. He then strokes up and down with a slow, rhythmic motions of his hand.

It doesn't take long for her to begin using the little freedom she has to rock her hips against his touch. "This is an effective masturbation technique, analogous to the conventional hand job technique on a man. When you're turned-on, pressure over the swollen tissue can be enjoyable."

He speaks like a professor, but his eyes watch her like a hungry animal. Ella Jane blurts, "Can Be?" and starts to giggle.

He pulls his hand away and delivers a sharp smack to her wide-open vulva, then resumes his caressing as if nothing had happened.

She gasps at the sudden impact, but it breaks her fit of laughter. "Sorry. Biology lessons were never like this."

"I should hope not. A flat handed smack to the vulva is an effective way of curing girlish giggles but very much a between consenting adults sort of a thing." His hand continues as he speaks. After her laughter it takes her body longer to be return to a state of high arousal, but his patience with her body is boundless. He slowly adjusts his pressure and pace until her body reacts and then maintains them.

Eventually her breathing hastens, and her tongue touches her lips. He carries on until her hips start rocking again. Then guides her hand to her opening and moves his away. This time she shows less reticence in masturbating while they both watch. She quickly finds a rhythm she likes. When she does, he commands her to mirror his actions as he cups and squeezes the underside of her right breast in time with the motion of her hand.

Before long, the matching caresses cause rivulets of pleasure to flow between the three erogenous zones. Her body starts to accelerate towards its release. Rather than let her cum though, he has her repeat the details of the lesson so far. She curses her lost orgasm in the privacy of her mind even as she answers. The entire time, she doesn't miss a beat of her caressing until he pulls her hand away.

He continues upwards placing the heel of his hand over the strong bone above her opening and leans a fraction of his mass down onto her there.

Ella Jane's teeth take a hold of her lower lip more tightly as he increases the force he applies to pubic bone. She knows what to expect, and her body doesn't disappoint her. Waves of pleasure build up in the dense bone and radiate out, first through her sex and then beyond.

She watches his hand on her until the welling up of suffusing heat from deep in the bone beneath his hand then lets her lids fall and breathes, "You love making me cum like this, don't you?"

Instead of asking Ella Jane or telling her he knows full well that she's partial too, he chuckles, "It's okay." Then he eases his hand aside and has her place both of hers, one on top of the other, in its place.

No matter how hard she tries, she can't exert the force he does, and the sense of lava flowing through her body dissipates.

"Some women like to lie face down and do this, so they can use their body-weight and the strength of their hips to increase pressure to a level where they can get a nice buzz going or even cum."

"Is that so?"

He lends her a portion of his physical power by pressing down over her hands and her body reacts instantly. "It is. Some men do the same. It's a fashionably androgynous erogenous zone."

Her cheeks twitch. “Do you deliberately include puns and rhymes to stop your demonstration models cumming?”

“To delay, not stop.”

“Mmm, Professor Cum.”

“You can get a more intense effect by going a little higher.” He uses his covering hand to ease hers to the top of her pubic bone, and a flood of desire gushes through her. “Good?”

“Fuck, so good.” There’s hope in her voice, but he soon dashes in by withdrawing his hand. Without it the energy her body needed dissipates.

He only does so though in order to pass her the steel toy from the table by the bed. “Put this under the heel of your hand and try again.”

She does, and the steels curve and hardness concentrate her strength enough to renew the flow. Though the joyous rush isn’t enough to prevent her teasing him. “You’re going to be even more insufferable after this, aren’t you?”

“I haven’t finished yet.”

He talks through what he does with her fourchette, perineum, and the outer part of her anus, using just his hands and having her repeat his caresses. In the process he brings her close, makes her laugh and then makes her edge herself again.

While she’s recovering from her denial, she asks, “Is the lesson over?”

“Nope, but you can have the quick version if you prefer.”

Her eyes narrow suspiciously. “That’s generous of you.”

“Not really, I probably want to fuck you as much as you want to cum.”

“Quick then.”

He beams and bends to kiss her lips, “If you like it, we can always do the long one another time.” Then he picks up the steel toy and the wand.

“What’s the slow version?”

He strokes her skin, and his eyes look into hers as if seeking to see her memories of their shared intimacy. “One, then the other, then some sensory play, and finally both for the main event.”

Ella Jane has no way to be sure what his eyes see other than herself, but the intensity of their focus raises a heat to her cheeks, one that her memories multiply. "You've already done that part to me more than once."

His voice as he answers is rich with honey contentment. "Is that a complaint?"

"No, just an observation."

He holds up the two toys one after the other and introduces them. "Dildo. Vibrator." He points both down at her waiting yoni. "Best job in the world!"

First, he tests the vibrator. It buzzes, and when he touches it to her, Ella Jane buzzes too. Certain that only the briefest use of the toy would enable her to achieve a much-needed orgasm, she volunteers. "Shall I show you how I use that too?"

"You seem to have grown less shy."

She touches her tongue to her front teeth. "It's your bad influence."

"Not your sweet nature coming out?" He runs the vibrator's tip along each of her outer lips in turn, making her squirm and squeak with pleasure. "You can show me in a while." With that he takes up the steel toy in his left hand.

She squirms and clutches at the bed and his arms as he traces each part of her vulva with the toy's rounded end, with the wand and then with the toy again, but with the wand pressed against it.

He encourages her, "If you're having trouble finding something to do with your hands, you can touch your breasts. Or I could tie them if you'd prefer?"

Ella Jane blasphemes again but does as asked. She also does her best to repeat the names of each place he touches.

He sandwiches her every part of her vulva between the wand's vibrating head and the dildos steel shaft and studies her reaction to each. Whether it sets her on the path to orgasm? How long it takes her to get close. Every time he edges her, then backs off and edges her again. Then he finally commands the increasingly desperate Ella Jane demonstrate her understanding. She reaches down. Each time he has her touch herself, her reticence fades, but the thrill of exposure and the sense that she's breaking a taboo remain. Having taken her close by the same method, and having made her cum so often in previous sessions, he sees the signs and is able to force her hands away in time to prevent her achieving the release she craves.

She sobs when, after a bare second, he pulls her hands away from sandwiching her hood between the wand and the steel dildo's hardness, and he reads it as a sign that she's endured all the teasing she can bear "Have we tried enough things?" She blinks up and he repeats his question.

Her eyes narrow suspiciously. "That depends."

His sudden smile almost does the job on its own. "Are you ready for your test?" He releases her hands and gestures that she's free to use them as she wishes. Then he lays his left hand over her pubic bone and takes a hold of her fourchette to perineum with his right.

Ella Jane resumes her self-touch using the two toys and does her best to drag this final build up out by sliding the toy past his thumb and into herself while she runs the vibe around her opening, each of their hands and the dildo. After getting so close so many times, and with their four hands and the two toys on her body, the tidal wave quickly overwhelms her, and in no time she begins bucking against her bonds and his grip.

She keeps the toy inside and vibrator against herself through several crushingly intense orgasms, or else through one long one with multiple peaks. He continues to play his part, until exhausted and sated, she pulls the toys away. He then holds her until her breathing calms before starting to release her from her bondage.

"So that was your female pleasure class?"

"The introductory one, yes. Well, a variation on the theme."

"Will I get to try the advanced edition?"

"If you're satisfied with my teaching, I don't see why not. It needs a little more equipment though."

"Hmm, you make a very good teacher."

"Do I?"

"Mhm. You could teach anatomy, just not to under-eighteens!" She puts her hand over her mouth and opens her eyes wide in faux horror, and they both laugh long and hard.

He transfers her from the makeshift couch to the room's emperor sized bed, and she snuggles up to him. "What equipment?"

"Hmm?"

"What extra equipment do you need for the advanced version?"

"Oh! Speculum, endoscope, Sybian, the cameras and screens."

"Have you taught it at one of Madame Alexandra's parties?"

"Not the big ones, but at a couple of gatherings, yes."

She leans her head against his chest and looks down. "It's going to take some getting used to."

"What is?"

"Other women. How they look at you. How some of them *know* you."

"Pretty much every man at the party would have loved to play with you or take you home."

She shifts uncomfortably and tries to do redirect the conversation. "Can I get another couple of things? This isn't exactly what I had planned."

"Oh? Do tell."

"Well, you were supposed to be this super-kinky, hot, older guy thing."

"Is this your way of telling me I'm not hot?"

Ella Jane winces. "No, but I thought just a thing, then a smile-making memory, not..."

His lips twitch with mirth. "Were you worried my heart would give out?"

"Ha! Not after I saw you naked anyway. Then I was more worried mine would! I thought getting together would fun, good, that we'd try some of the things we talked about, but just a thing. That or we wouldn't be into one another in the flesh. Why? What did you think?"

"I thought we'd see how things went, but it'd probably just be a thing for during the conference. I wasn't certain we'd sleep together, maybe just talk or talk and play."

"And that's why you had the invitations to the party?"

"I'd be in trouble if I came to New York and didn't see Alexandra. It was also an option for us, partly as a backup plan. It was a good party."

Her face falls. "It was..." She stops, blinks, and swallows. Then she tells him her first out and out lie, "But you decided we should leave after a couple of hours." Then waits to see how he takes it. She has to wait, but the annoyance passes from his face, and a wry amusement replaces it.

He puts his arms around her and draws her face to his shoulder so neither has to look into the others' eyes. "That was because I wanted to play with you in private."

Ella Jane sniffs but tries to recover her levity. "And in Central Park – so romantic."

He kisses the top of her head, and pours all the cheeriness he can into his, "I know, right?"

"I do." She gives him a squeeze and looks up. "You have nice friends in New York, you know."

"I suppose I do."

"Even if I'd never picture them as all being the same person's friend."

"Really?"

"Johnson, the van Beeks, Madame Alexandra."

He laughs at this relieved that she didn't mention any of the other women from the party then covers with. "Please don't tell Johnson he's a New Yorker."

She frowns. "There you go joking again."

"Then on a serious note, yes. They're different to each other, but they're all bright and thoughtful." He smiles at her again and touches a hand to her face to make it clear his words apply to her as well. "I value those qualities in a person."

His Plate and Her Interview

When Ella Jane gets downstairs, the breakfast dishes are laid out around a large space on the table top, and all but one chair has been taken away. That chair is by the large space.

She looks at the table and then at him. His face is wearing one of his self-satisfied expressions.

"You're kidding?"

He raises his eyebrows and blinks slowly.

"You aren't kidding."

He grins.

"Is this why you said I didn't need to do my hair?"

"It is."

"Because you wanted a plate?"

"Think of all the washing-up we could save."

"*You* could save?"

He agrees, "Yes." He blinks and looks at her with wide eyes.

"When other people do the washing up?"

"Yes, I suppose they do."

"And afterwards I'm going to need another shower?"

"That's right."

"I see some obvious flaws in your reasoning, Sir."

The muscles of his throat twitch with suppressed amusement, but he manages to keep his face almost entirely impassive. "Pray tell."

Ella Jane's hands half rise to her hips, then she looks away, draws in a breath, lets it out slowly and then takes another to power her voice before turning back to him and counting off. "One, like I said, I'm going to have to get cleaned up after. Two, I won't be able to feed myself, so you'll have to feed both of us. You'll have to. Three, er, we won't be able to have the butler unless you break your rules."

"Anything else?"

"Um, yes! Four, I need to get ready for my interview!"

"Ah, I see. And what makes you think I'm not trying to keep you busy and entertained rather than fretting about your interview, while I sneakily prep you for it?"

"You're serious about that, aren't you? You didn't just think that up, did you?"

"I'd love to be able to say I just thought of it, but you're smart enough to work out I said not to bother with your hair earlier."

"Very clever."

He preens, "We are. It's a burden."

And Ella Jane twists her foot on the carpet and frowns back. "And very thoughtful."

His smile broadens, but he looks over her shoulder as he answers. "That's more sort of a work in progress."

She steps right up to him, puts her arms around his waist and presses her head against him. "You're as thoughtful as you are clever, even if you don't like admitting it." Then she looks up seeking to kiss him. But his eyes evade hers, so she touches her lips to his chest and asks, "Now, how does my Sir want his plate?"

The question draws his attention back to her, and in no time, he has her lying on her back on the table with her legs parted, her hands palms up at her sides, and a small strawberry balanced on her lips.

Ella Jane doesn't know whether his intention is to test her patience or to provoke her into eating it, but she starts chuckling the moment he reaches away. She has to concentrate on neither biting it nor sending to tumbling onto the table.

She manages to restrain herself until after he's carefully poured a small dollop of thick cream onto the little fruit. Even then, she holds on until. While he's turned away pouring coffee, a drip of cream runs down to her mouth. Her lips open, and before she knows it, the strawberry is in her mouth cream and all. Only her fear of bursting into laughter and choking on the juice holds her back from biting into its sweetness.

It's the fit of stifled giggles that alerts him to her mischief. As soon as he looks her way the absent strawberry tells him what she's done.

He doesn't look at her face as he returns with glass in one hand and a pipette in his other -- not until after he's admired the way her mirth is making her breasts jiggle, though he does when he sits.

His disobedient plate looks at him, and he looks at her. They strive, unsuccessfully, to keep their expression impassive.

"Has your mouth started filling up with saliva?"

She nods.

He brushes the icy glass across her ribs, and she clenches her eyes as she fights to hold still. "You do realise I'm going to have to punish you, don't you?"

Ella Jane manages a small squeak of assent without choking herself.

A rotation of his wrist draws the chill hardness in a circle around the tip of her nearer breast. "I think you'd better eat that strawberry first though." She smiles her relief up to him as she bites. "Good?"

She nods again as she chews and swallows, though her eyes glance down nervously towards where a drip of condensation from his juice filled glass lands on the erect bud at the tip of her chilled breast.

"Ready?"

Having swallowed her delicious, and deliciously illicit morsel, Ella Jane is able to answer, "Yes, Sir."

"Good girl." After a final circle around her pert bud to get it as stiff as possible, he sips before carefully setting the glass down. Then he patiently draws a pipette full of juice from it and takes a hold of her by the nipple. "Open your mouth."

She does as commanded, and he lets a drop fall onto her waiting tongue. The sharpness of red grapefruit and the sweetness of clementines erupt from her taste buds. The blended scents flood her sense of smell as his fingers clamp tight on her vulnerable flesh and stretch her breast cruelly upwards. After releasing his hold, he sips from a cup of piping hot tea against and then strokes its heat over her chilled flesh.

He repeats his chilling and torture on her other breast and then on her opening and clit.

The combination of ritual, sensual delight and wicked pressure on her most sensitive flesh sends her rushing towards the edge, but he releases her a moment too soon and sets about soothing her tormented flesh.

His gentling with hands and lips doesn't stop when it brings her back to the edge. There's no further teasing, just a slow, confident build up to her crescendo.

The orgasm is gentle, sweet. He lets each crest rise, peak, and fade, rather than adding additional sensations and force until her nervous system is overloaded.

Its aftermath has a warm glow to it rather than the full on emotional and physical exhaustion he frequently drives her to. He praises her and strokes her hair as she recovers afterwards, then uses a second pipette to sate her thirst with thick, rich coffee, and kisses her lips before placing a second strawberry on them. "Can I trust you to behave this time?"

She nods yes, but her eyes tease, and she promises herself that someday, if he repeats this game when they have time, she'll take fruit after fruit into her mouth so she can find out what wicked things doing so will provoke him into doing to her. For now though, she has to content herself with the feather light touch of his lips on hers as he eats his strawberry from her lips.

He lays some pancakes onto her body, pours warmed maple syrup onto them, cuts and forks pieces.

She watches him with envy and anticipation as he eats, and consumes the morsels he feeds her with relish.

The pancakes are soft enough to cut on her without risk and hot enough to be *interesting* without burning, so he finishes the stack. Then he guides her hand to the wipe the residual sweetness from her skin and shares it with her from her fingertips.

Once he's out of pancakes, he lifts a sunny side up egg onto her and slices into it, sending hot yoke into her navel and running down her side.

Ella Jane smiles in relief that his care and the blunt knife keep her safe from being cut, and at the strange sensation of slow thick warmth on her skin. Then she chuckles as he curses and catches runaway drizzle of golden yoke with a piece of bread, which he then shares with her. "Have you done this before?"

"Yes, but not for ages. It takes someone with a real sense of fun to make it enjoyable." As he speaks, he carefully dunks another piece of bread into her belly button to make an eggy soldier. He feeds it to her with a strip of bacon. He then makes another for himself, which he eats while idly pressing a hot coffee cup against her opening and rolling its heat against her hooded clit.

She watches him, his enjoyment of the delicate morsel, of her submission and of her body. Then she closes her eyes and dreams daydreams inspired by the sensations in her body.

He lifts the cup away, drinks, feeds each of them, slices egg and wraps it around further strips of bacon which he shares with her. "Open your mouth and put your tongue out. Then stay perfectly still."

She smells the piece of bacon. Then her tongue registers its salty sweetness, and remaining still isn't easy. The bacon has set her saliva glands on overdrive. Another piece of lightly fried egg comes next, the soft yoke dribbling across her tongue.

"Last detail."

Finally, an ooze of maple syrup.

He strokes her face with a loving hand and breathes, "Eat," in a rapt basso rumble.

It's the most demeaning thing Ella Jane has ever experienced, or it would have been. Like a trick a circus performer might have taught a performing animal in a worse bygone age. But it's far from that. The little mouthful is a perfect piece of multitextured heaven carefully prepared to delight her.

"Good girl."

As he progresses through the meal, he pauses from time to time to caress her skin, idly diddle her, or play with her breasts. He also asks her questions he remembers facing from interviewers about his life as writer.

She answers, and he critiques until they're both content. But as their game continues, she drifts, and he allows their intimate silence to stretch.

Lying there, Ella Jane imagines herself in the role of banquet platter along with other slim, fit young men and women, punished if they move, or cum without permission, and only allowed to eat when a diner chooses to reward them. Her lips chase tid-bits of food, and dribbles of strong coffee and sweet fresh juice. And she greedily consumes those that pass her lips.

It progresses, and as it does, the experience and idea of being his plate grow on her. It's aided by his mischievous caresses easing her into an ever higher state of arousal. He runs out of eggs and cleans the last traces of them from her with licks and kisses which tickle and tingle and so does his stubble.

When he goes to kiss the taste to her mouth, she sees a residue of yoke caught in his two-day shadow moustache and takes the opportunity to lick back.

He protests, "Hey!"

She smiles, then touches her to teeth to her lower lip. "Sorry, you were eggy too."

He mutters. "Damn, I'm going to need another shower too."

The by now sticky all over Ella Jane gives him a narrowed eyed look which he blithely ignores as he carefully builds a small pile of pieces of fruit between her breasts.

"You're making me sticky again."

"So I am." The sudden touch of his icy juice glass on the outer curve of a breast jolts her out of her reverie. She starts, and the pile tumbles.

"Hmm, let me see." He slides the glass around her body touching it to each fallen morsel and counting as he goes. When he finishes, he declares, "Six. I wonder what I should do to you for spilling six pieces and stealing one of my strawberries?"

"We're going to be on the front page if you're still doing these things to me when that reporter arrives, you know!"

"I'm going to ask you seven questions about Abigail. You can escape a part of your punishment for each one you answer correctly."

"Funishment or –" His eyes narrow and the line of his mouth hardens, and Ella Jane cuts herself off.

She starts again. "What a good idea, Sir."

In truth, he only knows the answers to four of his questions.

Ella Jane answers the first six immediately and with a smug certainty. She then answers the last with so much thought and interest he believes that reply as fully as any of her others.

"She's almost real to you, isn't she?"

"I like that you understand that."

"Ha, it's a curse we bear. There are one or two of mine I know better than people in real life. Sometimes that feels like a loss and..." He winks.

And she finishes, "...and sometimes a blessing." for him.

He bends and kisses her lips. "Was that fun?"

"Yes, you..." Ella Jane doesn't finish saying *you know it was.* The mood is too serene. "Yes, more lovely than fun, but yes."

"Worth getting a bit covered in maple syrup and egg?"

She makes a face, but grins afterwards. "Yes. I definitely need to wash again though."

"Let's get you cleaned up so you can wow your audience." And just like that, she's his duchess again. They shower and dry one another. He neither lets her cum (because he wants her sharp for her interview) nor edges her (because he doesn't want her to bite the reporter). This time he lets her do her hair, though he suggests she put on a pair of jeans rather than dressing up yet, then leaves her in peace to get ready.

He's at the desk when she emerges. "Will they have cleared the things from downstairs?"

"Yes," he assures her. "Everything but the pastries and juice."

"Oh good." Having determined they won't be disturbed by the hotel's staff, Ella Jane heads out of their bedroom wearing just her jeans and his discarded shirt from the day before.

"We will however have to put something on in a bit, Cynthia's due at ten and that journo will be here to interview you at half past."

Ella Jane complains, "Why did we arrange for them to come so early?"

"So we could have the rest of the day to ourselves."

The comment wins him a softening of her expression. "Did I ever tell you you're too sensible?"

He kisses the top of her head. "Yes, more than once, I generally punish you for doing so."

She bites her lip and looks down as she sidles up to him. "Ha, well, funnish anyway."

"You're being too sensible now."

Her expression remains unrepentant. “I suppose I walked into that one.”

“I think you wanted to.”

“And you’re too clever by half.”

He swats her bum, then leans back and admires her naked form. “I suppose I’ll have to funnish you for that as well.”

“Yes please!”

“After we get done with *your* visitors.”

He picks up on the way Ella Jane fails to settle. “Why don’t you get changed. Maybe give your new suit an outing, or the green dress you and Amberlee chose. It goes well with the suite’s decor.”

Cynthia does a double take at him that makes Ella Jane smile. “He does that, likes to take charge.” She protests his suggestion though. “I don’t see why I need to dress up.”

He leans back and lets that irritatingly smug smile of his spread across his face. “It’ll set your head in the right space and impress the crap out of this journo.”

She looks to Cynthia for support but finds none.

Cynthia sets her face in motherly mode. “Don’t look at me. He’s right. Besides, dressing up will give you something to do besides getting more nervous.”

Outnumbered two to one and aware of her nerves Ella Jane gives in and makes her way upstairs.

He waits for her to be out of earshot. “Thanks for that. She’s brilliant; it’s just that this is her first go with someone from a major.”

“She’ll be fine. I’ll look after her.”

“I appreciate that.”

“It’s my job.”

He nods. “I suppose so. That’s what Roger tells me he does.”

“You’re his favourite client, you know that?”

That makes him chuckle. “Yes, but don’t let either of us know that.” He then goes back to reading his laptop screen until Ella Jane makes her entrance.

Upstairs Ella Jane goes to the wardrobe where she keeps the rented clothes. Each dress is in its neat protective bag. Even just opening the door does something to her; the prospect of dressing up in her borrowed finery is enough distract her from her nervousness. Realising he's right again, she feels a flare of rebellion rise, but her native common sense kicks in.

She takes the suit out and unzips its bag, the charcoal grey wool is pristine, and she knows from trying it on that wearing it would give her a much-needed extra sense of authority. But it's just too far from what she wants to say about herself when talking about her coming of age novel. She can imagine herself going to one of his functions wearing it, but not talking about her book.

With the suit discounted she takes the green dress out. It certainly doesn't scream accountant or manager, and it doesn't add years to her age, so she slips out of her shirt and jeans. Putting it and the matching shoes on is simple and delightful. So is looking in the mirrors and seeing herself wearing it!

The reflection is everything she'd seen in the store, plus the bonus of it having been adjusted to fit her slight form perfectly. It's everything Amberlee has said, young enough, just different enough to stand out. The modelesque blonde had also described it as not so out there a person wouldn't dare be seen in it twice. Not that Ella Jane can imagine herself ever being bothered at the thought of being seen twice in something so lovely or that fits her so well.

The journalist arrives early, but Cynthia insists that Ella Jane make him wait. She also demands that she should collect him from the lobby rather than inviting him directly up to the suite. "This is what you pay me for. I'll set the mood and make it clear who he's dealing with."

"He's dealing with a terrified first-time author."

"No, he's dealing with a woman who's clearly so successful that she's staying in one of the most expensive and beautiful hotel suites in Manhattan. He'll come in to find you natural, comfortable, relaxed and looking amazing in that dress. And when he speaks, you'll be confident and magnificent."

"I won't."

"Of course not. But you *will* act it." Cynthia checks her watch and observes, "Ah, time for me to go and fetch him."

He stands and moves over to Ella Jane, speaking as he does. "You really will be fine. This guy's not going to give you a hard time. He's just collecting a light piece that probably won't even see the light of day. Treat it is a practice run."

She pouts up at him. "That's easy for you to say."

"Well, I do have uncommon oral dexterity."

Despite her nerves the reminder of their conference moment makes her chuckle. "You're never going to forget that, are you?"

"No, nor seeing you try not to laugh. Do you want me to stay till he arrives or give you the floor?"

"What would be best?"

"If they see me, they'll want to talk to me and about us. We can do that if you want."

"You didn't answer my question."

"No, because it's your decision. Do you want to talk about us or have the interview they promised you and talk about Abigail."

"I should, shouldn't I?"

He grins and winks. "See, you didn't need any advice at all, did you?"

"You don't mind me using the reception room?"

"It's easier. I've got the little office upstairs, and if I need, the bedroom and roof terrace. This sort of thing is why I prefer a suite." He pecks her cheek and squeezes her hand. "Cynthia will sit with you, or she can hide in the spare bedroom."

"They could stage farces in your hotel room."

"We'll have to write one together after your interview." He picks up his laptop and kisses her cheek. "I'll be upstairs. Shout if you need to, but you won't."

Ella Jane squeezes his hand as he makes to leave. "Thank you."

There's a knock at the door a moment later and Ella Jane goes to open it expecting to find Cynthia and the man from the Post, but it's the butler service. She looks at the smartly uniformed woman.

"Drinks service, Ma'am?"

His voice comes down the stairway. "If that's the butler service, could you ask for a tray of sandwiches in an hour or so?"

It takes a second for Ella Jane's mind to process. Of course, He arranged it and did another of his not bothering to remember acts. . "Oh, yes, thanks, er... my guest will be here in a minute."

"Can I get you anything, Ma'am?"

"Er, just sparkling water would be great."

When Cynthia returns, the butler lets her in. The reporter arrives with a photographer in tow rather than on his own. "You don't mind if we take a few shots to accompany the piece, do you?"

The photographer is a middle-aged woman, and one of those people who has a talent other to relax by talking about the most trivial of things. In this case, she chooses the subject of New York taxis. Ella Jane somewhat cautiously confesses to only ever having been in two but doesn't go on to explain that the reason is that she's been ferried around in an assortment of luxury cars.

Once she has her relaxed and has taken photographs of her seated, on the grand staircase and looking out at the view over Central Park, she sits down with her and goes through the images on her tablet allowing Ella Jane to delete any she doesn't like. That done, she mentions the photographs taken of her at the Met and asks if she still has the dress. "I'd love to photograph you in it."

Ella Jane looks at the reporter who nods enthusiastically and then makes her way upstairs to change.

Hearing her in the bedroom he puts his head around the door. "Is everything alright?"

"Yes, they just want to photograph me in the blue dress."

"Oh, okay." He makes to leave.

"I thought I was supposed to be a writer not a model!"

"Hey, they just want a selection of pictures of you looking lovely. The more glamorous you look the more likely their editor is to publish the article."

She complains, "That doesn't seem quite fair." But her laudable sentiment doesn't stop her admiring her reflection, or bouffing up her hair.

He nods his approval and goes back to work with a *Go get 'em.*

"I'll try."

Downstairs, the butler has kept their guests comfortable. Ella Jane lets her top her glass up. Then, having asked their visitors if they'd like something to eat and have any dietary requirement, she lets the woman go with her thanks.

There are even more photographs, and another round of deletions. Cynthia requests for copies of the retained images could be sent to her. Then she asks, "Would you mind if I sat in? It's Ella Jane's first major interview."

The reporter looks across at the young author, sees her looking gratefully at her agent, and agrees. He starts off with some simple questions, checking facts and discussing the background to Abigail Leaving Home, all of which Ella Jane answers happily.

Things seem to be going swimmingly when he observes. "You'll forgive me if I say meeting you here and seeing you in the flesh. You seem a world apart from the shy, tomboyish Abigail who's capturing the hearts of Middle America."

"When it comes to shyness, I'm sitting here shaking with nerves. I didn't imagine being interviewed for the Washington Post."

"And her tomboy qualities?"

"I grew up in West Virginia. My granddaddy taught me to shoot, and my uncle took me camping. I let expectations turn me away from that part of my character. In Abigail I've let that girl grow up too, and through her I've rediscovered their joys."

"Does that mean the glamorous young woman in front of me isn't the real you?"

"Far from it. She's every bit the real me. Going through school, I experienced pressure to play down my femme side, just as teen culture pushed me to focus on it."

"Some people might say that paints a confusing image."

"They might. I think it's my coming of age though. I'm learning to embrace myself, celebrate the two sides of my femininity. The other day I went to a dress fitting in the morning and a gun club in the afternoon. They're both me. They're both things I cherish the memory of."

"It's hard to imagine Abigail in a designer suit."

"I'm not giving away any secrets about her long-term future, but there's nothing like that in her next adventure. Hers isn't the only story I'll tell though. Who knows, maybe there's a girlier coming of age waiting around the corner to capture my imagination."

The butler returns with a sumptuous array of sandwiches and nibbles including some things Ella Jane would have asked to have identified for her if she'd been alone with him or him and the butler. There's also ramp mayonnaise and a cold pasta dish made with that hometown favourite bacon and tomato. Fortunately, the butler doesn't leave her in any doubt as she goes through the selection pointing out which items are sourced from Ella Jane's native West Virginia.

Cynthia jumps in, "Miss Tyler thought it would help you get an idea of where Abigail comes from if you got to sample some of her home state's fine produce and local delicacies."

The butler offers, "I'm sure we can supply details of any producers if Miss Tyler can't recall."

Ella Jane takes a drink of water and hopes the reporter doesn't notice her surprise.

Pictures are taken of the feast, and the reporter continues to ask questions. , though, Cynthia now apparently considering the formal interview to be at an end fields any she doesn't want Ella Jane to have to answer *off topic.*

Farewells are said, and the butler shows their guests out.

Once they're gone, Cynthia gushes, "That was such a good idea with the refreshments."

Ella Jane is just confessing that she had no idea when He swans down the stairs. "Was that fun?"

"It was your idea, wasn't it?"

"The food? Just my suggestion. The details were down to my office and the hotel. Can I take it they excelled themselves?"

She purses her lips, both at his presumption and at the effect he seems to have on the world around him. "Everyone always excels themselves for you."

"Asking nicely and saying thank you go a long way."

Her eyes go around the room, and then back to him with his innocent look on his oh-so-not-innocent face. Ger awareness goes to the finery she's wearing too, and her lips start to move. Wealth, charm, physical power, and that voice of his that has people moving to follow his least instruction before their brains register what's happening, and he puts it down to asking nicely. Of course, that doesn't hurt, but... She shakes her head, "I think they do it for you too." and she kisses him so hard and so long she forgets Cynthia's presence.

"Ahem,"

Ella Jane lets out a little squeak.

He's smooth though. "Did it all go well?"

"Ella was brilliant, just feisty enough, and the home town girl act played perfectly."

The suggestion that it had been an act raises you young author's hackles. "It wasn't an act!"

Cynthia's eyes settle on her. "No, I don't suppose it was, was it. I'm sorry, I've spent so much time around people who want me to think this or that about them, that I quite forgotten. We coach our writers to come up with a *story*, but you..."

He steps in again. "She's quite something, isn't she?"

Her agent agrees, and Ella Jane goes a little quiet after the excitement. Not long after Cynthia says her own goodbyes and they're left alone.

"Did you mean that?"

"About?"

"About me being quite something?"

"Yes, didn't you have this conversation with Dr Jenkins?"

"I – I'm not."

He humphs, "You, yes you are, now, isn't it about time you took those clothes off so I show you how pleased I am with you?"

Ella Jane resumes her musing in the intimate interval while he dries her after their shower. "If I'm going to be your sub while we're travelling, what does that involve that I'm not already doing?"

"Play within our already agreed limits, personal service, attending some vanilla functions without misbehaving."

"I've never misbehaved for you in public!"

"No, you haven't, I wouldn't have made the offer if I thought you were likely to either, but this is agreeing not to."

"And personal service?" Ella Jane sucks her lips into her mouth. "I'm not brushing your teeth, and you are most certainly not brushing mine. I don't even like a hygienist doing it." She rushes out, "But bathing's okay." Then she offers an enthusiastic smile to make certain he knows she wants to carry on with the happy task of soaping and drying his muscular form.

"Bathing, hair washing, massage, scratching itches, applying sunblock, hair brushing, shaving..." He punctuates each activity with a kiss.

They stand by the twin sinks, doing their morning ablutions and Ella Jane having accepted that brushing one another's teeth is a step too far.

He stops and looks around when he registers that Ella Jane has become still. "Why are you smiling?"

"I like the way your cock moves when you're brushing your teeth." She does a little shimmy and gestures with a hand in front of her.

"Is that so?"

"It is." He's still not pouncing on her, so she tries again. "When you said a person should learn to enjoy being dressed and undressed."

"Yes?"

"Does that mean you want me to dress and undress you?"

"I will sometimes."

"My very own Ken doll?" Her expression makes the tease more obvious, but she makes no move to escape or defend herself. She doesn't even move her eyes from his until her turns her to face away so he can bind her wrists.

He secures her forearms together in a box tie. The bondage is strict, and the plug and internal vibrator are filling. The lecture he delivers on the subject of brattiness is long and whimsical while he caresses her bound body is lengthy. He punctuates it with tickles, edging and by inflicting little jolts of pain to various sensitive parts of her body.

Her confessions of guilt are frivolous, then serious but feigned, before his hands and his voice and the theatre coax her awareness into the role of penitent.

He teases so long and so ably that she buries her head in the thick pillows and sighs, surrendering to this latest new thing and breathes, "You're smiling, aren't you?"

"I am." His voice is warm. "You're making me happy." He touches her vulva for the first time – the first time, this time.

She has no idea how many times he's touched her in these last few days. He runs a near-pinched thumb and forefinger nails up her slit and between her inner labia, to, and then under her hood. She catches her breath.

"Even if you are being such a brat." The threat is there, and he feels her heart pounding and her legs tense with the temptation to try to protect herself. He rotates his hand, bringing the pads at the tips of his fore and middle fingers against her most sensitive place, sandwiching it.

He finds this spot and achieves this way of touching it as easily as she does herself. It's her favourite masturbation touch, though she's never told him, nor sent him a video. She recalls the one she made when he told her to record herself, the one he said she should keep secret unless they met. The one she's watched at least once every few days since.

By the time the first blow of the flogger lands, she's drifting.

And by the time he turns the vibe on, she's already in flight.

Her body is limp when he frees her, and when she floats back to reality and makes to clench herself comfortingly around the twin intruders, but they're gone, and she grieves for the lack of their solidity to press against.

Her messages

Ella Jane wakes alone, well, almost alone. There's a neat pile of printed sheets on his vacant side of the bed. She picks up the stack and reads the first page:

Little bit of reminiscence and maybe some fun if you decide to tag along.

The following page has a one row grid at the top. Each cell has one or more emojis in it. The far left has a being sick, the far right has the smiling angel and devil symbols, and the party popper. Those in the middle hint at levels of distaste and interest that range between. It reminds her of their long emoji filled online flirtations before they'd even decided to meet.

Below there are a series of paragraphs. It doesn't take her long to recognise their contents. They're messages she's sent to him, a few from the many hundreds, a themed selection, he must have spent an age choosing them.

The first paragraph begins:

> In my fantasy, my lover requires me to be naked whenever we're alone together, even virtually. He has me strip to answer the phone or video chats, be naked to message him, everything.

Another passage leaps out from the next:

> I want it to be so nobody else knows, but whenever I'm with him I want it to feel as though everyone does, As though if he were to tell me to strip in public, I'd do it no matter how scared I was, or how much trouble doing it would get me into.

Below there's a question from him and her answer:

> *How do you feel about the idea of not wearing underwear beneath your clothes, just a plug and the marks left by your last whipping?*

> I thought you said you didn't usually leave long-lasting marks?

> *I don't, just occasionally, and if my partner likes them.*

> I'm not sure I'd like it for real. [smile, see no evil] But right now I'm safe in my bed and feeling *tingly*.

It's okay to have things you like to fantasise about but will never do or will only maybe do some day with the right company, in the right place and time.

Do you think?

I know.

She circles the right-hand box and moves on.
On a later page, she reads her words from another exchange:

...To be completely in the power of an external force, chance or my dominant, know that his whim or the toss of a coin will determine whether I cum, whether I'm forced to work, bound or tortured, that no begging or pleading will alter my fate.

But that won't stop you begging?

I don't know. I suppose it depends how intense it is, but in my fantasies it either does me no good, or I'm punished for daring to plead for mercy.

She remembers her self-pleasure session after that. It wasn't long after he'd sent her a picture of his riding crop collection, and she'd used her vibrator for an age while she imagined him using them on her. After a moment spent enjoying that memory, she circles the right-hand box again.

Another page has their conversation on her delight in a dominant getting turned on by putting her into bondage, and on her conflicted urges to either revel in surrendering herself to her bonds or pretend she doesn't want to be tied. This time she not only circles the smiling angel and devil but adds arrows pointing to the box.

Further on, there are messages from him and her responses. They detail his twin fascination with tenderness and cruelty. Some of the things he'd said make her smile because she hadn't believed them at the time, but he's already done them to her. Others make her bite her lip because they're scary now that he's in her real life, not just her private fantasy. There are some that make her hand want to stray, but she stops it before it touches. She's conscious that he must have a reason for this, wanting to save herself for whatever that reason may be.

The second last has an exchange she remembers well in which they discussed extreme activities they would never consider and at the bottom a note in bold that reads, *Hopefully, we're still in agreement*. She circles the left-hand box with a laugh and moves on.

On the final page there's an exchange on a topic they visited frequently.

I want to take you beyond the need for pain.

But I like pain.

I didn't say I wouldn't give you pain, just that I'd take you beyond the need for it.

Isn't it better for me to torture you because you want me to, than because you need it?

I don't want to hurt you because you can't let me in without that. I want to hurt you knowing you're letting me hurt you because you want me to and because you choose to give me your pain and the power to inflict it.

I want your desire, more than your need.

Oh, is that all?"

"Only if we don't connect fully."

"And what if we do?"

"If that happens, I want to make you need again."

Of course, he'd taken her beyond that initial need from their first night together and done so with all the arrogance he displayed before and has since. But the reminder of that second need is a sharp stab. It's something new, something he hadn't mentioned before or since. Not even in their most intimate moments.

She tries to choose a box to circle, but it's too much. She leaves the sheet blank save for drawing a smiley face with a tear and a row of three X's at the bottom.

Having completed his little quiz, Ella Jane looks for him in the office first, hoping she'll find him there. When she does, he's sitting at the desk in a full-three piece suit. He doesn't look up, though she does see the corners of his mouth twitch as she approaches his desk. There are three trays on the desktop, one labelled *yes*, another *no*, and the third *maybe*. She lays all but the final two sheets in the tray marked yes. Then she holds the second last over the one marked no until he glances up and then puts it down with a smile she hopes she sees reflected in his eyes.

Simple choices made, she holds the final piece of paper in her hand while he watches her. Her hand drifts from yes to maybe and back. She blinks tries to read his expression, looks down, swallows and slowly lowers it into the as yet empty maybe tray.

He looks down and starts typing again. She lets out a long sigh, then stands back, waiting for him.

He makes her wait until she starts nervously hovering from one foot to the other.

"If you've nothing better to do while you're waiting..." He looks up, then down and tilts his head until she nods her comprehension before going back to work.

She smiles at the intimation. It's something from one of her messages, and lowers herself to her knees to crawl under the desk.

It's something he hadn't included in the quiz, and one she doesn't recall telling him about. Maybe if she'd known who he was earlier she would have, but yes, it's high in her private kinky bucket list.

Once in place, she looks behind herself and checks that her feet are neatly tucked in and her legs are spread just right. Nobody looking from the side of the desk would see, but anyone behind her would, and they'd see her hairless entrance glistening with desire.

Having settled in her place she moves her hands to his thighs and kisses him through the soft woollen material of his suit. They then go to his waist, which is circled by a heavy leather belt, as it has been every day since that first evening when she expressed her disappointment that it wasn't.

As she begins to unbuckle it, she asks, "Are you wearing this for me?"

"Ha, perhaps more because of you. You always seem to need the threat of something harsh to keep you in line."

She glances up, exposing her tooth whitened lower lip and sees him smile and wink down while she pulls his belt free. She passes the wide leather band up to him, then releases her lip to return his grin. "You are so strict, Sir!"

"Indeed, so you'd best concentrate more on your duties than your desire to get the sass whupped out of you." She chuckles, and he adds, "Did I use sass and whupped correctly?" Which makes her laugh harder.

"You did! And it would be easier to concentrate if you didn't keep making me laugh when I'm trying to suck your cock."

He reaches a hand down and strokes her hair. "Very well, I shan't talk with your mouth full."

"Stop it!"

In answer, he pulls his belt completely free, loops his it loosely around her neck, edges his hips closer to the edge of his chair, and returns his attention to his computer.

The office chair is even less accommodating to her efforts to rearrange his clothing than the armchair had been. But with his active cooperation, her guiding hands are able to lower his trousers to around his thighs. This still doesn't provide her enough access to do much, so when he makes another intended to be humorous comment, she tries to push his chair back so she can take undress him from the waist down.

"Hey!" The heavy muscles of his thighs tense as he pushes his weight and strength down on his feet stopping the chair's movement.

"Sorry. Please could you roll back a little so I can take your pants off?"

When he does, and she bends down Ella Jane finds that he hasn't double knotted his laces. She takes his shoes and socks off, tucking the socks into the shoes and setting them to one side then touches his thighs again.

He guesses her intent and raises himself on his arms while she strips his trousers and briefs down past his knees. Then he eases the chair back to make it easier for her to pull them over his feet.

Under the desk she finds folding his briefs and resting them on top of his shoes easy but bangs her head when she tries to fold his trousers. "Ow!"

"Are you okay?" He reaches a comforting hand down to her.

"Yes, just trying to fold your pants."

"Lunatic. Pass them up to me."

She does, and wryly observes. "This isn't as easy as I'd thought."

"I suppose it wouldn't be. You didn't have me as an anatomy teacher."

Beneath the desk, Ella Jane presses her glowing face to the smooth strength of his legs. "No, sir." Then places her hands on his thighs and eases them apart. Even with his hips forward on the chair she has to take a hold of his shaft to draw his cock to her lips. The confined space isn't suited to bringing him off in her mouth, but the situation is the stuff of fantasy. Knowing that if anyone were behind her they could see her openings between her parted legs and would know precisely what she is doing with her mouth. That they could only conclude that her body is his to do with as he pleases and that it is ready for him to do so.

She manages to lick, suck, swirl her tongue and stroke his shaft despite the awkward confines and his cock rewards her with twitches and surges in its hardness.

He himself lets out a series of sighs and chuckles while he either finishes whatever is keeping him from her or pretends to.

"Ah, all done!" He reaches under the desk and touches a hand to her hair, then waits. "I have a proposal, but it might be easier to discuss it if you were up here."

Ella Jane disengages herself from his cock and he rolls his chair back far enough for her to half crawl and half climb into his lap.

Once there she kisses the tasted of his pre-cum into his mouth and his hands play with her body.

"If you agree and come with me for the rest of my trip, I'll try to fulfil as many of both our desires as I can without harming you or landing either of us in jail. All agreed limits and safewords will remain in place. Unless there some soft limits your answers make you want to change.

She swallows at that, she doesn't think there's anything, but she'd been excited when she was reading, still, the safewords, and her trust... She shifts and nods."If I'm going to be travelling with you, will it be as your friend with benefits or your sub?" Then waits for some sign that he's eager.

His smile starts before he draws in a breath to speak. "You're invited as my friend – my, what did you say? *Something between a situationship and a dynamic* or as my sub."

"Oh my god, she told you."

"She did, yes, while she was telling me how sweet you are, and how I should treat you how nicely if you like that sort of thing. For my part, I'd like you to come as my sub and as my friend."

Her face's turn to betray her emotions, creasing in a smile despite her efforts to sound cool and businesslike. "So, if I say yes, you get to do anything you want to me?"

He rolls his eyes, "Anything you've agreed to, unless you safeword, or I decide to stop."

Ella Jane braves asking the question. "So you're doing what Alexandra wants?"

He leans forward an inch raising an eyebrow and lowering his head as, with those hard consonants in every word he answers, "I'm doing as I wish, with your generous consent, and bolstered by her good advice."

"So, not what she wants?"

"Alexandra is a keenly observant woman. She likes to advise people to do what they want to if she thinks it's a good idea. Then she can claim credit." His palm continues to tease tantalisingly around her breasts. "If you don't, we can carry on playing at you being my sub, or as my lover, or we can just travel as friends with or without benefits. I'm not going to kick you off your own book tour out of spite."

She listens to his offer and tries to put herself in each of the roles he offers. As his friend? Her mind shows her memories of Liselle, and Princess and Fancy. Even worse there's the possibility of seeing him with someone like the insufferable Brie, that would never do. And they've only known one another a scant few days, so lovers strikes her as being out of the question too. She kisses him and he kisses her. "As your sub then."

She lays back, the only part of her touching him a leg stretched out so that her foot is resting in his thickly muscled, just enough to preserve the contact. "May your girl humbly ask a question?"

"Certainly."

"When you aren't punishing or rewarding me?"

"Yes."

"You like giving me pleasure and pain and making me do things?"

"I do."

"So what will be different?"

"I'll still find excuses to give you pleasure and pain whenever I think you need, or either of us wants, but I'll be more formal with the rules we've only played at, nudity, self care, obedience, control of your pleasure."

She squeezes herself up against him. "Thank you."

After lying companionably together a while longer she rolls against him and touches her lips to his shoulder. "So I'll have to call you Sir from now on, not just like we're role playing?"

His lips curl into an unconscious smile, and she takes it for agreement.

"Sir," she says. She focuses on him, on his eyes as she speaks. She fancies she sees the darkness shine inside and knows she feels something inside her. Encouraged, emboldened, her fingers touch him, touch his already hard member. She pauses, breathes. Her face begins to smile, and she takes her bottom lip between her teeth. "Sir," she says again and wets her lower lip before sliding it between her teeth. "Sir!"

"Yes?"

Ella Jane scrunches up her forehead. "I like it, but I'm not promising anything." She then backs away a half a step. "Do you know how much meaner your face is than you are?" By some illusion or her imagination light blends with the darkness in his eyes, creating shadows and flashes, and as it does, she sees how total the blackness and focus there are.

His throat makes a low growl, though his smile softens and his low voice murmurs, "I think there's something there we can work on, little one."

The rich depth of his voice, the clear upper crust English accent, and the wicked glint in his eyes all melt straight through to her core. She smiles and flushes. Her eyes look down and then slowly back up to meet his. "Yes, Sir," she says, trying it again, and rubs her head against his shoulder both for the contact, and to hide the emotion of the moment.

With her eyes averted, he kisses the top of her head, and lets out a long slow breath.

Despite the assurances that her interview would likely never see the light of day that he'd given her in order to help with her nerves, the interview is published the next day.

The news arrives on his phone first, accompanied by a link, aided by his having people five time zones ahead. He loads the article on his tablet and wakes her, then videos her reaction to seeing her name and face.

Having spent five minutes bouncing around the suite like a demented jack-in-the-box, Ella Jane skims the article to make sure it isn't critical, and then sends the link to her parents and then to everyone she knows.

"I suppose you're going to want to get this out of your system before your morning exercises?"

She stares at him.

"Only I've asked them to send up a few copies and breakfast now."

Ella Jane's already reading one the printed copy of the Post He's had sent up before Cynthia calls to give her the good news, and she answers the phone with an excited description.

The printed piece is a thousand words, and there are pictures of her book, and glamorous ones of her face and of her posing in both dresses. There's even one of the elaborate, West Virginia focused buffet he arranged. In the article her agency, Thackeray and St. John and her publisher are both quoted as being pleased to have signed her and certain she has a big future. *Abigail Leaving Home* is described as a charming and popular first novel.

She alternately points details out to him and apologises for ignoring him and trying to be the centre of attention by calling his attention to passages and pictures.

He doesn't even pick up his phone, just quietly skims another print copy of the article while making sure she eats.

The version of the story is on their website has more detail and a number of lovingly taken photographs of Ella Jane, and their suite. There are also a dozen photographs of what the writer describes as:

...local delicacies from her home state that Miss Tyler requested the Plaza's talented chefs showcase to give an idea where Abigail Leaving Home comes from.

He wryly observes, "They've rather helpfully included the details of some of the producers. You might not have to buy another drink in West Virginia this year."

"I didn't do anything to deserve that!"

"They're small businesses. You gave them the kind of positive publicity that small businesses need."

"But you did it, not me."

"I'm pretty sure I just said, *hey, wouldn't it be cool if to serve some local dishes from West Virginia,* the details were down to the hotel, which gets some nice comments did wonderfully.

Ella Jane spends an hour before and over and after breakfast telling everyone she knows. With the last person told, she floats her way through her morning exercises without earning a single flick of his ever eager whip.

There isn't even her usual good hearted complaint at the way the bar stretches her open during the final part of their morning ritual or a light-hearted protest when he insists on using his oh-so-clever tongue to bring her to a series of orgasms while she's bound and stretched. This morning, in her mind, she deserves this, and he deserves it too.

Rituals performed, she asks if she can thank him for his help before they bathe, and spends an age doing so in every way she's ever shown gratitude to a man.

Thus it is that they don't get around to bathing until early afternoon.

Their visitor

Madam Alexandra arrives while they're bathing, and, almost as instructed, the butler admits her to their suite and serves coffee and biscuits. It's an unseasonably fine day, and Alexandra, being Alexandra, knows there's a terrace and decides that would be a better setting for her. She is not a woman to be readily denied, so they serve it out there, rather than in the reception room as He'd planned so Ella Jane could descent the stairs to greet her.

She selects what she considers the most favourable location and pose and messages Him.

> *On the terrace surrounded by your wicked Heath Robinson creations, darling.*

He receives the missive with amusement, kisses Ella Jane lingeringly, and leaves her to finish up, his fingers trailing regretfully over the curve of her buttocks as he goes.

Despite one of his dearest friends waiting, he doesn't rush to dress although he knows what he plans to wear, a soft blue cotton shirt, jeans, and trainers, all carefully designed so as to not look as though they were made to measure. A quick check in the mirror and a slight ruffling of his hair to make himself look a tad more rakish, he saunters out, drawing the curtains closed behind him.

"Alexandra, what a delightful surprise. You look magnificent!" It is delightful, though it's not a surprise either that she's come or that she looks magnificent, she's one of the few people he knows who owns more tailored suits than he does and looks better in them.

She rises and allows him to air kiss within a millimetre of her knuckles. "I couldn't not visit my dearest friend while you're gracing our fine city."

Formalities performed, he looks up with the devil in his eyes. "Have we been dazzling enough?"

"My dear man, we were born dazzling enough."

His wolf grin spreads as he pours himself tea. "I suppose you've come to soak up praise?"

"Was she pleased?"

The seamlessly perfect butler returns with a chilled white Burgundy and more refreshments.

He tastes the wine and nods his approval. "I don't think her feet have touched the ground yet."

Alexandra sips and preens. "You haven't tied them to it for safe keeping? My, you are slipping."

"You know I don't talk about private play, even with my favourite people."

"You're such a gentleman. I shall have to use my imagination."The elegantly dressed woman looks around, her eyes taking in their sumptuous surroundings, but settling on his DIY additions.

Point made, she graces him with a beatific smile. "Can I take it you two have got over my little faux-pas?"

"Just about, she's agreed to keep me company for the rest of my holiday."

"So easy to arrange when you bring one of your jets with you whenever you hop over the pond."

He winces.

Alexandra rolls her eyes and tilts her head. "You have told her about the Gulfstream?"

"It'll be alright. It's only rented."

"It's only rented from *you*!"

"I'm trying to introduce her to things gently."

She lets out a peal of disbelieving laughter. "You're staying here! And she must have seen a dozen films based on your books."

"That still doesn't come close to explaining everything."

"The van Beeks didn't let on that you're the money?"

He lets out a sigh of relief. "No."

Alexandra leans forward and lifts her glass, then enquires, "Do you like her enough that you might invite her to visit your home?"

His brow furrows, and it takes a moment before his eyebrows and the corners of his mouth rise a fraction. "You know, I just might. She's adventurous, and some time in England might help her career."

"How are you going to explain owning half a county and having two research centres in your grounds?"

"One piece at a time, I suppose."

"It's a good job you're a dominant. If you were my sub, you wouldn't be sitting down for a year after surprising me like that."

When Ella Jane emerges from the bathroom, the curtains leading to the roof terrace have been closed. She goes over to peek through. He's sitting at the table with a woman.

She recognises his friend instantly. She's not dressed in costume but still most certainly in style. She is suited in that way popularised by Annie Lennox, the one that hints at masculinity but nonetheless makes it entirely clear that she's far too much the woman to seem androgynous.

As how they have company Ella Jane goes back to dress. At first, she reaches for a robe, then thinking better of it, for her jeans. A thought for Alexandra's statement choice of attire prompts a second change of mind, and she dons one of the sets of lingerie he bought her and the black lacy dress she'd selected. Then she steps outside to join them.

He turns as soon as she opens the door. "Ella Jane, you remember Alexandra?"

Ella Jane stops on the threshold. The way the dominatrix looks at her makes her wish she had more on. "Of course, er, lovely to see you."

Alexandra rises and opens he arms, "Is that any way to greet a friend?"

Unable to think what else to do Ella Jane goes to the taller woman and accepts a formal hug and an air kiss.

"It's always good to get to know one of this old rascal's other friends, and doubly so to meet one who can walk and hold a coherent conversation after spending any time in his company."

"Don't! He's not that –"

"No, he's worse."

Ella Jane purses her lips.

And the older woman smiles. "See, you know he is."

"It sounds almost as if you're trying to warn me off him!"

"That thought couldn't be further from my mind. Not that there aren't a million perfectly good reasons to avoid him, almost as many as there are to avoid me, we're both terribly immoral people." The elegantly dressed brunette pauses and looks around the roof terrace taking in the various homemade items whose nature might confuse an innocent, but which the two women both know the other understands. "However, sitting here in your little alfresco play-space, I can't help drawing the conclusion that for you some of the reasons to stay away are reasons to stay."

"We have had a lot of fun."

"I'm sure." Alexandra then lifts the newspaper she's been keeping by her side. "How did you like the interview?"

Ella Jane almost bursts. "Brilliant! Did you see it?"

"Of course, I did. I had one of my little pets organise it by way of apology for the little faux pas at the party."

Ella Jane stares, then looks at him.

"Nobody does making-up quite like Alexandra, even when she's done nothing wrong." He winks at Alexandra. "Which is always. She has the biggest heart in the big apple. Just don't tell anyone, or she'll destroy you socially."

"I can't believe you did that for me."

"It was nothing. I made someone check if your book was good enough to not make me look like a fool first."

"You needn't have, but I'm very grateful."

Alexandra lifts her glass and casts a satisfied smile from Him to Ella Jane. "Of course, I needn't have, but I like to do things for good people. It worked out rather well. Your interview was a smash, so my little pet still owes me despite me calling a favour in."

"Would you ladies excuse me for a few minutes?"

Alexandra looks at him with a whimsical smile. "Of course darling, so long as we can borrow your butler service?"

"No borrowing required. Ella Jane is the lady of the house."

Alexandra watches him as he leaves with uncharacteristic slowness, and most of his attention focused on the petite redhead. "My! Lady of the House!"

Ella Jane answers robotically, "He's teasing me."

"He teases everyone, but he's a darling." She holds up her glass, lets her drift down the black dress. "And he has impeccable taste." As she speaks, her eyes go to the door he's just gone through before returning to her glass. Then she looks to Ella Jane and sees her equally fascinated with his absence and the portal he has just disappeared through. If he were submissive I could see myself become quite smitten, but then he wouldn't be him."

The words send a twisting through Ella Jane's guts, and she stays looking at the door until the feeling passes. When returns her attention to their guest, she sees the suited woman's eyes on her, and her sense of being underdressed rises once more. She quickly seeks to change the topic. "I'm sorry we had to leave your party early."

"That's alright, but you're both now obliged to come again and stay the night." She then settles into a smile.

"Are you laughing at me?"

"No, I don't laugh at my friends. That would be vulgar. Whatever expression I'm wearing is due to you both."

"So you're laughing at both of us?"

"It's more a case of waiting until I can laugh with you."

"You sound as cryptic as he likes to."

"Of course, my dear, all the best people do from time to time."

This time her face turns serious and she lowers her head so that her eyes are looking up at Ella Jane while the rest of her is looking down as if studying. "How are you two beautiful people getting along?"

Ella Jane colours, and Alexandra smiles. "Well, I take it?"

"It's exciting, and um?" Ella Jane lets her voice fade, she doesn't want to criticise him, especially to his friend, but she can't think of a concisely polite way of describing his way.

The suited woman offers her own continuation. "And um, he's the most arrogant man you've ever met in your life?"

"I didn't say that!"

Alexandra nods in acceptance. "If he weren't also one of the most formidable and one of the kindest, someone would probably have murdered him for it by now." Then she adopts a more confidential tone. "Now, tell me about yourself without his haughtiness listening."

"There isn't much to tell."

"That isn't true, you're bright and educated. You speak well and stand up for what you believe in. You've crafted a lovely story, one I have yet to receive a signed copy of I might add, and if I know anything about that old rascal you've started work on another."

"How did you?"

"Know? I read people." She looks around, "You also appear entirely at home with his naughtiness's taste for al-fresco pursuits."

Ella Jane laughs, "We had a session in Central Park after we left your party." then relates the tale of their adventure of her would-be rescuers.

The older woman joins in with her amusement and makes a delightful audience for her story but cautions her. "It's a good job I have a sense of humour, some hosts would be insulted."

"I'm sorry. I thought I wouldn't mind seeing him with someone else, I really did, but..."

"But he's done a version of his flogger plus trick with you too?"

Ella Jane glows.

"More than one?"

"Um, a few."

"It's a classic, and one of his favourites. One of mine too." Alexandra sips, closes her eyes and rolls her head before continuing. "There are so many ways to use the falls and wrapping, and so many things that can be added, a crop, dressage whip, a second flogger."

Ella Jane leaps in. "I love the second flogger-oops." Her eyes go wide as she cuts herself off mid confession.

"Don't worry, I'm hardly going to shame you." She pauses and her eyes rove appreciatively. "Of course, if either of you ever decide to share you with me, I will use my knowledge ruthlessly."

Ella Jane blusters, "How do you do that?"

Madam Alexandra laughs. "Talent and practice, I could make a statue blush."

"He does that too."

"I know, it's probably one reason why we're friends." With Ella Jane seemingly so content she takes an oblique approach to the question that has been vexing her since his admission about the pair's travel arrangements. "He tells me you're joining him on the rest of his trip."

"Yes, that is, where he can get flights."

Not one muscle of Alexandra's face moves for the second it takes her to formulate a reply. "I think you'll fine he's quite resourceful enough to arrange transportation."

Outwardly reassured, Ella Jane brings up her own concern. "Can I ask you something?"

"You can, but remember he is my friend."

"All those glamorous women –"

Alexandra raises a finger as she cuts across her, "*Other* glamorous women."

"Will he get bored of me when he's trained me to be his perfect little fuck toy, and you've made me famous?"

"My dear, men are like us in some ways. We just have to keep them thinking we're interesting and interested."

"But I don't see how?"

"You're pretty, clever, and amusing, and you're both writers. People have built a lot more than *situationships* on a lot less." The taller woman waits for her attempt at reassurance to take effect, and when it doesn't, she leans forward and touches a hand to Ella Jane's. "My little pet from The Post said you were utterly charming, and he's normally just plain jealous of pretty female submissives."

"I wish I'd never said situationship!"

"Everything starts off as a situationship: marriages, wars. If Jane Austen hadn't been in the situation of wondering about marriages and carriages, she'd never have written her books."

"I suppose not."

He offers, "Would you care to stay to dinner?"

Ella Jane's eyes go wide with disappointment, and Alexandra politely declines his invitation with a conspiratorial smile to the young writer. "I'm not going to play gooseberry on your last night in New York."

"Can I lend you Mr Johnson's services to drive you home?"

She sighs, "Thank you. Though I'd rather you leant me Mr Johnson. It's a shame that man doesn't like being told what to do any more than you do."

Once they're alone, he takes stock of his home made toys. "I suppose I ought to drop these down ready for shipping."

"We ought to pack as well, shouldn't we?"

"They're doing that for us."

Her eyes widen.

"Everything except the toys."

"Phew."

"Want a last go of any of these?"

She shakes her head. "Can we just us?"

He puts his arms around her. "Sure."

Their Last Night in New York

The butler service set out a candlelit dinner on the suite's roof terrace while Ella Jane bathes, and, having served, they have discretely departed, enabling Him to play the host.

He blindfolds her first. Then, after easing her out of her robe and ensuring she's dry, he leads her through the bedroom, guides her up the three steps and out into the warm early evening air, and sits her at the table. She makes no effort to cover herself or cross her legs.

She does ask though, "Can...may I take the blindfold off?"

He teases, "Not yet."

She hears the amusement in his voice and then the sounds of foil tearing, a cork twisting, and a bottle opening with a soft hiss. "Champagne?"

"Has to be done."

"Does it really?"

"Of course. There's so much you can do with champagne." He lifts the bottle and adds a little to each of their glasses. "And with the bottle. Then there's the ice..."

Ella Jane bites her lip.

He lifts her glass and moves close to her, so close that in her blindness she feels the heat of his presence and his breath as he speaks, "We haven't done much with temperature. Apart from talk, that is..."

His voice fades to nothing and the silence, and her blindness, Ella Jane reaches into her other senses. She lets out a small involuntary sound as her breasts detect the passage of something icy cold within a millimetre of their tips then her lips curl into a smile as the scent of champagne reaches her nose.

The warmth of his hand takes hers and guides it to the glass's stem and he touches his lips to hers. "Fun?"

She beams. "Mmm." And leans forward in search of another kiss, but he's not there. His glass is clinking hers. They each sip and his eyes study her as she does.

It pays off. The disappointment passes quickly from her face, and she exclaims, "Mmm, this is different." Then she tastes the wine again.

"It's a Rosé."

That tickles her. "You don't strike me as a rosé drinker."

"Sparkling wines are different."

His sureness prompts her smile, as well as her sense that she's stepping on, if not a landmine, then perhaps a launch button as she lets herself ask, "Is that so?" She runs a fingertip down the side of her icy glass and then uses it to transfer a little of the chill to her throat as she grins speculatively at him.

His breath whispers past her ear, "That might be considered an invitation."

The blindfolded Ella Jane teases, "Might it?"

"Yes, but I'm not going to let it spoil my dinner." He touches his lips to hers. "Are you ready to see?"

Her tongue moistens her lower lip and then her teeth take a hold of it once more. "I don't know, this is exciting."

She can't see him smile, but she does hear the low rumbling of his chuckle.

"Are you ready for me to see your eyes?"

His voice is gentle, and that gentleness reminds her more sharply that a reprimand might have, that no matter how much she's enjoying her experience, it's their experience.

"Can I keep the blindfold on while we eat?" She holds her breath after asking, without the use of her eyes there's no way of knowing whether her request has angered, amused or pleased him until he speaks.

"Very well, just while we eat."

Relief floods her at the warmth in his voice, and she smiles, a smile which he kisses before setting about cutting food for both of them.

He floats a question while they continue their meal. "Other than New York, and the cities we're already booked for signings in, is there anywhere else in the States you haven't been?"

"You do know how big the US is?"

"Sorry, yes. I meant the obvious places, Bay Area for example."

"I've hardly been anywhere, but I did always want to see Hawaii." Her brow furrows over her blindfold. "Why?"

He looks away, then chuckles to himself, as much at his needless instinctive response as at her answer. "I've got a few more places to arrange visits to while I'm over here, and I could put a word in with my publisher and my office to try and organise some excuses." He grins. "I mean signings."

"Oh, really? And why might that be?"

"Various reasons."

"Business or pleasure?"

"The odd interview, a few book signings, bit of business, a few days off and a couple of fun things I fancy doing but can make look sort of worky."

"Worky?"

"Yes."

"Such as?"

"That would be telling."

"You still haven't told me *why*!"

"Haven't I?" He takes her hand and starts lightly caressing her forearm.

"No!"

"Is that so?"

Her *Yes!* is loaded with exasperation.

He looks down at his glass then gives her a lopsided grin. "I thought you might enjoy it."

Ella Jane humphs, shifts in her seat, and then blinks and tilts her head. "Is that the only reason?" But she makes no move to withdraw her arm from his playful touch.

"Well, I got the impression that you like spending time with me when you're clothed and when you're naked, apart from rope and chains."

"Oh, so you think I like spending time with you?"

Ella Jane lets him pull her closer and doesn't resist in the least. He loosens her robe, exposing a breast. Her brow furrows as she tries to interpret the sound him working one of the candles out of the candelabra. Even when he cups her breast in one hand she doesn't divine his intention. It's only when her she registers the flames heat warms her sensitive bud that she understands, and all she does then is hold her breath in anticipation.

He angles the honey-white taper.

The wax drips.

She winces.

Smiles.

She continues to smile and let her tongue and teeth play with her lips as he coats the tip of her breast. Neither of them speaks until her bud and aureole are covered with hardened wax, and he has returned the candle to its place.

"I deserved that."

"You might have, if you hadn't enjoyed it quite so much."

Ella Jane bites back a smile. "Sorry."

He, on the other hand, makes no effort to control his amusement. "No, you aren't."

"No, but I accept that I should feel sorry."

This time he's the one to *humph*. "Close your eyes. He eases the covering from her eyes.

Ella Jane blinks until her eyes adjust. "Wouldn't it be hard to organise flights for everywhere?"

"I can ask my management, they'll sort something out."

"Your management seems to put up with a lot."

"They get paid a lot."

"I'm sure that's a comfort," she delivers tartly. She scrunches up her eyes a moment after it escapes from her lips. "Sorry."

"You are, aren't you?"

"Yes."

He looks down from her eyes to her wax coated breast, and gestures appreciatively with his hand, "They are wonderful, and I value them very highly." then looks back up into her eyes with a mischievous smile. "Er, my management team, that is."

She leans forward and pulls the other side of her robe back, exposing herself still further. Then she waits, lips parted and eyes on him.

He makes her wait too, brushes the backs of his fingers across the already stiffening bud until it hardens fully, and continues doing so until her breathing catches. Only then does he continue with the ritual. This time the candle comes out easily. He works just as diligently until the pink at the summit of her breast is fully covered. Then he adds a smattering of drips to the upper curves of her décolletage from differing heights (and so with differing temperatures) before setting the improvised toy aside again.

Ella Jane begins, "Can...," but stops when he raises an eyebrow. "*May* I ask if this is just an excuse to keep me with you, so you can keep doing whatever you want to me?" She then arches her back a little more and looks down, wondering where he might aim the next little stream of gleaming droplets to chastise her further.

He doesn't disappoint, but he does answer her question. "I'm inviting you because I want you to come, as well as because I like making you cum. My publishers also want to add you to some of the publicity things they've arranged."

"And a few extra signings and publicity opportunities wouldn't hurt?" Her shoulders and the corners of her eyes tighten after the words escape.

"I always have a spare bed or couch wherever I stay, so there's no obligation."

"That sounded ungrateful, didn't it?"

"It did." He slowly peels the mould from the tip of a breast and recoats it, holding the candle closer and making the sensation of the wax droplets landing on her tender bud more intense. "But not too unreasonable. Were you out of role when you said it?"

Ella Jane studies the intensity of his expression, the focus of his gaze, and her skin flushes in response to what her eyes see.

His voice is thick and soft when he observes, "You might have been out of role, but your eyes aren't."

"I can't always control my eyes, and I won't claim an excuse." The seriousness of his expression forces a sudden smile onto her face. "If I say yes, can we carry on?"

"We can," he rises, and hold out his hand to her, "But I'd like to go to bed too."

She smiles, takes it, and allows him to lead her inside.

He stops by the bed, and turns to face her, then just stands with his eyes her and a smile on his face.

Ella Jane lets him, and finds herself smiling back, and then blushing. Finally she manages to speak. "Should I take my robe off and lie down now?"

"I think that might be for the best, but perhaps we should put a cover down first." He goes to his wardrobes, takes out another case, opens it, unzips a panel and takes out a folded camping blanket.

Ella Jane's curiosity opens her mouth and asks, "How do you know where everything is?"

He shakes out the blanket and signals for her to take one side. "Do you want the truth or some domly bullshit about having a perfect memory?"

Having helped him lay it over the bed and smooth it out, Ella Jane takes a moment to try to gauge his mood and makes a call. "Which is funnier?"

"The truth, the domly thing only carries a person so far."

"The truth then."

"I got myself stuck looking through stacks of boxes filled with fun stuff when a scene happened on the spur of the moment one too many times. Trying to seem cool and in command when inside you're going, *shit, wrong butt plug* or *where did I put the batteries* isn't easy. These days they're all colour coded and labelled." He indicates a small mark etched into the case's frame.

"Is that so?"

Pointing to the now protected bed, he continues, "Yes, one poor lass thought I spent two who hours edging her when in fact I was hunting out the dildo and vibe combination I thought would give her the biggest orgasm."

Ella Jane lies down with her legs pressed together. "Poor girl."

"Don't feel too sorry for her, she got her orgasm, and said it was well worth, but my nerves were frazzled." As he speaks he takes a hold of each of her ankles and draws them apart.

"Did you tell her what happened?"

"Not at the time, we had a laugh about it later." He bends to kiss her lips and turns away to fetch the candlestick.

As soon as his back is turned, Ella Jane closes her legs.

He sees her face before he sees the reason for the smile plastered across it, but not long before. When he does he sucks his lips into his mouth and patiently sets the candelabra down on the beside and pulls her legs apart again.

The moment he lets go of her ankles, she starts to draw them together again.

Her act of mild defiance doesn't break his calm. But it does succeed in raising a chuckle.

"I thought you wanted to do this?"

Ella Jane's grin remains unrepentant. "I do."

His brow furrows, and he tilts his head, but he doesn't give up, and before long his lips twitch and the corners of his eyes crease with a smile of his own. "But you want me to tie you up?"

She nods vigorously.

"You could have asked, you know?"

"I like it when you smile and want to spank me at the same time though."

"How would you like to be tied?"

"Spreader bar."

"Which one?"

"The one you designed for me."

He assembles the new spreader bar, her spreader bar, and first sets it wide, to longer than the furthest she can spread her legs.

"Face down to start, I think."

She opens her mouth to protest, but he does that thing with his eyebrows, one rising while he half squints the other down.

"You wanted to be tied."

The currently only semi-submissive Ella Jane closes her mouth, but doesn't manage to make her body move.

"There's plenty of candlewax, and there are some fun places to pour it on your read too." As he speaks he draws a fingertip over her rosebud.

That's somewhere she's never experienced wax-play, and she turns over and does her best to put her ankles far enough apart, hoping that it's enough to satisfy him. Even someone taller and on their back would finds themself spread obscenely. But the elfin Ella Jane is face down, and even after he's shortened it, the bar keeps her unable to move by wriggling. She's truly as helpless as a tortoise on its back.

The only slight freedom of movement the bind leaves her with is the ability to raise and wiggle her bum, exposing her widely splayed openings and feeling like nothing more than a living invitation. She pictures herself and imagines how she looks, one-part wanton tart and one-part experimental subject.

He's there, and she and her most sensitive flesh are as exposed and vulnerable as she imagines possible to his seemingly endless desire and cruelty. The thoughts that tumble from her mind fantasy of the moment send a flood of heat through her, making her want him to take her, and to press her splayed legs together to gain relief. Reflexively she tries, but of course she can do no such thing and sighs her exasperation. She's his, there for the using in whatever way he pleases, but also there for him to ignore if he so desires.

She turns her head and manages to see him from the corner of her eye. By now, any of her previous lovers or playmates would have indulged either their lust or their sadism. But he still bides his time caressing her with feathery touches and passes of his candles without allowing any of the bright hot wax to fall on her skin, and, by doing so, builds her arousal.

His fingers stroke down the cleft between the moons of her bum. "Would you like me to touch your clit or pour a little wax here?"

The touch causes her to catch her breath rather than answering immediately and he responds by allows a few hot but harmless drips to fall directly onto her rosebud as his left hand cups her mons. He brushes her hair aside, and another trail of droplets runs the length of her spine.

Ella Jane swears and tenses as the sensation of burning heat splashes down and his fingers press beside and above her hood.

For him it is almost the perfect game, she's so available, and so turned on that her anticipation, pain and pleasure all work together to raise wash her closer. The pressure her arousal and his eagerness have build up is aching though, so he guides himself to her entrance and eases himself into her. He doesn't fuck her, just stays there, deep inside her body and draws comfort from the warmth and strength of her around him.

Ella Jane tries the rock back and forth but he stills her with a firm, "No." then leans and kisses half a dozen of the milky white splashes of solidified wax.

She manages to stop her fucking, but not the pulse of need that make her canal tense around him of its own accord and in response the per periodic swelling of his cock.

They stays like this, with him diddling her and decorating her skin, until she whimpers with need and carries on until she sobs before granting her release. He fucks her through her orgasm and holds her through the silence after.

He withdraws without taking his own pleasure, and she reaches behind and but he's already gone from inside her.

Having moved back he sees that her bum is once again without the decoration he has so carefully applied. "What a shame, the wax has come off here."

Ella Jane understands his meaning and divines his intention even with the way his touch brushes across her upturned buttocks and the furrow between them. An inexperienced submissive might have done differently, and an inexperienced top might have been surprised, but they both know what they're doing and her purring and the arching of her back are followed by his caresses and chuckled, "Good girl."

It takes a while for him to coat her to his satisfaction, largely because the first few times he sends droplets tumbling onto and around her rosebud she squirm as sighs so prettily that elects to peel the cooling wax from her skin. Eventually though he either tires of that part of the game, or decides he cannot wait any longer to enjoy the next.

In an effort to get her face up without causing the wax to crack or fall off he guides her up onto her knees and then lifts and somewhat awkwardly turns her without releasing her from the bar's bondage.

He arranges her with her head and shoulders slightly raised by the pillows and dims the electric lighting, then, still not satisfied he heads outside and fetches the second candlestick.

The young America has her hands behind her head and a relaxed smile on her lips when he returns. She watches him, counts the six large candles, and teases, "I don't think I'm big enough for all that wax."

His answer comes after failing to control his amusement, "I could always cover you twice, however," he bends and touches his lips to her, "I was thinking of the lighting."

Before he begins he runs his fingertips over her mons and gives her a wink. "It's a good job you're waxed."

She smiles. "Such a bastard."

The wax is different for Ella Jane when she can see the candle flames dancing in the darkness. Her experience enables her to judge how hot each sparkling drip and stream of molten wax will be when it touches her skin. She can see him and the way the creamy white wax paints her pale skin too.

What blindness had made a game of surprise is transformed into one of vision and communion.

He's just the same as since their first night; fascinating, fascinated and present with an intensity that is still new to her.

First he runs trails across her stomach and along the insides of her thighs, between her breasts.

She watches, breathes, anticipates, fights the urge to squirm under the sweetness of the almost painful streams, and waits for him to move on to still more sensitive parts of her body.

Her guess is correct, he breasts come next. He uses trails and single drips from different heights to decorate and then to cover them before taking two fresh candles and using their pooled wax to pour matching streams down length of her V where the skin is thinnest between her outstretched thighs and the eager swelling of her outer lips.

There's actual pain her, though it passes within a second of each droplet touching.

Then he sets the candles back in their places, bends and kisses her long and lovingly. They both know what's coming next, that he's going to pour the almost scalding liquid onto and between her lower lips, that neither her entrance nor even the half hidden tip of her clitoris will be spared.

However only he knows that for all the delicacy of those places, they are less sensitive to heat unless one causes burns, and he'd rather never play this most intimate of games again than cause injury while doing so.

He takes up a candle, eases her hood back and looks into her eyes as he carefully spreads her wetness through her folds and up and around the now exposed pearl at the centre of her awareness; reads the fear and the trust, sees her hold her breath, and pours.

For the first time she breaks from her stillness, bucking her hips, curses first at his cruelty in not telling her how little it would hurt, and again as the wax cools and hardens.

Despite the secret being out he goes on to coat her whole vulva before he puts his last candle aside.

Torment over, he kisses along the white trails on the insides of her thighs around her wax covered opening, which makes her mewl and over all of their favourite, but now protected places, which makes her giggle at the absence of the usual sweet sensations.

When he goes to tease her breasts in a similar way, she puts her arms around his shoulders, and he allows her to draw her up and into a passionate kiss.

"You're a cruel and wicked man, you know that?"

"I try to be that." He returns the kiss, "Speaking of which, I'm going to have to get some of this wax off you before we do anything or it's going to go all over the bedroom."

Ella Jane opens her mouth to tell him he could afford to pay for any cleaning, and then closes it again. They haven't known one another long, but she's sure he'd no more show such a lack of consideration than she would. Instead she asks, "Can I help?"

It takes a while, and she winces as they ease the hardened wax from her opening, then both express their regret and not preserving the cast better, and without thinking he suggests they could make a better mould some day.

Once the wax is cleared from her openings and the insides of her thighs he releases her from the bar and massages her hips and legs.

She peels the coverings from her breasts carefully and but the wax is thin and she fails to preserve the castes, though she does so well enough to be able to kiss the shapes of their tips. "I always wished I'd been a little bigger so I could try this."

He bends and kisses the newly exposed buds and, though she hadn't been fishing for compliments he declares them just right as they are as his lips brush and suck and his teeth nip. "Just the right size, shape and sensitivity."

Satisfied that they've removed as much of their mess as possible he folds it in his cover and puts it and the candlesticks well away from the bed.

Their bodies have lost the edge of their readiness, and they the wildness of need, but, flush with the enjoyment and intimacy of their play Ella Jane urges him to lie back and sets about stoking her own passion by bringing his fully to life.

Having got them both thoroughly ready she looks into his eyes with a question in her own, and when he smiles rather than making the pull her down and roll on top of her she lifts herself up and guides him into herself.

Ella Jane raises herself up on her elbows afterwards. "Can I get you anything?"

Usually the first to recover he strokes her shoulder. "I'd like that."

"What would you like?"

"Maybe a hot lemon and ginger."

She hops out of bed, and makes for the door from where she turns back and asks, "Do you trust me to make it?" before laughing and ducking through it to escape the pillow he throws at her.

Once downstairs she puts the kettle on, and, having teased him, carefully slices lemon and ginger into two mugs. She then makes her way to the second bedroom where the massage bed is still set up. She trails her fingers over it remembering the times she's lain on or been tied to it.

Hearing the kettle click off, she returns to it and pours the boiling water. She doesn't take the mugs straight up though, preferring to spend some time reminding herself of the suite and of the adventures she's had there.

Eventually he makes his way downstairs. "Everything alright?"

He finds her staring out over the darkened park, and she turns, "Yes, just saying goodbye. It's our last night here, this might have been goodbye."

Joining her he puts his arms around her waist. "But it isn't."

She kisses him. "No."

"Come on, lets get our mugs, we've got an early start."

On their way upstairs Ella Jane lingers, running her hands along the banister.

Rather than sleepily trying to entice or goad him into a final tryst before settling down, Ella Jane is quiet and spends time looking at the views from their suite.

When they get to their bedroom she undresses him and they kiss while his hands work out imaginary knots in her back. They lie down and she takes a hold of him, but does nothing more.

Unused to her staid response he strokes her hair. "Sad?"

"It's our last night here."

"Tomorrow will be our first in Dallas and the night after our last there." He touches his lips to her cheek. "We have weeks of first and last nights in places coming up." So long as she doesn't throw a fit when she realises why it was so easy for my office to make travel arrangements.

She casts another eye around their temporary home. "I suppose so."

And he pats her bum. "Just so long as you don't annoy me too much, or I don't wear you out."

"Hey!" Ella Jane starts, ready to protest that he can be annoying too, and that she can do her own share of wearing out. But he's chuckling, and he's warm against her side, and hot and hard in her hand, so she sets about trying to show him instead.

My thanks to Kate, Allie, Maria, Mira and others for their years of encouragement, and to those who have told me I'm the naughtiest man they've ever met.

I'd also like to thank Maria, Erin and Leanne at All Write Well without whom Ella Jane's may well have remained an ever-growing but never-heard story.

There are a couple of business which have also helped me hugely with advice and samples

Slagwerk Atelier – the amazing Dutch Whip Maker

Shiri Zinn – A UK based toy and restraint designer who makes unbelievably gorgeous glass toys

Him and Her Erotic Steel – who have been kind enough to produce some of my designs

Also By

The first book in his series is **Meeting Him** - I recommend reading this first
https://mybook.to/EllaJaneMeetingHim

Having been flirting and playing online for for some time with a mysterious dominant, young author Ella Jane finds herself on the way to a writing conference he's also attending. Not only that it turns out that he's a highly successful writer. She flies coach to New York to meet him while his Gulfstream arrows over the Atlantic.

Both of them are in for more than either expects.

Ella Jane's story continues in **Travelling with Him – due out September 2023**
https://mybook.to/TravellingWithHim

The erotic adventure continues as they leave New York to do a number of book signings around the US, and for him to visit various parts of his far flung business empire. On the way they continue to explore Ella Jane's boundaries and the limits of one another's endurance and imagination

If you enjoyed reading about Ella Jane, you may enjoy **Meredith's Journey Begins**

Meredith Webb has built herself a pleasant, though unchallenging life, with a decent job she doesn't strive too hard at. Oh, and she has two cats she loves very much.

William Farrow on the other hand, knows there's something missing from his.

Reader Comments:

"A richly crafted journey into passion"

"Tantalisingly teasing"

"Stylish, smart and captivating! Sprinkled with moments of spine tingling awkwardness and evocativeness."

Get it here: https://mybook.to/MeredithsJourneyBegins

About the Author

Edward has written technical papers and articles that have been read by millions. Now he turns his writing talents to the world of erotic romance by applying his thirty years of experience in massage therapy, fine dining, and as a bdsm practitioner to create stories with a uniquely rich sensuality.

In **Meredith's Journey**, he creates a relatable world with characters you might meet in the street. Meanwhile, in **Him and Her, the Ella Jane Stories** he tells a tale of exotic, high-living beauty, and in the **Black Choker Diaries** he investigates the pleasures and pitfalls of a three person love story.

Each is crafted in a way that will leave you begging for more.

Printed in Great Britain
by Amazon

25855689R00185